DON'T DATE YOUR EX BEST FRIEND

THE UNFOLDING DUET

BOOK TWO

MAHI MISTRY

Don't Date Your Ex Best Friend

Copyright © 2020 Mahi Mistry

Published by Mahi Mistry
Cover Design by Get Covers
Edited by Creech Enterprise
Proofread by Sisters Get Lit(erary) Author Services

QUOTE

There is no charm equal to tenderness of heart.
Jane Austen

Dedicated to all the mothers.

THE LETTER

Hey Ethan,

If you are reading this, then I'm sure that I did it.

I am gone. Just like that.

I have so many things to say to you, but it's ironic how I have no words. I know you have many unanswered questions as well but don't worry, E, you'll find out why I did it. And why I *had* to. Please do me a favor and read this journal.

I hid all of this from you and I deeply apologize for that. I wish I was brave enough to face you and talk to you about all of *this*. But I am not. I am coward and selfish. I am sorry. I hope you will be able to forgive me, Ethan.

These are the entries of my days and I'll be fair with you, you won't like it. Sometimes you will hate me and love me. Sometimes you won't feel anything at all. I was tired of keeping this from you, so here it is.

You were my everything, and I was nothing . . . I am sorry for losing you.

Love,

Kiara

PART ONE

"I was a mess. You were my saving grace, so I had to let you go."

20th May, Sunday

Hey Ethan,

You know the rush of feeling you have the day before your birthday? The excited rumble in your churning stomach? The dizzy, strange happiness in your brain? Before everyone surprises you?

Yeah, the one I feel every year before going to bed and crying on my pillow.

I used to hate my birthdays, wondering why I was even born. I mean, the world would be a better place without me, eh?

But then, *you,* the world's best friend, *my* best friend, always made it special.

You bought me zoo tickets last year, and we had so much fun holding the snakes. You were so scared to hold a Tricolor Hognose, you almost cried letting her go. That was so precious! And *yes,* I still have your scared photos, and *no,* I am not giving it back.

Remember how both of us tried to talk to the snakes? To see whether we were Parseltongue or not and you even glared at the guard who was giving us skeptical looks. We had so much fun. I loved every single moment with you.

But now, sitting on the roof with the cool summer breeze kissing my face, I wonder if you will have any time to go out with me. Times have changed now. You need to shave your stubble every three days. I have to shave my legs every alternate day. You are in a relationship. I have boobs now, like when did they show up? I also kind of hate how Ariana has wrapped you around her stupid manicured finger.

I really wish you were playing Scrabble with me instead. But I get it, she is your first girlfriend and you're really excited to date her. I know she makes you happy, I can see it in your face.

Bad thoughts keep coming to me and I hate it. I hate thinking. I wish we could hit a pause button on thinking sometimes and do nothing.

Still, I can't wait for tomorrow!

Love,

Kiara

2 *3rd May, Wednesday*
Um, hey E,

Sorry I haven't been writing since the night before my birthday. I didn't know what to write. Mainly because my birthday was a disaster. I wasn't ready to pick up the fountain pen my mom had gifted me when I was four. I didn't *want* to write.

Sigh. It's strange.

Everyone was busy with something, even Katherine. But she sent me the book I was dying to read since the last two months. Even you had to go on a last-minute date with Ariana. Yes, you asked me to ditch your date, but I was the one who smiled it off.

Isn't smiling one of my talents? Works like a charm. I hate myself for lying to you without using words.

Mom was busy with her drawings, Dad was in the hospital, and Karan with his internship. I didn't have dinner that day, even though it was my favorite panner sabzi.

I cried in the shower because I was weak. It hurt me to

stay on the floor, hugging my knees and hiding my face. I don't remember why I was crying. Hating myself or hating all of you? It was sad, painful and pitiful. To look at your reflection and all you see are tear-stained cheeks, a flushed nose and red eyes.

Then you came sneaking through the window. You gave me my gift. It was a scrapbook. You were secretly working on it for months and you had glued pictures of us since our birth. I can't imagine you out of all people making a scrapbook for my birthday. The thought itself makes me laugh.

There were so many pictures of us! Playing together with soft toys, your moms showering us, playing with paint, four-year-old Ethan kissing my knee when I bruised it, our first fight for the last slice of pizza, first bicycle ride, our birthdays, eight-year-old me fighting with Nancy Jones over you (I still hate her. How dare she call you her boyfriend!), getting braces, our Radha-Krishna pictures, your swim practice, my first trophy for winning that essay competition. I can still remember that you were standing on your chair in the first row and cheering me on, 'That's my best friend, Kiara! Go, Kia!'

Then we looked grown up in the next pictures, painting together in my mom's studio, the school summer dance, Halloween, Christmas, driving your car; it had *everything*.

The last picture was of us standing together. We were on the beach and you were kissing my hair, your arm around my shoulder while I was laughing at something with my eyes closed. It was *beautiful*.

I was in tears and jumped on you, wrapping my arms and legs around you. I gave you the tightest hug. You fell on my bed and started laughing. When I stopped crying, you cuddled with me and we watched 'The Princess Bride' mouthing the dialogue.

Just like that, I wasn't sad anymore. You don't know how much I appreciate your existence, Ethan Kane.

Love,

Kiara

CHAPTER THREE

2 *9th May, Tuesday*
Ethan . . . I can't anymore.
It hurts . . . it hurts *so* bad. I don't know what to do. I am so exhausted. I will just sleep it off.
Tired,
Kiara

CHAPTER FOUR

0th June, Sunday

Hey Ethan,

Sorry for not writing daily, I can't keep up with a journal, but I am trying. I hope I will keep writing this.

Anyway, I called you last night and . . . you seemed happy. Very happy. Also, you ordered me to bring *bundi ladoos* as a souvenir for you from India. Don't worry, I've already made a secret stash for both of us. I hope Eve's not sick anymore and it was just gas.

Well, life here is slow compared to San Diego, not like you haven't seen. My Nana and Nani are spoiling me with food, not that I'm complaining because I really missed them. Including the spicy Indian food. They asked about you and were sad that you couldn't come with us this year.

Nana told me a story last night while my Nani was doing *champi* on my hair. He still calls me his little lion in Gujarati, and I can't help but grin every time he calls me that.

Miss you,

Kiara

P.S. I am not sorry for stealing your cologne. It's with me. Because I knew I would miss you.

CHAPTER FIVE

1 *2th June, Tuesday*
Morning, E! Wondering how I woke up at six in the morning? Spoiler alert: It wasn't magic.

I'm writing this sitting on our special rock. Remember that big rock near the little pond on the outskirts of my hometown where we used to sneak off and throw pebbles eating *gola* (shaved ice). I am sitting right on that rock right now. I wished you could come with us and it seems like my overprotective cousins missed you.

The weather here is still fresh, and you can smell the cool fragrance in the air. Sadly, the pond dried out, and it has turned into a vast clearing. The tire swing we tied to the oak tree is being used by little kids.

Even though the life here is simple and lovely, I miss home. Especially you. Because it feels like for the longest time, my home is where you are, Ethan Kane.

Love,
Kiara

CHAPTER SIX

1*7th June, Sunday*
I am bored.
B
O
R
E
D

Can you feel me? BORED! There's absolutely nothing to do here. The heat is too much. I can't even wear a bikini to get tanned. There's no swimming pool around and the lake has turned into a desert. I eat ice cream all day, watch Hindi movies (okay I am not complaining, I can watch Hrithik Roshan all day and night) and I've already finished the books I had brought with me. I even watched my mom paint and then watched that paint dry.

I am tired of writing and need you here to cuddle with me and talk to me about your day. Did Evey barf on you? Pee in your arms? I want to know about that too. Just don't tell me you kissed Ariana with a tongue like last time. I don't know why I feel weird around you when you're with her.

Heck, I am your best friend. I should be comfortable with your girlfriend and talk to her, but I can't. I will just watch that paint dry.

At least we have Paneer Tikka Masala for dinner.

Bored,

Kiara

CHAPTER SEVEN

2*0th June, Wednesday*

Hey Ethan,

Somehow, you made me cry—in a happy way.

You came to the airport and hugged me so tight that you made me spill burning hot tears from my eyes. You kissed my hair and got worried when you saw tears sliding down my face but don't panic. They were happy tears. I was so glad to see you and hey, you got a lot tanner. It brings out your blue-green eyes and you look really cute hiding that blush when I said it to you.

My shirt still smells of you as we caught up and cuddled in your room. In fact, I am writing this while you are sleeping soundly, hugging a pillow.

Am I being a creep for taking a picture of you? Because you look absolutely adorable.

I can't wait to start the school year. I can't stand Ariana, but I will try to talk with her when she stops glaring at me every time I'm around you.

But I will try. For you.

Love,
Kiara

CHAPTER EIGHT

2 *3rd June, Saturday*
I can't write, Ethan.
I can't. I am exhausted. I am sorry.
Tired,
Kiara

2

5th June, Monday
I hope you forgive me.

CHAPTER TEN

8th June, Thursday

2 Did I ever tell you how much I hate your best friend? I despise him. I hate Liam so fucking much.

I . . . I wanted the pain to stop, Ethan. So, with that intention in my mind, I went to the Moonstone Bridge and yes; I was going to jump. I was contemplating my decision and obviously, my mind won. Everyone said to jump. Life would be easier and happier for all of us. I won't have to drag you into my problems, you'd be happy with Ariana and you know how much I hate to see you sad. I had decided that I would do it.

Be selfish for one time in my life.

I wondered who would come to my funeral. Would you be there? Happy, that I was finally gone. Or bitter that I am dead.

I shook my head and stopped my brain, my heart, those voices and stopped breathing. I was more than ready.

But, of course, he just had to drive over that bridge at the same time and stop me.

Hating myself,
Kiara

CHAPTER ELEVEN

3 *0th June, Sunday*

You ignored me when I snuck into your room today. I was hurt, but I kept myself together and explained to you I needed to be alone for two days. But I swear I saw a hint of a smile when I said that I'd brought you your favorite *bundi ladoos* to make peace.

As we both bonded over the sweets, I didn't dare to tell you about Liam. How he dragged me away from the edge. I kept hitting him and punching him, but he scolded me and dragged me to his car, locking me in.

I had fought with him, called him things, but he didn't listen and threw his jacket at me because my entire body was trembling. I had never seen him so red and furious. After driving aimlessly for a while and ignoring me, he stopped the car in our parking area and asked me one simple question,

'Why, Kiara?'

That's when I looked away and cried. He stayed silent as my sobs echoed in his car. He had asked me why and truthfully, either I had many reasons or no reason at all. I wanted to say something, but I couldn't. I wanted to scream at him and tell him it was my life and it's my decision if I want to end it or not.

But somehow, words betrayed me for the first time in my life.

When I didn't reply, he removed his seatbelt and hugged me. I hugged him back, crying on his shoulder as I kept muttering 'sorry.' What was I apologizing for, anyway? But he said nothing and let me cry. Rubbed my back, brushed my hair back which had stuck on my face and wiped the tears away.

I kissed him. I don't know who initiated it. But we were in his car, I was straddling him and he was holding my face in his warm hands. I kissed Liam, Ethan. It felt so good that I almost forgot why I was in his car in the first place.

We were both blushing red when we pulled away. He squeezed my hand and told me to promise him something—that I won't give up or try to kill myself. In return, he won't tell this to anyone, including you—only if I tell you first.

I knew that if I had told you I wanted to kill myself and I am suicidal, you'd never let me out of your sight. Stay by me 24/7 and make sure I get proper medication. Maybe, in the end, I would make you as crazy as me. Because who even considers that the 'Golden Girl' with the perfect family, perfect friends, perfect grades and perfect fucking smile is suffering from depression and anxiety? No one.

I am not sorry for lying to Liam about the promise. Because you're too good for me. You deserve so much better than me and it hurts that I can't give you anything because I have nothing left! And I would do anything but see you waste your time on my already broken self.

Sorry,
Kiara

CHAPTER TWELVE

3 *rd July, Tuesday*
Holy shit, Ethan!
I can't believe it.

You broke up with Ariana and ended your friendship with Liam. I wanted to let you know I felt the same emotions you were feeling when you realized that the person you had feelings for was sneaking behind your back. I held my tongue because Liam and I had shared just one kiss and I am sure it meant nothing to him. I wanted to fight him and as always; you held me back.

But I can't believe that my stupid drunken self-told you how I felt about you. It just tumbled out of my mouth. We were dancing. We were alone. We were grinning and happy. I can still remember the way my skin scorched wherever you touched me.

I still can't get over the fact that I said I love you.

Thank God you were drunk and didn't remember it the next day. But I did. And I hid it well. There's at least one thing I am good at.

I am glad we didn't kiss each other. Because I was already

in panic mode when I said it and . . . I am sure I would have told you everything.

Hai Bhagwan. That was a mess.

Well, now you know how I feel about you. How I have always felt about you since you punched Paul Corey and bought me ice cream, kissing me on the roof with your cold lips. I didn't tell you because it would steal you away from me as my best friend. Our friendship mattered more than a stupid emotion called love. But then Ariana happened, and you were so happy with her. So, I swallowed my jealousy with my feelings.

I don't want to lose you, E. That's why I will ignore my feelings until they go away on their own. Fingers crossed.

Love,
Kiara

CHAPTER THIRTEEN

5 *th July, Thursday*
I guess our age and hormones are taking a toll on us.

I had written six thousand words last night and slept at four in the morning, so I was pretty exhausted throughout the entire day. But it got worse after a little talk with Liam. He wanted me to tell you about the day I tried . . . you know what I mean. I ignored it and had to shut myself in a washroom because warm tears were sliding down my cheeks.

In calculus, you kept me awake by poking my arm in school. Thank you, Ethan. I couldn't stop thinking about our slow dance, my drunk confession, and not to mention you wanted to feel my breasts, which was funny.

We saw each other naked for the first time.

Not that it will ever happen again.

But it was brilliant. I mean, you are the first guy who has seen me naked and by your flushed face, I could only wonder if I was the first female to see you naked. I can't believe I saw a dick for the first time in real life. Unless you count Paul. I will not talk about it because that'd be awkward.

We skinny dipped. We were having so much fun and I almost told you to kiss me and you would have, but Katherine interrupted us.

I swear, I wanted to kill her for cockblocking us. But what you did at the dining table topped it off. You teased me and it was like you were a whole new person.

I hope you were happy after teasing me and not letting me eat. That was just plain rude. But I love you anyway.

Love,

Kiara

CHAPTER FOURTEEN

9 *th July, Monday*

    You slowed down. Again. Just when you were about to win, you let Liam win.

Why, Ethan?

You think if you don't tell me, I won't know. Well, you are very wrong. We grew up together and I know when you're lying. The pupil of your blue eye goes small like a dot, making your lid twitch on the side when you lie. Yes, I know I stare at you a lot, that's why I know that but don't act like you don't like me ogling at your handsome face.

But, ignoring that, something happened today. Between me and Liam, which got you riled up in the end. I am sorry, even though I know it won't change anything.

When I went to talk with Liam today, he was angry at me because I hadn't told you about me . . . trying to end my life. He would have told you and ended it then and there. I panicked and just snapped, arguing with him as if it would have solved anything.

I lost my mind and said that no one would care if I died.

Not even . . . not even *you*. I know it was a low blow, but I didn't care anymore.

After I said that, Liam whispered to me, 'He does,' and pushed me in the pool.

He was right.

Love,
Kiara

CHAPTER FIFTEEN

1 *4th July, Saturday*
Well . . . we did something last night.

I hope you don't regret it because I can't get our kiss out of my mind. Among other things.

You know Katherine chose the outfit for the party and judging by your expression; I think it damn well worked. I was pumped to party after what had happened with Liam earlier that week. He had come to apologize and talk to me when you left. He wanted me to come clean and tell you about everything. But you entered before he could say anything. Thank God, you did.

Enough about that. The frat party at Ryan's farmhouse was wild. I am not sorry that I chose Seven Minutes in Heaven with Liam instead of a kiss with Carter. Liam said some things and as always, threatened to tell you but I shut myself off in the bathroom and then you were there. Is it bad that I am happy Liam spilled nothing to you?

You both fought, and we made out on a bed. I am blushing just thinking about the way you cradled my face in your warm hands. My lips are tingling thinking about pressing them against yours.

One good thing that came out of last night is that we made a deal. A very weird but good deal, nonetheless.

Love,
Kiara

CHAPTER SIXTEEN

1 *5th July, Sunday*
Don't get me wrong, I love my mom, but she can be very truthful and honest sometimes. Like how she knows I love you and am too scared to admit it because I am too scared to ruin our friendship.

Only if it was easy to admit what we feel and stop over-thinking every decision we make. It would be so damn easy to confess my genuine feelings for you, E.

Speaking of, you don't appreciate my dry humor, Ethan.

When you asked me to swim with you, I replied that I needed the swim lessons. You got that angry look on your face saying that it was Liam's fault that he pushed me in the pool.

But how could I ever tell you it was my fault?

In his weird Liam way, he was trying to help me. He was right. You saved me. But it's sad that I didn't let you save me again as you are reading this.

As soon as you said it was his fault, I pushed you away. Even Katherine. Because that's all I know. Pushing away.

Running away. And just . . . jumping. Which I already tried, haha.

The truth is, I am drowning. I want you to save me again and again. I am so caught up in feeling each emotion that I don't know what's happening around me. But sometimes, I forget that you are a human and you need saving too.

So, I pushed those feelings away and tried to be happy around you, for your sake. You looked so happy and sad when you talked with Eveline yesterday on my phone. I tried my best to swim around you without having a panic attack, thinking about the last time.

Do you know how happy you looked when you were swimming? Or the time when you were cuddling with my stomach with your head on my lap? I don't care if you put on an intimidating, angry mask for the world because you were hurt in the past by those bullies. But when you're with me, it slips away and you turn into a beautiful, goofy guy who needs all the love he deserves.

I am sorry that those children bullied you and I wasn't always there for you, but I promise you I will always love you. Even when you're reading this, I want you to know that wherever I am, I may be happy—away from those horrible voices and I will love you.

Love,

Kiara

P.S. Do you know you purr adorably when I run my hand through your hair? Looking at your smile with a dizzy look on your face, I realized that I took a fart on my heart.

CHAPTER SEVENTEEN

6th July, Monday

Lots of things happened yesterday. I gave you a blow job, tried to do your rough sketch and when I was about to give last touches—Karan came and ruined it explaining to me how it was the worst thing I've ever done and showed me my mistakes. I let him. I wanted to scream at him for ruining the sketch I had worked hard on for hours.

When I went to his room to give him a piece of my mind, I saw that he was crying. I thought Rachel was 'The One' for Karan, so much to my surprise when he said that she broke up with him.

After crying with him, I realized something, Ethan. Everyone in this world is suffering from something. Life itself is suffering. But it's our choice if we want to show our suffering to the world or not. Like me, some hide the pain behind their smile because that would make them forget about their own suffering. Even for a little while.

Then, there are some like Karan. The bullies. Maybe in his own crazy way, he forgot about his suffering by ruining my sketch and hurting me ten times more in the process.

You know, everything was going smoothly. I was trying to be happy with you—*no*; I was happy. More than happy. I found my happiness with you, Ethan. I considered this as a ray of hope. A small step ahead toward a bright and happy future. But then, there it is. Always lurking behind my happiness.

One small step forward . . . ten huge steps backward.

The worst part was that Karan didn't even realize why I was crying with him, so I let him believe whatever he wanted. I was on the verge of an anxiety attack when I got back to my room. Feeling brave, I wanted to tell Karan that I was having an anxiety attack and I needed his help. When I went back to his room to tell him, I stumbled on my words.

Before I could tell him, his friend called, and he said, 'We will talk later. This is important.' Guess what I did? I smiled. Brightly. When he closed the door in my face.

I sat on the edge of my bed and I don't know how many tears left my eyes, but I knew they weren't enough to let anyone know how I felt during that moment. I helped him but when I needed help . . . he left me broken. He didn't even see how numb and void my eyes were. How numb and void I was. I am.

I knew no one would care, so I wiped the tears and grinned like I was a perfectly normal person. I mean . . . that's what I do, eh? Pretend.

So, pretending I am happy, I came to your room, and I hated every inch of my body as you looked at me as if there was something worth looking at. You saw past me, Ethan. Like I was transparent, and you knew what I was feeling every fucking time, and I hated that.

So, I lied. Again.

Telling you about Karan and Rachel's breakup. You believed me because I was crying on your shoulder, hiding my face from you. Because I was scared that if I let you see me, you would hate what you're looking at and you would know.

I am sad, Ethan. So sad . . . it hurts. Why does it hurt so much?

Maybe because I feel everything and nothing.

Love,

Kiara

CHAPTER EIGHTEEN

2 *7th July, Friday*

I don't know if you know this, but I like you. Like crazy. It hurts me that only you can make me so vulnerable and weak. But that's okay because I like you, you lovable fool.

Love,
Kiara

CHAPTER NINETEEN

6th August, Thursday

I know I haven't been writing lately, but we were all busy with homework, projects and . . . stuff like exploring each other's bodies.

Did I ever tell you how much more attractive you become when you're playing with Evey? Don't get me started. God, your mothers have raised you so well! You know, as weird as it may seem, if I have a non-existent future, I would want a son like you.

I just made it awkward, didn't I?

You must be wondering why I pushed you yesterday when you told me to take some rest after a long evening with Eveline. I wanted to save my virginity till marriage, even though I know how cliché it sounds. The feeling of becoming one soul with a person you love, cherish, worship, the one you call husband. Cherishing each other's bodies, not because of lust, but because of love.

Ethan, I was ready to give up my virginity to you, rather than anyone else. I was ready. Far more than ready, physically and emotionally. But when you said that you wanted me to take a rest, the sick part of me thought you don't like me that way. Or didn't want to have sex with me.

Everything came crumbling down and all I could think about was the negative part of it. I couldn't see that you really cared about me, and not just because of my body.

But fuck me for having a mini anxiety attack. It's three in the morning right now and I can hear you shuffling in your room. I could hear Eveline cry faintly and without even seeing you, I know you are holding her in your arms and soothing her to sleep.

I don't regret anything that happened between the two of us, E. I really hope you feel the same.

Love,

Kiara

CHAPTER TWENTY

1 *7th August, Friday*
I can't believe we had sex. Wow. I still feel that it was all just a dream. Let me pinch myself—

Well, it was real. I mean, we stayed up all night. Having sex, cuddling, laughing, dizzy talking. To be honest, the first time was a little uncomfortable, but soon we practiced enough to know why the world was so obsessed with sex. It was so euphoric and you lose calories without working out!

But I hated how you teased me on my weird penguin walk. My, oh my, was I sore? Still, it was a good kind of sore. Not painfully sore, if you know what I mean. I am rambling, sorry.

If I said I loved you before then, I think I am more than in love with you after yesterday. The rose, the 'I am Jedi!' lightning neon condom, your main purpose to make me comfortable, making me laugh and your gentleness after we did the deed, everything you did makes my heart flutter.

I am made for your love, Ethan Kane.

Love,

Kiara

CHAPTER TWENTY-ONE

2*0th August, Monday*

I won't apologize for not writing daily because I can't keep up with a routine—you of all people know that.

Seems like we all are hiding secrets from each other.

But my question to you is that, are you keeping it a secret to protect me? Because you know why I kept all this shit from you, to protect you. From me.

I don't think you are protecting me by hiding it. I can see the words *slut* written on my locker, E. You can't just go around punching every guy who passed by my locker. But it's okay. They are just words and I am fine with it.

You don't have to do anything about it. I am fine.

Love,

Kiara

CHAPTER TWENTY-TWO

2 *5th August, Saturday*

Did I ever mention that you would make a great boyfriend? Not that we are in a relationship, but I could tell from eighteen years of us being best friends . . . and doing other deeds.

Yeah, just wanted to get that out. I'll get back to cuddling you because you're already whining in your sleep. Even though you're three times my size, I don't mind being the bigger spoon, just saying.

Love,

Kiara

CHAPTER TWENTY-THREE

5th *September, Wednesday*

I am so done with this life. She's dead. My mother is dead . . . oh, God.

I can't keep going on like this, Ethan. I am tired. Fucking exhausted. The worst part is that when she was in pain, I was busy having sex with you in the school cubicle. I hate myself. I hate this body. I hate everything.

It broke me to see my dad cry, hear my brother's muffled sobs and your warm tears on my skin when you cried, hiding your face in my neck. I couldn't cry but let silent tears slide down my face.

I got angry with myself when you said you didn't want to touch me like that or even help me forget. I hurt you using my words, but you didn't run away.

Why didn't you? You can't let me do that to you, Ethan. Maybe it's a good thing I left in the end.

I want nothing but the hurt to swallow me whole and drown in my own tears.

CHAPTER TWENTY-FOUR

5 *th October, Friday*
It's been a month since my mom passed away. It's also been a month since I stopped writing. How could I when the pen and my reflection remind me of my dead mother?

I thought things would change, but most of it has stayed the same. The world goes on whether or not you're suffering.

Thank you, Ethan, for scolding me and getting me to eat, and to stop pretending to sleep all the time. I would wake up with a nightmare and you'd always be there, calming me down and bathing me in warm water if I had a panic attack. You are truly an angel.

I know you saw how skinny I had become and heard me puking out the food as soon as I ate. You are stubborn when you want something. Even if it means taking care of me and learning how to make Indian food for me. You burnt the curry yesterday with the pan, but I forgave you because you looked adorable with a sheepish smile.

I gave you your sketch I was working on. Before Karan ruined it and I had the guts to sketch it again.

But, hey, you loved it, so that's something. You showed it through something else, which was a bonus.

Even though we broke my bed and my dad grounded me for 'jumping too much on the bed.' I knew you were holding your laugh standing buck naked in my closet, you loveable fool!

Sigh. Is it bad that I forgive you for breaking one thing I love more than you? It's like my favorite thing broke my other favorite thing. Even though you're not a thing to me, you already know that.

In case you're wondering, we have already ordered a new bed for me and it's tougher than the last one but please, don't break this one, too.

Love,

Kiara

CHAPTER TWENTY-FIVE

1 *1th October, Thursday*
So . . .
I had my first and last lesbian encounter.

Remember, we had rough and almost jealous sex in your car after we left the library? I know I was riding you hard (you didn't complain) but I was jealous, okay? Probably you were, too.

That is why we had so much fun with the chocolate cake. You know what I mean.

Love,
Kiara

CHAPTER TWENTY-SIX

2nd October, Monday

2You know what scares me the most other than losing myself and dying? *You.* Losing you. And I almost did today.

I know you didn't mean the words you said to me when you saw Liam hugging me and hearing me confess that we had shared a kiss. But they still hurt. Not to mention, my father wanted to go back to India and I just couldn't handle it all.

It hurt me more when you said you didn't want to see any of us. But I stayed put. I was scared that if I moved an inch, something would happen to you and I would blame myself for it. I was fuming with anger, pain and hurt when I saw you on that bed. I never want to go through that again, Ethan.

Yes, I let the words slip out about how I feel about you in anger, but don't you ever scare me like that again.

It was the scariest incident of my life. Even scarier than me being suicidal because I might lose the only thing I was living for.

Love,
Kiara

CHAPTER TWENTY-SEVEN

2 *6th October, Friday*

Today is the most special day, E. Today, eighteen years ago, you were born covered in blood and screaming your throat out. Yes, I wanted to make sure you cringed.

I can't imagine growing up without you by my side. I've successfully completed my first ever book so I could give it to you as your birthday gift. Ignore the mistakes, grammar Nazi. I may or may not have written their first intimate moment from personal experience . . . if you get my drift.

Even though I am a mess, I hope you know that you mean everything to me.

Love,

Kiara

CHAPTER TWENTY-EIGHT

2 *9th October, Monday*
I went to school today and . . . some stuff happened. Nasty stuff. Which I don't want to tell anyone about. *Ever.* But I can't hide it from you either.

You were getting discharged today, and we were happy about it. I had decided to take personal care of you and Katherine teased me to wear a sexy nurse outfit for you. I'm sure you would have liked that very much.

I think I would have worn it if I was not harassed by Dave Cooper, the one and only dearest son of principal Inez.

I can't talk about it so I am doing what I am good at. Writing about it. I may or may not have told him off in the canteen when he and his friends were making fun of you. I couldn't stand it, so I insulted him in front of his friends. I get it; I overstepped a line. But what he did to me . . . was far worse.

He must have followed me to the girl's bathroom when I was alone and, um, tried to force himself on me. He called me a slut, whore and what-not. For a moment, I was scared. I was frozen with what seemed like fear running in my veins. I was terrified when he grabbed my wrists and shoved his tongue down my throat. I knew I was crying, tasting the salt in my mouth and trying to push him away when his . . . oh God, his hand lowered to my jeans.

I bit his tongue and pushed him away as hard as I could, covering myself from him and his disgusted eyes. What he did next shocked me. He looked genuinely surprised when he saw how terrified I was of him. He seemed to get out of his trance.

He stared at my tearful eyes and said that this was supposed to be a prank and that he didn't mean any of it. Like yeah, groping someone and forcefully kissing them while they cried to get away is supposed to be a prank.

Dave Cooper and his friends are worthless pieces of shits. For doing this to me and God knows how many other girls they have pranked. I don't know how many times I washed my face, hands and mouth trying to get rid of his touch and scent.

I realized that I can't always be Jhansi Ki Rani.

I somehow got home without getting scared of any guy who walked past me. I apologize for not being there to take you home when you were discharged. I was too busy hating myself and my body.

I picked the blade. I won't go into details, but yes, I cut myself. It was just in the moment when all the dark thoughts came. Like I said before, one step toward happiness and ten big steps backward into the darkness. You know it's ironic how the voice in my head told me to cut myself but it was also the one who said that I am not alone just lonely.

I am such a crazy person to befriend that voice, aren't I? Or was I too desperate for someone to feel my pain and understand it?

3 *0th October, Tuesday*

I love how your face lights up like the fourth of July when you see me laugh or smile, especially when you are the reason behind that smile. I really do. It's like you have achieved something impossible that you are proud of.

But you can't always do that, Ethan.

When we were kissing today and going to do more intimate stuff, I remembered that I had disgusting cuts on my thighs. I didn't want you to see them and ask me what had happened because I knew I would have told you. About everything.

That's why I tried to push you away when you were about to remove my pajamas. But that's not the whole point. I saw Dave's face every time you kissed me and felt his rough hands when you held me.

It was wrong, but I was scared. I am sorry you had to see me cry and almost have an anxiety attack. I couldn't help myself.

I didn't sleep that night until I had enough guts to face you. So, I took my blanket and snuggled with you. As your warm body cuddled with me, all the bad thoughts went away. Just like that. I apologized to you and I meant it.

I pushed you away, but you stayed and now I wished I had stayed too.

Love,
Kiara

CHAPTER THIRTY

It's been such a long time since I opened this book and made myself vulnerable. Maybe I was a coward, or maybe I was busy. You'll never know.

I have decided, Ethan. I have already hurt myself, Liam, and a little part of you. I can't do that again anymore.

Today was prom, and it was great.

I almost tripped on my heels when I saw you tonight. Your green and blue eyes were shining so brightly with a slight curve on your lips that made my heartbeat faster. I wanted to cry seeing you like that, as you gazed at me with so much adoration in your beautiful unmatched eyes. Because, soon, I would lose the one person I breathed for.

I wanted tonight to be just us. I ignored the guilty stares of Dave and his friends, the longing gaze of Liam, and lost myself in you.

I love how you didn't complain when I stepped on your toes and told me to sway at the music. You're too good to me, Ethan.

Maybe this was a good thing. Because if I would have

stayed, I would pretend to be normal, and you'd never know how I felt all this time.

I would never forget about tonight, Ethan. Wherever I go, I will always have tonight locked in my heart. It was so hard not to spill the truth when you hovered above me and looked at me with your unmatched eyes like I was everything and more you wished for.

We both were crying at the intimacy and pleasure as if it was our first time. In a way, it was. We made love today. Not to each other's bodies, but to our souls. Every part of it was beautiful.

It hurts to know that I will never experience it again.

I hated waking up and getting dressed while you slept. A goofy smile curved on your lips. Maybe dreaming about our future. It hurts to know that I won't be with you the next morning, or in your future.

With a heavy heart, I crossed the distance between us and held back my tears as I let myself open up to you. I hope you forgive me and know that I love you.

I am a mess, Ethan. You don't deserve me. You deserve someone better and more. A person who won't lie to you every single day. A person who won't hide their true self from you. Maybe I am worse than Ariana to do this to you. You are my saving grace, E. I can't stand the idea that I let myself hurt you so much, I am sorry for losing you.

I hope that tomorrow when you wake up, you might understand why I had to do it.

I love you.

END OF PART ONE

SIX YEARS LATER

I saw you today, and it almost made my heart stop.

Your hair is longer than before and your smile is even wider. You looked so breathtaking, laughing without a care in this world. The same old dimples I loved—deeper than before as they poked your cheeks. Your golden skin was glowing.

Should I come talk to you? Would you scrunch your nose in that adorable way I know when I struggle to stumble words out of my lips? Would you look at me like a past lover or a stranger?

Maybe I shouldn't get my heart broken today. Well, *too* late.

Ethan

PART TWO

"I wish I had never loved you."

1. YOU WILL USE THE SAFE WORD

ETHAN

I stared deadly at the pen stand, my heavy-lidded eyes barely staying up. *Fuck.* I need to sleep. Then I remembered how I had slept last night and smiled.

"Ethan!"

My skin jumped, my eyes fluttering open and blinking at my agent, Elliot Warner, with wide innocent eyes. I rubbed my eyes and shuffled in my seat.

I drawled, "What now? Am I getting detention again?"

He sighed audibly, a sign that I had fucked up badly this time. Not going to lie, I had been fucking up since last year, so he has been sighing a lot. I wouldn't be surprised if I was the reason behind the white thinning hair on his sides.

"Not detention. But our sponsors are cutting the endorsement deals," he ran a hand through his hair and sat down behind his massive oak wood desk and lit up a cigar.

The stench of smoke woke me up from the hangover, my skin crawling with the need to put the cigarette in between my lips and inhale—*No, we are not going there, Ethan.*

I replayed his words twice in my head and drank a glass

of water. "Why the endorsement deals? I scored a gold medal, didn't I?"

I don't know why I even bothered asking that when I knew the answer.

I had fucked up. *Big time.*

Elliot smiled at me like a father would at his son. "You punched Richard fucking Jane. Did you forget about that when you spent time with Aretta last night? Seriously, Kane, what the fuck were you thinking?"

I slouched in my seat, looking at the lollipop wrapped in sparkly red paper. *Of course, I remember it.* How could I forget punching the famous celebrity reporter, Richard Jane. It felt so good doing it that I forgot his cameraman had the footage and leaked it on the internet, so I was on every celebrity news.

Ethan Kane, the twenty-five-year-old swim athlete and a model, punched Richard Jane, fleeing away from the scene to spend the night with the famous pop singer, Aretta.

I remember how it all started. Liam and I were invited to the VS fashion show as we were top swimmers after passing USA Swimming Olympic Trials with A-Level qualification standards. But he bailed on me at the last moment as he had some issues with his family to deal with and couldn't arrive there.

"How did you sleep last night?" Elliot asked, his voice stern while he watched me with his piercing coal black eyes.

I smiled thinking about last night. About Aretta. I ran my hand through my hair and smirked at him, "I slept like a baby."

He gave me the briefest smile. "Touché. Hope you had fun last night, Kane, because you need to clean up your act or your sponsors are cutting you out of the endorsement deals."

I frowned, my head still throbbing slightly from the little alcohol I had last night. "Clean up what act?"

He leaned back in his chair and I knew I was about to get a lecture. "Oh, let me think. Last month you slept with Chris Moore's wife, and then your dick didn't have enough so you slept with his twenty-one-year-old daughter a week later, officially removing you from his modelling gig. Not to mention, *Julian.* You were drunk and flirted with a female cop and slept with her in the back of her cop car. Do you know how hard it was for me to clean that up? And last night, you punched Richard *fucking* Jane in front of his cameraman, and every news, fashion and fitness magazine is talking about you."

I flashed him a grin.

He glared at me.

My grin dropped. I sighed, keeping my elbows on his large oak wood desk. "Okay, first of all, Chris Moore's wife is hot; you have seen her. How could I resist when she wanted me to fuck her on her bed? And the daughter was really sweet. We were both tipsy after a party and it just happened. About Julian, *um,* long story short. Someone caught her with her handcuffed to the door because we lost the key. Not to mention, Richard deserved it."

My nerves twitched just thinking about Richard, the oh so fancy reporter who I hated with all my guts. Especially after what he did last night.

Elliot, my agent and a good friend, knew I wouldn't have resorted to violence without a motive. His jaw ticked when he said, "HR doesn't care about that shit, Kane. They want you to clean up your act."

Of course, they wanted me to clean up my act. I *needed* to clean up my act. I could imagine my mothers' faces when they saw the news and called me later to talk to me about it. I closed my eyes and wondered how everything went to shit.

The music was too loud at the after party of the VS show. I took a flute of champagne and downed it in three gulps. My bow tie was itching me, so I took it off, tugged at a few buttons and kept it in my pocket. The air felt too heavy with perfume, alcohol and something female and musky. I could smell the hair products from the striking lady sitting beside me during the dinner.

I jumped when her hand landed on my thigh and gave it a squeeze. I smiled, turning to her when she flashed me a toothy grin, her red lipstick perfect for her lips. But there was something in her gaze, which I didn't want right then. Especially when her claws painted in the same shade of red trailed upwards.

I held her wrist, leaning closer to her and whispered in her ear, "Slide your hand anymore further and I will make sure that your ass is bruised with my belt marks till next week."

Pulling away, I flashed her a small smile, watching her gape at me. She clearly didn't expect that and moved her hand on her lap when I let it go.

After the dessert was served, I looked at the chocolate mousse and felt bile rising in my mouth. I quickly excused myself to the washroom and splashed some cold water on my face. *It is nothing, Ethan. Just calm down. Count to ten.* I wiped my face and stared at the blue-green eyes across me.

The door of the washroom opened, and I closed my eyes when it was the same lady who had sat beside me during the meal. Chris Moore's wife, Sadie Moore. I clenched my jaw when she trailed her hand on my arm, but I still felt her touch through my suit. I straightened up, easily towering in front of her, and she dropped her hand.

"I . . . I would like that," she whispered, her eyes wide with lust.

I tilted my head.

"I want you to do that, Ethan. I have heard rumors about—"

Waving her off, I said, "Not tonight. Go find someone else." My eyes raked over her curvy frame and met hers. I smirked, "You wouldn't be able to handle it, anyway. Goodnight, Mrs. Moore. Tell your husband I said hello."

Her cheeks flamed with embarrassment as I left her alone in the washroom. I checked my phone, seeing three missed calls from Aretta and one from my mom. After letting my agent know I was leaving, I made my way out of the hotel and breathed in the warm crisp air of Los Angeles. The atmosphere was dark with few glowing lights decorated along the porch of the hotel. I wondered whether I should pack my bags to go back to San Diego, visit my family, or go visit Aretta. I looked up at the night sky and waited for my driver.

I frowned, hearing a commotion over my shoulder. My mouth set in a grim line when I saw who it was, Richard Jane. Sliding my hands in my slacks, I turned toward them and saw that the hotel security was far away from the reporter, his cameraman, and the model they wanted to interview. I was about to turn away, thinking it was an everyday thing when I heard her words.

"Please move away," her voice was stern. Her heels clicked against the cobblestone when she took a step back as he got too close to her.

My jaw clenched and palms turned into fists when the cameraman zoomed in on her face. But I had my doubts that he was zooming in on something else.

Richard's voice was low and heavy, his face wrinkled with age as he was nearing his fifties. Still the best Hollywood reporter out there. He leaned in and asked, "Just answer one question, Ma'am. Did you or did you not frame the nip slip at Coachella?"

I rolled my eyes. *Are you fucking kidding me?*

She flinched away, giving him a disgusting look. "I am not

going to answer that, and it's none of your fucking business." Her hands were on his chest, trying to get away from him, "*Seriously*, move the fuck away."

Images flashed in my mind. Her wavy brown hair mussed, puffy eyes stained with tears, lips quivering and her hands in fists. *Just because of men like him.* I swallowed the lump in my throat thinking about that diary page which had blurry words because her tears had smudged the black ink on the paper.

I couldn't watch this any longer.

"She told you to move, Jane."

The cameraman turned toward me, so did Richard and Emma. She was an aspiring model, and after working with her on a couple of shoots, I knew how sweet she was. He stepped back from her and flared his angry red nose at me.

"Shove it, Ethan. Is there something going on between you two? It will make a great headline. Ethan Kane strikes another model's pussy again," he chuckled, his yellow-stained lower teeth grinning at me.

I didn't feel like giving him a reply and raised my palm for her. She accepted it with a small smile, and I pulled her closer, away from Richard.

"Let him be, Ethan. He is an asshole," she whispered when I turned to escort her away from there.

"What did you just say, you bitch?" Richard spat.

A small smirk tugged at the corner of my lips, but Emma yelped when she was pushed down from behind. I helped her up, seeing a slight bruise on her knee. I asked her if she was okay. She was not. She looked like she was about to cry.

I looked at him, anger boiling inside me, and without even thinking, I threw my fist at his nose. He screamed, but I held his collar with my throbbing knuckles and said, "Dare to even think about touching someone like that again and I will break your arm." I pushed him away, glaring at him when he whimpered, trying to control the bleeding from his cracked nose, "Watch your fucking tongue."

I helped wide-eyed Emma away from there.

I asked, "You okay?"

She was shaking.

"You didn't need to punch him. He will press charges against you."

"I would love to see him try."

The driver was waiting for me in my Mercedes. I opened the door and said to her, "Get inside. You were clearly waiting for someone to arrive, but I am not letting you wait out here alone. Tell him the address and he will drop you off."

Her eyes widened, and she shook her head, "I can't have that, Ethan. I am really thankful for this, but you don't have to."

I gave her a firm look and tilted my head to the open car door, "Get inside the car, Emma. I have to be somewhere else, anyway. You need to get home safe and clean up that cut."

I was surprised when she leaned up and hugged me. I froze when she whispered, "Thank you, Ethan Kane. You're not as bad as they told me."

She gave me a brief smile and sat in the comfortable leather seats. I closed the door for her.

I am as bad as they told you.

Running my hand through my hair, I replied to Aretta's text and told her what to do. I stared out of the window of the taxi and clenched my palm. It still stung from the punch. I don't know how I lost my control so easily. It was *her*. She made me lose my control. Even after six years, she still had that power over me. Just a few little words and I turn into someone I hate.

Closing my eyes, I sighed and leaned back in the seat.

The cabbie glanced at me from his rearview mirror, "What has you sighing like that, young man?"

Someone must have added some kind of truth serum to my food when I told him, "Nothing, just remembered someone harassing my ex-girlfriend and I couldn't do anything about it."

What the fuck, Ethan?

He nodded. He looked over fifty, small lines of wrinkles etching his face when he frowned. "Ah, that is a sad thing. If she said that to you, then she must have truly loved you."

"No, yes, maybe," I paused. "She left me."

My heartbeat wildly every time I tried to talk about her. My stomach coiled tightly and a small headache was churning in my head.

The cabbie smiled at me through the rearview mirror, a sad smile. "All troubled women do. Must be hard, but at least you have sweet memories of her."

I smiled sadly, thinking about those memories. Now tainted with nothing but sadness, regret, and guilt. "A lot, actually. We were best friends."

"Cherish them, young man, and I hope you will find love again," his words were sincere when he stopped the car at the hotel. He grinned back at me, "I have to go, my wife's been waiting for me to eat this mean steak she makes."

"How long have you been married to her?" I asked, nodding at the sweet picture of them together, probably in their twenties, over the dashboard.

"Thirty years and still counting."

I smiled at him and paid him with a hefty tip. "Take care and thank you for this."

I didn't know why I said that. He didn't ask what I meant by '*this*' because my nerves snaked in my body, and as soon as I said it, I left the car. I exhaled sharply and checked the time. Five minutes left.

Telling myself that this was what I needed, I went to the corridor of the corner room on the eighth floor. It was time. But I waited for two more minutes, just playing with her mind.

I needed this right now. I needed to gain control back. I craved it like a druggie who promised it was his last dose but still went back for more.

Turning the knob, I stepped inside.

Good, she had obeyed to keep it unlocked. I closed the door behind me with a slam and her body gave a small shudder. I smiled and stepped inside the suite, her naked body glinting in the moonlight as she stayed still. Bent over the balcony with her hands holding the railings.

I teased, "Well, look at what we have here."

Her ass arched up in my direction even though I stayed perfectly still near the door. I wanted her like that. Desperate and needy. Her eyes were blindfolded like I had asked her to do. Keeping the door unlocked, she would think anyone would enter and see her that way, and I wanted her to think like that. Even though I had paid the hotel manager to make sure that the eighth-floor stayed empty and no one stepped in here.

I went to the minibar and poured a glass of scotch. Taking a slow sip, savoring the burning taste on my tongue, I walked toward her. The room was chilly and the air was tinged with her fruity perfume. I stood exactly behind her, watching her chocolaty body quiver with excitement. Her dark curls brushed her lower neck when she arched her body back at me.

Putting the empty glass on the table, I brushed my fingers down her back, goosebumps rising on her skin. I lowered them between her creamy thighs. She let out a small gasp when I rubbed the slickness of her pussy—so wet and ready.

"Sir, please?"

I stopped. "Did I allow you to speak?"

She shook her head, her knees buckling slightly.

Her thighs trembled when I edged her, rubbing her engorged clit and squeezing her ass with my other hand. We both sighed for other reasons when I smacked her ass.

"Spread your legs, Aretta," I said, "Let me see your dripping cunt, how greedy you are."

She moaned, her legs spreading wider and my cock pressing tightly against my pants when I saw her bare pussy, dripping with arousal and grinding herself on my fingers.

I pulled my hand away and stepped closer to her. I grabbed her curls and pushed my fingers inside her mouth, making her taste herself. She groaned and sucked them clean when I rubbed my hard length on her through my pants.

I did it again, this time spanking her on her other cheek and rolled her tight nipple with my fingers, which were wet with her saliva. She moaned louder.

I whispered gruffly in her ear, "Did you touch yourself, thinking about me? How I would spank this pussy of yours? Fuck you when you are nothing but a moaning mess?"

Pulling away and letting go of her hair, I smacked her in between her thighs, landing it perfectly on her sensitive clit and her body bucked. If she wasn't holding onto the railing, she would've lost her balance.

"I did, Sir, please, I am so close!" She breathed, pushing herself back, trying to find me and rub herself.

"No. Turn around, you've been bad for not following my orders," I said and held her elbow when she straightened. Her knees were buckling, and I didn't want her to fall. I removed her blindfold. "I am going to spank your ass. You can use your safe word."

Her pupils dilated, and she licked her lips, watching me for the first time tonight. Her fingers trailed over my shoulder to the hard planes of my chest. I raised my eyebrow but let her continue. She cupped me through my pants, and I watched her palm stroking me.

"Can I use some other way where you don't need to punish me?" She whispered, her voice breathy.

I shook my head, "No, you should've thought of that before touching yourself. Get on the bed. Face down, ass up."

She frowned but followed my demand, lying down on the king-size poster bed. I told her to keep her hands above her head while I removed the cuff links and my jacket. Her eyes followed me when I rolled my sleeves above my forearms and unbuckled my belt.

Standing at the edge of the bed, I looked down at her and kissed her back. "I will use my belt, Aretta," I whispered lightly, noting her reaction.

She trembled, a shaky breath leaving her plum lips, but she didn't fight.

"Use the safe word," I reminded her and stepped back, looping the belt in my hands, readying myself.

She smiled back at me, "I won't."

I tilted my head, "You will."

And landed the first *smack* on her ass.

She gasped, and I only allowed two seconds for her to recover before I set into my rhythm, making sure I never went too close to her sex or strayed far from the soft skin of her ass. It was hurting her, I could see it in her clenched fists, furrowed brows, writhing body and crying moans. But it was also turning her on. Her dark nipples were hard, and her arousal was sliding down her inner thigh when her ass turned into a light hue of red.

I was panting too, waiting for her to say her safe word, my smacks getting harder and rougher. The only sounds in the room were of her cries, my increased breath and the sound of leather smacking sharply against her ass.

"Red, red, red," she blabbered, her voice thick.

I stopped, dropping the belt, and went toward her, "Told you, you will."

Gently gathering her in my arms, I let her hide her face in my neck as she cried. I rubbed her back, soothing her, "Shh, stop crying, it's over now. Close your eyes and feel. Take deep breaths, Aretta. You did so well."

She nodded because she knew I meant using the safe word, not the spanking. She knew I honored using the safe word more than the punishment.

We both took a shower together. I held her close, fingering her, gazing at her beautiful face when she came apart in my palm. Cleaning both of us, I told her to apply chamomile lotion on her ass. I ignored her sad frown when I got dressed back in my clothes and kissed her on her forehead. I was gathering my wallet, phone and keys when Aretta breathed sharply over my shoulder.

She was checking her phone, sitting naked on the bed.

"What happened?"

She looked up at me and my right hand. "You punched Richard Jane?"

I pursed my lips, "*About that.*"

Clearing my throat, I blinked back at my agent. That was last night, and my knuckles still throbbed. My only regret was that I wish I had broken his nose.

"So? What do they want me to do? Knowing HR, they've already planned something for me. Are they cutting me out?" I asked with a devious grin.

They would be idiots to cut out a pro athlete like me.

Elliot chuckled, "They are not that much of idiots, Kane."

Knew it.

"So?"

This time, he grinned back at me, "You have to do some volunteering."

"Volunteering?"

Elliot nodded as if he was talking to his ten-year-old daughter. "Yes, community service to show the media that you are not going off the bat by punching reporters. They need to know that you are still sane."

I rolled my eyes. "Yes, Daddy."

"You give me more grey hairs than my daughters," he muttered and stood up, gathering some papers. "I will talk to HR and you have to decide where you want to work."

He was about to walk out of his office when he paused, "And, Ethan? You can have that lollipop."

Fucking scored it.

2. BEDROOM EYES

KIARA

I gathered all the test papers I had graded last night and organized them according to the students' names while two pairs of eyes watched me from their tiny desks.

Sighing, I raised my brow at them, "What happened? Why are you two frowning?"

I couldn't blame them. They were the only kids left in my classroom while others were in the cafeteria, having fun with their friends and eating lunch.

Ben swung his legs, sitting on the desk. It wasn't allowed, but I didn't mind. "Do you really have to call in my mom, Miss Kiara?" he asked, his voice small.

I gave him a reassuring smile and cleaned up the desk. "Yes, Ben, you know the drill. We call in parents when teachers need to talk to parents about some stuff."

I didn't need to tell him all the details. He was still a kid. I would talk about it with his parents.

Andrew Wu stopped doodling in his notebook. His light brown eyes, similar to his mom's, narrowed in confusion. "What will you tell Mom? You talk to her every day."

I did because he and his mom were my roommates for the

"

past two years. We were more than roommates.

"I do, but this is related to school and Mr. Davis personally asked me to call and talk to them, so I have to."

I asked if they took the notes of the adverb clause I had taught them today and cleared up the whiteboard. I checked the time and heard the little growls in their stomach.

Walking to my handbag, I pulled out my lunch box and kept it on my empty desk. "Who wants to eat gulab jamuns?"

The legs of the desk squeaked as they shuffled out of it and ran for the sweets covered in sugary syrup. I smiled at them as they fought for the last piece after stuffing it in their mouths like squirrels. It almost reminded me of me and Eth—

My stomach coiled, and the smile wiped off my face. I sat down on the desk and tried to count to ten. He still slipped into my brain. Six years and I still couldn't forget him. My therapist had told me I never would. Too much had happened in too little time. I could never forget him.

How could I when he was the most important part of my life?

Ben and Andrew were distracted and having their own lunch, talking about a new anime they were watching while I pulled out a small journal and wrote what I felt about thinking about him all of a sudden. I wondered if I should check in with my therapist and sent her a quick text. Her reply came fast as it was lunch hour. She told me not to worry too much. Fragments of memories were inevitable, and I didn't need to worry about it every time I thought of him.

My stomach clenched with nerves. I knew something was missing. Shaking my head, I decided I would figure it out after school. I needed to be at my best right then.

After finishing the lunch with Ben and Andrew, who were now grinning from ear to ear because of the sweet gulab jamuns, I made a quick trip to the washroom and cooled down before two more classes.

I was on my way to my class when I saw a kid trip down the stairs because of his shoelace. I rushed to him and helped him on the stairs, looking for any wound. He had bruised his elbow a little. He seemed about seven to eight years old, much younger than the kids I teach.

I gently inspected his elbow, his shoulders slouching as he tried hard not to cry. "It's okay, love. I will help you clean it. Come on, I have a bandage in my bag just over here."

I helped him tie up his shoelace, and he followed me quietly. He said he was going back to his class after having lunch with his friends, but he wanted to go to the washroom first. I smiled and sat him down on my chair, pulling out a bandage and cotton from my bag.

As I cleaned the minor wound, I asked, "So, what's your name? I am Kiara."

"Rahul," he mumbled, biting his lip.

"That's a really good name," I said. "I have a friend in India named Rahul."

"Oh," his dark brown eyes widened. "I bet he doesn't trip like I do."

"I will tell you a secret, Rahul." He listened to me and I whispered, "He is worse."

A fit of giggles escaped his lips, and I grinned at him.

"But don't be afraid to fall, okay?" I said. "It is okay to fall. You know why?"

He shook his head, his attention fixed on me as I took a small bandage.

"Because you have the courage to stand up again."

He nodded and looked at his elbow where I had applied the bandage. He gasped, "Spiderman!"

"Yes, Spiderman. Just like him."

His grin was so wide, I could see the freckles splattered over his small nose and cheeks, his chocolate skin glowing. "Thank you, Miss! I will show this Spiderman to all my friends, they will be so jealous."

I let out a soft chuckle, and he kissed my cheek before rushing out of the classroom.

"Watch your steps!" I called after him, but he was already out of earshot.

I gazed back at my empty chair and nibbled on my lip. I took a deep breath and focused on the next class, which was about to begin.

After the last students left, handing me their assignments, I erased the board and solved the question one girl had. She thanked me when I helped her with my own notes and allowed her to take a picture on her phone. I watched her leave and saw a gorgeous blonde woman in fitted trousers and a blouse as she smiled warmly at me, knocking lightly at the door. I let her in and saw Ben following his mother. I could see the resemblance between the two. Same golden blonde hair, small nose and deep blue eyes.

Her voice was sweet when she introduced herself. "Hello, I am Ben's mother, Stacy, and I am so glad to finally meet you. Benny can't stop talking about the new English teacher, and because of you, his grades have improved a lot. Thank you so much for all the extra lessons."

My cheeks flushed. "Oh, I am sure it's because of all the hard work Ben puts in his studies. I am very proud of all my students. He worked hard to get the grades he has."

Andrew kept doodling as Ben went to stand beside him, talking to his friend. Other kids' parents had already talked to me, but Ben had told me that his mother wanted to personally meet me.

I handed her Ben's test papers and heat bloomed in my

chest when I noticed her face light up. I could see it all. She was proud of her son for all the A's he scored, way better than the C's from last semester. She would kiss him on his cheek and maybe treat him with junk food on their way back home. Or their family would go out for dinner, or maybe she would make his favorite dish.

I swallowed the lump in my throat. My mother used to do that when she was alive. She would make delicious Indian sweets for me and Ethan when either of us scored good. Or not. It didn't matter. She loved to spoil us with sugary goods, and my dad would banter playfully with her while he helped her make the sweets.

Snapping my mind out of the old memories, I focused on talking to Stacy about the next month's meeting when Ben stood close to his mom and whispered in her ear.

"Mom, can we please hurry? Dad's visiting us for dinner today and he promised he will play video games with me."

I smiled at him and looked at Andrew. My heart felt heavy. He looked down at his doodles. I knew that he was longing for his father too, with whom he could play video games and talk about all the boy stuff. But how could I tell him that his father was a douchebag who left his mom as soon as she told him she was pregnant.

Stacy patted his hand and calmly said, "Of course, sweetheart. I am thanking your teacher for helping you with the essay."

I tucked a strand of hair behind my ear. "Okay, I won't hold you guys longer. Be sure to come to the meeting. The principal, Mr. Davis, is very strict about it as we will discuss the syllabus and chat with every parent."

She promised she would, and I was surprised when she hugged me before walking out of the classroom with Ben as he waved at his friend and me.

Andrew didn't want to talk, and I decided not to disturb

him while he worked on his sketch. I asked him if he wanted me to call his mom, but he just shrugged.

It relieved me when she walked into the class, slipping off her sunglasses and nodding at me. She was in her I-am-a-lawyer-and-I-am-all-business dress code with a nice fitting suit for her slender frame, her sleek black hair in a perfect long bob.

Andrew rolled his eyes at his mom. "About time you got here."

Anya Wu narrowed her eyes at her son, pinching his ear. "Watch it, you."

I grinned at them when he whined, "Ow, Mom. Not in the school."

She let go and turned to me, "So, what did he do this time?"

"Have faith in your son, Anya. He is doing really great at his studies, but Davis wanted to call in all the parents and make sure they are present at the meeting next month. Show how serious we all are."

She nodded and helped pack up her son's stationary. "I will be there," she ruffled his hair and smiled at me, "Come on, let's go home."

I always let Andrew sit in the passenger seat as Anya drove the car back to the apartment we lived in. I had rented it two years ago when Anya, with her son and twin sister, shared the three-bedroom apartment. As Leni Wu was getting married, she had emptied her room and rented it to me.

But soon, I have to empty it too.

Smiling, I tried calling him, but his phone seemed switched off. Probably on a flight. He was coming back to San Diego from New York, and he had told me to get ready for a date. My stomach knotted with excitement. I would see him after two weeks.

I helped Anya and Andrew in making the dinner, cutting the tofu and watching her make a delicious curry while rice cooked in the rice cooker. I showered, applied lotion and changed into a navy-blue dress which hugged my body, accentuating my curves. My makeup was minimal, and my hair was down. Wearing black sandals, I waited for him.

Jake would be with me soon.

I smiled giddily, thinking back to the moment we had first met. Lina, Anya and I were traveling to Las Vegas for her bachelorette party and waiting for the gas to fill.

Why did I agree to come to Vegas for a bachelorette party with these crazy twins? Oh, yes, because I wanted to get laid.

"I hate my life!" Lina Wu wailed, and I resisted my urge to throw a sandal at her. Anya patted her sister's shoulder. The weather was so dry and humid, it made me crankier than our car getting beaten up when we stopped for gas at a gas station in the middle of a highway.

I shook my head and looked at our beaten-up Mini Cooper and kicked the tire. It shook, making me stagger back, tripping on my sandals. I squeezed my eyes, ready to hit the pavement and start the *wonderful* bachelorette party.

But the fall never came.

"Woah!" A deep husky male voice whispered, catching me in his arms. I held the fabric of his shirt for dear life, feeling his warm breath caressing my ear.

I opened my eyes and stared back at the most stunning pair of crystal blue eyes. They gazed back at me with dilated pupils, making them look almost black if you weren't staring closely. My eyes traveled to his sharp cheekbones and sensuous lips. My breath hitched in my throat and I felt a shiver slither down my spine from his touch on my waist, traveling down to my core, making my toes curl in delightful pleasure.

Bedroom Eyes. That was the word for those beautiful eyes.

The type of eyes that parents warned about and poets wrote about.

"Wow," he breathed out, gazing at my face and noticing every curve and flaw as if he wanted to remember me whenever he closed his eyes.

I blinked at him and mustered an awkward smile. I pulled away and felt my knees wobble at the sudden closeness of this gorgeous man. The musky scent of his cologne wafted through my nose. Yet somehow, I stood on my own legs while we stared at each other. More like, I stared up at him because of my short, closer-to-Satan height.

Brushing away the strands of my hair from my face, I noticed his sharp features and lowered my eyes to his v-neck black t-shirt. It hugged his broad shoulders, stretching over them. I clenched my fists trying to control my hormones and looked down at his long legs clad in pants and sneakers.

I felt heat surge my face under his scrutinizing gaze and chuckled nervously, "Um . . . thank you for catching me."

I ignored the sound of Lina and Anya as he smiled warmly at me, his teeth gleaming like white pearls, "It was nothing really, I feel honored."

Smiling at him, I felt my insides melt at his smooth, sultry voice as if he wasn't even trying to make his voice sound deeper. He was—what I like to call, 'Fuck-pussy on legs', just another idiom of 'sex on legs,' because I could imagine myself riding hi—

PG-13, Kia. PG-13.

I looked away, heat rushing to my face, neck, and ears as I sneakily checked his left hand to look for a ring and sighed in relief when I found it empty.

His voice snapped me out of my dirty, filthy thoughts, "So, what are you doing out here?" His voice traveled down to my core, and I had to clench my thighs because I wasn't wearing underwear.

Fuck my life.

I cleared my throat and pointed to the Mini Cooper we had rented for our drive to Las Vegas. "We were traveling to Vegas, but it broke down after we paid for the gas, and now we are hanging out here until the car service shows up." I looked at Lina who was crying about her no-bachelorette party and looked back at Blue-eyes who was gazing at me.

He watched me longingly and finally looked over my shoulder at the twins like it was a hard task to take his eyes off me. I blushed instantly, thinking about it, and bit my lip when his eyes dropped to them, making me release it instantly.

Why the fuck am I acting like a teenager?

Licking my lips, I straightened myself, and I swear I saw him hide a smile as his eyes glowed with mischief.

"Bachelorette?" He even checked my left hand for good measure.

I bit back my laugh, "Yeah, it was . . . but I bet it won't happen. The twin in the red top; her wedding is next week, and she's been acting like a bridezilla since last month."

"That's sad," I looked back at him and saw him biting his lip as he ran his hand through his smooth raven hair, "This is weird, but we have some space in our Safari and we're going to Vegas too."

I noticed his sleek black 1957 Pontiac Safari—*my God*, a hot guy with a hot car? I also noticed that he said 'we'. But as I squinted my eyes, I saw a ginger head guy bobbing his head to some 90s jam he was playing. I looked back at Blue-eyes and found him staring back at me with patience. Well, he didn't look like a serial killer. But who am I to judge a person to know whether he was a serial killer?

"Oh, and—" I almost jumped back when he stepped toward me. *Almost.* "I am Jake," he extended his hand to me. I stared at it like it was a baby dragon about to blow fire on me.

Not to mention he already blew fire on my pu—

I raised my hand, ignoring the zing of pleasure when he squeezed it. "Nice to meet you, Jake. I am Kiara." I smiled and realized how wonderful his name sounds from my lips.

It would sound much better if I was moaning it.

I clenched my thighs and let go of his calloused hand. Jake smiled, "Pleasure is mine, Kiara."

Was it bad that I wanted to hear him groan when I—*hold your thoughts, Kia. He is a respectable gentleman and he could be gay for all you know. He's a fine ass man with a fine ass, but don't forget that God created fine ass men as gay.*

I just said fine ass three times in one sentence. I needed to get laid. *Oh, Lord.*

Almost six months later, we were dating each other and next month, after the parents' meeting is over, I had asked Mr. Davis for a week vacation because—

My phone lit up with a text message, and I felt bubbles in my stomach seeing it was a text from him. My excitement died down when I read the text.

Jake: *Sorry, sweetheart. Flight is late. Might not make it.*

I groaned into my pillow and sighed. I removed my earrings and replied,

Me: *It's alright. Missing you.*

He didn't reply, and I quickly changed out of the dress into my pajamas. As soon as Anya saw me in his hoodie, she narrowed her eyes at me and kept her hands on her hips. This look was her special mom look, which was only meant for Andrew. Not for me. But I snuggled up to her and wrapped my arms around her and told her that his flight is late. She patted my hair and told me to sit with Andrew on the couch.

We all ate our dinner together, and I helped Andrew with

his homework while Anya read through one of her case files. I finished reading a fantasy novel and started braiding Anya's silky black hair.

She groaned, dropping the case file, "I swear to God, your hands have magic in them. Keep going."

I snickered and continued doing the *champi* on her hair without any hair oil, relaxing her. Andrew saw us and demanded it too, so his mom massaged his scalp while I did hers.

Another memory flashed in my brain. My mom applying hair oil on my hair, doing *champi* with her soft hands and me doing the same to Ethan's hair.

Closing my eyes, I tried to shake off the shivering feeling and excused myself to my room, sliding under the covers. Someone knocked on the front door and I heard muffled voices, but I ignored them. Why was my brain still not over him? I guess it had to do with spending most of my life with him.

"Kiara, your boyfriend's here," Anya knocked and opened the door, keeping her hand on her hip and glaring at Jake when he kept his suitcase down and came to me, hugging me in his arms.

"Fiancé, Anya," he corrected her.

I smiled and nuzzled my face in his sweater. I heard the door close, leaving us in our own bubble as I breathed in his musky cologne. This was what I needed right now. *Him.* His hands tightened before he moved back, kissing me on my lips. I melted in his arms, cupping his face, his lips soft on mine.

"I missed you," I whispered and pulled away to look at him.

His wavy onyx hair was tousled, blue eyes bright and shining, little stubble peppering his sharp jaw and cheekbones. A wide grin tugged his lips. "So did I," he kissed me again, "I brought something for you."

"You did?"

He nodded and pulled away to show me a box. I started drooling at the scent of cocoa in the air when he opened it and wriggled his eyebrows at me.

"Ta-da!" He exclaimed, bringing the chocolate cake closer to me.

"You're the best fiancé ever!" I said and grabbed the cake box, digging in the chocolate goodness with a spoon he offered me.

He told me he bought one for Anya and Andrew as well. We both ate it together, sharing it and feeding it to each other while he talked about his New York Fashion Show. When we had first met, I had told him he might be a pornstar because he looked famous. He had laughed at me and told me he was a model, and then it had clicked. The man who had saved me from a fall at a gas station was none other than *the* Jake O'Neal.

"Babe, what are your plans for next week?" Jake asked, his arms on my waist as we cuddled on the bed.

I shrugged, "The usual work stuff. Why do you ask?"

"Did you talk to your agent about your second book?" he said, his hand running through my hair.

I shook my head. After finishing university, I had published my debut novel and within the first three months, it had sold over a million copies all over the world. Even though I was glad to have writing as my job, I moved back to San Diego to teach full time.

"Later. I will talk to her later." I promised and trailed my hand on his sweater, feeling his heartbeat.

Jake faced me, his sharp, handsome face glowing in the dim light of the lamp. "I need to ask you about something."

I waited, wanting him to continue.

"There is this fashion event next week," he started but paused when he saw I was about to deny him. "Babe, just listen. It is a fashion event but also a fundraiser for children who have cancer. I am invited, and I wanted you to be my date for the event."

I wondered about it for a moment. I would definitely go for the fundraiser, but going with Jake also meant that the media would finally know about our engagement. As Jake was one of the best models in the fashion industry, we had decided to not let the media know about our engagement. I didn't mind it because it meant less attention on the both of us since he proposed to me on my twenty-fifth birthday.

"Are you ready to let . . ." I didn't need to finish the sentence.

He kissed my knuckles. "Yes, Kiara, I am. I want the entire world to know that I am getting married to one of the most brilliant women I know."

Shaking my head with a grin, I kissed him. "Fine, I will go with you. But you better feed me chocolate cake after the event."

He winked. "You know I will."

I admired his handsome face and blurted, "Jake . . . do you, do you want children after marriage?"

His eyes widened, and he stared at me. "Children?"

I nodded.

"Of course, babe, I want children," he said. "But I would rather wait for a year or two when we are both settled in our own home. I don't want to rush it."

I agreed, humming to him as I fell back in his arms. It will be *our* home when I move in with him next month. Anya had already found a better house for her and Andrew, which was closer to her law firm and the school.

As we both dozed off, I kept thinking about having children and hearing their tiny giggles in our home.

3. SHE WAS MY SAVING GRACE TOO

ETHAN

"So, you mean to tell me you punched him and went to cuddle with Aretta?"

I glared at his smug grin through my sunglasses. "Yes, Liam, I went to meet Aretta but for other reasons. And I don't cuddle."

"Yeah, right, as if I didn't catch you cuddling Evey last month," he said, opening the door of the café, the scent of freshly ground coffee wafting in my nose as I followed my friend.

"She is my little sister."

I missed her a lot because I had to leave San Diego for NYU, and then I couldn't spend as much time with her as I would like to. But I made it up to her and my parents every time I visited them. I met Liam again at NYU. He had applied for the same swim program that me and Rio had, so it was no surprise to find him there. Soon, we talked out everything between us, and since then, we have been good friends.

We sat in the corner booth, because we didn't need to draw attention to ourselves, and ordered breakfast.

"So, how serious is HR?" He asked, sipping on his black coffee.

"As serious as HR can get when they find their athlete punching a reporter and threatening to cut his arm."

He grinned at me, but his grin slipped off when he looked down at the styrofoam cup. I knew something was bothering him. His shoulders were tensed, and he couldn't look me in the eye.

"What is it?"

"Did you check up on that model?"

Sighing, I raked a hand through my hair and removed my sunglasses. "Her name is Emma. I haven't, actually. I will call her today."

He glared at me with his piercing grey eyes. "You could ask her to tell what happened, you know? You wouldn't be—"

"And then what?" I clenched my jaw. "They harassed her for fuck's sake, Liam. I will not ask her to tell the media what happened if she's not comfortable with it. I punched him so I will deal with it."

He stared at me for a moment, studying me, and nodded. "Okay. But how did it feel to punch that jerk?"

I grinned, "I wish I had done it before."

We laughed and ate eggs and bacon. We both were starving after our morning swim practice, but I knew I would let Liam take the lead at this Olympic. As we talked about swimming, modelling gigs and the endorsement deals, I realized I hadn't told him about the volunteering work I had to do.

"I have to volunteer for community service, or HR will cut off my sponsorship and endorsement deals," I said, waiting for his reaction.

"Of course, they would, Ethan. Remember Lee? They cut him loose because of a scandal. And this is big." I knew what he meant. "People are still talking about it even though it happened two weeks ago."

"I know. That's why I need your help to find me any service, so far what I have come up with doesn't fit with swim practice. Now is not the time to miss any of them."

I thanked the waitress when she cleared our empty plates from the table as Liam thought about it. After a moment, he grinned at me, "Did you search for any swimming related volunteer work?"

Now I knew where to look.

AFTER BREAKFAST WITH LIAM, I was back in the home I had bought as soon as I came back to San Diego. It was love at first sight. It was a two-story house, with a backyard pool and a small place for a barbecue. The lower floor had a large glass door which led to the pool and backyard. I remembered when I didn't have furniture for the house, I would sleep on the couch looking out of those glass doors. This home was my sanctuary.

I kept my car keys in the bowl and went upstairs into my room to check any emails. I also researched for any volunteer work related to swimming. I told Elliot about it, and he said that his assistant would send me the list before evening.

Ignoring Aretta's missed call, I took a quick shower and changed into sweatpants. My eyes went straight to the locked drawer in my closet. My jaw clenched and my pulse increased even thinking about it.

I shouldn't. But I needed it right now.

It was as if her words, her diary had invaded deep into my brain, my heart and my soul, that I knew I would forever be tainted with the memories we had spent together.

With a heavy heart, I unlock the drawer and take her

diary in my hand, already feeling the weight of her words on my body. I remembered the first time I read it on the flight from San Diego to New York. I had to rush to the washroom and puke out the breakfast I had. It was not because it was disgusting; it was because I had hated myself for not being the guy she could trust to tell me all about it. Later, I had realized that it was not my fault. None of it was. It depended on her, whether to tell me about it. We were just teenagers, high on love.

Taking a deep breath, I sat on the edge of my bed, my body already feeling stiff and foreign. I opened the old leather and flipped through the pages with blurred ink smattered across a few of the pages with her tears. I felt out of my body. As if I was nothing but a floating head in the room watching someone open the diary of his ex-lover because even after six years, he was not over her.

Will I ever get over Kiara Sharma? No, I won't. She loved me, I loved her, and it was nothing but a hurricane and storm striking together, ruining each other in the process. I did not want to forget her.

She was my saving grace, too.

Even now, as I opened the diary entry that had made me puke six years ago in an airplane, her words cut deep in my heart, bringing tears in my eyes. I blinked them away and read the last line of that entry.

I pushed you away, but you stayed and now I wished I had stayed too.

For years, I had wanted the same thing, but I knew that it wouldn't have helped her. She would have never been strong enough to talk to me about it, any of it. I hate it that she left so suddenly, but I knew she needed it.

I needed it too.

Closing the diary, I put it in the drawer and slammed it shut. I let out a sharp exhale and closed my eyes for a few moments. Just like every time I read one of her entries, I stalked her name on the internet. A small smile lit up my face when I read one of her interviews.

She was a teacher now. I chuckled thinking about Kiara Sharma, who had hated school for half of her life, teaching students, being their English teacher and grading essays. I remembered when I had seen her book, her debut novel, in the bookstore and bought it while I was in my last year of university. I was so proud of her I had finished it in two days. No wonder it was an International bestseller.

But then I read the acknowledgements and read how she wanted to thank young Kiara for falling in love with one of the best persons in this world. I was furious reading it, but it all died down in a few minutes.

I still had that copy in the same drawer. Locked away like a box of old memories. I would visit them like a nostalgic wounded lover in dark nights and early mornings, holding on to each page as if trying to figure out how she must have felt writing it down, pouring her heart out in blank pages.

Feeling overwhelmed, I called Emma and ignored the clipped warning from Elliot when I asked for her number. She picked up on the third ring, asking who it was. She was relieved when I said my name.

"How have you been?"

Words clogged my throat, thinking about large hands forcing her down, bruising her lips, icy fingers sliding down the skin.

I cleared my throat, "Are you okay?"

Emma didn't reply for a while. "Yeah, I am. Thank you, Ethan, but don't worry about it."

Her voice was too firm, but I didn't want to push her. "Okay. If you want to press charges against him, I have a lawyer who can help you."

I heard her laugh, "No, Ethan Kane. I am not some big

shot celebrity who can press charges on Richard Jane for manhandling me. Seriously, it *is* okay. He wouldn't be the first guy to do that, and certainly not the last."

"Emma."

"Why do you care, anyway?" She sighed. "I am glad you stepped in that night, but it's been two weeks."

"I care because I saw how shaken up you were." I paused and looked at my closed closet, where the diary was locked inside a drawer. "Something similar happened to a girl I once knew."

"Oh." She stayed silent for a while and asked, "Did she press charges against him?"

My silence was her reply.

"I am grateful for your support, Ethan, but I just want to forget it and move on."

"Alright, Emma. As you wish. Take care."

I ended the call and before I could toss it on my bed, I saw my mothers were video calling me and a smile lit up my face. We ended up talking for an hour because Eveline wanted to talk to me about her school, her ballet classes, and her new friends. I listened to her and wanted nothing more but to go see them soon.

"When will you come visit us? We all miss you," she whined, her curly blonde hair clipped back from her face.

I smiled, "Soon, sweetheart. I am planning to visit you soon after an event I have to go to."

"Which event?" My mom piqued in.

"It's a fundraiser for children, I want to be there."

They wished me good luck, and I ended the call after waving them goodbye. Elliot's assistant had sent me a list of volunteering work related to swimming. After going through it, a small grin tugged at my lips.

4. I FEEL LIKE I KNOW YOU

KIARA

I finished my look by adding gold hoop earrings and leaving my neck bare. Staring at my reflection in the mirror, I made sure that my hair and makeup were perfect and the red satin dress, which Jake had bought for me for this event, hugged my body perfectly. The material was soft and the full-length dress looked gorgeous with my golden skin. Straps of the dress were thin. The neck was a little deeper than I would like, but it showed a bit of my cleavage without looking too revealing with the low cut back.

It was the Friday night of the fundraising gala where I would join Jake as his date. I felt a nervous tug in my belly and ran a hand through my dark brown hair tumbling down in waves over my shoulder. I didn't know why I was so nervous suddenly. I had agreed to go with him because of the children fighting cancer.

Taking a deep breath, I gave myself one last look in the mirror. I had subtle makeup on but a little red tint on my lips to match with the dress. My almond-shaped eyes looked hooded with the eye makeup Anya had helped me with.

Wearing my black strappy heels, I walked out of my room

with a small clutch in my hand which held my phone, chap-stick, a tampon, and a check for donation.

"So, how do I look?" I asked the duo sitting on the couch working on Andrew's assignment.

Andrew's eyes twinkled with awe. "Like a beautiful Indian Princess!"

My cheeks flushed with his honest compliment, and I ruffled his hair, thanking him. Anya stood up and gave an appreciative hum, her pale fingers brushing over my hair as she fixed them over my shoulder, smiling at me.

"I would be surprised if Jake doesn't take you to his house instead of the fundraising gala," she whispered with a mischievous twinkle in her dark eyes.

My fingers tightened over the clutch. "He won't do such a thing," I said and added. "And I wouldn't mind if he did."

She grinned at me and went to open the door when someone knocked. I felt the nervous churn in my belly again. I looked down at my left hand, the diamond ring glinting on my finger.

"My God," Jake whispered, his cobalt blue eyes trailing over my body and face as he walked closer. His eyes turned a shade darker when they rested on my chest, and he gave me a secretive smile. "You look stunning, Kiara."

I chuckled nervously when he wrapped his arms around me, his strong cologne making me feel heady. "You don't look so bad yourself," I whispered, taking in his navy-blue suit and polished shoes.

He looked handsome with the five o'clock stubble and his high cheekbones. Cupping his neck, I pulled him closer as his eyes twinkled with adoration, looking over every inch of my face.

I kissed him, a slow peck because I knew we had an audi-ence, and pulled away when he closed his eyes and kissed the corner of my lips. My nerves relaxed when I heard him whisper,

"What did I do to deserve you?"

"Stop for gas?"

His ocean eyes twinkled with humor when we said our goodbyes to Anya and Andrew. She yelled from the living room, "Be back before eleven, kids. And no funny business."

I hid my grin against his shoulder when he squeezed my hand and replied to her, "I can't promise you that, Anya Wu."

The fundraising gala was on full buzz when we arrived in Jake's car, cameras flashing on both of us. Jake held me close, his hand squeezing mine when we entered the hotel. The hall was humongous and decorated with beige and satin where everyone mingled with each other, servers moving around with champagne, and there were many people from the fashion industry. It looked more like a fashion event than a fundraiser as I recognized designers and models from all over the world.

"You doing good, Kiara?" Jake whispered in my ear, his arms wrapped around my waist.

I gave him a reassuring smile, and he pecked my temple. We met his agent, his friends. Even the host of this event, Mr. Stone, who was a sweet, kind man in his early sixties and wanted to help kids. I talked with Jake's friend but slipped off, needing something to warm up my throat.

I don't know why I am being so nervous.

Thanking the server, I gulped down the bubbly champagne, which left quite a burn in my throat. I watched Jake laugh with his colleagues and talk to them. I smiled and let him be as I ventured to hand over my donation check for the children.

I had a nice chat with the warm lady who explained to me where the money would go and how it would help aid kids fighting cancer. I asked for their office card so I could visit their office personally and see if I could volunteer or help them in any other way. She was taken aback by my answer and thanked me, even though I should be the one thanking her for supporting this alternative.

Mr. Stone arrived as I hugged sweet Olivia goodbye after talking to her.

"Among all the three hundred people, you are one of the few who came forward to donate, Ms. Sharma," he said in his soft voice, walking beside me in his pristine suit.

I assured him, "I am sure more people will come after the dinner."

He huffed, "You are being too optimistic. I wish that would happen, but unfortunately, most of the people are here for their popularity. At least it will get the word out."

I agreed and my eyes drifted to the tall, bronze-skinned man with a beautiful raven-haired woman in his arm. I tilted my head to him, "Well, Khalid Al-Latif is here, so you shouldn't worry about it. The press will do its work."

He smiled kindly at the towering man who was busy whispering something to the lady in his arms, her cheeks flushing red. "Even as the Prince of Azmia, his paintings have made over two billion dollars for the fundraisers, so I believe it will go well."

Khalid Al-Latif was not only the Prince of Azmia, the country that bleeds gold, but he was also the brother of Sultan of Azmia. His paintings are inspired by grief, death, and a sad notion of life which my mother always found intriguing even though he was barely twenty at that time. I had seen his artwork for the gala; every painting had a child in an abstract form, blended beautifully with sharp, contrasting colors that made your eyes hazy if you kept looking at it. I knew from the start that most of the donation would be collected because of his paintings.

Mr. Stone asked, "Would you like to dance with me?"

I grinned at him and held his hand, "Of course, Mr. Stone. I wouldn't dream of declining your request."

He chuckled, the sound raspy and throaty as he led me to the middle of the floor where other couples were dancing and swaying to the soft music. We swayed together for a while, talking about the other initiatives for the children all around the world.

"Mr. Stone, may I please borrow my fiancée for a dance?" Jake appeared beside me, smiling at the old man.

"Of course, Jacob. Take care of her, she's an angel." He squeezed my hand when my cheeks flushed at his compliment. He patted Jake's shoulder and walked to his husband, who was well known for his luxurious fashion brand.

Jake stepped closer, wrapping his arms around me, and raised his eyebrow. "Flirting with Mr. Stone, are we?"

I let out a soft laugh, "Don't tell me you got jealous of him."

He shook his head, swaying me and pressing me much closer to his body. "You should see how men are staring at you right now. I needed to step in and let them know that you are marrying me."

My hands tightened around his. "I am one lucky woman," I smiled up at him.

"I am a lucky man to have you," he whispered, his eyes glinting with adoration. He kissed my knuckles softly, "I love you, Kiara Sharma."

"And I love you, Jake O'Neal."

Before he could reply, our dance partners changed, and he was whisked away by another woman. I smiled at him and was about to walk off the stage as I didn't see anyone when someone held my palm, sweeping me back on the dance floor, twirling me around.

My breath hitched in my throat at the touch of his cold, firm hold when all the lights turned off. The only source of light was the huge glowing chandelier above us. I swallowed the lump in my throat at the strange sensation, my nose wafting with musky woodsy and cinnamon cologne. I couldn't place it, but I knew there was something familiar about it.

Something familiar about this person.

With the drifting shadows of the light across his face, I marked his sharp features gazing up at him. His wavy onyx hair was slicked to perfection, but it seemed he had raked his hand through it a lot tonight, tousling it in the process. No matter, it suited his fierce face well. High cheekbones, pointed manly nose, slight stubble peppering his sharp jaw and his dark eyes glinting under the lights as he looked straight back at me.

His eyes. A small smile appeared on my lips when I stared up at them. They didn't know which color they wanted to be, at one moment they were dark blue like the ocean or moss green like a forest. They were beautiful.

He was beautiful.

A shudder ran through my body when those dark, feral eyes raked over my body, his cold yet gentle palm sliding down my bare back, touching me skin to skin. I instinctively arched up to him because of his touch, my front pressing up against the smooth fabric of his shirt, and I sighed at the feeling of his muscles stiffening. He hummed, the sound rumbling from his throat making me shiver. His hand dipped down my dress to stay at my lower hip. My hand tightened around his other palm, and I looked away from his piercing, probing eyes.

It felt as if he could read me. Could see through me.

My eyes trailed down to his broad shoulders swathed in a black suit which didn't help hiding his muscles. He was wearing a crisp black shirt underneath the suit, and the top few buttons of his shirt were open, revealing a hint of tan skin. Blood warmed my cheeks, and I looked away from his body, trying to keep up with his graceful dancing.

Who are you? My mind wondered. *Do I know you? I feel like I have known you all my life and not at all.*

This strange, handsome man took me by surprise as he twirled me around, almost forcefully, but caught me in his arms. I gasped and searched for his eyes as my palms flattened on his shirt, feeling his wild heartbeat. I could feel him gazing down at me, searching for something.

"Who are you?"

We both asked the same question. His voice was a rich timbre, much deeper than I predicted. My mouth went dry when I trailed my hand up his neck to cup his jaw. He didn't mind because he was doing the same. We had stopped dancing and were standing in the corner, away from the glowing lights of the chandelier, in the dark where his palm cupped my cheek, making me look at him, demanding his attention. His touch was soft but firm, warming my cheek and neck.

I felt hot and cold when I blinked up at him. "I feel like I know you."

I know you by my heart.

His arm around my waist tightened, and I bit my lip when my breasts pressed up against his shirt. I shouldn't be here, standing in the dark corner, leaning up on a handsome stranger. I was about to push him away when his hand lowered to my neck, his finger brushing up on the crook of my neck, feeling my increasing pulse as I felt his heartbeat.

"I have known you for my entire life," he muttered darkly,

his voice rich and smoky, "Haven't I? I am not so sure anymore."

Lights flickered on in the hall and I saw him.

That voice. Those eyes. That hair. Those lips.

A sharp exhale escaped my lips and my heart thumped loudly in my chest. I stared back at him, his dark pupils widening. Blue and green eyes gazing at every little inch of my face, my skin.

No, it couldn't be.

But it was happening.

His heterochromic diamond-like eyes drilled into me as if I was naked and bare and he could see me. See everything that I was feeling right now.

After all these years . . .

I shivered when he exhaled sharply, warm breath caressing my bare neck.

"Ethan," I whispered.

"Bella," he whispered as if it was a prayer.

5. I MISSED YOU

ETHAN

That voice. Those eyes. That hair. Those lips.

Her pupils widened, warm dark brown eyes gazing at my face, her body pressed against mine in a familiar way. The scent of black vanilla and coconut wafted in my nose, and I wanted to press her closer and lean down to bury my face in the crook of her neck and that familiar scent. Her fingers tightened over my shirt, scrunching the fabric when she let out a whisper of my name.

"Ethan."

"Bella," I replied, whispering her name like a prayer.

I would have closed my eyes, but I was scared to open them and find her gone, just like waking up from those nightmares I used to have. I slid my palm over her back. She shivered. Her hair was much longer than before, brushing over my hand.

She was truly here. With me. In my arms.

"You are here," I managed to say, my eyes raking over her stunning red dress. "You look beautiful, Kiara."

"You look . . ." her soft husky voice paused, her eyes darkening, but she closed them, shaking her head lightly.

I wanted her to finish the sentence.

Gently grabbing her jaw, I murmured, "Finish that sentence, Bella."

Her skin felt warm under my touch, the pulse in her neck increasing as she opened her eyes and said,

"You look just like I had been dreaming about."

How is it possible for this tiny woman to say a few words and make me forget about everything?

I wanted to ask her so many questions, yet I stayed silent, still overwhelmed with the feeling of having her back in my arms and whispering those sweet words to me.

Abruptly, she pulled away, her eyes looking anywhere but my face. "I should go."

I nodded, she should. But a second later, I regretted letting her go when I watched her turn around, walking away from me. My heart was still beating wildly when she disappeared in the crowd. My palms were tingling where I had touched her back and cupped her cheek.

Fuck. *Snap out of it, Ethan. It's been six years and you're still not over her.* I chuckled at my conscience and grabbed a flute of champagne. One does not just *get over* Kiara Sharma. Especially when you loved her as deeply as I did.

It had been six years since I last saw her, made love to her, watched her cry and then sleep peacefully in my arms. But I knew that since then, both of us had changed. Her eyes were a similar shade of brown but seemed mature. Her hair was longer and there was something about her that I knew she was doing well.

After reading her diary in the airplane, I had puked out my breakfast in the washroom because thinking about what happened to her still made my stomach clench. After three months of refusing to answer my calls and texts, she finally replied to one text.

Me: Are you okay?

She had replied when I had landed in New York for the first time since she left.

Bella: *No. But I will be. Take care of yourself, Ethan Kane.*

Somehow, that text had made me smile, knowing what she meant. She needed to get better on her own, and she was such a stubborn ass that I knew she would do this on her own. Be okay with herself and get better.

Me: *You too, Kiara Sharma.*

My hands clenched in a fist. It had been six years, so why was I still stuck on her? I had moved on. But seeing her a few moments ago with her soft voice and brown eyes and that familiar scent of black vanilla and coconut, it overwhelmed me.

I shook my head, *no. Nothing is happening. Nothing has changed. I just met my ex-best-friend-slash-ex-girlfriend after six years. No big deal.* Drinking down the champagne, I marched toward the hall to distract myself of all the thoughts.

"Ethan?" I paused and turned around to see none other than Jake O'Neal, the man who helped introduce me to modelling. "How's it going, man?"

I smiled at him as we hugged and patted each other's back. He grinned at me, his blue eyes twinkling as we talked about the event, the gala, and the fundraiser, and what was going on in each other's life.

I caught the ring around his left hand and raised my eyebrow, "Getting married, huh?"

Jake looked down at the glinting ring and smiled warmly. Damn, he was whipped. "Yes, we got engaged at the end of May, glad she said yes. We are getting married next month."

I grinned, seeing flustered Jake for the first time in my life. He had always been confident and charming, but to see his cheeks flush just talking about his fiancée was an odd sight. "Congratulations, I am happy for you."

"Thank you, you are definitely invited to the wedding," he

said and looked around. "She's right here, come on, I will introduce you to her."

With a small smile, I went along with him. It was good to see him after such a long time. He seemed more mature than before. I could still remember the time when Elliot had contacted me for the first time for a modelling gig, when Liam and I had made it to the A-Level of qualifications. I had flatly denied. He had sent Jake to talk with me as he was also a basketball player before he focused on turning modelling into his career. He had always been a good man and to see him engaged, with the lovey-dovey look on his face, made me happy for him.

"Ah, there you are," he murmured. "Babe, meet my old friend."

I turned to see who he was calling, and my heartbeat stuttered to a stop when I saw his arm wrapped around her waist. She faced me and my gut tightened when I saw her wide eyes, her smile washing away. My eyes dropped to her left hand, and sure enough, there was a diamond ring glinting on her ring finger that I hadn't noticed before.

Fuck.

"Ethan," she said my name in a way that she was about to explain this to me, but I shook my head. She didn't need to explain herself. She had done that enough already.

"Oh, you two seem to know each other," Jake said, noticing the obvious tension in the air.

I clenched my jaw and looked at him and then fixed my gaze on Kiara.

"She was my ex-girlfriend."

"He was my ex-best friend."

I couldn't help it, a humorless chuckle escaped my lips. *Ex-best friend? Right.* Kiara's lips pursed as Jake tried to ease the crackling heaviness between us.

"Oh, well, I will let you guys sort this out," he said and bent down low to whisper something in her ear, kissing her temple. He offered me a smile before walking away and leaving the two of us alone in the middle of the crowded hall.

I glared at her and looked away. I wanted to be angry, but I wasn't. Yes, I felt like throwing things around, but I didn't. Kiara was getting married. My Bella—*no, now Jake's Bella,* was getting married to him next month.

Does he call her Bella? What sweet name does he whisper to her when they are alone? Do her eyes light up with golden flecks in them—

No. Stop it.

My anger flared away when her palm wrapped around mine, pulling me from my thoughts as she took me away from the crowd to the open balcony with a gorgeous scene of city lights. Cold breeze brushed my face, and I wanted to thank her for bringing me out here, because I knew I was about to lose my shit in there. Judging by the look on her face, she knew it too. After all these years, she still remembered.

We both stayed silent, watching each other. I could still feel the soft pressure of her hand holding mine, my palm tingling at the sensation, now feeling bereft without her.

I looked away first. Clenching my jaw, I said, "So, you are getting married?"

"I am sorry, Ethan."

My eyes met hers, "What are you apologizing for?"

She took a deep breath, and I hated myself for noticing the way her chest rose and the top of her dress tightened around her golden skin. *She is engaged, asshole.*

"For a lot of things," she sighed and went to lean on the marble edge. "I should have opened up to you about my anxiety . . . about all of it. But I didn't and left you like a coward." I saw the bob in her throat as she gulped before adding softly, "I should have called you. Told you about the book. About Jake. *Everything*."

I leaned beside her, watching her tuck her hair behind her ear because of the chilly wind. "Yes, you should have, Kiara, but I have come to an understanding as to why you did what you did. You . . . you needed to get better on your own because you are stubborn and wouldn't ask for help. How is it now? Does Jake know?"

Kiara looked at me, the corner of her lips twitching as she gave me a small smile. "Yes, some nights are better than the others, but therapy helps. Jake knows." She squeezed her eyes shut and shook her head, "I am terribly sorry, Ethan. I should have called you, talked to you, but I was scared."

"Stop apologizing, Bella. You are in a better place and I can see that you are happy." *Happy with Jake.* "Why were you scared?" I asked softly, not liking the sad frown etched on her face.

"Scared that you would be angry at me. Hate me."

Fuck, I hated the way her voice wavered. Kiara Sharma was a lot of things, but a coward, she was not.

"I can never hate you, Kiara Sharma," I said truthfully. "I was angry at you first, but then, just disappointed."

She let out a weak chuckle and looked away. "God, I am a terrible person."

"No." I stepped closer, holding her hand and brushing my thumb on her knuckles, "You are not a terrible person. I forgave you a long time ago because I now know that you would have never told me about your anxieties and depression if we had stayed together. You would have bottled it up and let it eat you alive. In a way, I am happy that you left me, because it made you into who you are right now. I . . . I am proud of you, Bella."

Thousand times. I had imagined us meeting thousands of different times, each scenario different from the other, each word planned out to woo her, see her smile before I see the dimple I desperately missed and take her to see my moms and then kiss her. But never did I imagine *this*. Seeing her here, with Jake as her fiancé.

"You're proud of me?" She whispered those words as if she didn't believe me.

I smiled. "Yes, I am. You published the book."

"I did," she whispered and blinked at me. "I watched you. I saw you during your swim trials and when you were selected for the Olympics." My heartbeat increased when she squeezed my hand, a dimple forming in her left cheek as she grinned at me. "I am so proud of you, Ethan Kane."

I don't know why hearing those words from her lips brought the same warm feeling in my chest as when my moms said that to me.

I was surprised and relieved when she hugged me, wrapping her arms around my waist and burying her head in my chest just like old times. I smiled and pulled her closer, hugging her tight and enjoying her lingering scent, black vanilla and coconut.

Her voice was muffled when she said, "I missed you."

She pulled back to look at me and I watched the tiny gold flecks in her warm brown eyes. I ran my hand through her hair and cupped her cheek, whispering, "I missed you too, Bella."

Kiara held my palm, a small smile playing on her lips. I wanted to kiss her. I wanted to savor the feeling of her lips against mine and see if she remembered the times I would kiss her just because I missed her lips pressing against mine. But I couldn't. I wouldn't. She was engaged. We both had moved on.

Yeah, I was lying to myself.

I pulled away from her first and kissed her forehead. "Are you hungry? I heard there's gulab jamun for dessert."

And just like that, it felt like we had never lost each other in the first place.

6. I PROMISE

KIARA

Ethan was right, there were gulab jamuns for dessert after dinner.

Jake invited him to sit with us when the dinner was announced, but he let us know that something urgent came up and he had to leave. Jake brushed it off, but I had spent eighteen years of my life with Ethan. I knew he was lying. He left because he didn't want to create anymore tension between us, especially as I was engaged to Jake.

"Hey, you have been thinking a lot." Jake's words snapped me out of my stream of thoughts, and I turned to him as he drove the car. "You okay, sweetheart?"

We were going back to his house for the night, and my gut tightened into a ball and I didn't know why. He entwined his hand with mine and kissed my knuckles.

I smiled at him, squeezing his warm hand and adoring the ring on his finger. "I am more than okay. But I never thought I would see Ethan there."

Jake held my hand as we walked into his cozy house. Pictures of us smiling at each other framed in the bookshelf we had cleared last week, because I was going to move in with him soon, and he wanted to offer me as much space for books as he could.

"If you want to talk, I am here to listen, Kiara," he whispered, kissing my neck.

I took a deep breath and turned around. His blue eyes were dark under the dim lights of his house. I tipped on my toes and pecked his lips. "I am going to go take a shower."

Upstairs, in the master bedroom ensuite, I had kept the door open for him to join me if he wanted to, but he hadn't. In a way, I was thankful that he didn't. I needed some time to think.

I met Ethan tonight. Ethan Kane. The boy I loved, who had grown into a mature, handsome man. I closed my eyes, trying to keep my emotions at bay. I had left him. He wasn't mad at me, he was disappointed, but now he had come to terms with it.

Shaking my head, I changed into one of Jake's t-shirts and let my wet hair down. I needed to stop thinking about him. Yes, we had a history together, but I was engaged to Jake. *I am getting married to him next month, I need to focus on that.*

When I stepped out of the bathroom, Jake was still in his suit, removing the cufflinks and talking to someone on the phone. I smiled at him and he smiled back mouthing 'I love you,' which made me giggle. He went back to answering the person on the phone while I hung up the dress that I had worn tonight in his closet, now, *our* closet space as he had helped me clear it up last week. Only my dress, a box of tampons and a few pairs of underwear were here. I would move my things from the apartment next week so that Anya and Andrew would have plenty of time to shift into their new home, and I wanted to help them as well after the wedding.

I was reading a fantasy romance with only the lamp on when Jake stepped out of the bathroom smelling clean and manly with a musky scent. I wasn't surprised when he gathered me in his lap and kissed me. Cupping his cheeks, I kissed him back. I wanted to cherish his gentle touch on my thighs, his warm breath on my neck when he tasted my skin, but I couldn't.

Swallowing the lump in my throat, I pulled away from him. "Babe, can we not?"

He looked at me for a while, surprised by what I had just said. He kissed my forehead and placed me down on the bed, "It's about seeing Ethan today, isn't it?"

"I am sorry, but I am overwhelmed right now."

"Don't apologize for it, love," he massaged my skin, holding me close. "Tell me, why are you overwhelmed?"

I thought about it. I was overwhelmed because I didn't expect to feel those emotions rush in as soon as I laid my eyes on him. I was overwhelmed because he knew everything about me, my secrets, read it and didn't run away when he saw me. I was overwhelmed because I wanted him to be angry at me and push me away, but he didn't. I was overwhelmed because he had accepted and understood my decision to leave him and told me that it made me into a better person. I was overwhelmed because he missed me. I was overwhelmed because I had missed him more.

Instead, I replied, "We were best friends before it grew into something more." I paused before whispering, "We lost our virginity to each other."

"Ah, so you were high school sweethearts?"

"You could say that."

Jake's lips curled. I leaned closer, "What? Why are you smiling like that?"

He turned to me, still smiling, but now that smile turned into a sad smile as he tucked my hair behind my ear. "I lost my virginity to my high school sweetheart, too. Unfortunately, it didn't work out. We both wanted different things."

Huh, he never told me that before. But again, I hadn't told him about my first time with Ethan.

I grinned at him, "You wanted to be a basketball champion."

"Damn, right," he stopped smiling and cupped my cheek. "Look where I am now."

I held his hand and snuggled closer to him. "You are one of the world's best models and one of the sweetest men I know, Jake O'Neal." Peering into his eyes, I kissed his cheek with a small smile, "I am proud to be getting married to you."

He stayed silent for a while, watching me with his dark eyes before pulling me closer to his side.

"I love you," he whispered, kissing my head.

"I love you, too."

"What? More books?" Jake asked, shocked when I lifted the duvet and the cover of my bed and pulled out the boxes of my books which I had kept underneath the bed because I had no space to keep them.

"How many more are there? Should I check the attic?"

I snorted, opening up the box. "We don't have an attic in the apartment, Jake. Come on, help me with them. You promised you would."

He huffed and sat beside me on the floor. "I was thinking more of finding your old pictures, diaries, and even lingerie."

His look was heated when he whispered the last word, making me shiver.

"I already packed most of them except my lingerie and books," I replied and awed at the old Harry Potter book set my mom had bought me on my birthday. It was old but still held so many memories. Memories of me and Ethan sprawled on my bed or my bedroom floor reading books together, guessing each other's Hogwarts house.

It was Friday afternoon. As the classes were over before noon, I had called Jake over to help me pack all my stuff for the move. Anya would have helped, but she was in her office and had called in to make sure Jake and Andrew were behaving.

"Is that Harry Potter?!" Andrew exclaimed, rushing into my room and leaning down to see the books with his big brown eyes.

I grinned at him and let him see the books. "My mom gifted it to me when I was ten."

He grinned at me, "No way! My mom gifted it to me too. I love Ron Weasley!"

Our book fangirling came to a stop when my cell phone started ringing. As I was on the floor, Jake passed it to me from the dresser. Not before seeing the name flashing on the screen and raising his brows at me. I saw the name and my heart came to a halt.

I picked it up, "Hello?"

"Hey, Bella, what are you doing right now?"

My cheeks burned under Jake's eyes as I replied, "Oh, um, I am packing my things and books with Jake. I have to move into his house next week."

Ethan didn't reply for a second, and I heard a shuffling on his side. He finally said, "Oh, that's good. I called you to meet up with you. We can do this later if you're busy."

I almost forgot about this. *Okay, I am lying*. I didn't forget about this. We had been texting each other since that gala, and even Jake was happy that we both were getting back on speaking terms. Jake presented the idea of meeting up with Ethan and catching up with him, so we had been planning to meet up even though I turned into a nervous wreck whenever I saw a text from Ethan.

This was the first time he called me.

I looked at Jake who was smiling at me with a raised brow and he mouthed at me, 'Call him over.' I stared at my fiancé and back at the phone in my hand.

Taking a deep breath, I pressed it back to my ear and said, "I-if you don't mind, why don't you come over?"

God, I sounded like a nervous teenager asking her crush to hang out at her place when her parents were away.

I held my breath and waited for Ethan to reply.

"To your apartment?"

Even he was confused by my offer.

"Yes, if you want."

I could hear the smile in his voice when he said, "Text me the address, I will be there in half an hour."

I sent him the address and exhaled a deep breath after keeping my phone aside. I waved off Jake's grin. "Stop smiling like that." I paused and narrowed my eyes at him. "Why do you want me to get along with him so bad?"

Jake came closer and pinched my cheeks until I batted his hands away. "Because I know he is important to you, and I know he is a good man despite what the media says. I would like you to have him as your friend because our wedding is next month, and I have already invited him."

I knew that, we had already talked about it. I also knew how many tabloids turned him into a person he was not. Yes, he had a wonderful taste in dating a new woman every month, but that didn't mean he was a heartless player. Not once had I read an article that his relationships were bitter with any of the women he dated. Paparazzi only shared what they wanted with their audience to feel about him. He had a bad rep as he had punched one of the famous reporters, Richard something. But I knew he wouldn't just go around punching reporters for no reason.

Ethan arrived at the apartment sooner than expected, and

it was Andrew who opened the door, exclaiming, "Hey, Kiara! An Olympic Swimmer is at our door. And he is asking for you."

"Andrew, let him in! He is my friend."

My cheeks were warm with blood when I introduced Ethan to him, who was inspecting Ethan as if he was a new species. Jake and Ethan exchanged a few pleasantries while I tried to focus on going through my books and deciding which ones to keep and which ones to donate.

Ethan helped me and exclaimed when he picked out the classics we had read together for our English assignments. The pages were annotated with both of our messy handwriting.

"God, I hated reading classics," he said, closing yet another book and keeping it in the growing pile.

"I thought you were always excited to read the next one as soon as we finished one."

Ethan looked at me, his blue-green eyes warm in the sunlight splattered across my room. He gave me a small secret smile and said, "It's because I loved reading them with you."

My breath hitched in my throat hearing his words. I stared at him while he picked up another book from the pile. I didn't know that teenage Ethan was excited to read classics because he read them with me.

I did not like knowing that.

I heard Jake pick up his phone and looked at him as he stopped taking out my jewelry and accessories from the drawer. I frowned when he ended the call and looked at me.

"You have to leave?" I asked, trying to hide the fact that he would leave me with Ethan alone, even though Andrew was in the living room, playing video games.

Jake nodded, pocketing his phone and came closer to me and pecked my cheek, "Sorry, sweetheart, I have to meet my agent for an urgent meeting. Don't wait up for me, I will call you as soon as I can."

I didn't like the sound of that, but I agreed because he had taken a month off for our wedding, so work was piling up for him, and he wanted to get it done before the end of this month. Jake left. Ethan and I went back to talking about books, organizing them and laughing at the old times when we used to read books together.

He told me how he and Liam were friends again, how he and Liam made it to the Olympics. How Jake met him and presented the idea of doing modelling on the side and how it worked out for him.

I told him how I moved to London, finished my bachelor's and my debut novel. How I impatiently waited to hear from a publisher for a year while doing small, odd jobs in London and moved back to San Diego when I got the book offer. How I became a teacher and wrote part time and how it worked out for me.

I sighed, dropping the last box of books in the corner of my room which looked empty without them and turned to Ethan who had helped me arrange them and tape the boxes.

I wanted to hug him like old times. Instead, I said, "Thank you so much for this, Ethan. You are staying for dinner tonight. Anya Wu makes a mean chicken satay and you will love it."

He flashed me a grin. "You know me, Bella. I love free food."

Ethan and I played video games with Andrew, who was more than excited to win every round against us. Anya arrived home cursing at a racist client she had to deal with.

"Oh, wow," she paused and looked at Ethan who was sitting beside Andrew with a gaming console in his hand. "And who must you be?" She asked, keeping her hand on her hip, giving Ethan her mom look.

No matter how handsome the guy was, she wouldn't get wooed unless she was sure that her son was safe and sound in good care. I knew because her parents had shunned her as soon as she told them she was pregnant at the age of seventeen. I had tried to get her dates, play her wing woman, but it never worked because she was always worried about her son. Still, in the past I had seen handsome men leave her room when Andrew was staying with her sister.

"Mom, he is my new friend, Ethan. Do you know he is Kiara's childhood friend? He even swims and has two moms and a sister. How cool is that!"

I smiled warmly looking between him and Ethan whose face was flushed. God, even at twenty-five, he blushed just the same. It was adorable, and I wanted to pinch his cheeks. I quickly scolded myself for having that thought. *No.* No pinching cheeks.

I knew Anya had accepted Ethan to be around her apartment when she told him to stay over for dinner. I had to excuse myself from them because I had a video call therapy session with my therapist, Sabrina Young. Ethan's face was hard to read when I announced that.

By the time the session was over, I felt lighter, like I did every time after a session. I had told her about Ethan, and after listening to me, her suggestion was to talk to him.

Great.

When I stepped out of my room, Anya and Ethan were in the kitchen. They both paused and looked up at me as if I had interrupted their important talk. I narrowed my eyes at her while she smirked at me and showed him how to marinate the chicken. I asked her if she needed any help, but she denied. Ethan just gave me a warm smile, making my gut churn.

How could he still smile at me like that after I left him?

Dinner was served on the dining table and we all thanked

Anya for it before we tasted the delicious satay. Ethan sat across from me, beside Andrew, while Anya sat beside me.

"So, I heard you punched a reporter."

I coughed and swallowed the food before glaring at her. Ethan seemed to be amused by it.

"Yeah, I did," he shrugged and looked at Andrew who stared at him with wide eyes. Poor kid had the same reaction when his mother explained to him that Santa wasn't real.

Ethan cleared his throat and added, "I punched him because he was harassing a woman."

His dark eyes flickered to me when he said the last words. I clenched my hand in a fist under the table. I didn't know that there was a woman involved when he punched the reporter.

My friend smiled at Ethan, "I am glad you punched him then. So, that's why your image is bad right now in the media."

I kicked her leg underneath the table, but she kicked me right back. What was she up to? Why was she grilling him with questions? This was none of our business.

"Ethan," I said, "You don't have to . . ."

He flashed me a small smile, "I don't mind, Bella." He looked at my friend and answered, "You are right, my sponsors have paused my endorsement deals until I volunteer for some community service."

I talked to him about the charity for kids fighting cancer and that I had their office card too. I had yet to pay them a visit, so taking a deep breath, I asked him if we could go there sometime together.

"Andrew, didn't you complain about the swimming coach needing help for your school?" Anya asked and then looked at me, "Didn't you say this too? That the swim coach was going on her maternity leave?"

"I did, she is already on her maternity leave, so Mr. Davis

is looking for a swim coach to fill in for a few months," I explained.

Then it struck me. When I saw the mischievous glint in Anya's dark eyes.

But I was too late.

I snapped my head at Ethan, and he was looking at me, searching my face for any emotion while Andrew exclaimed, "Wait, Mom, Kiara! Ethan is a swimmer, right?"

"Why don't you ask him, Son?"

"You are a swimmer, right, Mr. Ethan?" he asked politely.

Ethan smiled at him, his cheeks flushing, "Yes, I am a swimmer."

"Then can you be our swim coach?"

Ethan turned to me, raising his brow. Then Anya and Andrew looked at me. When I didn't give in, they tried harder with their puppy-dog eye looks.

I sighed as if it was my decision when it clearly wasn't. My lips curled into a small smile. "I will give you Mr. Davis' number and talk to him about you."

Andrew cheered and started rambling how he was going to tell Ben and every one of his classmates that he knew Ethan and that he was my close friend. I hid my face with my hair when he said that and focused on eating. But I could feel Ethan's warm gaze on me.

It was late when I stepped out of the elevator with Ethan to bid him goodbye. The night air was chilly. It was a polite thing to do, and I needed to thank him for today.

"Are you sure about me being a swim coach?" Ethan asked.

By the tone of his voice, I knew he thought he wouldn't be able to do it or might be a bad influence on the kids. My heart tugged at the vulnerability behind his voice.

I grinned at him and nudged his shoulder, "Of course, E,

you will be a great swim coach, and I am sure Mr. Davis would accept you in a heartbeat. So would the kids."

He gave me a relieved smile, and when he opened the door of his car, I told him to wait. Without thinking, I leaned closer and wrapped my arms around him.

"Thank you for today, Ethan. I missed you."

His arms embraced me tightly, and I felt his lips on my hair, kissing it. "I missed you too, Bella." He pulled away to cup my cheek and my breath hitched in my throat at the intensity of his piercing blue-green eyes. "Promise me you won't leave again."

I squeezed his hand on my cheek, "I promise, E. Never again."

As soon as those words left my mouth, I knew I would keep this promise no matter what happened. Ethan was important to me. Losing him once had wrecked me, and I didn't want to go through that again. He meant too much to me, even after all these years. He was still one of the few people who truly knew me, understood me and accepted me for who I was. So, for him and me, both, I wouldn't even dream of leaving him again.

7. I NEED YOUR ASSISTANCE

KIARA

"And this is the swimming pool . . . as you can see," I said, watching Ethan's eyes light up when he noticed the pool and the bleachers.

It was the next day after our dinner and Ethan had agreed to join the parents' meeting in the school, because somehow in the span of a few hours, he could be the school's interim swim coach. He had picked me up after lunch. Jake still hadn't called. I had sent him a voicemail in the morning, but he hadn't replied.

Ethan walked around the empty swim hall, his hands in his pockets. "It reminds me of our school," he whispered to himself, a small smile playing on his lips.

"Yes, it does," I said and walked toward the side to show him the locker room and the small office, keeping far away from the pool, because if I tripped in these heels, I was sure I was going to ruin my beige dress which I had chosen just for the parents' meeting.

"These are the male and female locker rooms. Mr. Davis said you can take over this office for the time being."

The office was small, but it had a desk, shelf, and in the storage room behind it, all the necessities for swimming.

"It's small, but you don't have to use this if you don't want to. You can come over to mine whenever you want," I said, turning around.

A small gasp escaped my lips when I saw how close Ethan was standing. I swallowed the lump in my throat when I noticed his familiar cologne. The mild musky scent with cinnamon and something woodsy. When I trailed my eyes over his black shirt, which was stretched across his broad shoulders, I found his dark eyes pinned on me. It took my breath away. I forced my legs to stand and not tremble when he stared at me like *that*.

He took a step closer to me, my chest brushing with his shirt, and stepped around me to look around the tiny room. I released the breath I was holding and fixed my dress, noticing how big Ethan looked in the office.

I tucked my hair behind my ear when he surveyed the desk and smiled at me, "It's perfect. Thank you, Kiara."

I returned his smile, my heart beating faster than before. "You don't have to thank me for it, Ethan." I glanced at my wristwatch. "It's time for the parent-teacher meeting. Are you ready?"

"As ready as I can ever be."

ALL THE KIDS were seated beside their parents while Ethan and I stood beside each other behind the table of the classroom. Every teacher had to explain the syllabus regarding their subject. I had just finished explaining my syllabus for this semester and also told the parents how they could help their kids with their academics without pressuring them into studying more.

"Any questions?" I asked, trying to ignore the way Ethan was looking at me from his side. Throughout the whole thing, I had felt his heavy gaze on me, warming my skin, but I had tried my best to stay professional and not let him affect me.

But I was failing badly. If I could, I would tie my hair in a bun and fan myself with something, because I was turning into mush.

Why is he affecting me so much?

One mother raised her hand and wriggled her eyebrows at Ethan with a dirty smile. "Who is that fine man?"

Ethan offered a smile. "Hello, I am Ethan Kane and I will volunteer here as a swim coach for a couple of months."

One of the women said, "Oh, is it only for our kids or can we join too? I need some lessons in correcting my positions."

I bit my lip and looked at Anya who wriggled her eyebrows at me. Even though my cheeks were flushed, I couldn't deny that Ethan was handsome and reeked of raw masculinity that could make any woman into a puddle if he just looked at her. The mothers of the kids had always been playful flirts with all the male teachers, so Ethan was not an exception. I knew this would happen. Even Anya had warned me to protect Ethan.

Now's the time to play my role.

I announced, "Oh, look, it's time for the one-on-one meetings, why don't you guys come to my office?"

The kids and the adults immediately started talking among themselves while I took my files and looked at Ethan who was surveying me.

"Come with me."

He smirked, "I thought you wanted me to stay here and look after—"

With a firm voice, I said, "I need your assistance."

He raised his eyebrow. "Assistance, you say?"

Rolling my eyes at him, I walked to my teacher's office, which was similar to the coach's office but still had a bigger space. It was beside my classroom, and if I wasn't teaching, I was in my office most of the time.

One parent after another, I talked to them about their kids and made sure both the parent and the student left the office with a smile on their lips. Ethan sat beside me and answered parents' questions about how they could help their kids reach Olympic trials. I watched him explain all of it and was proud of him when he heartily talked to them.

When Anya and Andrew came, I tried my best to be professional even though we live together. We couldn't help it and discussed what we should have for dinner. Once again, she invited Ethan as we were going out, and even Jake would join us. Ethan wasn't sure, but he promised he would let us know as soon as possible.

Only Ben was left, and his mom had called to say that they were going to be a little late, so I didn't mind. But I did mind when my office looked smaller than before with Ethan sitting beside me, his knees brushing with my bare legs whenever I tried to shift. Not to mention, even sitting down, he looked tall and muscular enough to make the room look smaller.

"Hey, Kiara."

My eyes snapped at Jake's when he entered the office, looking between me and Ethan.

I stood up. "Jake, what are you doing here? Where have you been?" I closed my eyes and cleared my throat, "We need to talk later, today is the parent-teacher meeting."

He stepped closer to the desk and said, "I know. I need to talk to you." He surveyed my face, and before he could speak again, Ben rushed inside the room with a big grin on his face.

"Hello, Ms. Kiara!"

I smiled at Ben, his blue eyes sparking with delight when he saw me.

"Look, meet my daddy! Daddy, this is my favorite teacher, Ms. Kiara. Ms. Kiara, this my daddy!" Ben exclaimed, his hand holding Jake's as he made the introduction.

I looked between Jake and Ben and Stacy, Ben's mom, when she entered and looked at all of us.

I shook my head to clear my brain, "Jake . . . I—what did he just say?"

Jake took a deep breath, "I needed to talk to you about this. Ben is . . . my son."

"Huh."

My eyes were wide as I stared between my fiancé and my student. I didn't notice before, but looking at them side by side, they both had the striking sapphire blue eyes and I knew Ben would grow up to be as good looking as Jake. The only difference was Ben's hair, which was golden instead of Jake's black curls.

"So you have a son and didn't think it was important to tell me before . . ." I stopped, took a deep breath even though my whole body was knotted in nerves and all I wanted to do was get out of there.

I knew Stacy was Ben's mom, so Jake and Stacy must have been together. Or they were together, judging by the way they stared at each other and back at me. I hated it. The way Jake made me feel in front of my student and Ethan.

"I am so sorry, Kiara, but we need to talk—"

I sat down, glaring at him. "Later. This is a parent-teacher meeting, and as a parent you should know that we are here to talk about Ben. Love, why don't you sit down with your parents?" I said, addressing Ben as he seemed confused, looking between me and Jake, his father.

For the next few minutes, I tried my best to ignore Jake's presence and acted as if he didn't exist. I talked to Stacy and

Ben, trying to remain calm because Ben didn't know what was happening. When Ethan made his introduction, it was curt and short, his voice clipped. Judging by the clench in his jaw, I knew he was angry.

Did he know that Jake had a son? I clenched my hand in my lap. No, if he had, he would have told me as soon as possible. He didn't know.

After finishing up, I gathered the papers on my desk aimlessly and let them know that the meeting had ended. I was ready to get out of there. My skin was itching, and I wanted to do something instead of sitting there and realize that even though I was engaged to him, he didn't have the need to explain to me about Ben. We were getting married in a month, for God's sake.

"Kiara, we need to talk."

I gave him a saccharine smile, "It's a bit late, don't you think?"

Stacy had told Ben to go hang out with Andrew, who was still in the classroom. That meant Anya had sensed trouble when she saw Jake here and was waiting for me to finish up.

Jake's pleading eyes met mine. "Sweetheart, please, let me explain."

I flinched at his words and looked at my desk. "You have a son, Jake. That you forgot to mention when you slipped this ring on my finger!"

I pulled the diamond ring off and grabbing his palm, I handed it to him. "You can keep it."

Taking my purse, I was ready to get out of there, ignoring Jake's shocked face when Stacy stopped me.

"I know what he did was terrible, but we were together a long time ago. We didn't know we had conceived, and we had already broken up," Stacy said. Her eyes were filled with sadness as she looked at me as if she understood my pain. "He had moved to New York and was working on his career, so I didn't tell him. H-he found out when Ben was a year old."

"Ben loves his father because from what I know, he talks about him every time he comes back home from his business trip," I shook my head. "I should have known. You are either always late or miss our dates because you were with Ben."

"Kiara, please let me explain," Jake said, "I was meaning to tell you about this. That's why I was going to meet them and let them know about you. Please don't break this engage—"

"Jake," I tried to say without a quiver in my voice, "It is *too* late. You could have told me when we went on our first date that you have a kid and I would've accepted you. Even before our engagement, I would have. But we are, *no*—we *were* getting married next month, and now you have the audacity to show up and tell me you were planning to tell me that you have a son!"

Jake seemed taken aback by my outburst.

Well, what did he expect would happen?

"Don't bother to show up at the wedding. It's *over*."

As soon as those words escaped my lips, I left the office.

Anya saw me, saw the tears glistening in my eyes, but I shook my head when she approached me. I needed to get away from Jake, even though I knew he was behind me.

Holding my elbow, Jake made me look at him, "Please, Kiara. I never meant to hurt you like this. I didn't know how to tell you about Ben."

I glared at him through my tears, "With your fucking mouth, Jake. You hiding this for such a long time means only one thing. I am not important for you to tell me about your son." I wrenched my arm from his grip and managed to say, "I don't want to marry you."

He shook his head, but I was too busy thinking if he ever loved me. He did, I knew that, but you don't hide such a big thing from the person you truly love. That's why I had to tell

Ethan about my anxiety through my words and leave him, because I could never tell him the truth if I had stayed.

You don't hurt the people you love. And I had already done that.

My throat closed up as I gulped nervously and looked down at my hand, the empty ring finger. The night he had proposed to me was my twenty-fifth birthday and one of the best nights of my life.

He was watching me with those same eyes I had seen so many times, I hated it. He was pitying me.

"I'm . . . I just need to leave." I stammered, swallowing the lump in my throat and turning away from him.

I knew exactly how I was feeling. The day I saw Paul Corey on an ice cream date with Shaely. The day I saw my father and brother cry when my mother passed away. The day my brother, Karan, left for university without a word. The months without seeing my father's face because he was grieving by drowning himself in work. The day I left Ethan, my best friend. The day I received the news that my unborn baby had died. It felt all the same. This feeling of dread, guilt and pain. *So much pain.*

I wanted to drown in this pit of sadness and never hurl myself out again.

I should have listened to myself. I was better off alone. *Why didn't I?* This is my fault. I didn't listen to myself, loved Jake, and now this breakup was my fault too. Thirteen-year-old Paul was smart enough to stay away from me. My mother left me alone. My brother pushed me away. My father was afraid to look at me because I reminded him of his dead wife. I pushed away Ethan and now he hates me. And now, Jake.

He saw all of it and didn't want it.

I should've known. I was supposed to be smarter than this.

Why did he have to shatter my trust like this? Why did he have to ruin it? Was I not enough? *Was I ever enough?*

I couldn't stop it when a sob broke out of my throat and I covered my face in my palms, my legs giving out under me. I knew I was about to fall, but I didn't care. Strong arms held me from falling.

Jake mumbled in my ears, "Oh, honey . . . please don't cry."

I shook my head, more tears falling out, "Don't touch me, Jacob. *Please* don't."

My shoulders shook with heart-wrenching sobs. "I don't want to see you or touch you. Just . . . *go away.*"

Jake's eyes turned grim when he looked at my tear-stricken face, "Kiara . . . please, don't do this."

I squeezed my eyes shut as more tears leaked out, hearing the small tremble in his voice. That hurt me as much as what he did, what he had already done.

"You don't hide things like this from the people you love, Jake. Why did you do this?" I asked as more sobs threatened to pierce through my throat.

"*Kiara.* Babe, please, we can talk this out. We can a-adopt Ben if—"

I took a sharp breath, my eyes wide, "Are you hearing yourself right now? You want to take Ben away from his mother just because . . ." I shook my head and wiped the tears, "I don't know you. I wish I had never loved you, Jake."

He looked like I had slapped him. I might as well have. I turned and walked away from there. Tears slid down my face as I clutched my hand in the straps of my purse.

What am I going to do?

My eyes were blurred when I walked away from him in the empty hallway. I still couldn't wrap my brain around the fact—the *reality* that Jake was the precious father Ben always talked about. I couldn't process what was happening.

I stepped out of the school, and the evening breeze dried up my face, which was feeling heavy. God, I must look like a mess. *What would I do now?* Anya was supposed to move out at the end of the week, and I was supposed to move in with Jake. But not now. *Where will I live?* Shit, this is a mess.

Cinnamon woodsy musky scent wrapped around me and flowed in through my nose, calming my brain. I met his sharp, fierce eyes which clouded with smoldering anger, looking down at my face.

"It's alright, Bella. I got you," he whispered, kissing my hair and crushing me against his chest. He let me hide my face in his warm shirt, "Come on, I will take you home."

Temporary home. I mentally added.

I didn't know what to say or how to thank him when he buckled me in his car and held my hand while he drove silently. I was clutching his hand so tight that I wondered if it hurt him, but he didn't complain. I needed to hold on to something as more silent tears escaped my eyes.

"Come on, Kia, we are here," Ethan mumbled softly in my ear and gently coaxed me out of the car as if I was a fragile china doll. Maybe I was, because he knew I was at my breaking point, and I would either end up shouting at him or breaking something. I hoped neither of them would happen.

"Thank you, E," I mumbled through a sniffle as he opened the door to the apartment with the key from my purse and sat me down on the couch. He told me to remove my heels and gave me a glass of water, sitting down beside me.

"You don't have to thank me, Bella," he said, keeping my empty glass of water on the coffee table. He frowned at me and leaned closer, "Let me help you with that."

I held my breath when he touched my hair and gently removed the pins which were holding the sides of my hair in place, tucking them back. I sighed in relief when he ran a hand through my hair, tucking the loose strands over my ear.

I swallowed the lump in my throat, and I knew the tears were welling in my eyes while I desperately tried to hide them in front of him. But he knew how I felt. He always knew how I felt by just looking at me. We were best friends and more than that. Sometimes he knew me better than myself. I used to hate that when we were teenagers, but not anymore.

My body tensed when he held my cold palms in his warm hands. I fluttered my eyes to him, and he saw he was looking down at the white, tan line on my ring finger.

His eyes flickered to mine and leaned closer. My body stilled at the intensity of his eyes pinning me to the spot. His warm breath fanned on my skin, his hands cupping my face and gently wiping the tears.

"Please don't cry, Bella," he whispered silently.

My eyes averted to his hands and saw the swollen bruise on his right knuckles. Clenching my jaw, I held it and observed the swollen cuts on his hand.

I glared at him, "Why?"

Ethan sighed, *"Because."*

God, he and his stubborn ass.

I stood up to get the medical kit from the bathroom and tried to ignore my reflection in the mirror. He said that it wasn't needed, and it was just a few scratches, but he stopped arguing when I gave him a blank stare and clasped his hand to clean it up.

After cleaning the wound and blood from his knuckles, I didn't want to imagine how Jake must have looked.

"How was he?" I asked, wrapping a Barbie bandage around the injury with gentle fingers.

He was giving me a funny look for the pink bandage, but he could handle it with the big man ego of his.

"I gave him a split lip. He will be fine," Ethan said as if he did this every other day. *As if he had not just punched a model.*

Taking a deep breath, I held his hand in mine. "You didn't have to do that, Ethan."

"Yes, I did. Any guy who hurts you will have a warm welcome with my fists," he said without a hint of any guilt. He looked at me and my dress, "Come on, go take a shower. I will clean this up."

Anya and Andrew stepped in the apartment. She took one look at me before sending Andrew to his room, telling him that she would explain everything later. She took me to my room and before I could explain, she said, "You don't have to say anything. I figured it out, Ben is his son. That stupid jerk. I knew there was a reason I didn't like him that much."

"I thought you told me that you wished you had wooed him with your oral ski—"

She glared at me. "Not now, Kiara. That was before. I wished Ethan had punched him again. Now go take a shower. I will order some pizza and we can watch action movies together."

I hugged her because that's exactly what I needed. During the shower, I tried to ignore looking at my mirror, but I couldn't help it. My eyes looked red and puffy because of all the crying, and my face was flushed red.

I stood under the shower, squeezing my eyes shut as I thought of all the good memories I had made with Jake. The first meeting with him, the night I had spent in his suite that night, drunk and laughing and cuddling with him. All the dates, my birthday, our engagement, the dinner with our family. But not once did he tell me about Ben. I wondered if that's why he closed off when I talked about children with him. God, I was so stupid.

A sob pierced out of my throat. I closed my eyes and let the tears wash along with the soap. I slid down on the floor, hiding my face and wondered if I was ever enough for him that he had to hide that he was a father. And he wanted to take Ben away from Stacy, his mother. My head felt heavy with all the overthinking and my heart crumpled. I didn't want to do anything. I wanted the water to wash away the sadness.

A knock on the door snapped me out of the whirlpool of my thoughts. I turned off the shower and stood up. I walked out of the shower stall which was steamed with fog and covered myself in a thick, towel robe.

Opening the door, I saw Ethan. His eyes drilled into my face, and I didn't avert my red eyes because he would know if I had cried or not anyway. He always knows.

He clenched his jaw, trying to hide his anger, and swallowed the lump in his throat. "When you get ready, come and join us. I made Italian hot chocolate for you."

I gave him a small smile and watched him walk out of the door, closing it shut. I sighed and looked at my almost empty room. All the boxes were still there, as I had been way too busy to move them to Jake's house, and I was thankful for that. At least I wouldn't have to face him again.

But where am I going to go?

Changing into sweatpants and a baggy t-shirt, I combed my wet hair and wondered about all the apartments I had looked through when I came back to San Diego. Maybe some of them are still empty? I shook my head. That was a fool's wish. Looking at my tired reflection, I decided. I would only mope around for two days at the most. Then I would start looking for apartments because I didn't want Anya Wu to let me stay here as long as I wanted, because I knew she would do that. No, I would find a way, I wouldn't let this breakup affect me.

I WAS LYING. It affected me too much.

After stuffing my face with pizza with Anya, Andrew and Ethan, we all had Italian hot chocolate for dessert and watched a mafia action movie with me sobbing and whining at the heroine who fell for the mob boss just because he saved her life from a bullet. Ethan had to calm me down while Andrew Wu asked his mom what was wrong with me.

I started crying all over again. But this time it was ugly sobbing, and my body shook and trembled so hard that I puked out my dinner in the toilet.

Ethan held my hair, stroking my back. "It's okay, Bella. Get it out. It's alright."

My friend checked up on me when I brushed my teeth and handed me aspirin, ordering me to go to sleep. I did it without arguing because I was exhausted and my body felt numb. Ethan stayed by my side, flipping pages of my book in my desk chair and glancing at me every five minutes just to make sure I was there. I don't know how I managed to tell him to cuddle with me, but he did.

My heart calmed down when I laid my head on his chest, his arm wrapped around me and gently rubbing my back, soothing me. Taking a deep breath, I peered up at his face, "Ethan, why are you so nice to me?"

He furrowed his brows at me. "What do you mean?"

I licked my lips and looked away from him. "I left you. I chose myself over our relationship and yet you are . . . *here*. Why don't you hate me?"

He didn't reply for a while, and his heartbeat increased under my palm. He cupped my face and made me look at him, his blue-green eyes intense.

"I can never hate you, Bella. You would do the same if I were in your place." He paused and gave me a small smile, "And you are my best friend."

Hearing those words did something weird to my stomach. I grinned and kissed his palm, tucking my head in his chest. Ethan was asleep with his arm loosely wrapped around my waist when I thought about all the events that happened that day.

I knew that I needed to stay away from any close romantic relationships. Either I would hurt that person, or that person would end up hurting me. It wasn't worth it for all the pain and hurt. All I wanted was to feel normal again without having any romantic feelings for anyone at all. I needed to be stronger than before and not fall for it. I don't want anyone to hurt me like that again.

Like Paul had when we were thirteen. Like the passing of my mom, my family pushing me away, and leaving Ethan when I was eighteen. Like how Jake hid being a father. *I won't allow it anymore. I will be stronger even though I have to keep people at arm's length.*

I clutched my heart, curling into a ball, the void getting bigger and bigger, and fell asleep with warm tears staining my pillow.

PART THREE

"I want your baby."

8. I WANT TO KISS YOU

ETHAN

Kiara moved into the guest room I had offered. She was stubborn, but I was persistent, and the school was much closer to my house. We had agreed on her paying the rent for her stay until she found a place of her own. I didn't mind. She could stay as long as she wanted.

For the next week, I helped her move into the room next door while she helped me with the school stuff. Being a swim coach to kids was fun and stressful. I loved to teach them new swim strokes, but I had to stay on my toes all the time. Still, I enjoyed it.

But what I didn't enjoy was seeing Kiara in tight dresses or formal pants every day. When she turned to grab the mug from the cabinet, I couldn't help my eyes when they fell down to her tight ass in the form-fitting trousers or skirts. I closed my eyes and mentally groaned when I felt a twitch in my sweatpants.

Not now, Eiffel. Stay down.

I came back from the gym and saw Kiara making eggs and bacon for both of us. I tried to avoid seeing her in the morning because I had to take a cold shower and stop my mind from thinking about her or her body. She didn't need to know about my cold showers and what I did in them.

It had been a month since she called off her wedding.

The wedding that was supposed to happen today.

I cleared my throat and thanked her for breakfast. We had fallen into our usual routine of making breakfasts for each other. We rarely had lunch together as she would either be in the school or have a lunch date with Anya and Katherine. She invited me, but I would either have photoshoot gigs or swim practice that I couldn't miss. We would either cook dinner together or order takeout and watch a movie on the couch with beers.

It almost felt like old times.

Almost because when she would lean over me to grab the remote of the television while we are on the couch, I would feel the brush of her chest on my arm and mentally groan every time I saw the cleavage from her t-shirt. Then I would eat the dinner with a pillow on my lap while she critiqued the main characters of the movie.

"What is your plan for tonight?" I asked, eating up the last part of my eggs.

She looked at me, her amber eyes seemed distracted and her lips were in a sad frown. I clenched the fork. She was still not over him. That stupid jerk who decided it was a good idea to hide that he has a son. I hated him when he made Bella cry in the hallway and thought she would accept him after hiding such a big thing.

"Why? It's a usual weekday." Her voice was clipped.

I reached for her hand and held it. When she looked at me, her eyes were guarded, but she let me rub my thumb on her pulse point.

"How about we have some Indian cuisine tonight? Panner Butter Masala with tandoori naan?"

Her eyes lit up and a small smile tugged her lips, "You want to have Indian tonight?"

"Mmhmm. I will cook."

Her eyebrows raised, "You will cook Indian?"

"I may or may not have taken some cooking classes after university," I brushed my lips on her knuckles, noticing the sharp intake of breath. The thin white blouse tightened across her chest and I forced myself to think about sharks. "So, it's a deal. Tonight, Chef Ethan will cook for you."

Kiara squeezed my hand. "You don't have to do all this, Ethan. I will help you with dinner."

She kissed my cheek before taking her handbag and walking out of the house. I sat there, staring at the empty stool where she had been sitting a few moments ago. I touched my flushed cheek where I could feel the slight pressure of her lips.

My skin burned, and I didn't regret thinking about her in the shower. On her knees. Using those same full lips and soft hands on me, making me groan with pleasure. I let my mind wander and think about all the dirty things I would do to her and her body if I had the chance to be with her, even for a night.

Would she like being spanked? Being told when to come and not? Would she like being punished by me if she came in my hands or mouth without my permission? Would she like being clamped, padded, and tied up naked for me?

I came with a low groan, my sharp breath panting on the cold wall. My hand was still lazily stroking my cock, and I glared down at the mess I had made. I should not think about all that. It was Kiara. My best friend. The woman I have loved. Even if she was attracted to me physically, I didn't know if she was into the kinks I enjoyed. She was kinky, I knew that, but times have changed.

I need to stop thinking about her. No matter what.

"SINCE WHEN DO YOU HAVE BICEPS?" Kiara smiled giddily and poked the said bicep she was smiling giddily at.

I didn't expect a very tipsy Kiara while I was preparing dinner. The taxi driver was nice enough to ring the bell and let me know about a very drunk woman who was whining about men for the past twenty minutes. I didn't expect *that*. Sure, she must be bummed about the breakup, but she had been nothing but calm and collected after the day she called the marriage off and handed Jake her ring.

She must have reached her breaking point.

I helped her in, ignoring the way her breasts covered by a thin blouse pressed against my arm. She watched me cut vegetables for the Panner Butter Masala and ogled at me. Trust me, neither I, nor Eiffel minded the ogling and the casual lingering touches from her, but she was drunk.

"I loooooooooove your becups, Ethan!" She hiccupped and continued trailing her finger on my right bicep.

My Bella is a horny drunk.

I sighed, and holding her wrist, made her sit down on the stool. "They're called *biceps*, Kiara." She kept looking at me with her half-lidded hooded brown eyes. "How much did you drink?"

"*Sixty-nine.*"

"What?"

She licked her lips and took a long time doing that. My eyes fell on her plump lips. I clenched my jaw and looked away.

"I want to try sixty-nine."

Yes, she was definitely horny. And drunk.

I ignored the images of sixty-nine with her and straightened up. "You're coming with me." I didn't wait for her to reply and helped her in the bathroom, turning on the warm bath for her while she leaned on the frame of the door.

"Get inside."

"You first."

"No, Bella. You need to take a bath. It will clear up your head."

An adorable pout framed her lips, her amber eyes looking up at me from beneath her lashes. "Won't you join me?" Her voice was barely a whisper, but I felt it deep within my skin. I wanted to join her. *Fuck.*

She is drunk.

My eyes darkened, and I stepped closer to her. "I would have thought about it if you weren't drunk right now."

Kiara stubbornly pressed closer to me, her hands clutching the side of my t-shirt, scrunching the fabric. "I am not drunk. I just need to feel you. Skin to skin," she whispered sultrily, her eyes darkening with lust. "And maybe try sixty-nine."

I closed my eyes. *This is the worst torture for mankind.* I could try to handle Kiara, but a horny, drunk Kiara? No chance. With as much control as I could muster, I held her shoulder and turned her toward the bath.

"Get undressed and take a bath. I will check up on you in a while."

"Why don't you help undress me?"

I glared at her and said with a firm voice, "Kiara. Get in the bath. *Now.*"

She seemed stunned by this and blinked at me. Kiara giggled, "Whatever you say, Daddy."

I gaped at her and her words. *She did not just*—Kiara turned her back on me and removed her blouse, her wavy hair tumbling over the nude bra strap. *Okay, this is my cue.* I quickly backed out of the bathroom and closed the door behind me, breathing a sigh of relief.

Somehow, I knew tonight was going to be a long night.

As promised, I went to check up on Kiara when she didn't step out of the bath after half an hour. I had already prepared the sabzi, and the naan was ready as well. All we had to do was serve it and eat. But Kiara was still in the bath. I knocked and waited. She didn't reply, so I called her name, but still, she didn't reply. Should I let her take her time? She seemed sad before leaving for school today.

What if she is not okay and sad?

Fuck it.

I opened the bathroom door and walked inside. Kiara was in the bathtub, but she was naked and wet. I felt like a teenager looking at breasts for the first time, even though her body was covered under the foamy water.

"Oh. I knocked, but you didn't say anything; and it had been too long, so I wondered if I should check up on you," I rambled like a complete idiot.

Way to go, Ethan.

Kiara's eyes seemed brighter than before, and she looked a little better. She pursed her lips, her wet hair clung to her wet skin.

She smiled at me, not at all bothered by my presence. "It's alright, Ethan. I loved the bath and found it too relaxing to get out of it. I'm sorry, I lost the track of time." Kiara blushed, the water in the bath splashing when she moved. It took all the control in me not to avert my eyes from her face.

"It's fine, I'll leave you to it," I said, my voice deep and husky.

"Oh, no. I am done with the bath, I was about to get out, anyway."

My eyebrows raised when I noticed the subtle change in

her tone, and my lips fell open when Kiara stood up from the bath. Her naked body dripped wet with water as she stepped out of it and walked toward me. I couldn't help but watch her perky breasts pouting toward me with her hard nipples as they bounced a little with each soft step she took. Her stomach was taut, and her body was toned and curvy in all the right places. I wanted to touch and lick every part of her golden, soft skin.

"*Kiara*," I warned, my voice heavy with arousal.

I clenched and unclenched my fists while I watched her dry her naked body with a towel. If I could, I would get rid of the useless towel and eat her out against the wall while she writhed in my arms, moaning my name and begging me to make her come in my mouth. But I wouldn't for her teasing me like that.

"What, Ethan?" she asked in her sultry, mischievous voice, teasing me with a dirty glint in her eyes. "It's not like you haven't seen this before."

I closed my eyes and took a deep breath to control myself from pouncing on her like a wild beast. God, this woman made me lose the ability to think straight.

Shaking my head, I pinned her with my gaze and gritted out, "Dinner is ready."

I turned and left her in the bathroom. In the kitchen, I gulped down a glass of cold water. The images of her wet naked body flashed in my mind. If she kept teasing me like that, then I would have no choice but to give in. I shook my head. No, she thinks she has the upper hand here, but not again. I have much more self-control than she thinks I do.

Kiara had dinner with me, and she was much more sober than before. She tried her best not to meet my eyes or even look at my face, hiding hers with the curtain of her damp hair.

Did she regret pulling that stunt in the bathroom?

"Kiara, what happened back there?" I asked when she loaded our empty plates in the dishwasher.

She pursed her lips and her shoulders tensed. "I am sorry I flirted with you like that. I wasn't thinking straight."

I would have accepted her statement, but her voice was too firm and sounded too robotic.

Holding her elbow, I made her face me, her eyes guarded. "What happened back there?"

She parted her lips to reply, but I said, "Be honest."

Kiara paused and gazed up at me, her dark eyes softening. "I am sorry, Ethan. I can't play being your best friend or even have a platonic relationship with you."

My face must have shown how hurt I was after she said that. I took a step back, but she shook her head, taking my palm in her hand. "No, Ethan, listen to me. I am apologizing to you because as much as I want to be your friend or go back to how we were, I can't do it. I loved you. You were my first . . . *everything*."

"What are you trying to say, Bella?" I whispered, pulling her closer, the pulse on her neck beating faster. "Why can't you be my friend?"

"Because I am still attracted to you."

Time slowed down, and my ears rang with her confession. *Because I am still attracted to you.* Kiara Sharma, my Bella, was attracted to me.

I could see her brain turning, her dark brown eyes looking up at me and waiting for my reply. I released the breath I was holding and said, "Come visit my parents."

"What?"

"Yes, Bella. Come visit my parents. Eveline. Tomorrow."

"Ethan, I just told you I am—"

"I heard you, Kiara." Pushing her back on the island, I caged her with my body and made her feel the bulge in my sweatpants. Her rosy lips parted, my muscles clenching and fighting the urgent need to kiss her and take her on the kitchen floor.

"I am attracted to you as well, Kiara."

Before I could go any further, I pulled away. "But I want to take this slow. Come meet my parents and Eveline with me tomorrow."

I didn't wait for her reply and walked to my room, closing the door. I might have been pushing her a little, but I wanted her to know that this was serious for me. I was either all in or not at all. I was more than attracted to Kiara Sharma, but this time, I wanted to play all my cards right. I wanted her to spend time with my family, take her on a date, and kiss her when the date was over.

THE NEXT MORNING, silence filled the car ride to my parents with a very fidgeting Kiara. I would glance at her every two minutes because she looked gorgeous in a peach summer dress, her tan skin glowing and begging for my touch. Even though she had agreed, she was holding the seat belt and clutching her handbag. At one point, she even made a low braid with her hair because she couldn't sit still.

"Are you okay, Bella?"

"I am perfectly fine and not at all nervous."

I smiled. *I couldn't wait till she saw my moms and Evey.*

As I had expected, my moms took Kiara in a big hug with tears in their eyes while Eveline stared at her the same way when Cinderella from Disney World took a picture with her. Not a single minute had gone by, and my family already accepted Kiara back with open arms and cookies.

We had sat down for lunch and were piling our plates with food when my mom looked at me and Kiara who was sitting beside me. I raised my eyebrow at her when she glanced at her ring finger. Before I could tell her to not ask about it, my mom smiled at Kiara.

"Ethan told me about your engagement, Kiara."

Kiara tensed beside me, and I squeezed her hand under the table. Her palm was cold.

"*Ma*," I said in a clipped voice, warning her not to prod.

Kiara clutched my hand and smiled at her, "Yes, I called it off."

Lucy, my mom who was observing us, spoke up with a bright smile. "Well, if you must know, I almost got engaged to another woman before realizing how much I loved Helen."

I sighed in relief when my moms looked at each other, their eyes full of love and adoration, making Eveline giggle.

Swallowing the lump in my throat, I stole a furtive glance at Kiara. She was doing the same. We both let go of each other's hands at the same time and stayed quiet during most of the lunch.

We had an apple pie for dessert and then Eveline demanded Kiara to see her nail polish collection. I was sitting on her small bed, her room painted lilac purple, while my sister and Kiara sat on the soft rug, going through the various colors of the bottles.

"I think black will suit him the most," my sister said after a moment.

What were they thinking?

I frowned, "No, I think—"

Kiara gave her the sweetest smile and my heart felt heavy when her eyes glinted with mischief, "Yes, you are absolutely right, Evey! We can use this pink as well."

Sitting up straighter, I shook my head at them. "Actually, I'd rather not—"

My little sister gave her a toothy grin, taking the neon pink bottle in her hand. "Kiara, you're brilliant!"

Oh, no.

"Now, if you have had your fun, can you please remove this?" I asked Kiara as soon as Eveline ran downstairs when Mom called her.

Kiara and Eveline had painted my fingernails in alternating colors of black and neon pink, giggling to themselves while I scowled at them. Just after one meeting, they were like best friends, and I was already scared that they might braid my hair the next time or apply makeup.

But deep down, I knew I would let them, just to make them happy and hear their laugh again.

She looked up from my sister's little bookshelf to my face. A grin tugged her lips when she took in my outstretched hands, my fingers colored in horrifying nail polish.

"You don't like it? I thought we both did an outstanding job adding glitter here," she teased, pointing at my middle finger.

"Hilarious." I deadpanned.

Kiara snickered and took my hand in hers after dabbing a cotton ball in acidic solution. It had a strong smell which I tried to ignore and focus on Kiara's mild perfume twanged with coconut and black vanilla. While she removed the nail polish, I gazed at the way her eyebrows were furrowed with concentration. She had undone her braid after lunch, so few strands of her hair brushed her cheeks.

I raised my hand which was already clear of the nail paint and tucked her hair behind her ear. She paused for a moment and continued wiping the color from my nails. The pulse of her neck had increased, and her breathing had changed.

"See?" She said, her voice breathy, "It's all clear now."

My nails were the same as before, but I was focusing on her, why her neck and cheeks were flushing. Ignoring everything around me, I lightly tugged the strand of her hair and whispered, "What are you thinking, Bella?"

Her eyes flickered up to me, and the intensity of her deep brown eyes caught me off guard. Her hand was still on my lap as we were on the floor when she cleaned up my nails, and she was trying to ball her palm in a fist. When she looked away, I knew she was closing off and trying to hide away from me.

I didn't want that. I wanted those golden flecked brown eyes on me, to look me straight in the eye, and tell me what she was feeling.

Leaning closer, I felt her take a shuddering breath. I tipped her chin toward me and dug my fingers on her waist, her body tensing at my touch.

I tilted my head, my eyes following the path of her creeping blush, down her slender neck to the cleavage of her dress and landing on the hardened tips of her nipples. My eyes met hers and I whispered, "Are you thinking what I am thinking?"

"What do you mean?" She replied, her voice a soft whisper on my lips. Her eyes were hooded and pupils dilated.

"Do you want me to kiss you, Bella?"

My hand slid up her waist, wrapping around her tiny body and pulling her closer to me. She was almost on my lap, her breasts pressed up against my shirt and her palms on my shoulder, bracing herself. I waited, my eyes on her parted lips, her hazy eyes, her heaving breasts. I rubbed the pad of my thumb on her bottom lip, brushing it lightly and feeling the softness of her pillowy lips.

I want to kiss you.

It was written all over my face. But I waited. Waiting for her to make a move because it was written all over her face too. How her eyes moved from my eyes to my lips, her hands holding my shirt tightly, afraid of letting me go and how she pressed up against me.

She closed her eyes, and I trailed my hand to cup her cheek. I watched the slow bob of her throat and she opened her eyes, her hands touching my neck, angling my face and pulling me close.

I waited.

Her lips parted, "Ethan, I want to—"

"Look what I found!"

Like two frightened teenagers caught watching porn, we both scrambled away from each other when Eveline entered the room. Thank God she didn't see anything. Kiara's face was flushed, and she was hiding it with her hair and asking my sister about the photo album that was in her hand. She had found the album of when we were kids.

I ran a hand through my hair and tried to talk with Eveline and be interested in watching young Kiara and Ethan in every picture, but I couldn't. Because I was dying to know what Kiara wanted to say before she was going to kiss me. I wanted her to complete that sentence. I wanted to hold her in my arms again. Feel her warm, soft body press against me. Feel the whisper of her breath on my skin.

I wanted her to kiss me. I wanted to kiss her.

As soon as the main door of my house locked behind us, I pushed her against the door, her eyes wide with surprise.

"What are you doing, Ethan?"

I dropped the keys and her handbag on the floor. I didn't care about it at that moment. I wanted to know what she was going to say in Eveline's room. I caged her against the door, my arms planted on either side of her, "What were you going to say?"

Closing her eyes, she shook her head, her hands pressing up against my chest and pushing me away. "I can't say that to you, Ethan. It was wrong."

I followed her in the dim hallway, "What was wrong? That you flirted with me, that you're attracted to me, you want to kiss me?"

Kiara turned around, tears glistening in her eyes, "Yes, Ethan, all of it. I want to kiss you, but I can't."

Taking a slow step toward her, I cupped her face and asked, "Why can't you, Bella?"

Her voice was barely audible when she whispered, "Because I am afraid I will ruin you."

"You won't."

"How can you know that?"

"Because I want to kiss you too."

I kissed her.

It was nothing but a soft pressing of our lips against each other. The tight clench in my body released as I pulled her closer, running my hand through her hair and holding her there. She leaned against me, kissing me back with more fervor. Kiara released a small sigh, her hands clutching my shirt and pulling closer as she tipped on her toes to press herself against me. Electrifying goosebumps spread across my body when I licked the seams of her bottom lip, biting it with my teeth.

Kiara moaned, and I pulled away, both of us breathing heavily as we gazed at each other with hooded eyes filled with lust. I pushed her back on the wall, my hand wrapping around her slender throat, and slammed my lips against hers. I wanted her to know how much I craved her and how much I wanted her. I swallowed her small moans, her fingers tugging my hair making me groan between our hot, wet kisses.

The lack of oxygen made me pull away, breathing hard and noticing her mussed hair, flushed face, and gleaming eyes. A tear on her cheek.

I wiped it with my thumb, "Why are you crying, Bella?"

9. I WANT YOUR BABY

KIARA

A gasp escaped my lips when Ethan wrapped his hand around my throat, his lips pressing against mine. He swallowed my moan. The intensity and passion of his kiss amazed me, rocked me to my core, making my toes curl in pleasure. I pulled him closer until there was no space between us and kissed him until I felt dizzy in my head. I wanted him to know how much I had missed him for all these years. I wanted him to know that I still remembered our teenage days. The last night of the prom. And the way we had made love during that night. I wanted him to know that I could never forget that or him.

I felt heady after the kiss when he pulled away. My breathing was heavy and my eyes hazed. Ethan's hair was tousled, his shirt ruffled, but his blue-green eyes were light and clearer than ever before. They were staring straight at me, making my legs tremble.

His thumb brushed over my cheek and he whispered, "Why are you crying, Bella?"

I blinked up at him. Ethan. I kissed Ethan.

"I kissed you."

"You did."

My eyes widened, and I looked at his handsome face, his sharp jawline, and cheekbones which I was cradling in my palm moments ago. A shiver spiraled down my body and I pressed my back on the cold wall. I touched my lips and felt the tingles of his lips when they kissed me, biting them.

I shook my head, "I kissed you. *Oh, God.*"

Ignoring the sudden dizziness, I pushed him away, rushing to my room. He followed me, "Kiara, what happened?"

"I am sorry," I said and closed the door behind me, my heart pounding in my ears. I stared at the reflection in the mirror. My face and neck were flushed. I cupped my mouth where I could still feel the lick of his tongue, the delicious pressure of his lips on mine, and the soft bite of his teeth.

"Bella." His voice was soft and almost pleading, "Tell me what happened, what's going on in your head?"

I swallowed the lump in my throat. "I am sorry, Ethan."

"What are you apologizing for? Was the kiss that bad?"

My cheeks heated thinking about moments ago. That kiss was electrifying and had rocked me to my core. I shook my head even though he couldn't see me.

"That kiss was . . . everything, Ethan," I replied, not knowing how to put it in words.

"Open the door, I want to see you," his voice was firm, all the softness gone.

Nerves balled up in my stomach as I unlocked the door and looked anywhere but his face. But I should have known that Ethan wouldn't want that. He made me look at him, his hand on my jaw, holding my face. His face looked sharp with rough edges under the dim hallway lights, which made him look much more intimidating than before.

I licked my lips, waiting for him to say something or do something.

Ethan gave me one last look before tucking my hair behind my ear. I took a sharp intake of breath when he leaned closer, his lips pressing on my forehead. I missed the warm heat of his body when he pulled away.

"I am taking you out on a date tomorrow. Be ready at seven."

My eyebrows raised and before I could stop him or ask him about the date, he turned and went to his room, closing the door shut.

I stayed there, my lips parted, as I stared at the closed door of his room. Closing my door, I leaned back and exhaled the breath I was holding. I knew that he meant it. He would take me on a date tomorrow.

What am I going to do?

THE DATE WAS in the evening, but Ethan had to meet his agent at the last moment, so he had called me and told me he wouldn't be able to pick me up. I searched for the address of the restaurant he had sent me, and my nerves tightened. He was pulling all the strings right. If his plan was to woo me then so far, he was succeeding. The restaurant was Italian and luxurious where you had to make a reservation a week in advance to get a terrace view table overlooking a beautiful lake.

I didn't know how to dress up for it. I was confused, conflicted, and overwhelmed. Ethan was pushing me out of my comfort zone, breaking my walls, and pressing all the right buttons. Two hours left till the date, but I wondered if my plan was going to fail or not.

But he was Ethan, he would understand. Or even try to

understand. He would do it. He would agree with me. I trusted him.

Take a deep breath, Kiara. It's all going to work out.

For the first time in a while, I grinned to myself and couldn't wait for it. I was excited and scared. In the next two hours, I showered, pampered myself, and washed my hair, giving it a blow-dry. I changed into a short black dress with a neck deep enough to show my little cleavage. The dress fabric was thick enough for me to skip wearing a bra, so I did. He wouldn't be the only one pulling all the strings tonight. As the hem of the dress ended on my mid-thigh, I wore black sheer stockings and hooked them with lace garter belts.

With black sandals, gold earrings, and bold red lipstick, I was ready. I felt and looked great even though I was a nervous mess on the inside. I tugged the dress lower and pushed my wavy hair over my shoulder. I closed my eyes and counted to ten.

I was going to do it. No matter what happened, I would ask Ethan tonight.

When I entered the restaurant, the waiter led me upstairs where Ethan had reserved our table. I noticed a bar in the lower level when I walked to the stairs to go up. The interior was warm with extravagant details in the paintings hung on the dark red wallpaper. All the lights were muted and glowed with a soft light, making the cadence of the restaurant cozy.

My mouth dried when I noticed Ethan. He was wearing a black suit over a crisp white shirt with two buttons undone, revealing a tanned neck. I licked my lips and thanked the waiter when he left us. Ethan stood up. His eyes were hard to read when they roved over my body, staying far too long on my legs and chest. He loomed over me, his face inches away from me. I clenched my jaw, breathing in the musky scent of his cologne, and tried my best not to lean up and lick his throat.

I balled my hand in a fist, trying to stop all the dirty thoughts. He leaned down, brushing his lips against my ear as he whispered and pulled the chair for me. "You look fucking beautiful, Bella." I took a shuddering breath at his deep voice, "And if we were alone, I would want you laid out as my personal feast."

My cheeks warmed with blood when he pulled away. I watched him sit across me, looking calm and reserved while I was clenching my legs and already wondering if I should bailout.

No, Kiara. Ask him.

Clearing my throat, I asked him about his meeting with the agent. We both fell in a smooth conversation about work and colleagues while he also talked about Liam. Even though the main course was delicious with the sweet white wine, I couldn't ignore the low thrumming in my stomach. My legs clenched at the way Ethan looked at me, like he knew I was wet. For him.

But my mind was on something, noticing his good looks, his manners, and the relationship he has with his family. It was confirmed when I spent the day with him and his family yesterday, and that kiss last night was only the beginning.

I took a sip of wine, relishing the sweet burn in my mouth and throat for one last time. I looked at my empty plate and decided that it was time.

My mind went back to my mother, the pain of losing her, the pain of leaving Ethan alone, the pain and hurt of being in London alone. I clenched the fork in my hand and decided that I didn't want to be alone anymore. I wanted something much more. Especially after the breakup with Jake, I did not want to be alone.

Not anymore.

There was only one way I could achieve it, by having something, someone of my own.

Taking a deep breath, I looked at Ethan. "I want to ask something from you."

His eyebrows furrowed, but he nodded, his eyes intense.

"I want your baby, Ethan."

10. I WON'T BITE

ETHAN

I had thought about thousands of ways on how this date with Kiara would go, but listening to her asking for a baby, for a child from me was not what I had expected. My eyes blinked at her because I thought I misheard her. *"What?"*

Kiara licked her lips, her pillowy lips, which were painted in red. *Fuck, she looks hot.* I cleared my brain and focused on her when she repeated,

"I want a baby. *Your* baby."

I stared at her for what felt like a minute before a soft chuckle escaped my lips. I had forgotten how Kiara was when she wanted to be, and she was pulling my leg.

But then I looked at her expression, her almond-shaped eyes were not crinkling with humor. They were serious.

"Kiara, what the fuck are you saying?" I asked, shocked, and surprised by her.

She wants a kid. A baby. *My* baby.

I don't understand.

Kiara took a deep breath and explained, "Yes, you heard

me. I want a kid and I know I sound insane right now but hear me out."

"I am listening."

"I . . . I have wanted a baby for a while. Jake and I broke up and I am thankful for that. But then I saw you yesterday with Eveline, and I knew that—"

"You wanted my sperm inside you?" I asked, my brain still processing all of it.

Her cheeks flushed, and she looked down at her plate, her hair covering her face. "Yes," she muttered.

I stayed silent for a while and frowned. "Why didn't you try it with Jake?"

Kiara looked at me and tucked her hair over her shoulder, giving me a full view of her cleavage. I clenched my jaw and listened to her, "We wanted to wait for the marriage."

I raised my eyebrow.

She continued, "We never had sex. We decided together that it would be better after the marriage . . . and you know the rest."

"You guys . . . never had sex?"

"Yes, Ethan."

"*Huh.*"

I leaned back in the chair, staring at her. I could never understand how Jake controlled himself when he was with Kiara. Just sitting across from her made me want to splay her across the table and ravish her.

"Why didn't you look for insemination?" I asked. "You could have asked my mothers."

She shook her head, "I have researched about it and really thought about it, but I don't want a baby through insemination."

I forced a smile. "*Right.*"

Kiara winced. "No, Ethan, I—look, I didn't mean it like that. I am asking you because you are a great person and you have been nothing but nice to me since we met. I appreciate everything we have together, and . . ." her cheeks flushed, "I would love to have a baby who is like you. I would be honored to have that."

"*No.*"

I don't know why I was angry all of a sudden.

Her eyes snapped at me, "What?"

I tilted my head and glared at her, "I said no. My answer is no, Kiara."

I wanted a kid, to have my own children, but not right now. I wanted to settle down with a woman I love, marry her, have our own house, and then think about kids. Having kids right now didn't settle with me. I had always used protection during sex. Only with Kiara, I didn't use a condom because she was on the pill, but after she left, I always used protection.

"Can you at least think about it?"

I shook my head, "No, Kiara. I don't want to have kids with you or anyone right now." Shit, I didn't mean to sound so angry when I said it.

Kiara's eyes turned glassy, and I hated myself when her lower lip trembled.

"*Bella,*" I tried talking to her.

She swallowed the wine in one go, my eyes widening when she glared at me and stood up.

"What are you doing?" I stood up, watching her leave her credit card on the table even though the cheque was already paid, "Kiara, where are you going?"

She turned to me, giving me a saccharine smile, "Don't wait up for me, I will catch a cab and probably arrive tomorrow morning."

Kiara left me without waiting for my reply.

Fucking great, Ethan.

WHEN KIARA LEFT, I stood there waiting and wondering what I could do in this situation. I needed to have some drinks before asking Anya where she could have gone. I didn't want to even think about her having a one-night stand with a stranger and arriving at the house tomorrow morning.

As the cheque was already paid, I went downstairs. To my surprise, I found Kiara sitting on a stool and drinking a cold glass of water. I could see the sadness on her face and the way her shoulders were deflated. She must have wanted a baby badly.

Anger coursed through my veins when I saw a guy talking to her, laughing, and flirting with her. I huffed when he said something that made her smile.

Oh, come on.

The man was probably in his mid-thirties, ogling at the little strap of her garter belt which was peeking from her thighs because of her dress. Now that I could see, other men had already noticed her, too, watching her from afar and wondering if she would go home with them.

No, she won't, you pieces of shits.

I wanted to go there and haul Kiara on my shoulder, taking her away from those men. I strolled there, glaring at the man who was sitting beside her, and held Kiara's elbow.

"You're coming with me," I said and dragged her to the corner before she pinched my hand.

"What the fuck do you think you are doing?" she asked, her eyes blazing with anger. She crossed her arms, her cleavage getting deeper, and she looked hot.

"I should be the one asking you that."

"I am looking for potential partners."

I chuckled and nodded at the guy waiting for her to come back to the stool, "You want to have his kid?"

Kiara glared at me, "Why do you care?"

I raked my hand through my hair, frustrated. "He's wearing fucking shorts while you're dressed like you just came from a Victoria Secret's after-party."

She narrowed her eyes at me, "Of course you'd know about that."

I glared at the tiny woman in front of me and at the man in shorts. I turned to her, "He has an 'I love my mom' tattoo on his fucking knee."

I don't like to judge someone by their outer appearance, but that guy with shorts was getting on my nerves and I had never spoken to him.

Kiara frowned at me and noticed the tattoo. She bit her lip, "It shows that he is a family guy."

I couldn't believe this woman.

"No. It shows that he has mommy issues." I took a step closer to her, "Do you *seriously* want to think about his mom when you go down on him? Do you want *that* to be the father of your baby?"

Her nostrils flared at me, and for a moment I was scared that she might kick my family jewels or slap me. But what she did was *worse*.

Kiara leaned up and whispered in my ear, "I will let you know tomorrow, Ethan."

I glared at her, her dark eyes daring me, challenging me to do something when she went back to the bar, sitting beside the man in shorts. I clenched my hand in a fist and slid it inside my pocket. All I wanted to do was take her over my knee and spank her until her ass turned red and fuck her until she was pregnant. Then fuck her more so she knew that it's *my* baby growing inside her womb.

Fuck, I am going wild.

Whatever happens, Kiara is coming home with me.

I sat down beside her nursing a glass of scotch and shot daggers through my eyes at the man who was trying to flirt with her, talking about his family back in Texas and how he makes a mean barbeque sauce that she should try one day. Kiara agreed, my knuckles turning white because I was holding the glass too tight. I knew she wasn't flirting with him because she kept glancing my way with a guarded look in her eyes.

I thought about her previous words. *I want your baby, Ethan.* Kiara wanted a baby for some time, and she would have had one with Jake, but she thankfully didn't because of the breakup. She saw me with my family and decided that she would rather have my sperm inside her than someone else's.

But if I denied her, she would ask other men. Other men with shorts and 'I love my mom' tattoos on their knee who would not think twice before going bare inside her. The thought made my stomach clench in a tight ball. I bet if she asked him about having his baby, he would agree.

No, I wouldn't let her. And I had told her I didn't want a baby.

The mild scent of her exotic perfume wafted in my nose when I leaned closer to her. I ignored the furious look on the man's face when Kiara faced me, my finger tucking her hair away.

"What would I get?"

She swallowed the lump in her throat, "What?"

I gave her a lazy smile and raked my eyes down her body, keeping my palm on her thigh, feeling the slight tremor under her skin through the stockings.

"What would I get for putting a baby inside you? For getting you pregnant, Bella."

My cock pressed against the confines of my pants when I

said it. My muscles tense with the idea of going bare inside her, coming inside her and making her pregnant.

Kiara took a sip of cold water and completely faced me. "We can have lots of sex . . . until I get pregnant," her eyes were dark and pupils dilated when she whispered in her sultry voice.

I narrowed my eyes at the choice of her words and stood up. "Come with me, I have a proposition for you."

She stood up, my eyes zeroing to her ass when she said her goodbye to that man. I held her hand and pulled her close while we waited for the valet to bring my car.

"What is the proposition?" she asked.

"Something that will benefit both of us." *Hopefully, if you agree*. I added mentally.

The drive back home was tense and filled with silence. I had decided that if I was going to get Kiara pregnant and if she agreed with my proposition, then I wanted to be selfish with her and her body.

"Sit down, Kiara," I said, switching on the low lights of the living room, noticing how tense she was. Bending low, I whispered in her ear, "I won't bite unless you beg me to."

She exhaled shakily, sitting down on the armchair, away from me, which made me smirk. I unbuttoned my suit and sat across from her on the couch.

"If I am going to get you pregnant, Kiara," I paused, staring at the way her amber eyes lit up, "I want something in return."

She frowned, "Okay, and what's that?"

"You and your body. I want to fuck you whenever I can."

Kiara crossed her legs, clearly aroused when her cheeks flushed. "Until I get pregnant," she added.

"Yes, until you get pregnant."

"Okay, I agree with you," she answered without missing a beat.

I smiled and shook my head, "No, Kiara. I have different kinks."

Her face went scarlet red, and I wondered where else she was red.

Hold it right there, Eiffel.

"Kinks?" she asked. "Can I ask what they are?"

Better yet, I could show you. I clenched my jaw at the images flashing in my mind and controlled myself.

I licked my lips and answered, "I am a dominant, Bella. I like to control my partner while having sex and ordering them around like when and if they can come. Or not at all."

11. OKAY, BIG DADDY

KIARA

Ethan's words echoed in my ears, my legs clenching together. Images of eighteen-year-old Ethan hovering above me, asking me with a flushed face if he could tie my hands flashed in my mind. Of all the times when he would tease me, edge me to orgasm then pull away until I begged for him to touch me. Now, sitting on the couch, legs wide, his body donned in a dark suit with piercing eyes. He was tall and big, and even though he had always been a gentleman with me, I felt intimidated by his size and his aura.

Of course, Ethan is a dominant.

Clearing my throat, I met his guarded eyes as if I would judge him for his kinks. It shook me to my core, and I knew he was more than serious. "I kind of realized that, Ethan," I tried to say in a calm voice.

"You did?"

I flashed him a grin, "You asked me if you could tie my hands when we were eighteen."

He leaned back on the couch, his eyes noting the subtle clench of my legs. I took a shuddering breath. I knew that he knew that I was turned on. He met my eyes and said with a small smile, "I am glad you didn't run for the hills."

"Why would I?"

"You tell me."

Was he ashamed of his kinks? If so, I wanted to nestle myself on his lap and kiss him softly, holding his sharp jaw in my hands and let him know that his kinks did nothing but turn me on. He was still the Ethan who made me breakfast this morning and asked me about my father. Nothing was going to change that.

I licked my lips and removed the strap of my high-heeled sandals, putting them aside. I sighed pressing my feet on the soft rug and said, "I slept with a guy once who was dominant."

When the silence stretched in the room, I lifted my eyes to see a delicious clench in his jaw. I curled my toes, crossing my legs.

"Who?"

"My classmate from university in London."

"What did he do to you, Kiara?"

My stomach clenched at the tone of his deep baritone voice. I met his challenging stare and replied, "He tied me up and he was rough . . . and he spanked me."

But I had enjoyed it.

"Okay, I needed to know if you have been in a real scene before. Can I ask you something?"

I gave him a slight nod and waited.

Ethan leaned forward, his elbows on his knees, his polished black shoes glinting in the lights with his hands clasped together. The way his eyes arrested me with one look made me want to go closer to him, press myself against him, feel the hard planes of his muscular chest on my soft curves.

"Did it turn you on? When you had no control over your

body, and he could do anything he wanted to do with you?" he asked, his voice serious. "Did you like being controlled?"

My body squirmed underneath his piercing gaze, wetness pooling in my thong. I replied to him with a small murmur, but he couldn't hear me, so he stood up and came closer to me, my heartbeat increasing.

He cupped my jaw, making me look at him as he said, "Say it again, Bella."

"Yes, I want to try it again." I licked my lips and added, "Probably with someone who is experienced and knows me."

Take the hint, Ethan.

His lips curled in the corner, giving me the barest hint of a smile. "Are you sure you want to do this?"

"Have kinky sex with you and get pregnant? *Yes*, Ethan."

"Okay," he replied and kept staring at me, his eyes a whirlpool of emotions. His thumb rubbed my bottom lip, and before I could take it in my mouth he said, "I am going to kiss you."

His lips met mine in a soft caress, my body melting in his arms when he held me close to him. Ethan settled me on his lap, my legs straddling him and feeling the bulge in his pants. I kissed him back, licking his lips as my hands feathered his thick locks. I sighed when his hands explored my body, creating tiny explosions of heat and pleasure underneath my skin wherever he touched. A soft moan slipped past my lips when he licked and kissed my neck, his hands squeezing my ass, his fingers digging in my skin as if he couldn't get enough of me. A sharp gasp escaped my lips when his finger pulled the garter belt and let it smack onto my skin. I raised my dress a little to spread my legs more and moaned softly between our kisses when I brushed my aching core on his hardened length.

Ethan swore, his harsh, warm breath fanning on my neck.

He pulled away and cupped my cheeks, "Before we go further, I want you to know your safe words."

"Safe words?"

He gently sat me down beside him on the couch, my dress in such disarray that I was sure he had seen my thong. I tugged my dress down while trying to hold some breath in my lungs.

"Yes, safe words. Something you will use when you are uncomfortable and want to stop the scene." His tone had changed. He was serious even though there was a prominent bulge in his pants. I nodded. "Red, yellow, and green are common, but we can have our own safe words. Green is to let me know that you are perfectly okay with the scene, you can use yellow when something is uncomfortable for you and you want to take some time. And you will use red when something is out of your comfort zone and you want me to stop whatever I am doing."

His eyes were fierce, the sharp features of his face looking more stark than usual. I nodded, my mouth dry. What would he do that I would need to use those safe words?

Ethan must have seen the fear and excitement in my eyes. He held my hand and kissed my knuckles. "I would never do anything to harm you, Bella. I need your complete trust. And I am trusting you to use safe words when you need to, okay?"

"Yes, Ethan," I replied looking at his hand holding mine. "I want to use other words."

He waited, looking at me from his thick lashes. I ignored the itch to lean closer and kiss him and said, "Black, grey, and white."

His thumb stroked the pulse on my wrist, "And what are you feeling right now?"

I didn't miss a beat. "White."

Ethan stared at me for a few moments and stood up, his

tall, muscular body looming over me. I licked my lips and met his piercing gaze.

"Give me your thong, Kiara," his velvety deep voice traveled down my body and stroked my throbbing sex. His tone was a pure command that I gladly wanted to obey.

I lifted my dress, his pupils dilating. We were gazing at each other, our eyes never leaving each other's face. We both heard the small clink of my fingers unclipping the garter belts. I shifted and hooking my fingers on the lace, I trailed it down my legs covered in stockings and handed the black lace to him.

His eyes finally moved from my face down to the sheer garment in his palm. I watched him lift it to his face and take a deep breath, taking in the scent of my feminine arousal. I clenched my legs together, my naked sex throbbing painfully for his touch as he let out a low growl and flashed his eyes to me and my legs.

"Spread your legs," he ordered, keeping my thong in his pocket.

I did, the tight dress constricting my thighs to stay closer. Goosebumps raised all over my body when Ethan leaned down and pulled my dress up to my upper thigh, his masculine scent wafting in my nose. I wanted to get close and breathe him in, but he pulled away, his eyes glaring at me to spread my legs wider. I bit my lip and spread them, shivering when the cold air brushed against my naked core. He couldn't see my bare sex as the dress still covered it, but he didn't need to see my pussy to confirm that I was dripping for him.

"Good. Now I don't want you to move your hands or I will stop. Understood?" Ethan asked in his stern voice.

I nodded, clenching my hands in fists.

He narrowed his eyes at me. "Use that sweet little tongue of yours, Kiara. Or else I have a much better use of it."

It seemed like my pussy had grown a heartbeat after hearing his words. My body thrummed with the need of his touch and the promise of his words.

I licked my lips before asking, "Like what?"

Ethan gave me a small smile before kneeling across me, his large hands stroking my stocking covered legs. His touch tickled, and I wanted to shut them closed because he looked different. Ethan's broad shoulders looked magnificent between my legs. I would never tire of this view, his handsome face peering between my thighs, searching for his prize.

My body trembled when he softly kissed my thigh, removing the stocking with ease and throwing it away. His lips were soft, but his kiss turned rough when he bit my skin, licking it sweetly afterward. My hands dug into the soft couch, and I knew my nails might get imprinted on the leather. Having Ethan kiss my thigh and not touch him, tug his hair, dig my hands in his shoulders was harder than I had thought.

But I had always loved a challenge—OH GOD.

I covered my mouth at the loud moan that tore through my lips. But I failed and moaned again, watching Ethan's hand under my dress, his fingers rubbing my slick lips and toying with the clitoris. I clenched my legs and squirmed on the couch, but he was holding my other leg and lightly smacked my thigh when I tried to pull away from his erotic touch.

"Use your words, Bella," he reminded me, "Where are you?"

I breathed, "White."

His exploring fingers stopped for a moment. A whimper tore out of me when he lifted my leg off the floor to plant it on the couch, baring me all to him. He let out a low groan, his fingers dipping inside me and slowly moving in and out. I didn't hold back my moans anymore. My hands went from my hair to my aching breasts, his piercing eyes watching me as I watched his hand move back and forth. Curses flew out of my mouth as I begged him to touch me or let me touch him, but he was persistent in torturing me.

"God, you're so fucking wet," he whispered, "I can't wait to taste you."

Tears welled in my eyes when his thumb played with my clitoris, his lips kissing my neck and trailing down to bite the soft flesh of my cleavage.

"Ethan, *please*," I whimpered, my hips rising up to meet the slow, languid strokes of his fingers. "It's not fair, you're touching me, and I can't touch you."

He hummed throatily; the vibration reverberating through my body and making my toes curl. "You can touch me as much as you want when I tell you to. Not right now," he pulled away, his eyes taking in my face, "I love seeing you desperate, your pussy clenching my fingers tightly to make you cum."

"You're being mean," I said breathlessly and squeezed my eyes shut when the pad of his thumb rubbed against my swollen bud.

"Open your eyes and look at me," his hand wrapped around my throat, his voice deeper and rougher.

My orgasm was so close, I was on the edge as I gazed at him through heavy-lidded eyes, my mind hazy.

He stopped and looked at my hand holding his palm, which was wrapped around my throat. I shook my head, "Please, *no*, I am sorry." I rambled and pulled my hand away, but Ethan had already pulled out his fingers, leaving me bare and horny for more.

He placed his ring finger on my bottom lip. The sharp scent of my feminine arousal wafted in my nose as he met my eyes.

"Suck."

Looking at him, I took his finger in my mouth and sucked it clean, moaning at the taste, the way his eyes darkened making them look onyx. I swirled my tongue around the pad of his finger, licking it clean and pulling away. Ethan watched me as he licked his middle finger clean from my glistening juices, a low groan rumbling from his throat as he tasted me. I took a shuddering breath watching the erotic sight and wondered if he would mind if I rubbed one out in front of him.

I was just planning to slide my hand underneath the dress when Ethan stood up, lifting me up with him, my breasts pressing against his shirt, feeling the hard planes of muscles.

He leaned down and whispered in my ear, "Go to sleep. And don't touch yourself."

Before I could process what he had uttered, he kissed my temple and left me in the low light of the living room. I sighed when I heard the door close to his room and felt the painful throb in my core.

I woke up an hour later, gasping as I controlled my breathing, when I remembered my wet dream. A crazy wet dream. My body was thrumming with desire as I felt the familiar dampness in my underwear. I tried controlling my naughty mood and pressed my thighs together because my dirty mind had another idea. It was well past twelve. Ethan was probably asleep by now.

Swallowing the lump in my throat, I opened the closet and pulled out a small bullet vibrator from my underwear drawer. It was small and easily fit in my palm, but its girth was thick, and it came with different powerful levels of sensations. I slid under the blanket and took a deep breath, closing my eyes. *He is asleep, Kiara. Stop thinking too much.* Before I could talk myself out of it, I removed my shorts and spread my legs.

I was wearing a nude-colored satin camisole. My hardened nipples pebbled through the top when I switched on the vibrator and turned it on to the lowest level.

The bedside lamp was on, giving a soft glow to the bed. Closing my eyes, I imagined Ethan standing over the edge of the bed and ordering me to use that toy on my soaking pussy. I was breathing hard when I lowered the vibrator to my hips, my stomach clenching at the powerful sensation on my skin. I slid it lower where I needed it the most.

"Oh, fuck," I mewled, my toes curling in pleasure when I brushed the toy on my sensitive nub. The reverberating vibrations on my clitoris were so overwhelming that it made me edge to my orgasm within seconds.

My volume of moans increased with time. I turned the settings on the second level and my hips jerked up at the powerful vibrations. I groaned softly, fondling my tender breasts through the flimsy top. I pinched my hardened nipples, the soft sharp pains sending bolts of pleasure directly to my heated sex. My mind felt dizzy as it solely focused on the sensations my body was riding through.

I couldn't control my whimpers and groans that escaped my lips when I felt the mind-shattering orgasm rolling through my body. I tried to stifle my loud moans in the pillow, but I knew I was loud.

I opened my half-lidded eyes and registered a soft click followed by a knock before I heard Ethan's husky voice rumbling through the door.

"Hey, Kiara, are you alright? I heard you groan." Sincere worry laced his voice while I bit my lips.

Unfortunately, at that exact moment, the bullet vibrator brushed over my sensitive clitoris on level three. A loud and very clear guttural moan escaped my lips and I closed my eyes shut when I felt how achingly good it felt.

"Ohmygod," I blurted out breathily when I felt my orgasm crushing through my body, mind, and soul. I wrenched the sheets underneath me and pulled away from the vibrator, my legs trembling and my hips rocking me through the earth-shattering orgasm. I tried to keep down my moans by biting my lower lip, but even then, I couldn't control my breathy hums.

"Kiara? You don't sound well. I am coming in," Ethan said, still worried as he stepped inside the room and looked at me.

I was too busy checking him out through my post-orgasmic mind and watched the hard contours of his abs and the way his biceps bulged ever so slightly when he closed the door with a small click. He was shirtless and his hair was damp. He must have taken a shower.

Now I was thinking about him showering naked.

His forehead creased a little as he frowned at me, "Are you sick?"

Before I could tell him that I was fine and he should go back to sleep, his eyes fell on the bullet vibrator that was still on the floor. I clenched my legs to hold off the moans because I was wet all over again.

Ethan picked it up and his frown deepened before he snapped his eyes at me. "Are you . . ." he trailed off, and I desperately tried to act as if I hadn't just orgasmed.

I licked my lips when his darkened unmatched eyes roved over my face, chest, and my shivering legs which were hiding underneath the blankets.

"May I?" Ethan asked, standing at the edge of the bed.

The scent of my musky arousal tinged in the air made my head dizzy.

I don't know what was running in my orgasm phased mind as I nodded, allowing him to remove the blanket. A small gasp escaped my lips when he yanked the blanket off of me and cursed softly when his eyes dropped between my thighs. His gaze was nothing but predatory as I wondered if I should close my legs and back away a little.

"You are such a naughty girl, Kiara. Can I touch you?" he asked, licking his lips and gazing at my aching breasts which were pouting in the air through the camisole and to my face.

I breathed, "Yes, please."

He brushed his thumb on his bottom lip, his eyes never leaving my face. "What do you want, Bella? Soft or rough?"

I swallowed the lump in my throat and answered, "I need both."

His eyes swirled with hunger as they turned feral at my answer. "Come here," he said, patting his lap when he sat down.

My lips curled at the side as I whispered, "Yes, Daddy," and crawled onto his lap.

Ethan glared at me and wrapped his hand around my throat. I smiled at him, my hands cupping his cheek. "You are trouble, Kiara Sharma," he whispered, his eyes softening as he gently kissed me. "Don't call me that again," he warned, pulling me into a toe-curling kiss.

I savored his lips, his mouth when our lips parted and our tongues collided in sweet unison. I tasted the hint of the mint of his toothpaste and feathered his thick hair in my fingers. He bit my lip and peppered kisses down my throat, his hands sliding underneath the thin camisole and cupping my breasts. I squirmed in his lap, rocking my hips back and forth on the tent in his sweatpants.

Ethan removed the satin top and took my hardened nipple in his hot mouth, licking it and biting it slowly, teasingly while his hand pinched my nipple. I gasped at the sweet pleasure and dug my fingers on his shoulders.

As much as I wanted him to have raw sex with me and make me pregnant, I was also enjoying foreplay.

"Do you like being spanked, Bella?" he crooned, his hot whisper tickling my ear.

Blood rushed in my cheeks as I blinked at him, not able to form words and answer his question.

His hold on my waist tightened, "Only one way to find out."

I bit my lip when he laid me down on his lap, my stomach resting on his thighs, feeling his hardened bulge on my skin. I squirmed when he raised my ass, my toes barely touching the floor.

Holding my breath, I tried to relax when he stroked my ass, massaging and squeezing the skin. "I am going to punish you for touching yourself when I told you not to. Use your safe words when you need to, understood?" he asked, his deep voice rumbling through my body.

I nodded.

Smack

"Oh!" I groaned when his palm smacked my ass, heat rushing on my skin and warming my core. *Holy shit.*

"Use your tongue, Kiara. Do you understand using your safe words when you need to?" He asked, his voice rough while he stroked my ass.

"Y-yes, Ethan, I understand."

He hummed and pulled me close, wrapping his other hand in my hair and lightly tugging my head back. I couldn't hold back my groans and little yelps or shrieks when Ethan's palm met my ass in alternative strikes. *Smack. Smack. Smack.* My ass got sore and scorched more with each strike of his palm.

I was heaving for breath when he had to hold my wrists on my lower back with his palm. I moaned louder when he told me he wished he had some rope with him right now. I was curious and aroused to know what else he wanted to do and try with me.

I squeezed my eyes shut when he stopped for a while and made me gasp loudly when the same hand caressed my burning ass, which felt like it was on fire. He rubbed my skin and soothed some pain, "You're a real screamer, you know that?"

Yes, Ethan, I know that.

Sadly, I could hear myself over the slaps of skin when he spanked me. Maybe that was an exaggeration, but I didn't know this would hurt like a bitch. Not to mention, I could feel my juices sliding down my inner thigh. I was getting turned on by this, by the pain.

I swallowed the lump in my throat and closed my eyes so that the tears would stop pooling in my eyes. A small whimper escaped my lips when Ethan took me in his lap, wrapping his hands around me and rubbing my back.

He kissed my hair, "You did so well, Bella. How are you feeling?"

"Overwhelmed," I replied, listening to his heartbeat.

Ethan laid me down on the bed and kissed me lightly. He looked in my eyes and asked, "Which color?"

"White."

He clenched his jaw and pulled away.

"Spread your legs," he said, "Wider."

I willingly obeyed, staring at him, and the pure command lacing his husky voice. My eyes were half-lidded as goosebumps spread across my body just looking at him while he gazed at me and my dripping pussy as if I were his last meal.

"Are you going to fuck me?"

Ethan hovered above me, settling between my legs. "No, not now," he said and held my wrists, raising them to the headboard. I took a long whiff of his musky male scent. "Don't move your hands until I tell you to."

"Or what?"

He inclined his head, a strand of his coal-black hair falling against his face. Oh, fuck my kink. "Or I will have to see that you don't move your hands until I am done with you."

"Got it, Big Daddy," I replied, my voice breathy with a sultry undertone which made a vein pop on his neck. At that moment, I had a surreal amount of desire and lust to lick that vein, bite his ear, and scratch his back as I rode us both to insanity.

I pursed my lips from saying that out loud. I, Kiara Sharma, was seriously and literally fucked.

My hips bucked up when Ethan landed a sharp smack on my bare pussy. "Don't. Call. Me. *That*," he growled, spanking my aching sex with each word he said, holding my legs open when they trembled, and I writhed underneath him.

He kissed me, swallowing my groans and holding me down while slowly rubbing his fingers on my sensitive, sore clitoris. I shivered and opened my eyes, finding him gazing at me.

"You love being punished, don't you, Bella?" he asked, knowing the answer as his fingers dipped inside me, my eyes widening.

"Yes, Ethan," I moaned softly, moving my hips with his digits as they fucked me slowly, gently, opposite to the harsh spanking he had given my ass and my pussy.

"You're so fucking wet, Kiara." He groaned, kissing my neck and rubbing his thumb on my aching bud while fucking me with his fingers.

Ethan's lips descended to my naked breasts. He didn't waste any time devouring, biting, and kissing my hard nipples, eliciting whimpers from my throat. I clenched his fingers, willing myself not to move my hands from the headboard.

"*Ethan*," I said with a breathy groan, "Please, can I come?"

He didn't even lift his head before kissing down my stomach and flatly answering, "No."

"I am close. Please let me come," I begged him, my hips rising to meet his fingers, but he held me down.

"Not yet," Ethan replied sternly, a strand of his hair falling against his forehead. He bent down and licked my dripping pussy from my lips to my clitoris.

I whimpered, my legs trembling. This was too much. "Oh, fuck me, please!"

Ethan smirked like the sadist he was and did it a few more times, each time slowly as if he was having his favorite ice cream and had all the time in the world. Each time, a low groan dragged out of my throat, surprising me with my vocal capabilities. But he didn't complain and looked like he was enjoying it very much as the pace of his fingers fucking me increased, the tip of his tongue rolling around my swollen nub.

"*Ethan*," I half-moaned, half-screamed when he bit my clitoris, the sharp sting of pain and pleasure numbing my head as I felt endorphins taking over my body. "Please . . ." I begged, clutching the headboard, ". . . *more*."

His soft chuckle reverberated through my soaking sex, making me shiver. He leaned away a bit and looked at me. "Fucking hell, Kiara, you're so responsive," Ethan said, his voice deep and husky as I tried to control my breathing. His eyes averted to my breasts as he licked his lips and murmured, "I should try clamps on you. You'll love it."

My eyes widened. "A what?"

I never got a reply as he was back to town, eating me out like a starved man and only stopped to hold my inner thighs away from my sensitive core.

I shivered when his glare met my eyes, "Remind me to tie your legs next time."

"Next time?"

Ethan narrowed his eyes at me, "If you think this is a one time thing then you are very mistaken. And I can't even tongue fuck your pussy without your legs snapping my head." My face went scarlet hearing his words as he squeezed my thighs and demanded, "Don't move them."

I didn't but the thought of Ethan tying my legs apart and baring me to him for hours to no end as he teased and tortured me to his liking turned me on, making me squirm. But a sharp swat on my inner thigh snapped me out of my head. I looked at Ethan who was inclining his head, his hand massaging the stinging skin on my thigh making me sigh.

"You are imagining it, aren't you, Bella?" he asked, his voice smoky as a smirk tugged his lips. "You would love being tied up by me. Letting me tease and use this pussy of yours however I want. Spanking it . . ." My entire body flamed with lust at his words as he slowly fucked my pussy. "Licking it and fucking it . . ." I gasped with each sharp thrust of his fingers, clenching my muscles. He slowly added, "Or inserting a vibrator inside you and leaving you tied up on the bed."

I shook my head. "Please, no."

A small glint in his eyes told me he would do that, if needed. I gulped nervously, hoping he would make me come right now and not leave me with a vibrator.

I was waiting for his reply when Ethan leaned down and sucked on my clitoris, curling his fingers inside me, making a 'come here' motion as they scraped against my g-spot. I didn't know what I was moaning or begging for him to let me come as I moved my hips toward him, his tongue flicking the sensitive nub.

"Come for me, Kiara," Ethan said at last.

My resolve broke, and a loud groan escaped my lips when I orgasmed against his fingers, tongue, and lips. It felt like I was on the edge of the cliff and finally jumped, landing on the orgasmic clouds of cloud nine.

When I opened my eyes, I was panting and shivering. Ethan sucked soundly on my pussy, drinking my juices and dragging out my orgasm as long as he could. My mind was whirling with dizziness as exhaustion hit my body, making me sleepy while he pulled out his fingers and sucked them clean.

A hum escaped my lips when he hovered above me, capturing my lips in a tantalizing kiss. I could taste myself on his lips and tongue. He held my hands, kissing each wrist and massaging them with his fingers. I almost cried at the gesture.

Ethan gathered me in his arms as he tucked my hair back and pecked my forehead, "You did so well, Bella. Watching you come apart was breathtaking." He kissed my lips again, pulling the blanket over us as his hands continued to massage my waist.

"How are you feeling?" he asked softly.

I smiled with half-lidded eyes, "Like I am on cloud nine and . . . *strange*."

He nodded, running his hand through my hair, making me melt in his arms, "During the entire scene, did you ever think about using your safe words?"

Opening my eyes, I looked at his face, which was a hair's breadth away from me. I cupped his cheek and kissed his nose. "No, not even for a moment."

Ethan sighed in relief when I ran my hand through his hair. "But promise me you will use your safe words when I push you too much, okay? I don't want to hurt you."

"You can never hurt me, Ethan. And I promise I will use them when it gets too much," I said truthfully.

A small smile appeared on his face, his eyes glittering

with what I could decipher as happiness. "Good girl, now sleep. You must be tired."

I pursed my lips and settled comfortably with him.

"Was that an order or a request?"

"*Both*. Go to sleep, Kiara."

Now that was an order.

I smiled. "Okay, Big Daddy."

Ethan pinched my butt, making me snicker as I watched him smile at me and snuggle me into his chest.

12. WHAT'S YOUR MIDDLE NAME?

ETHAN

I was having a hard time focusing on simple things since last night. Like getting hard thinking about Kiara or not burning the eggs in a pan. Or my favorite, having a cold shower without getting hard because that shit hurt, and I did not want blue balls.

Last night's date took a whole different turn than what I had imagined. Kiara wanted a baby, and she wanted *me* to put a baby inside her. My jaw clenched thinking about it. I wanted to know what would happen after she gets pregnant.

Would I see her stomach grow each day? Would she let me talk to the baby growing inside her womb? Would I hear the child's first words? First steps? I wondered how he or she would look. If anything, the baby should have Kiara's smile with that dimple.

"Good morning."

My body tensed when Kiara's arms wrapped around my torso, her body pressing against mine as she hugged me from behind. I snapped out of my thoughts and cleared my throat.

I switched the fried eggs to the plate beside the chopped avocado and juicy strawberries and turned around to find a very sleepy Kiara, hugging my chest. I smiled and pulled away to see that she was wearing absolutely nothing underneath the blanket she had dragged to the kitchen.

Six years had passed, and Kiara was still not a morning person. Some things never change.

"Really, Kiara? Parading naked in my house already," I teased and set out plates on the marble countertop of the island.

Her hair was in a bun and she looked like she had washed her face with cold water but still couldn't wake up her brain even after brushing her teeth.

"I am so tired," she mumbled.

I sat down, pushing her plate toward her to have her breakfast. Instead of sitting down on a separate stool, she tipped on her toes and settled on my lap, making me grin at her. Her small body fit perfectly on me as she leaned on my chest. The blanket covering her slid down a little. I took a sharp breath gazing at her cleavage.

Don't you dare stand, Eiffel. Stay down.

We ate our breakfast in comfortable silence until Kiara opened her pouty lips and my ability to think straight went down the drain.

"So, I was thinking about last night," she started and licked her fingers, making me clench my jaw as I imagined her using that tongue and lips on her knees near my—

Bad Eiffel!

"And?" I asked impatiently as she closed her eyes, her eyelashes making shadows on her cheeks while I softly massaged the skin on her thighs. So smooth and soft. The dirty part of me wondered how red her skin would become when I flog her and she begged me to make her come again and again and again.

Gazing at me with her half-lidded hooded eyes and sultry look on her face, Kia whispered, "I want to return the favor."

My eyebrows raised as she turned toward me. The blanket fell over her left shoulder, my eyes taking in the delicious view of her perky left breast, her nipple hard. I licked my lips and flickered my eyes at her face, a small smirk tugging her lips as she straddled me, holding my face in her warm hands. I knew that dirty glint in her eyes. Because I had the same look while I was eating her out. And my Bella wanted to devour me right now.

I took a sharp breath when she leaned closer, pressing her body against mine making her soft breasts squish against my bare chest. She brushed her lips against the shell of my ear and exhaled softly as tingles shot through my body.

"I want to be on my knees and . . ." a soft groan escaped my throat when her palm cupped my hardened shaft through the sweatpants, rubbing her hand back and forth as she added, her voice husky, "Suck your cock until you make me swallow your cum."

"*Kiara,*" I warned, my voice strained hearing her dirty talk, my hands fisting in my lap. I wasn't even touching her because if I did, I would throw her on the island and have my favorite breakfast, spreading her thighs.

Her hand slipped under my waistband, now stroking me gently and making me sigh as I gazed at her. My eyes widened a bit when she pulled her hand up to lick her palm with her tongue. I gaped at her, watching in awe and lust as she slid her wet hand back and forth on my erect dick.

Her dirty brown eyes met mine, the pad of her thumb brushed my bottom lip, "What? Let me pleasure you."

"*Oh, fuck.*"

A soft moan escaped my lips and I wanted to close my eyes when her fingers ran over the head of my cock, massaging the frenulum. I gazed at her through my pleasure-filled haze as she wet her lips with her dirty tongue and leaned down to lick my neck and kiss my adam's apple before trailing her kisses to my collarbone.

"Let me worship you, Ethan," she whispered breathily, "Please. Let me suck your dick. I will make it worth it."

I wasn't going to deny at first, so sure, go ahead.

Swallowing the lump in my throat, I nodded, "Yes, Kiara."

I had dirty talked with most of my sexual partners, but Kiara was the first one to dirty talk right back, and it was a huge fucking turn on. I could come by hearing her dirty, filthy words.

As soon as I confirmed the blowjob, which was going to happen if she asked me or not, Kiara pulled away from me and stood up. I frowned at the loss of her body heat against mine.

She eyed me up and down, biting her lip. "Stay here."

"Yes, Ma'am," I muttered under my breath, too excited to move an inch. I watched her ass when she walked toward the refrigerator and pulled out an ice tray. I frowned when she pulled out ice cubes in a small bowl with a bottle of chocolate syrup and walked back to me.

"Spread your legs," she demanded, making me raise my eyebrows.

Well, okay. I would let her have the upper hand in this.

"First remove that fucking blanket. I want to see you naked."

Only a bit.

A sexy smirk tugged her lips as she slid the blanket down her shoulders and let it pool around her ankles with a soft whisper. My eyes roved over her bare body. I smiled at the small love bites peppered over her neck, breasts, stomach, and legs, remembering last night.

Kiara went down on her knees when I spread my legs, still sitting on the stool. I bit my lip when she removed my sweatpants and licked her own lips as she hungrily stared at the length of me.

Her hooded brown eyes flickered to my face. "Have you ever received a blowjob with ice cubes?"

Well, no, but looks like I am about to.

I had to blink twice to realize what she was asking. Have I given oral with ice? Yes. Have I received one? No. I shook my head, too speechless to answer a verbal reply as Kiara smiled and sucked a cube of ice between her lips.

Oh my fucking God.

Clenching my jaw, I watched her stroke me with her hand, her fingers circling the head, and I couldn't help my long sigh. I gulped nervously when she leaned on her knees and spread them, my eyes flickering to see wetness pooling between her thighs as her cold lips wrapped around the bulbous head of my dick.

My entire body reacted at the feeling as I held her head. "Holy fuck, Kia!"

I had never experienced a sensation like it before, and my body was reacting strongly toward Kiara's hands and lips. Her free hand held my thigh, her eyes averting to my eyes as she sucked me deeper, her cold tongue flicking against the tip, making me moan when my lower abdomen clenched.

I had to control my heavy breathing when she pulled away, only to take a cold ice cube in her mouth and suck me. This time, I didn't dare to hold back my groans when the cold walls of her mouth took me deeper. My hand tightened around her hair, tugging her closer when her nails dug in my thighs.

"Oh, yes, Bella," I whispered throatily, my voice deep and smoky as the ice turned into cold water inside her mouth, dribbling down her lips to her neck and down the valley of her breasts.

Kiara repeated her actions with another ice cube, making

me jerk at the new sensations. Her muffled moans made me shiver when they reverberated through my cock to my entire body.

"Fuck, do that again. Moan with my cock inside your mouth," I groaned and felt hot all over my body when Kiara followed my command, moaning and moving her hips as her head bobbed up and down my veiny shaft.

She pulled away only to uncap the bottle of chocolate and drizzle it over my lower stomach and cock. God, she was going all dirty for me. Relaxing back in the stool, I closed my eyes and swore loudly when I felt her hot mouth lapping over my lower stomach, biting my hips just for the tease.

I looked down and met one of the most erotic sights ever. Kiara's messy waves were down, brushing her back as she hungrily licked and kissed me as if she was worshipping me as she had said before. *I want to marry this woman.* The thought of her being with anyone else made me furious and jealous if she had ever given them a blowjob like this one.

I didn't like the thoughts running in my head. I fisted her hair in my hand and said, "Keep your hands behind your back."

Kiara momentarily pulled away, licking her lips and blinking at me through her lust dazed eyes. "What?"

"Keep your hands behind your back and then suck me," I explained, my eyes devouring her naked body kneeling at my feet. "And spread your legs. Wider." I nodded when she struggled to keep upright, her chest arching toward me with a clouded expression in her eyes.

"Good girl."

As if my comment affected her, Kiara leaned down and took me deep and hard in her mouth, her cold tongue flicking on the underside of my shaft, making me groan in pleasure. I couldn't help but lead her head on my veiny cock, her muffled whimpers and moans turning me on as she desperately tried to sit upright while pleasuring me.

I enjoyed the small trail of her juices on her inner thigh when I slowly started fucking her tight mouth. I paused and let her relax when she gagged as my head grazed the back of her throat and did it again until she was deep throating me. I cursed and swore when I went faster, holding her hair as tears welled in her eyes, her legs shivering when our groans echoed in the room.

But I wasn't done here. I pulled away, her eyes wide, "Stand up, Bella."

She frowned but stood up, holding my hand. She let out a small yelp of surprise when I held her waist and placed her down on the marble island. I spread her legs, holding them away with my hands, and licked her soaking pussy.

I increased my rhythm when a garbled moan escaped her lips, her hands tugging my hair. I sunk my tongue inside her wet cavern, my fingers tightening on her legs. I pulled away and laid her back on the cold marble while I slowly uncapped the chocolate syrup bottle, her eyes widening. She licked her lips and watched me devour her with my gaze.

"What are you doing, Ethan?" she whispered, leaning up on her elbows when I kept the bowl of ice cubes on the empty stool.

I smirked and kept my hand on her chest, I gently pushed her down and wrapped my hand around her throat. "Having my breakfast," I answered, watching her gasp when I drizzled the chocolate syrup on her breasts, stomach and pulled away to let it drop over her hips and inner thighs.

Kiara breathed, "Don't miss any spots."

My smirk widened when I held a few ice cubes in my hand and replied, "I won't."

I dived in. Licking, nibbling, and kissing all the chocolate from her trembling body while she writhed, moaning my name and twisting around when my mouth landed on her soaking pussy.

When I was tired of the same chocolaty taste on my tongue, I twirled an ice cube on her pebbled nipples and sucked on them until the only name Kiara knew was mine.

"What's your middle name, Kiara?" I asked between teasing her and licked her inner thighs, my fingers kneading her soft breasts.

"Uh . . . uh, it's—*mngk*, ohmyfuckinggod, *Ethan!*" She half screamed and half moaned.

I chuckled and released her swollen clitoris from between my teeth. I flicked it with my tongue to make her feel better and continued to eat her out. I took a sharp breath when her hand wrapped around my stiff member, making me hover above her, her bottom lip wedged between her teeth.

Leaning down, I kissed her, moving her hair away from her body as our chests pressed against each other, her free hand roaming over my abs when I moaned her name. Her palm was massaging my dick as I sunk two fingers inside her dripping pussy. A whimper escaped her pink lips.

"What are you doing, Kiara?" I asked, my voice gruff when I continued to fuck her with my fingers and curled them ever so slightly to scrape against her g-spot.

Her beautiful pink breasts were heaving up and down as she pleaded, "Fuck me, Ethan. *Please.*"

My eyes darkened, and it took a significant amount of self-control to shake my head. "No, Kiara. Not right now."

"But why?" she whined. Her lips went 'O' when I curled my fingers in a come-here motion. A long moan elicited from her throat.

I gave a small thrust in her hand, "Because I said so. I don't want to have our first time on a fucking kitchen island."

Kiara gasped in pleasure and went back to stroking me

with her hand as her eyes gleamed, "But we can go to your room."

"I said no," I narrowed my eyes at her. "I want to explore your little body. Tease you, clamp you, gag you, flog you and spank you before I sink my cock inside this tight pussy." Each time, I thrust in her palm and fucked her as I felt her getting wetter at what I had just said.

Kiara's expression was a mix between frustration and desire as she replied, licking her lips, "Okay, Ethan."

I closed my eyes and let out a small groan when I felt myself getting closer to orgasm. "Ugh, *fuck*, Kiara. I am so fucking close," I whispered when I fucked her tight hole faster and deeper, her moans increasing with mine.

"Oh, God, I am going to come!" Kiara gasped, her hips moving in rhythm to meet mine as her back bowed from the marble.

She groaned deeply as her orgasm washed over her little body, trembling and shaking with the aftershocks. I clenched my jaw, jerking and moaning her name when I came all over her taut stomach and breasts. We both watched with our half-lidded eyes as I kept spurting on her body until I sighed in relief, leaning on the marble.

I licked my lips when I watched Kiara twirl my semen around her nipple and lick her finger with her tongue and slightly spreading her legs. I blinked out of her seduction and scooped her in my arms before she literally rode me to hell for the sinful thoughts.

"Let's get you washed up," I muttered, kissing the top of her head and marching toward my bathroom. I ignored the pout on her lips as we stood against each other when I turned the knob of my shower.

13. I NEED YOU

KIARA

Katherine sipped on her glass of water, "I always feel wet."

My eyes widened, and I looked past her enormous baby bump to see if she was wet or not. She was six months pregnant, so I was sure she couldn't have her water break but what was she talking about.

Anya, who was sitting beside me, nodded at my friend and sipped her wine. "I understand. And not even the sexy wet."

"Yes! It's like I might have peed myself, but I know I haven't."

I exhaled a sharp breath looking at my friends, "*Wow.*"

We were all invited to Katherine and Ryan's co-ed baby shower. By we, I mean, all our high school friends and it was like a reunion. I had already met Rio, Volt, and Becky with his two sons and Liam. There was noticeable tension between Liam and me, but Ethan was by my side making it less awkward. They both had arrived together after their swim practice while Anya, Andrew, and I arrived together.

Katherine rolled her eyes and adjusted her satin dress

which hugged her beautiful curvy body. I was almost jealous. "Oh, hush, you. When you get pregnant, you will know what we are talking about."

My eyes darted to my stomach, and I clenched my jaw. I took the glass of water placed on the table and gulped it down. I wanted to be pregnant and hoped I would be as soon as possible.

Anya cleared her throat and asked, "So, how is everything going with Ethan?"

"Ethan, *huh?*" Katherine gave me a sly smirk and glanced at the round table next to us.

The baby shower was held in their backyard and decorated with baby blue and white flowers and curtains as she was pregnant with a baby boy. Ryan, Ethan, Liam, Rio, and Volt sat at the other table with their other friends. My eyes couldn't stay away from Ethan, and I clenched my legs as I saw him grinning at something Rio said. He looked absolutely beautiful and devilishly handsome when he was happy.

Fuck, it should be illegal for him to be this handsome.

He turned my way, his blue-green eyes twinkling in the warm evening sunlight. I took a sharp breath when he winked at me and eyed me shamelessly. I felt a hot prickling sensation, and even though I was wearing a dress, I felt naked under his piercing gaze. I looked away first, trying to forget how delicious he looked in a crisp white shirt.

I cleared my throat and replied to Anya's question. "Everything with Ethan is going great. More than great, actually." I squeezed my legs together, desperate for some friction, and surprising myself when I found my thong drenched. "We are getting along well."

Really well.

Ethan's determination and stamina were way beyond the previous partners I had shared a bed with. I missed the way the body gets sore after a solid day of excessive intimacy. I cherished it.

Katherine cooed, "The way Ethan has been looking at you, it seems like high school all over again. Reminds me of good old days."

I made a face that made both of them laugh at me.

Anya leaned toward Katherine, "Oh, really? How was Kiara when she was a teenager?"

Here we go.

"Oh, she was a spitfire. She still is, but she is more tamed."

I heard Ethan cough in his fist, trying to stop himself from grinning. I shot him a glare and fixed my eyes anywhere but on my friends or him.

Katherine continued, "She had this, I am sure she still has it, huge crush on Ethan, and Ethan had a crush on her as well, but they didn't want to ruin their friendship. They were so cute, I swear to God. They still are! They can't even stop looking at each other—"

Thankfully, Ryan came to my rescue and kissed his wife's cheek. "Okay, stop it you two. Kiara has turned into a tomato. Come on, it's time for cake."

WATCHING EVERYONE REUNITING, eating sweets, and congratulating Katherine made my heart melt. Andrew was playing with Volt's sons while Anya subtly tried to update me about Jake. I had tried to stay far away from the media articles and videos regarding our breakup because I knew they would be filled with rumors. When Anya told me he was doing well with Stacy and slowly reuniting with Ben, despite all that had happened between us, I was happy for him. He had a family to take care of and hopefully soon, so would I.

I was trying to hide in the washroom for a while

because I needed some time to myself before going outside to mingle with everyone. It had been overwhelming to see so many kids and hear mothers coo at Katherine's cute baby bump. I missed my mother and couldn't stop myself from thinking about how I would look during the pregnancy.

Someone knocked on the door, and I jumped. I patted my hair in the mirror's reflection and muttered, "I'll be out in a second!"

"*Bella*," Ethan said, "Open up, I need to see you."

My heart ached in my chest as I swallowed the lump in my throat. One of the major reasons I was hiding was because Ethan was affecting me. He didn't leave my side for a second unless either of our friends needed us. He had wrapped his arm around my waist and pressed me tightly to his robust chest, muttering, "I can't wait to see you pregnant with a baby bump." It had brought tears to my eyes thinking about it.

I unlocked the door and before I could step out, Ethan leaned in and closed the door, locking it.

"What are you doing?"

Ethan stared down at me, his blue-green eyes piercing, "I should be the one asking you that. Why are you hiding in a bathroom?"

My cheeks flushed, "I am not hiding."

He pulled me closer, cupping my cheek and making me look him in the eye. "Tell me the truth. What's going on in your head?"

My bottom lip wedged between my teeth, my eyes dancing across the exposed skin of his golden chest. "I was thinking about how I would look when I get pregnant."

Even when I said it out loud, a small smile tugged my lips, and I watched Ethan's electric eyes sparkle. His hands caressed my skin, trailing down to squeeze my ass. "I am sure you'd look beautiful with a baby bump." His voice was rough, his hips pressing against my stomach.

A small gasp escaped my lips when I felt his hardened length. He leaned down and emitted a low groan that made my toes curl in my sandals. "Fuck, Kiara, you've no idea how much that turned me on. I can't wait to see you pregnant with my baby."

My breath froze at his words. *My baby.* But before I could say anything, Ethan's lips pressed against mine. He lifted me on the marble counter, pressing me against the mirror as he devoured my lips. His lips were soft against mine, our heady passion fighting with each other, my fingers threading in his hair and pulling him closer. With heart pounding in my ears, I cupped his cheeks and leaned back to look at him.

His diamond-like eyes were clouded with lust, but the way they crinkled with a small smile on his lips, I knew Ethan wanted more. More from me. I swallowed the lump in my throat at the sudden realization. I couldn't fall for him. I would ruin both of us if I did.

So, instead of pushing him away, I licked my lips and said, "Let's get out of here."

The way his handsome face lit up, I knew I was too late.

WE SAID OUR GOODBYES, and I ignored the sly smirk on Anya and Katherine's lips when Ethan held my hand and dragged me to his car.

The ride back to his house was heavy with anticipation and raw, carnal hunger for each other. I craved his touch, and I wanted to mark mine on his body. It was heady, and I had never felt like this before with anyone except him. I knew I would never feel like this with anyone else. He had ruined me for others. The thought made me shiver as I pressed my legs together.

We needed no words entering the house. Our lips and bodies did the talking. Tracing unspoken words on each other's skin with tongue, teeth, and rough hands. Fingers gripping, shredding, taking. For tonight, I was his, and he was mine. To please, worship and ruin.

"*Ah!*" I cried out when Ethan pushed me on the wall, kneeling between my legs and throwing them over his shoulder.

His fingers were gentle and exploratory despite how rough his actions were. My hands gathered his hair when his middle finger slowly rubbed me through my wet underwear. He groaned, kissing dirty lines on my thighs as he kissed his way upward.

"Hold your dress up," he ordered, fisting the lace of my thong in his hand and ripping it apart.

I half-gasped and moaned when his fiery mouth landed on my dripping sex. The way he looked at me paralyzed me to my bone, his intense blue-green eyes watching me from beneath his dark lashes. Hot white lust flooded in my veins when his expert tongue gave me gentle flicks, my legs trembling in his wake.

Ethan leaned back on his heels. His smoldering eyes captured me while his long fingers toyed with me, teasing me, torturing me. I panted and squeezed my eyes shut when he placed the pad of his thumb precisely on my throbbing clit. The erotic sensation crawled up from my spine and released in a quiver. My back arched from the wall, but his hold was firm on my legs.

I whimpered, "Please Ethan, I need you."

"I know, Bella," he said softly. He smoothed his hands over my thighs, tracing my curves with the pads of his fingers before he cupped my ass in his hands and squeezed the cheeks. I jumped when he gave a quick, harsh spank on my left cheek.

I tugged at his hair when a small cry left my lips, arousal pooling on my core, wanting him to remedy it. As if reading my mind, his slick, warm tongue circled my clit, sucking it in his hot mouth before giving it playful flicks. All the breath left my body, abandoning me as Ethan toyed with my clitoris, his tongue tasting me languidly.

"So fucking sweet." He breathed me in as if he was savoring the taste of me.

My cheeks flushed red. I watched him through half-lidded eyes. My blood felt hot and heavy with hunger when he finally caved in, increasing his pace and inserting two digits inside me at the same time. My head knocked back on the wall as I anchored myself, holding his hair. The tension in my stomach finally exploded in his mouth when he pressed his tongue flat on my sensitive nub, giving me a gentle kiss.

I climaxed, moaning his name. My body convulsed, then went limp against the wall in his arms.

When I opened my eyes, Ethan was hovering above me in my room, softly kissing my neck. I had forgotten how his oral skills were enough to exhaust me into a deep slumber. But not at the moment.

I wanted him. *Needed* him.

Cupping his cheek, I leaned up and kissed him on his lips, breathing in the musky feminine scent of my arousal. Our bodies pressed against each other, desperate for more. My hands clutched the fabric of his shirt, and I removed it out of the way when he unzipped my dress, helping me out of it.

Ethan took a sharp breath, looking at my breasts, "What's this?"

I peered down, finding breast tape that I had used to wear

underneath the dress. I pursed my lips and slowly removed it, wincing at the bit of pain, "These are called boob tape."

He frowned, "Why are you making that face?" He took one from my hand and I bit back my laughter when he tried it on his own nipple. "Does it hurt? I don't feel any pain."

After removing my other tape and being naked with him, I grinned at him. He was shirtless, hair tousled, cheeks flushed, and lips swollen from our kisses, yet he wanted to know how breast tape worked.

Biting my lip, I ripped it off, watching his face fall as he moaned in pain, clutching his nipple. "Are you sure?" I teased at his scrunched face.

"What the fuck, Kiara?" He groaned, "That fucking hurt. I don't know how you manage to wear this shit."

I giggled, "Who told you to try it? You are such a dork."

While he was busy patting his nipple, I decided to do something. I laid him down on the bed, straddling him, and whispered, "Let me kiss it better."

His eyes darkened hearing my sultry tone as I pressed my body down on him and kissed his throat, the beating pulse of his neck, licked his golden skin. Ethan's hands squeezed my cheeks as my lips lowered to his nipple, kissing and licking it softly until he delivered a spank on my right cheek.

"You are such a fucking vixen, Bella," he whispered, his husky voice slithering down my spine, encouraging me to kiss down his robust chest to the six hard blocks of abs. I pulled away to admire his lean, muscular form. Scratching my nails down his abs, I watched his muscles tense and leaned down to kiss the same trail with my lips, licking it sweet.

Before I could remove his belt and unzip his pants, Ethan flipped us over, his eyes clouded with lust as he pressed down on me. I exhaled sharply at the long length of him. I knew he was well endowed and how sore I would feel for a few days every time I would sit down. I wanted to cherish that soreness.

With dazed eyes, I watched him remove his pants and boxers, my lips wetting and throat going dry at the naked sight of him. Ethan Kane was truly magnificent. And at that moment, I wanted his throbbing magnificence inside me.

The bed dipped as he hovered above me, my eyes watching him, the guarded expression in them. I clenched the sheets between my fists, seeing that. We had made sure we were clean and even showed us our tests just to be clear. I trusted him.

Swallowing a small gulp of air, I whispered, "Be gentle, E."

The guarded expression melted away into a soft one, his muscular frame pressing against my soft curves. He kissed me, softly, gently, nipping at my lower lip before whispering, "Of course, Bella. I wouldn't want it any other way."

My body melted underneath his, his fingers entwined with mine as he pulled them above my head, pressing down our adjoined hands in the cold sheets. He pushed his hips forward, aligning himself between my thighs as I spread my legs for him, locking them around his waist.

My breathing increased when he coated his tip with my wetness, our eyes never leaving each other as if lost in our passion of galaxies. My lips parted when he pushed himself inside me, slowly, achingly, tenderly as my walls stretched to accommodate his wide girth and length. It hurt, my body burned with the pain, my hands squeezing his as he felt the pressure of it. I was thankful for his fingers entwining mine when he thrust into me in one slow thrust, shoving past my walls and reaching deep inside me.

I whimpered, closing my eyes shut at the intensity of his.

"*Fuck,*" he groaned, "You feel amazing, Kiara. Your tight walls clamping me." He enveloped my mouth in a demanding kiss as he withdrew from me before pushing forward, sliding inside me with such force that he had to squeeze my hand when my entire body rocked on the bed.

"Open your eyes and look at me," he ordered, slamming inside me once again with a punishing thrust.

Tears welled in my eyes as I watched his sharp face, my heart thudding loudly in my chest. I clung to him, clenching my velvety walls around him and cherishing how wonderful he felt inside me. Raw carnal hunger ignited within me. I moved my hips matching with his slow, deep rhythm. His husky, low groans encouraging me.

I cried out when he rolled his hips and bumped against the secretive g-spot inside me. Noticing my reaction, he repeated the same action again and again. I writhed underneath him, his hard body pressing down on me, watching me come undone as my body shuddered through bliss.

I was overly sensitive after coming twice in a span of a few moments, but Ethan wasn't done with me. He kissed me, swallowed the moans of my orgasm, and leaned back to watch my heaving breath. His fingers massaged my soaking core while he was still inside me, throbbing.

"Ethan, please," I shook my head.

"Come on, Bella," he said, "Give me one more. I love watching you climax."

"Come with me," I pleaded when he pulled me closer, my legs locking around his strong waist. The pad of his thumb pressed on my sensitive clit as he began slowly moving in and out of me, his thrusts deeper and sharper than before, angling straight toward my spot he was well acquainted with. His mouth descended on my bare chest, latching on to the nipple while his other hand pinched and tweaked the other, eliciting soft groans from me.

My hands wrapped around his neck when he increased his rhythm, our moans and groans echoing in the room. His hand held onto the headboard as it repeatedly slammed against the wall. The air tinged with the heavy scent of our arousal, and I couldn't get enough of him when I pressed my nose against the crook of his neck.

The built-up tension was too much, and I was overly sensitive as a cry left my lips, my body shivering with the need to let go. Ethan wrapped his hand around my throat, "Not yet, Kiara, hold it," he ordered.

The sounds of our skins slapping against each other followed his command, and I quivered, my hand holding his arm as he continued to plow into me. I felt him then, releasing my throat to dig his fingers in my hips as he pushed himself to the brink and gave a small jerk. I let go at the same time he did, spilling his warm spurts of climax inside me. I squeezed my eyes shut to the white-fiery lust when we came together after chasing our own high. I was sure that I was lost in the bliss when I heard him let out a low groan, pulling himself out of me.

I peeked my eyes open, finding his predatory stare between my thighs. I shivered, wanting to shy away and cover-up at the way he looked at me.

Oh no.

The walls I had destroyed for him stood guarded when his eyes softened when they landed on me. He frowned when he saw the guarded expression on my face. The way he had been behaving for a while, I realized that he wanted more out of it.

My baby.

I shivered at the cold washing over my body. I couldn't fall for him.

"What happened?" he asked when he placed two pillows underneath my legs. "Keep your legs elevated for a few minutes."

Even though my resistance melted at his sweet actions, I couldn't ignore the reality as I had done before. It would end up destroying me. Or worse, both of us. I couldn't go through that again.

Shaking my head at his previous question, I covered my body with a blanket, "Nothing. I . . . I am tired, that's all."

He frowned, "Are you okay, Bella? Do you want a massage? Why didn't you tell me you were—"

"Ethan," I stopped him, "I am fine, just tired."

He paused, turning around to give me a stunning view of his muscular back. I gazed at the way the slabs of muscles and prominent hard lines moved and tensed as he wore his boxers and pants. He looked at me, the air turning cold in the room as his gaze hardened.

"What do you want, Kiara?" he asked, his voice hard and devoid of any emotion.

"I want a baby." I lied, my voice betraying my emotions.

He nodded to himself, "Right. I will see you tomorrow."

With that sharp tone, he left, slamming the door shut behind him. I shivered and hugged the blanket. Somehow, I knew that even though we had talked about this earlier, tonight had changed everything between us. Even the deal of having his baby. With tears welling in my eyes, I fell asleep with his scent overpowering me.

14. I PUNISHED HER

ETHAN

Walking out of Kiara's room while she hid under the covers must be one of the hardest things I had ever done. I had known something was off when she stared at me with her golden wide eyes. She was pulling away and I could see that. But hearing what she wanted from me gave me a cold shower of reality that we were doing this for a baby. *Her* baby. All I was meant to do was put a baby inside her and move on.

I clenched my fists, turning the shower to cold. I didn't know why I thought she was opening up to me. All her flirty eyes, secretive smiles meant nothing now. It wasn't even her fault for saying the truth to me. We both had been clear about our needs from before. I get to play with her body, and she gets to have a baby. Simple as that.

Then why does my chest feel hollow?

Kiara Sharma surrounded me with her feminine scent. She was all over me. *Fuck, I can still taste her sweetness on my lips.* The feel of her tight walls clamping on me as if her body didn't want to let go of me. I wanted to go back to her room and take her again, demanding that I hadn't played with her. The need to control her was overwhelming, but I knew I would ruin whatever we had if I acted like a caveman right now.

I would deal with her tomorrow, taking and controlling her body however I wanted.

MY COACH CALLED Liam and me early in the morning for extra laps. This time, I surpassed Liam with ease, and he congratulated me for it. After showering in the locker room and changing, Liam asked me, "So what happened?"

I shrugged.

He sighed. "Did something happen with Kiara?"

I glared at him, "How did you know? Did you talk to her?"

Liam smirked at me, his grey eyes glinting with mischief. "I don't have a death wish, Kane. It's all over your face. You pushed past your limits because something is on your mind."

As we made our way to our cars, I paused before replying, "Something happened. Talk tonight?"

"Dinner's on you. I will let Rio and Volt know." Sliding his Ray-Bans over his eyes, he got in his Aston Martin and roared out of the lot.

I rolled my eyes. *Show off.*

I had an afternoon practice to do at the school as the assistant swim coach. While I was making sure that the students kept kicking their legs and did not drown, I felt a tingle in my back and knew someone was watching me. I closed my eyes. *Control yourself, Ethan, this is not the time or place.* I talked to myself before opening my eyes and looking over my shoulder to find a very nervous Kiara.

Fuck.

She looked stunning in her tight trousers and formal blouse which did nothing to hide her curves. Her hair was in a ponytail, and I wanted nothing but to wrap my hand around it as I took her from behind. Clenching my jaw, I looked away and scolded Eiffel down. I was coaching kids for fuck's sake.

"What do you want?" I asked, toweling myself dry as she nervously bit her lip.

Wish I could grab her jaw and bite her lip instead.

Calm down.

"I wanted to talk with you about last night and apo—"

My humorless chuckle cut her off. "This is not the time and place for that, darling," I whispered, "I don't care about last night. All you want from me is to fuck you and put a baby inside your womb. I will do it, but in return, I want your body however I please."

Heat flushed her cheeks, and I wanted to trace the path down to her slender neck. I added, "Be ready by ten."

With that, I left her standing by the bleachers, her cheeks flushed and thong drenched.

DINNER WITH LIAM, Rio, and Volt had been nothing but easy. Ryan couldn't arrive as he wanted to spend a day alone with his wife. Volt was whipped with Becky and seeing him talk about his kids made me really happy for him and wish I could have a family in a few years as well. Rio had moved in with his boyfriend and by the look of it, he looked deeply in love. Liam didn't want to settle down, something we had discussed when we became best mates. I had been the same, but seeing Kiara and me together at Katherine's baby shower, they didn't bring it up. I was thankful for that.

After taking one glass of scotch, I blurted, "I don't know what to do with Kiara."

Rio and Volt audibly sighed as they gave me a pitiful look. Liam, on the other hand, cocked his head at me. "What do you mean?"

"Becky couldn't stop talking about both of you, she ships you both," Volt muttered, "I can't believe it's been six years and you guys don't have babies."

I choked on my drink.

Rio smacked his head, "Volt!"

Liam patted my back, giving me an odd look as I coughed and swallowed a mouthful of water, rubbing my chest.

I cleared my throat, "Volt, you know what happened. She was engaged when I met her."

He rolled his eyes, "Then she broke up with the model dude to be with you. Didn't she move in after a week when her engagement ended?"

My silence was enough to make him nod. "*Exactly.* Women are simple. So is Kiara. If you have the same feelings, which I know you do, *tell her.* If you don't, which is a lie, then don't complicate shit between you two."

I stared down at my empty plate, processing his words. Even Rio was gaping at him while Liam called the waitress for the cheque. Whatever Volt said might be true, but Kiara was no simple woman. She had asked to have my baby, not a relationship where I could even dream about settling in with her. No, she just wanted me for the baby. That much was clear by how she closed herself off from me last night.

When I reached back to the house, I took a couple of deep breaths, controlling myself before facing Kiara. Yes, I wanted to control her, but not when I was angry at her. I wondered if I should let it go, but as soon as I saw her worried face and her large amber eyes, I knew I wouldn't be able to sleep without touching her, having her writhe underneath me.

"Ethan, can we talk now?" She asked, her voice small. Her eyebrows were furrowed with worry as I dropped my car keys in the bowl and walked toward her.

My eyes shamelessly roved over her tiny body. She was wearing a long t-shirt that ended on her thighs, her face devoid of any makeup and her wavy hair tamed down.

Threading my hand through her hair, I pulled her closer and pressed my lips on her. The kiss was rough as I took her in my arms, savoring her taste. Her breath was minty, and I knew she was preparing to sleep after talking to me. Not anymore.

"Ethan," she gasped when I took her to my room, "we . . . we, *uh*, we need to talk."

I squeezed her ass, growling when I found nothing but tiny underwear. "Shut up, Kiara," I breathed, "Let me fucking kiss you."

I kissed her, licking her lips, biting them until she opened up to me, allowing our tongues to dance with each other. She sighed against the kiss, the soft sounds eliciting from her lips making me go insane while my feet padded toward my room.

It had sliding doors that opened up to the pool in my backyard. The air was cool in the room as our bodies pressed against each other, her nipples hard as pebbles against my shirt. I only leaned away from her to turn on the soft lights near my bed.

"*Ethan.*" Kiara let out a small gasp of pain and pleasure when I yanked her hair back, glared down at her with feral hunger in my eyes.

She took a sharp breath and released a small whimper when I clenched my jaw, wondering about all the filthy things that had been running through my head. I could smell her sweet feminine arousal as she tried to clench her legs for some friction. *Cute.*

Lowering my head, I kissed her ear, biting the earlobe

and pressing the pads of my fingers on her scalp, gently massaging it. Her body shivered in my arms, making me smile. She was always so responsive to my merest touch.

I brushed my lips on her cheek. "You are mine for tonight."

Tracing my other hand underneath her t-shirt, I continued, "No Jake. None of your nightstand. No rough sex, no lovemaking, or any shit." A sweet moan slipped past her lips when I pressed my middle finger directly over her clitoris through her drenched underwear. "Just us, Kiara. Fucking until either of us passes out."

Kiara looked at me as if she was about to orgasm, her knees buckling, but I tugged her hair. "Understood?"

She nodded.

A rough growl emitted from my throat, my teeth scraping on her slender neck, over her beating pulse. "I need words, Kiara." She stayed still, breathing hard as if she was under some kind of spell. "Do you want me to use that tongue somewhere else, *hmm*? Is that what you want?"

I squeezed her ass and landed a harsh spank on her ass, making her jump.

She trembled and clenched her jaw. "Yes, Ethan. I understand. I am yours." Her golden-brown eyes glared at me through her thick lashes when her hand lowered to my pants, cupping my raging hard on. "Only if you're mine for tonight."

I sighed when her palm stroked me through my pants. "It's cute that you think you are in control tonight," I whispered, kissing her lips one more time before I pulled away.

"Strip out of your clothes," I said, unbuttoning the top buttons of my shirt.

Her feeble fingers tugged on the hem of her t-shirt before she pulled it over her head. My eyes devoured the way her soft golden skin glowed, begging me to flog her and to see a red hue on them. I licked my lips, watching the strands of her hair brushing over her perky breasts when she removed her thong. The scent of her feminine arousal hovered in the air.

So fucking sweet.

"Aren't you going to undress?" she asked, her eyes trailing over my clothes.

"Not yet," I said. "I want to play with you first."

She fidgeted and looked so vulnerable, alone, and nervous. Good, I wanted her to feel vulnerable so I could break that tension when I fucked her. With my finger, I traced the spine of her back, loving the way she trembled, her body reacting to my small touches.

"Close your eyes," I whispered, standing behind her and gathering her hair over her shoulder. When I was sure she was keeping her eyes closed, I wrapped black silk around them, tying it securely. The way her breathing had increased, I knew it was affecting her more than she let on.

Good, I wanted to test her limits.

Opening the chest of drawers from the corner of my room, I pulled out a coil of rope and sharp scissors to cut it in half. Making sure her wrists were pressed against each other, I took the rope in my hand and slowly passed it around her hands, binding them together.

Kiara tensed. *"Ethan."*

"You can use your safe words." Tugging on the rope, I looked at her and asked, "Too tight?"

She tried pulling her hands free and shook her head. Kiara looked stunning with her eyes blindfolded and wrists bound, completely trusting me with her body. But not her mind. We would get there soon enough. There was so much I wanted to try with her that I knew tonight would fall short.

She desperately tried to feel or hear what was happening around her. Her body squirmed with anticipation and lust. She bit her lip and her slender neck bobbed as she swallowed nervously. I enjoyed seeing her like that, restrained and not knowing what to do, under my control.

Her flushed body was begging me to touch her, devour her and fuck her. But not *yet*.

I trailed the flogger over her tanned legs, letting her feel the tips of leather brush against her soft golden skin while her breathing grew erratic. It was black leather and medium in size, not too large or small for her. The end of the tassels would bring her both pain and pleasure. I saw her tongue flick out to wet her lips when I trailed the flogger over her inner thigh, working my way up and stopping abruptly. I started all over again from the other leg. I bit back a smirk when she sighed in disappointment, teasing her again.

Her body trembled when I let the tips of the leather trail over her arms, a soft sigh releasing from her lips. Kiara was enjoying the slight brushes of the flogger. I struck the flogger on her inner thigh without a warning as her back arched, and a soft groan left her lips. There was a pink hue pelt where I had struck, and I did it again but on the inside of her other thigh. I made sure it was a light smack just to get her body to release more endorphins and nothing more.

I repeated the smacks and strikes on her legs and arms, sometimes on her stomach, her body arching a bit every time as she bit her lip.

"Raise your hands," I ordered. Her bound wrists lifting and making her tits arch.

With a flick of the wrist, I gave a swift and sharp smack to her left breast with the flogger, and she moaned with the mixture of pain and pleasure. Red hue bloomed on her breasts, her back arching again as I repeated my actions on her other breast.

"*Oh, Ethan,*" she whimpered.

"Take a deep breath, Bella."

She did and exhaled sharply as the tips of the flogger

struck on her erogenous zones. We were in a rhythm. I struck, and she converted the pain to pleasure. Soon, her body relaxed and wanted more. I watched in awe as she let out a long moan. Her breasts were a soft hue of pink, heaving up and down as her sex glistened with more arousal. Even her round ass had red prints of the flogger on it.

"Stop wriggling," I said, flogging her on her heated sex.

Kiara heaved a sharp breath. *"Please . . ."* she breathed, struggling with her binds and standing still, "I am so close."

I flogged her again on her aching pussy. "You are not going to come until I tell you to."

I wasn't done, even though I could see her legs shaking when she bit back a moan. Sweat sheeted her taut, golden skin as I continued flogging her with little smacks, just teasing her as she held back her orgasm for me. When a small sob escaped her lips, I stopped, panting hard and watching her body quiver. Red hues flushed her golden skin.

Dropping the flogger, I gently lowered her arms and massaged the skin to get the blood flowing. I kissed the slope of her neck, her breathing coming back to normal.

"You okay?"

She nodded, looking away from me, and I knew she was not okay. She was just flogged by me, and the endorphins and other hormones were confusing her mind.

I laid her down on the bed. She hissed when her burning ass met the cold sheets. "I want to see you," she muttered, her voice breathy when I made sure she was comfortable.

"Not now," I replied and kissed her temple, tucking her hair behind her ears, "Stay here."

When she heard the door open, she asked, "Where are you going, Ethan?"

"I will be right back, Bella. Lay down on the bed and get some rest, you'll need it for the rest of the night," I said and walked to the kitchen with a bulge in my pants.

I took a cold bottle of water, and in the room, I watched her naked, flush body squirm on my bedsheets. Her thighs rubbing each other for friction made me let out a small groan. She stopped as soon as she heard me and looked away, biting her lip.

Fucking vixen.

"You dirty fucking girl," I growled, yanking her legs away, seeing how soaked she was, "You are so fucking wet." I lapped my fingers in her slick juices as she raised her hips for more. I pulled away, giving a harsh spank to her pussy.

"*Ah!*" She cried out, trying to close her thighs.

I held them as I wrapped the rope around her ankles and tied them to each leg of the bed. She moaned and squirmed, trying to move her legs. I tied Kiara spread eagle on my bed, her eyes blindfolded and her silky dark hair sprawled across the pillows. Her lips were red like rose petals with a slight pink hue of blush on her cheeks and her slender neck. I trailed my eyes toward her perky breasts, the pair of dusky nipples poking the air with each heavy breath she took. Her stomach was taut and flat as her breathing grew heavier.

"Use your safe words when you need them," I reminded her and took her bound wrists to bind them to the headboard. "I don't want to hear you whining, or I will use a ball gag."

"Ethan, please, no," she said, shaking her head, her silky hair fanning out on my pillows.

She looked vulnerable and had willingly submitted herself to me. Knowing that I would cherish and worship this woman made me jizz in my pants like a high schooler. I shook my head. I couldn't believe how much she affected me, even if she was doing nothing.

I kissed her soft lips, my hands wandering to her pebbled nipples. The sweet moans from her lips made blood rush to my nether region as I fondled and kneaded her breasts. I slowly caressed her soft mound before roughly groping it in a possessive hold. Instead of shying away from my roughness, she arched her back, all but thrusting herself into my hand. Kissing the nipple and twirling my tongue around the soft areola, I took her other nipple between my fingers and pinched harder until her moan turned into a hiss of pain. Kiara gasped, jutting her chest to me as I blew air on the red nub.

I repeated my actions on the twin until they were hard, slicing the air and red. I straddled her lithe body and moved my hands over her restrained arms, kneading the sore muscles when small breathy gasps escaped her lips. I wanted to try clamps on her tonight, but she was already riding on her subspace and I didn't want to push her too far. I couldn't believe how much my commands affected her. I always knew Kiara was submissive in bed and loved to be cherished and cared for.

Cupping her cheek, I asked, "Do you want some water?"

She cleared her throat and nodded. "Yes, thank you."

After taking a sip from the water bottle, I held the back of her neck and pressed my lips to hers. She parted her lips for me and arched up when the water slid down her lips. She smiled up at me, my heart thudding loudly at the sight of her smile, her dimple poking her cheek. When I repeated it again, I heard her hands rattle with the bonds, wanting to touch me.

I pulled away to see her lick her lips. Some water had slid down her jaw, creating a small trail on her slender neck. Pressing kisses down her jaw, I licked it away, her soft mewls arousing me and making all the blood in my body run south.

Caressing her breasts, I asked, "Do you want more water?"

She shook her head, biting her lip from smiling as I kneaded, massaged, and warmed her skin. I couldn't stop touching her. Her breathing grew erratic when I sweetly massaged her burning ass, her stomach, thighs, wherever I had flogged her. Her body relaxed, and she gave in to my touch. She was mesmerizing. I loved the curve of her body, the shape of her. I never wanted to stop touching her.

If only.

I wanted to lick away the red hues of the flogger on her thighs when I noticed the small sniffle. I stiffened and watched tears slide down her covered eyes as she turned her head, trying to hide away. I kissed her then, wiping away her tears and slanting my face so I could press my lips against hers. I caressed her hair, holding her cheek and deepening the kiss.

"Do you want to go further, Kiara?" I asked, brushing my thumb on her cheekbone, "You are already going down into your subspace, and I don't want to take advantage of that."

"Please don't stop," she whispered, her voice husky with the tears. "Why do I feel like crying?"

I kissed her once more and wiped away her tears. "Because none of your partners took care of you before fulfilling their needs. I love touching you, Kiara. You are breathtaking, tied up, and soaking wet for me. I wish I could never stop touching you."

A low growl emitted from me when I ravished her soft golden skin with my hands, squeezing, fondling and spanking her. My mouth kissing, biting, and licking the scorching skin. She writhed beneath me, tugging at her bonds and moaning my name when I licked the valley between her breasts.

A surprised moan escaped her lips when I lowered myself and tapped her dripping pussy. Smirking, I squeezed and kissed her inner thigh, her body shaking with need.

"Ethan . . . please, I want you!"

My hands slid down between her legs, so close to her aching sex. "I want you too, Bella. Have patience."

She nodded. I admired her courage for taking the scene so far and moved my face closer to her dripping core. Her breathing was labored when she felt my breath fan over her dripping pussy. My tongue licked her slicked lips, flicking her swollen nub as I tasted the sweet yet tangy nectar between her thighs.

"Fucking delicious," I grunted and held her thighs. I kissed and teased her lips, making her body writhe in pleasure when I let my tongue wander inside her, moaning at the taste.

"Oh, Ethan," Kiara moaned. Her entire body was quivering with pleasure, her cheeks flushed, breasts red, stomach taut and her legs shaking vigorously.

"Don't come, Kiara. You are not allowed to until I say so," I growled in a low voice and smacked her wet sex before plunging two fingers in her clenching pussy, moving them in and out. Her hips arched, wanting and craving more.

Leaning down, I licked her clit, sucking the tight nub in my mouth and giving it tiny flicks in different patterns. My fingers fucked her clenching sex and before I knew it, she had exploded in my hands with her intoxicating musky scent surrounding me. I let her ride out of her aftershocks, a whimper leaving her lips when I pulled out my fingers.

"You didn't ask for my permission, Kiara," I said, sucking her juices clean from my fingers. My cock pressed against the zip of my pants, begging to get free.

She breathed, "I couldn't hold it, Ethan."

"Which color are you right now?" I asked, getting a tiny vibrator from my nightstand, knowing well that she could handle it.

"White," she muttered sulkily, trying to close her legs.

"Good, how many times have you climaxed in a row?"

Kiara took a sharp breath, "Three."

I smirked and removed the blindfold from her eyes, letting her eyes adjust as she blinked up at me. She flushed under my gaze and saw the vibe in my hand, her amber eyes widening.

I turned it on and placed the tip on her nipple, her gasp of pleasure higher than the sound of vibrations. "You are going to come for me five times in a row, Kiara. That's your punishment."

She shook her head, "Ethan, no, I . . . I am sensitive—*oh!*"

She broke into a groan when I placed the vibe on her clitoris, her body convulsing, "Ethan! Please, I am going to come."

I pressed it harder, sucking on her nipple and watching her gaping, flushed face as she came, her bound body rocking on the bed. I pulled the vibe away to spank her pussy, "Count. You don't want to repeat the orgasm, do you?"

She whimpered as I placed the vibrator once again on her swollen clitoris, "T-two."

"Good girl. Three more to go before I fuck you."

Her eyes widened and before she could reply, a loud moan tore out of her throat, and I had to place my hand on her stomach as she orgasmed again. I was in awe at her body as she rode through her multiple orgasms. She looked stunning, her skin glistening with a thin sheen of sweat, her face and neck flushed.

"*Three,*" she finally heaved out, her eyes wide when I continued circling the small vibe around her red clit with increased vibrations. She thrashed on my bed, tugging hard at the bonds.

"You will bruise your skin if you keep tugging, Bella," I scolded her, inserting my middle finger inside her spasming pussy, loving the way her tight walls clenched it.

I knew that she was experiencing both pain and pleasure

as her body rocked through her fifth orgasm, her tiny body heaving with breath and limp in my bed. She let out a sigh of relief when I stopped the vibe to put it aside and let her have a slight break. She watched me with her heavy-lidded eyes when I unbuttoned my shirt and removed my pants with boxers.

I chuckled at the small whimper she made staring at my throbbing cock, "You can handle it, Bella."

She nodded, "I know, but I am scared to walk tomorrow."

My eyes darkened. I crawled above her naked body and teasingly brushed my length on her soaking sex. "I can't wait to see you in school tomorrow. Walking and teaching with a sore pussy. Feeling the spanking on your ass every time you sit and drenching your thong every time you remember this night."

Her lips parted while listening to me, and a part of me wished that I could make her long for me as I longed for her. Clenching my jaw, I turned her around, not wanting to let her see the raw emotions baring my face. I lifted her ass up, making her fall on her knees.

"Ethan," she looked over her shoulder, "Please, *no*, I want to see you."

I held the back of her neck, planting her face on the pillow, not wanting her to see me fall apart. "No," I said. "Not today."

Kiara whimpered, clenching her hands in fists above her head as I rubbed my raging, bulbous head over her slicked slit. Squeezing her ass, I gave her a harsh spank, watching her tremble beneath me.

"Ethan," she whispered in a hoarse voice that made me leak a bit of pre-cum. *Ah, shit.*

My hand held her throat, giving a slight pressure on her pulse. She relaxed after a while, trusting me with the air she was breathing. I hated that she could trust me with her body but not with her heart. Loosening my grip on her neck, I slammed inside her, relishing the way her velvety walls enveloped me, clenching me. Kiara gave a small hiss of pain at the sudden intrusion, my hand lowering down to rub her clit.

I slowly pulled out before giving a hard thrust, her body rocking further in the bed. I groaned at the pressure of her walls. I loved going raw with her, the way she gripped, afraid of letting me go, turned me into a caveman.

"Please, Ethan," she whispered, "I am so close."

"Hold it, Kiara," I warned, spanking her ass once again.

I wrapped her hair around my wrist and pulled her head back, her breasts touching the sheets. In a way, I was punishing her. I didn't want her to see me. She only wanted a baby out of this, and that is the only thing she would get.

"*Ah*," she cried out when I fucked her.

I leaned down to kiss her shoulder, licking the spine of her back and growled, "You love this, don't you? Feeling my cock slide inside you, fucking you hard."

She groaned but didn't reply. Letting go of her engorged clit, I held and squeezed her ass as I rocked inside her, yanking at her hair as perspiration coated our bodies. I could tell she was close when her body started shivering with the oncoming climax.

I let go of her hair, holding her hips and groaning at the sight of my cock fucking her, covered in her arousal. "Don't come yet, Kiara. Hold it back for me."

She squeezed her eyes shut, her hair covering her face. I leaned down, our bodies touching each other while I rolled my hips and angled myself to press against her g-spot with each thrust. I loved hearing her low groans when I pinched her nipple, her walls clamping around me as we both came closer and closer to our orgasms.

I kissed the corner of her neck, supporting myself with

my arms. Kiara whimpered when I started taking slow, deep thrusts, going deeper and harder with each slam.

"Come on, Bella, come for me," I said in a low, smoky voice, her body relaxing as she let go of herself. I groaned when she came, hiding her face in the pillow and milking and clenching me in a vice grip.

I grunted, jerking inside her and orgasmed, spurting my warm sperm inside her. I gave a breathy chuckle when she held me close, soft moans reaching my ear as her body writhed in pleasure, our bodies sleek with sweat and arousal. My arm was tightly wrapped around her waist, and I let go of her, gently laying her down on the bed as I slowly pulled out.

Swallowing the lump in my throat, I wiped the sweat on my forehead with my forearm and went to the washroom to clean myself up. After taking a cloth dipped in lukewarm water, I gently cleaned her up, caressing her back. I cut the rope and untied her bound wrists and ankles, rubbing the red marks of twisted rope that had dug into her skin. I would need to apply lotion to them and her breasts, thighs, and ass.

But before I could, she turned away from me, covering herself with the blanket.

"Bella," I said, hating the way she was hiding from me. "What happened?"

She shook her head, but I had already tugged on the blanket covering her face. Tears were glistening in her amber eyes and the tips of her ears had turned into a light shade of pink. As this was her first real scene, I knew how conflicted and confused she might be.

I settled Kiara on my lap, her arms tightening around my torso as she hid her face on my chest. I let her be, running my hands through her hair and back, waiting for her to cry it all out.

"What happened, Bella?"

"I don't know."

I pulled back, gazing at her. "Okay, can I bathe you?"

Her cheeks flushed when I wiped away her tears, "Why?"

"Because I want to take care of you and you can tell me how you really feel."

She smiled, her dimple poking her cheek, "Okay, I'd like that."

15. LET ME CELEBRATE

KIARA

I leaned my back on his warm chest after he rinsed the shampoo from my hair. His firm hands massaged the sore spots on my body, asking me if it hurt me anywhere else. I couldn't believe that half an hour ago he was dominating me, wielding my body to his commands.

"What are you thinking?" His warm breath brushed my ear.

"How gentle you are being right now despite what we did moments ago."

Ethan stood up from the bathtub, rivulets of water droplets coating his muscular body as he helped me up. While patting my body dry with a towel, he explained, "I can be gentle and rough depending on the scene, Kiara. I know you wanted to look at me during sex, but it is a dominant's duty to give what the submissive needs, not necessarily what she wants."

"I don't understand."

A mischievous glint formed in his eyes and I let out a gasp when he pushed my back on the cold wall, his one hand wrapping around my throat and other lowering to my heated sex. I held his arms when his fingers teased my nether lips which were wet with my arousal.

"You want me to take you here, don't you?" He whispered, his fingers teasing and playing with my swollen clitoris.

"Yes, Ethan, please," I moaned, my legs trembling.

But he pulled away, a small smile curling on his lips. "But I won't because you are sore and tired, still conflicted about how you feel. Okay?"

I understood what he meant. I needed to talk to him as well.

"Okay, Big Daddy." I pressed my lips against his and felt him smiling against my own as we made our way back to his room.

"Ethan?" I said when he finished drying my hair. He had applied chamomile lotion on my ass and my body where he had flogged me. After making sure, I wasn't hurt anywhere else despite me telling him, he tugged one of his t-shirts over me as it was more comfortable. "I wanted to apologize for what I said last night."

He peered down at me, "Regarding what?"

I made him sit on the edge of the bed and gently patted down his wet hair with a dry towel. "I know I hurt you when I said that all I wanted is a baby."

"Kiara, you don't have to—"

"No, I have to apologize, Ethan. That was mean and a terrible thing to say." I took a sharp breath, "Especially if it was a lie."

His hands wrapped around mine when I glanced at his face, his sharp features prominent. "What do you mean by lie, Kiara?"

I focused on the way his thumb brushed on my wrist, soothing me. "I want the baby but not at the cost of losing whatever we have between us. I like you, Ethan. But I am afraid too."

"Look at me," his warm hand cupped my cheek, his blue-green eyes softening. "Now tell me, what are you afraid of?"

"Of what would happen afterward. I know I sound crazy right now, but I am scared to know what would happen—I mean, if we have a baby then what?" My mind was whirring with thoughts, and I knew my therapist would say I am interpreting, and I should rather focus on facts, but I couldn't.

Ethan smiled at me, pulling me closer, "Then we will take it one step at a time, okay? And if you are scared or have any doubts, come to me and we will talk about it. How does that sound, Bella?"

I frowned at him, "You are serious?"

He nodded, his lips pressing against my forehead. "I am one hundred percent serious. I talked to your therapist if that's okay."

"You what?" I pulled back, looking at his sheepish face, "But why?"

He took a deep breath. "I wanted to know how you were doing and how could I help you if you needed someone." My heartbeat increased and warm tingles erupted in my belly at the thoughtfulness of the man in front of me. He continued, "She also told me about facts and interpretation."

She must have. It was one of the things that differentiated from a normal human brain to the mental health of someone suffering from depression or anxiety. Like me. Because of her, I had taught myself to listen to what my brain was saying and decided if they were facts or interpretations. If someone told me they liked me, it was a fact I could believe, but often-times when I assumed that someone liked or hated me was an interpretation. Dr. Sabrina had advised me to ask for the facts rather than interpreting.

I bit my lip, "So you know I was interpreting?"

Ethan nodded, "I know I don't fully understand what

you're going through mentally, but I want you to know that I am not leaving. If you are scared, come to me. We will take it one step at a time, okay Bella?"

I hugged him, hiding my face on the crook of his neck as his powerful arms wrapped around me, cocooning me in his warm embrace. "Thank you, Ethan," I said, my voice muffled. I felt like I was eighteen again, feeling everything and nothing. But this time, Ethan was supporting me by my side.

We cuddled on the bed as I listened to his velvety voice talking about how Volt, Rio and Liam were doing. How some of them secretly shipped us. I told him about my day and how guilty I felt for telling him I was using him just for a baby. We kissed and made up until he asked me about the tears that had appeared after we had sex tonight.

"I don't know, I feel bad," I whispered, watching his fingers trail on my bare stomach.

"Why do you feel bad?"

"Am I a freak to like all of that? I don't know what to feel about it, Ethan. All of that felt like a hazy dream and I don't even know what happened to me."

He listened to me and asked, "Did it feel like you were drunk?"

My eyes widened, "A little. But I wasn't drunk."

Ethan chuckled, "No, Bella, you were not drunk."

"Then why do I feel like it was a dream?"

"That's because you were in a subspace, Kiara," he explained with a proud smile. "I wasn't sure if you would go to subspace in the first scene, but you did. Your body and mind were very responsive."

I blinked at him, "I don't understand."

"When you experience pain and pleasure together your body can get all kinds of crossed-wires in the brain, dump a bunch of happy chemicals into your brain like endorphins and enkephalins. All those hormones produce a sort of trance-like state and you and your brain converted all the pain to those hormones, and you felt like you were drunk or as if you were high," he calmly explained.

"I stopped flogging you as you were in subspace and you could have never used your safe words because you were off to la-la-land. And as soon as it was over, you were exhausted."

I nodded, blushing. "I still am."

Ethan smirked. "But I needed to make sure you were alright, so I had to bathe you and take care of you."

I squeezed his hand and snuggled up beside him when I asked, "Then why did I feel like crying for no reason?"

He ran a hand through my hair as I sighed in relief, relishing in the feeling, "Because you got off that high from subspace. It's called a drop and I have to make sure you were okay, Bella."

"I am more than okay, E."

"I don't want to make you cry," Ethan paused, and I held my breath, "I hate seeing you cry. Especially if I am the reason you're crying."

My hand lingered on his heartbeat as his muscles tensed. I whispered, "You didn't make me cry, Ethan. You said it yourself. It was the hormones over-working in my brain."

With my cheek pressed against his chest and his hand running through my hair, I couldn't stop that nagging question which has been echoing in my mind for so long. So, I had to ask him.

Gulping nervously, I lifted on my elbow. "Why don't you hate me?" I asked, my voice a small whisper.

He clenched his jaw, his eyes dancing over my face when he replied truthfully. "I did, Kiara. For so long, that every time I heard your name, I felt like punching a wall." I pursed my lips when he added with a small smile lingering on his lips, his hand cupping my cheek, "But after a while, I was fine with you leaving me because I wouldn't be here if you had left me. I would still look for you to validate and support my every decision, and I would never learn to be on my own. Yes, I missed you very much, but as I had said before, I can go through that all over again if it means having . . . *this*. Being with you and holding you in my arms."

Ethan wiped the small tear that left my right eye. I chuckled and leaned closer, I kissed him to let him know that I missed him for all these years as much as he had. "God, you make me horny when you go all cheesy and corny on me," I whispered, removing the blanket from our bodies and straddling him. Holding the hem of his t-shirt I was wearing, I removed it, baring myself in front of him.

His eyes lit up as he gazed at my naked body still basking in post-coital glow with small marks imprinted on them. "Are you sure you're ready for this? Aren't you sore?" he asked teasingly, his hands caressing the skin on my waist when I moved my hair over my shoulder.

Biting my lower lip, I shook my head as I slowly humped him, waking him up and giggled when I felt him poke my ass. Ethan narrowed his eyes at me. I gasped when he rolled us over, his warm muscular body hovering above mine. I loved how big and strong he was compared to me and still cared for me as if I was a fragile doll. I cupped his face, kissing him on the lips and spread my legs.

"Make love to me, Ethan," I whispered in his ear when his hands rested beside my head.

His lips brushed against my ear. I admired his handsome, rugged face when he whispered, "I will make love to you all night, Bella. Every fucking day of my life."

A long moan escaped my parted lips when Ethan slowly slid inside me, his eyes never leaving my face as we made love, holding onto each other's bodies and groaning each other's name until we forgot our own.

I was sure Ethan Kane was ruining me for good the next morning.

As I was getting ready for the school, I had to stop myself from wincing at the sweet soreness from between my legs and the light pink hue on my ass. My cheeks were as red as tomatoes as I applied the lotion he had used last night to help with the healing. *I will remember him every time I sit or move today.*

Blood rushed to my cheeks as I took my handbag to the living room, making sure I had all my notes, books, and my laptop with me. When I turned to the kitchen to make break-fast, I noticed a big parcel wrapped in a red ribbon with a note,

I know you always wanted this edition. I hope you like it.
P.S. Breakfast is on the pan.
E

A smile lit up my face as I tugged off the red ribbon and opened the gift paper to reveal a beautiful hardcover of one of my favorite authors, Jane Austen. It was *The Complete Novels of Jane Austen* in lilac purple leather-bound hardcover. The book was heavy, but I was in utter awe at its beauty and the intricate design on the front cover. I loved it. I adored it, and I knew if I could, I would keep this edition on a pedestal.

Ethan had gifted me with this beauty. My heart melted, and I re-read his note once again, his handwriting sloped and perfectly aligned. His penmanship had always been beautiful, and I was always jealous because my handwriting changed on every page. I bit my lip when I read the last line again. Had he made breakfast for me?

I opened the lid of the pan to see fried eggs in a heart shape. I chuckled at the eggs and served them on a plate he had already readied for me with the buttered toast and avocado.

Did he make all this? How did he have the time to wake up before me, get the book, and make breakfast?

I shook my head at the breakfast and the book.

Somehow, I knew today was going to be a long day.

I WAS RIGHT.

My eyes widened when I saw a lunchbox on my desk in the classroom. The students giggled when I hurriedly kept the lunchbox in my drawer and pretended as if Ethan hadn't kept it. How did he know I wouldn't bring lunch today?

Ignoring the urge to open it, I focused on today's class, giving them a stern look when they groaned at today's assignment. I helped them when they solved it, raising questions so they could solve it on their own. I was proud of every student in my class and adored everyone. They always worked hard on their tests and never stopped asking for questions.

I had a break after two lectures, so I worked in my office and wrote. I still hadn't opened the lunchbox to read another note or even see what he had cooked for me. I needed to focus on my writing.

Someone knocked on the door. I smiled, lifting my eyes from my laptop screen to—

"Ethan, what are you doing here?" I asked, my voice a bit squeaky because I didn't think he would be in school today.

Not to mention, he looked extremely edible in a charcoal suit and a crisp grey shirt underneath it. The first two buttons were undone, and my mouth ran dry when I noticed the hint of his tan chest. *Fuck, I have it bad for him.* He smiled at me, closing and locking the door behind him. I swallowed the gulp as he loomed in front of my desk, his tall height making the office look cramped.

Walking over to my side, he leaned down, his sharp musky male scent wafting in my nose. I took a greedy inhale of his delicious cologne when he kissed my cheek and purred in my ear, "Hello, Kiara."

I crossed my legs, clenching my sex, and managed to say, "Hi!"

Yes, I definitely had it bad. And he knew that too.

Ethan smiled down at me, turning my chair toward him, making me face him. "How are you feeling now?" he asked, his voice less mischievous than before.

I lifted my eyes from his crotch to his face and leaned back on my chair, as far as I could lean back. "I am feeling good, actually."

He hummed, his intense eyes gazing at me, my underwear flooding with arousal as I clenched my fingers on the hem of my skirt. His blue-green eyes flickered to them, and a small smirk tugged at the corner of his lips.

He knew.

"Are you mad at me?" he asked, his voice deep and smoky, rumbling a sexual urge deep inside me.

I shook my head, my mouth going dry when he kneeled in front of me in his expensive suit.

He looked so beautiful and handsome, it made me want to weep. It should be illegal to look that good. Especially walking out in the open wearing that suit.

What the hell, Kiara? I am spouting rubbish in my brain now.

"Why are you here?" I asked, my voice higher than usual.

He let out a small chuckle before pulling me closer by dragging my chair toward him. I took a sharp breath when he spread my knees, settling his hands on my waist. With glittering eyes, he said, "Emma, the model who was harassed by Richard Jane, pressed charges against him and his cameraman. She told the truth that I punched him for pushing her down."

I cupped his cheeks, my grin wide, "That's wonderful news, Ethan! I am glad you won't be portrayed as the bad guy anymore. I am happy that she told what truly happened."

He smiled at me, his eyes bright with green and blue colors dancing in them. They were mesmerizing, and I could never stop staring at them.

"So am I."

"I am here to celebrate with you," he said, which sounded more like an order than a plea.

"How are you going to celebrate?"

His eyes clouded with lust when he lifted up my skirt, "With my tongue inside your pussy."

My eyes were wide watching his fingers pushing up my black skirt, his skin warm against mine. I bit my lip, holding the hem, and squirmed when his dark eyes pinned on the wet spot of my underwear. I tried closing my legs, but his hold was strong as his eyes raised up to meet my face.

"Ethan, what if someone comes in? We are at school," I said weakly.

"Kiara, we fucked in a school bathroom stall. I need to taste you. Let me."

My face turned red remembering young Ethan taking me from behind in a stall, thrusting inside me so hard that the door rattled. A gasp left my lips when his finger pressed over my tight nub, slowly rubbing it through the lace. I breathed loudly when he pulled away to remove my underwear, sliding it down my legs and tucking it in his pocket.

"You are insatiable," I whispered when he threw my legs over his broad shoulders.

Ethan smirked, his face close to my bare sex. "You love it, Bella," he said, pressing soft kisses on my thighs.

I watched him, his silky onyx hair gripped tightly

between my fingers when his warm breath fanned over my hip bones, his mouth closer to where I wanted him the most.

I would always remember this celebration.

"Always soaking wet for me," he said, his finger sliding over my slicked lips. He pushed it inside me, a soft moan leaving my lips.

"Tell me, Kiara, do you want my tongue in your cunt?" he asked, his voice a silky whisper.

I shivered at his tone and his words, which pulled at something darker within me.

My legs parted of their own accord and I stared at him with my half-lidded eyes, "Yes, Ethan."

Two of his fingers pressed inside me, his digits fucking me slowly when a lazy smile crossed his lips.

Oh no.

"Oh, *yes*," he purred, kissing my clitoris. "Hello, mate. It's been long, eh?"

I tugged at his hair, "Ethan, no, you said you were going to celebrate—*ah!* Fuck, that feels so good."

His thumb rubbed my nub when he leaned back to grin at me. "I am. Say what you want, and I will give it to you, Bella."

I muttered quickly, but he didn't hear me.

"Louder, Kiara."

"I . . . I want your tongue in my pussy."

I couldn't meet his gaze when I was so flustered. I can't believe I just said that.

"Good girl."

His fingers pulled out of me and were replaced by a pair of lips. The tantalizing electric sensation of his lips, tongue, and teeth on my sensitive nub shot a bolt throughout my body. My back arched from the chair, but Ethan held me, his tongue lapping over my soaking lips as if he was licking his favorite candy.

"So fucking sweet," he growled between his kisses, and I had to stifle my loud moan when his tongue fucked me.

My body trembled beneath him, my abdomen clenched with the anticipation, and my legs trembling as he increased his pace. I jumped when his palms held my ass, holding it lightly and lifting me up so he could get the right angle.

"Oh, fuck," I panted, my eyes squeezed shut while I tugged at his hair, "Ethan, I am going to come!"

"Let it go, Bella, cum on my mouth."

Ethan sucked my pleasure nub, flicking it with his tongue as my body exploded with an orgasm, white-hot lust blinding my eyes. I tugged at his hair and groaned loudly when my body trembled, aching in sweet, pleasurable bliss. Thankfully, Ethan had muffled my groans by cupping my mouth and now he was licking me up. I let go of his hair and wiped the tears that had escaped my eyes.

I could never forget the sight of him between my legs.

When he pulled away, satisfied, he had a Cheshire grin on his face. Cat got his cream, perhaps.

"I am not satisfied with this celebration, should I continue?" he asked, his fingers already dancing at my entrance.

I shook my head and tugged down my skirt before his fingers could seduce me again. "No . . . no more," I said breathily, knowing there was no end to his 'celebration.'

Ethan gave me a small pout and he looked so ridiculously funny that I laughed at him. His hair was all over the place, tousled, with his suit ruffled. He smiled at me and tugged my skirt back to its place, running his hand through my hair and patting it down.

Then he kissed me, grinning between our kisses as I tasted myself on him. I shuddered when he licked my ear, "I am keeping your thong. I want you to remember who tongue fucked you when you are teaching," he pulled away, smiling at my dazed expression, and kissed me once more. "And when you come back home, I will take the entire night and morning celebrating with you."

"Are we still talking about celebrating?" I asked, straightening his suit and fixing the collar of his shirt.

"Yes, we are," he pecked my forehead. "Be home soon, Bella. I will be waiting for you."

Ethan stood up to his full height, and I blushed like a teen when he winked at me before leaving through the door.

That man was going to be the death of me.

16. I AM SORRY

KIARA

I groaned, covered my face, and squeezed my eyes shut. Was it possible to have cramps when you get pregnant? *Or am I getting my period?*

I didn't know.

Another small moan of pain escaped my lips when the insides of my abdomen churned. This doesn't feel good at all. Thankfully, I was alone in my teachers' office so no one could see me like this. I decided not to take any painkillers and focus on working and arranging the worksheets for my next class.

I frowned, looking at my stomach. Why wasn't I getting pregnant? Ethan and I had been having sex like rabbits since he teased me and *celebrated* with me with his tongue while I was sitting in that same chair. He had been gentle but rough when I begged him to. The sex was definitely amazing, and neither of us wanted to part ways in our post-coital bliss so we would wake up next to each other almost every day.

Then why am I having such bad cramps?

I checked the calendar on my laptop and realized I was two days late for my period. I bit my lip and noticed that I had to visit Sabrina Young, my therapist, for a session. I had contacted her this week and had a virtual session, but I knew I needed to go see her in person and talk to her. She was my father's friend and one of the best in her field.

My attention diverted to my phone when someone sent me a message. I unlocked the screen and read it.

Ethan: Something special is baking for you.

My eyes widened at his words, and I looked down at my stomach. *Did he know? No, of course not. He must have meant something else.*

Me: I wonder what that is . . .

Ethan: Come home early to find out. I will be waiting, Bella.

Despite the mild cramps, I was smiling when I went to my next class.

WHEN I ENTERED THE HOUSE, the first thing I noticed was the delicious smell of something baking in the oven. It smelt like a bakery.

"How was your day?" Ethan asked from the couch he was sitting on, his laptop perched on his lap. He removed his eyeglasses and smiled at me as I gingerly walked toward him.

"It was okay," I muttered and peered in the kitchen to see what he had baked.

I took a sharp breath when he stood behind me, his hands wrapping around my waist and making me face him. His eyes were bright and clear, his shirt clean with his washed pair of denim.

"Do you want to talk about it?" he asked, nuzzling his face and pressing a small kiss on the pulse of my neck.

Taking a shaky breath, I pulled away from him. "Not really. I will go get changed."

Ignoring his frown, I rushed inside my room and taking

my pajamas, I locked myself in the washroom. I gripped the edge of the sink when I felt another burst of cramps in my lower stomach. How could I ever face him again? After knowing the truth, he would hate me. Forever.

But I knew I had to tell him. It was eating me alive.

I took a quick warm shower, and I wasn't surprised when I saw Ethan sitting on the edge of the bed, waiting for me.

"What happened at school, Kiara?" he asked in his deep, husky voice. It wasn't a command, but he wasn't going to leave without hearing my answer either.

I sat beside him. "I got my period," I mumbled, looking down at my hands.

For a while, he didn't say anything and then enveloped my hand in his big ones. I sighed, feeling the soft pressure of his lips on my forehead.

"I am sorry, Bella. We can try again."

"Don't apologize, E."

I squeezed his hand and took a deep breath before facing him. "I need to tell you about something else."

He nodded, waiting patiently for me.

"Promise me you will think it through."

Ethan lifted my hands and kissed my knuckles, "I promise, Bella. Now, tell me what's bothering you?"

I thought back to that day in London and tears welled in my eyes. "When I was in London, I was driving with my roommate at the time, Lea. I stopped at the red light, and we were talking about her crush when—"

A teary sob escaped my throat, and he squeezed my hand, "Tell me, Bella."

"I am so sorry, Ethan," I sniffled. "We got into an accident. The driver of the other car was drunk. I had moved in time to cover Lea, but . . ."

"Take a deep breath," he ordered and left my hands to stand up, "One more, Bella. Here, drink some water."

When my breathing came back to normal, I remembered the harsh impact of the other car, the scream of Lea, and the sticky blood coating my fingers. The heaviness of my body when someone dragged me out of the car and how the last thing I had seen before losing consciousness was a shard of glass in my abdomen.

Swallowing the lump in my throat, I tried my best to gather myself. I had to tell him. I looked at Ethan's worried face and said, "I saved Lea, but unfortunately my head had taken a blow. I was concussed and a shard of glass had pierced my abdomen."

He took a sharp intake of breath, and his eyes went to my waist. "It's better now. I woke up the next day, and the injury healed within a few days. But that's not important." My bottom lip trembled when I continued, "When I woke up, the first thing the doctor said to me was that he was sorry for my loss."

Ethan shook his head, "I don't understand."

"I was pregnant, Ethan."

As soon as I voiced out those words, silence settled in the room. Ethan stared at me, his body frozen. He blinked and shook his head.

"*What?*" he asked, his voice a mere whisper.

"Yes, he said I was eight weeks in and the fetus had died on impact as . . . as a shard of glass was impaled in my lower abdomen," my voice broke and warm tears slid down my face.

"You were pregnant," he whispered, staring between me and my stomach.

"We didn't use a condom that night, Ethan. I was still on birth control pills, but I—" A sob broke out of my throat as I said, "I am so sorry, Ethan."

"You mean to say . . . that we made a baby while we made love to each other?" Ethan said more to himself.

"I am sorry I hid this from you. I wanted to tell you, but I didn't have the courage."

"Until now," Ethan said sharply, his eyes blazing with anger. "Until *today*."

I tried to hold his hands, but he shook his head. Ethan stood up and paced the room, running his hands through his hair. "I need some time, Kiara. I am going out."

"Ethan, please don't."

He slammed the door shut behind him as I slumped on the bed, hiding my tear-stricken face in my hands. I covered my stomach with another hand as I cried for our unborn child like I had on that day and the reality that I couldn't save him . . . *or her*.

We had made love the night of the prom and I had left the next morning, but a part of Ethan had stayed with me, and I didn't realize that the signs were all there. I had puked and my breasts were hurting and blamed the signs on jet lag or sudden weather change. That accident still shook me to my core. Even though I had saved Lea, I had let my baby die.

No, I had let our child die. I was the one responsible for it.

17. I AM HERE, BELLA

ETHAN

My heart felt heavy with lead as I drove around aimlessly. Kiara was pregnant with my child. *Our baby*. We had created a small life on the night of prom when we had made love with each other. My eyes welled up and I wiped a tear with my sleeve. I parked the car in the garage and turned off the engine.

Kiara was probably inside her room, crying for the unborn baby she couldn't save and blaming herself. I knew her too well to know that she was blaming all this on herself.

Fuck.

I would have been a father right now. Would she have told me if she knew that she was pregnant? She would have. She would have flown back to New York to tell me she was pregnant. But she wasn't. I don't know how she coped with the pain of losing a baby all alone. I wonder if this was the first time she was telling anyone else.

I needed to be with her. I couldn't stand her blaming herself for everything.

With my feet padding against the floor, I opened the door and clenched my jaw. She was curled up in a ball, her hair hiding her face and clutching a pillow to her. Closing the door behind me, I laid down beside her on the bed. I finally sighed in relief when the feminine, musky scent of her black vanilla and coconut wafted in my nose. I ran my hand through her silky hair, tucking strands back from her face. I moved the pillow away, which was wet with tears and wiped her cheeks.

Even sad, she looked like an angel sleeping on the bed.

I kissed her forehead and leaned back.

She stirred beside me and gazed at me through her half-lidded eyes, "Ethan?"

I cradled her to my chest and whispered, "It's okay. I am here, Bella."

Her fingers clutched my shirt, "Please forgive me, Ethan. I am sorry. I never wanted this to happen."

Rubbing her back, I said, "Go to sleep, Kiara."

When she relaxed in my arms, I kept my hand on her stomach and tugged her closer to me.

WAKING up with a petite body pressed against you was one of the best feelings in this world. Taking a deep breath, I opened my eyes and looked at Kiara who was snuggling with my chest. Her cheek was pressed against my heart, lips agape, and her long soft hair was splayed against my arm and the pillows. She smelt like coconut and black vanilla, reminding me of the days when I used to wake up cuddling with her or on the floor because she had accidentally kicked me off the bed.

I gently ran my hand through her hair, remembering last night. She was pregnant with our child. The child we had made with love. But she didn't tell me she had a miscarriage.

"What are you thinking about?"

I looked down at Kiara, her face was propped up against my chest. Swallowing the lump in my throat, I said, "I was wondering how our life would be if you had delivered the baby."

A small smile tugged at my lips as I continued, "We would buy a house with a white picket fence and I would propose to you. I would drop our children at school every morning and stay up late to make you Italian hot chocolate while you are busy writing your novels. We would have movie nights while cuddling with our kids." Tears glistened in her gold-flecked brown eyes. I cupped her cheek, wiping the tear, "And we would make love in the afternoon because that's the only time we will have no kids running around."

I let her cry at this fantasy of ours as she sat up, turning her back on me. My throat clogged up as her shoulders shook with the small sobs that she was trying so hard to hide.

I sat up and kissed her shoulders, "Please don't cry, Bella. I . . . I didn't want to make you cry."

She shook her head and looked at me, tears leaking down her eyes, "This is all my fault, Ethan! If I would've never left, then there would have been no accident and our baby would not have died. We would still be together, married, and living happily in our own home."

Her voice made my heart crack as I realized she was blaming herself for everything. I pulled her closer and made her look at me, her eyes were red with tears. "Kiara, listen to me. I forgive you for pushing me away for all these years just so you could be in a better place and be happy with who you are. I don't regret anything because it's alright, love. You did what you thought was better for yourself . . . for *us*. I admire you for having the courage to stand on your own, publish your novel, and teach younger minds. That car accident wasn't your fault, Kia. Stop blaming yourself for everything."

She said nothing for a while before blinking her eyes, "How could you say that after all I did and left you?"

I cupped her cheeks and gently wiped the tears with my thumbs and whispered, "It doesn't matter anymore because you are here right now. I forgave you for everything, and I could go through that all over again if it means having you in my arms *right now*."

Her brown doe eyes widened when she gazed at me for a long time, her pupils dilating as she glanced at my lips. I leaned my face closer to hers, breathing in her scent. Soft rosy blush reddened her cheeks and neck and I wondered how low that blush went. Her lips pressed against mine with soft, pliant pressure. I sighed and pulled her over me, holding her from the waist while my hands ran over her hair, which kept falling on my face when I kissed her.

Kiara pulled away first, dimple poking her cheeks as she shyly smiled at me and my eyes danced across her face to see a shy side of her. Gulping nervously, she sat up and mumbled, "I am going to go take a shower."

Right. She was on her period and didn't want me to go further.

I smiled at her when she closed the door to the washroom. When I looked down at my trousers, my smile faded away and I let out a groan, running a hand over my face. I had a raging boner just from kissing her.

Damn it, Eiffel.

WE HAD muffins and eggs for breakfast because neither of us had eaten the muffins, which I had baked for her the day before. We were sharing similar longing glances at each other and smiling and blushing like teenagers. I wanted to strip her naked and make love to her on the floor, but I knew she wasn't ready to be so intimate after telling me about the miscarriage. She was on her period, so she wouldn't let me touch her.

Later that evening, we snuggled on the couch after having pizza for dinner. We were watching an action romance movie, and I had Kiara sit on my lap, my arms wrapped around her. Her fingers lightly trailed over my arms, and it oddly turned me on that she couldn't stop touching me as much as I couldn't get enough of her.

"Did you know I had sex with you for the first time after two years?" she said.

My smile dropped, and I blurted, *"What?"*

She chuckled and pressed her back against my chest, "Yes. I stopped sleeping around once I got the job and then I met Jake."

"So you guys never had sex. What about oral?"

"A few times, but we never had sex with each other. Even if we wanted to, we both held back."

"Huh," I said, "I am surprised."

"Nothing is surprising about this, Ethan."

Little did she know there was. If she wanted to wait till marriage, then she was sure that she wanted to settle down with him. She would have if that idiot hadn't hidden his son from her. Thank God for that. But that also means that she trusted me to be gentle with her. She was more serious about the baby now than ever.

I kissed her shoulder and promised myself to give whatever she wanted from me.

After a while, I had to hold her down when she started squirming. "Kiara. You need to stop grinding on me like that."

Her cheeks flushed into a beautiful shade of pink. "I . . . I am not grinding on you." She said while grinding on me.

A small smirk tugged at the corner of my lips as I pressed

her butt closer to my bulge. My smirk widened when I heard her soft gasp and pressed my lips on her neck, kissing her skin. I lifted her top and skimmed my fingers on the smooth skin of her stomach, then trailed my hand until I could feel how hard her nipples were.

"*Ethan*," she moaned sweetly, arching against my touch.

I palmed her breasts, massaged the soft skin, and lightly pinched her pebbled nubs. She squirmed and groaned instantly, her skin extra sensitive.

"*Shh*, Kiara," I whispered when she shook her head. "Close your eyes and relax."

With one hand kneading her breast, I lowered my other hand down her shorts to her underwear. Her breathing stopped. I bit her ear, licking the earlobe. Kiara shivered when I slowly rubbed her clitoris, her pleasure nub was more sensitive as I pressed down on it, her hands gripping my forearms.

I slowly circled it, her legs trembling and her lips eliciting small, sweet sounds of pleasure that drove me insane. If she would have been comfortable, I would have taken her in the shower, but she wasn't so I didn't want to push her.

"Ethan," she gasped, "If you don't stop . . . I-I, *oh, fuck!*"

I tweaked and pinched her nipple and repeated the same action to her sensitive clit, her back arching as I held her close to me. Kiara trembled in my arms and when I rubbed the swollen nub, she exploded with an orgasm, her body writhing, overpowered with hormones. I kissed her skin and massaged her waist as she slowly calmed down.

I was surprised when she turned around to give me a brief kiss and smiled in between the kisses. "Thank you, Ethan," she whispered, her amber-brown eyes shining. "*For everything.*"

Smiling at her beautiful face, I whispered, "You too, Bella."

18. PANCAKES FOR DINNER

KIARA

My fingers pressed on the cool black and white keys of the piano, soft melody pouring out of it. I closed my eyes and breathed out as I played the last notes, ending the music with soft strokes. I smiled when his lips pressed on the crook of my neck.

"That was beautiful," he whispered, his hands running on my waist, warming my body.

I pressed a chaste kiss on his lips, "Thank you. What's for dinner?"

After telling Ethan about the miscarriage, I had a one-on-one session with Doctor Sabrina. As I had expected, I cried and came back home refreshed. Ethan had cuddled me to sleep that night, and I remember waking up in the middle of the night to see my hands clutching his t-shirt tightly. Somehow, letting him know about the truth had made us get closer to each other. He didn't hate me.

Closing the fallboard, I turned to him, loving the way his eyes smiled at me. Blue and green melting in his piercing orbs.

"What do you want to eat?"

"Pancakes."

A hearty chuckle poured out of his mouth, my eyes dancing over his handsome face and the tan skin of his throat. "Pancakes for dinner?"

"Yes, do you have a problem with that?" I asked and stood up to stretch my body. I smirked to myself when I found him staring at me.

He straightened to his tall height and kissed my ass while I bent down, touching my toes. I giggled, standing up as he wrapped his arm around me. "I don't have a problem with eating pancakes for dinner. Help me?"

"Of course!" I said, "I will make better pancakes than you."

His dark eyes twinkled with a challenge, "We will see about that, Bella."

We made different batters for our recipe and I eyed him as he chopped some strawberries. I continued making my batter by cracking two eggs and making sure that the batter wasn't too thick or too thin. After half an hour, our pancakes were ready, and we decided that we would judge each other's pancakes, and the winner got to do anything they wanted with the other for an hour.

I was excited to win because as much as I enjoyed the dominant side of Ethan, I wanted to know how he would react if I tied him up and had my way with him. I was sure that if he won, he'd do the same or . . . I didn't even want to imagine.

"Ready?" he asked as we both stacked a big bite in our forks with the maple syrup dripping down on the plate.

I nodded, and we both took a bite together. I chewed and almost moaned out loud at the delicious taste of strawberries and something buttery, melting in my mouth. It was delicious.

When I opened my eyes, Ethan had the same expression. I eyed his lips when he licked them, my body warming and aching for his. We hadn't had sex for a few days because of my period, but now, I needed him more than ever. I wondered if the feeling of having him beside me all day would ever fade. I wondered if he felt the same way or not.

"It's okay, too sugary," he said, shrugging at the pancakes I had cooked.

"*Liar.* If you don't like it, then I will eat it."

He grinned at me and ate another forkful. I chuckled at his goofy expression. We ate pancakes, sharing the ones we had made, and concluded that both the recipes were delicious and both of us were winners.

"No, I am the winner," I said firmly, craning my neck up to narrow my eyes at him. "My pancakes were a little better than yours."

He raised his eyebrow, "Didn't we just agree that it was a tie?"

Keeping my hands at my hips, I asked, "Did we? I don't remember."

Ethan sighed, "Okay, fine, you won. Why do you want to win so badly?"

I let out an evil laugh that earned me a side glance from him as I helped him load the dishwasher. "It's because I want to tie you up, silly."

He froze and glared at me. "No, not happening."

My smile fell, "Ethan, no! You promised that the loser has to follow the winner's command for an hour."

He crossed his arms, trying to intimidate me, and a part of me wanted to tell him it was working. I scowled at him, "You tie me up all the time. It's not fair. Maybe I want to play with you too."

A hint of a smile appeared on his lips when I pouted. "And how do you want to play with me, Kiara?" His voice was low and playful that made my stomach somersault.

Swallowing the lump in my throat, I said, "I want to tie up your hands."

His expression darkened, and the kitchen became a lot smaller when I took a step back, the marble counter digging in my lower back. He towered in front of me, smelling like pancakes, blueberries with a hint of his musky male scent. Wet arousal pooled in my underwear.

"And what will you do after tying my hands?"

I took a shuddering breath and met his eyes. They looked darker than mine as they pinned me to my spot. "You have to agree to let me tie you up first," I countered.

Surprisingly, he agreed, but with safe words. I almost laughed at him because I wasn't going to do anything extreme at all, I just wanted to tease him a little.

Okay, I am lying.

I want to tease him a lot.

"Remove your shirt, I want you shirtless," I ordered and even spanked his butt for the effect. My palm zinged with heat because of the rough denim.

He narrowed his eyes at me, "Too much, Kia."

I kissed his cheek in return and told him to lie down on the bed. Ethan was probably three times my size. If he decided it was getting too much, then it would take him no effort to pull me underneath him and I would be helpless. If I wanted to do this right, then I needed to tie his hands to the headboard so he couldn't run away from me. Hehe, I was loving how the roles had reversed. Even though it was only for a while.

"Why do I think this is a bad idea?" He whispered to himself while I tied his hands to the headboard, straddling his bare chest. His prominent muscles tensed and hardened when I leaned down to kiss him on the lips and pulled away when he wanted to deepen it. He glared at me.

"Stop pouting, E, you agreed to be a good boy," I said and

stood up from the bed, marveling at the sight in front of me. Now I truly understood why he loved tying me up so much.

Ethan Kane was half-naked on the bed with his hands tied up. All for me. My mouth watered. I wanted to do my best to please him, make him come in my mouth. He looked exquisite and edible. All for me, I reminded myself, crossing my arms and removing his t-shirt that I was wearing. I watched his eyes rove over the dark red lace lingerie I had donned that morning. He let out a groan when I removed my shorts, revealing tiny red lace underwear.

Ethan tugged at his bonds, "Kiara . . . *fuck*, you are killing me here, babe. I want to touch you."

I smirked, running my hands down my breasts and over my stomach, "Too bad, *eh*."

"*Kiara*," he warned, his face etched with anger and arousal.

"Yes?" I asked him sweetly when I crawled up the length of his body and lightly kissed his hip bone.

Keeping my eyes on him, I licked his skin. His hips arched when I peppered small kisses on his abdomen. My hands roamed over the slabs of his prominent muscles and scratched his abs. I kissed, licked, and left hickeys, all the while hearing his sharp intake of breath and small groans. By the time I reached his waistband, he was hard as stone and a spot of pre-cum had stained his boxers.

"You are so fucking hot, Ethan," I whispered and removed his boxers.

"*Finally*," he muttered under his breath. His hooded eyes watched me lick my lips at the sight of his beautiful cock. The tip glistened with pre-cum, his girth solid with angry veins surrounding it. I stroked him slowly, relishing the hard touch of his velvety skin.

"Take me in your mouth, Bella," he rasped, "I want to see those lips suck on my cock."

His crude, dirty words aroused me further as I followed his directions. I lowered my head and took him in my mouth, his musky male scent exploding on my tongue. I moaned at his taste and licked his head, sucking it while my hand continued to stroke him.

"Like that?" I asked, licking my lips before pulling away,

Ethan groaned at me with his half-lidded eyes, "Yes, Bella, don't fucking stop."

Smiling to myself, I leaned down and licked his length, his body tensing underneath me. He let out a sound of protest when I pulled away from him to unhook my bra and remove the thong.

Ethan swallowed, "Kiara, if you don't fuck me right now—"

I silenced him with my finger on his lips. "Or what, Ethan?" I purred, his eyes glaring at me but getting distracted as they landed on my breasts. I giggled when he tried to bite my finger.

"You are being a tease. Take me inside you," he said, his voice smoky and deep, arching up to me.

I shook my head and grabbed his jaw to kiss him. The kiss was savage with our tongues and lips clashing against each other. I tugged at his hair and moaned when he bit my bottom lip, licking it better with small flicks of his tongue.

I pulled away before he could make me untie him. Taking a deep breath, I gathered my hair in a bun as he shot me a confused look.

"What are you doing, Kiara?" he asked worriedly.

Turning around, I went on all fours, straddling him with my naked sex facing him. He took a sharp breath. Looking over my shoulder, I grinned, "I am giving you a blow job, Ethan."

"Not like that, you aren't! Untie me, Kiara. *Right. Now,*" his voice was menacing, and I knew I was going to get it bad when I untied him afterward, but his hands were restrained. I wanted to do nothing but please and worship him.

"Kiara, I—*Fuck!*" he groaned when I sucked him in my mouth, swirling my tongue around the thick head and relaxing my throat before I took him in little by little. Tears burned in my eyes when his hips arched, and I had to pull away a little to take a deep breath before diving in and taking him inside my mouth again.

I was slow and deliberate in pleasing him because I wanted to edge out his climax as he did to me. I could hear the tug of his hands, trying to remove the bonds from his wrists when I sucked his balls in my mouth, squeezing and slowly massaging his long length. It still surprised me he could fuck me without ever hitting my cervix and hurting me. This made me realize that his thrusts were always angled and precise so I wouldn't feel anything but pleasure.

My warm puff of breath fanned on his glistening skin as I leaned back and went all-in for him. I wanted this climax to be one of the best for him. I never wanted him to forget this. I wanted him to remember *this*.

With that intention, I was about to suck him in my mouth when I heard a rustle behind me. I turned around, but it was *too late.*

"*Ethan!*"

I squealed when he pulled me closer by dragging my thighs and spanked my ass.

"You fucking tease," he growled at me as he smacked another cheek and pulled my bare sex closer to his mouth.

I trembled and gasped, clutching his muscular thighs when his wet tongue lapped at my dripping juices. Heat surged at my core and my stomach clenched with anticipation for more. The warmth of his spanks had scorched my pussy, and I writhed when he grazed his teeth on my swollen clitoris.

An evil chuckle poured out of his throat that made me shiver. I didn't even dare to look at him. He thwacked my ass again and said, "Don't you worry, Kiara, I will punish you later for teasing me, but right now, I want you to suck my cock while I eat you out. Understood?"

I nodded and hummed.

"Good, sit on my face, Bella," he whispered.

Biting my lips, I did, his fingers digging into my soft skin as he breathed me in, "My Queen."

Heat flooded my cheeks hearing his words, and I moaned when his mouth covered my pussy. He remembered. Determined, I licked my lips and took him in my mouth. I licked, kissed, and sucked all along his glorious length while he bit, laved, and sucked at my naked sex.

Both of us were competing, wishing the other would climax first.

Too bad I still wanted to win.

I took a deep breath and sucked his cock in my mouth. I relaxed my throat when he brushed the back and kept going with tears burning in my eyes. I clenched my hands on the sheets and moaned when he rubbed my clitoris, thrusting himself inside me more.

"I am going to come in your mouth if you don't stop," he panted, inserting two fingers inside me. I jumped, my muscles clenching them.

I didn't reply. Instead, I pulled back and bobbed my head over him, preparing myself to deep throat him again. This time, tears streamed down my face when he flexed inside my mouth, my orgasm teetering on the edge, his hot, warm mouth sucking on my pleasure nub.

I let go first, coming on his mouth as I trembled above him, my body rocking through the aftershocks when his legs tensed, and he exploded in my mouth. I squeezed my eyes shut and swallowed his cum, licking his length clean until he was soft. I sighed and jumped when his tongue poked out to lick me.

"Ethan," I warned, even though my voice was an inaudible whisper, "I'm sensitive."

He gave me a lazy smile similar to a cat after licking cream and turned me around to cup my face. His eyes darkened when they landed on my chin and before I could do anything, his thumb swiped on the corner of my lips and brushed it over my bottom lip. Not looking away from him, I licked the glistening bead from his thumb, my inner muscles clenching for more.

"You are trouble," he whispered, smiling at me with a dazed expression.

I smiled at him when he kissed me softly, his fingers tugging down the lazy bun I had done and running a hand through my hair. I sighed in content when he pulled me closer to his chest, wrapping his arm around me,

"Kiara?"

"*Hm?*"

"Let's go on a date tomorrow."

I stayed silent for a while before I moved to look in his different colored eyes. One date couldn't hurt, right?

Nodding, I pressed my lips against his. "Yes, we should," I breathed between our small kisses.

"AND THAT'S how he woke up cuffed to his bed," Ethan grinned, shaking his head as bubbly laughter poured out of me. I clutched my stomach and tried to control my laughter, but I couldn't.

Nearby couples eyed us with envy, Ethan's fingers stroking my hand and watching me grin.

Ethan had just told me the story of Liam having a threesome in Las Vegas and waking up hungover while cuffed to the bed. He had to call Ethan while he was naked, and Ethan had to cover his crotch before he helped him out of the cuffs with a key he found in Liam's pants from the night before.

"You guys seem a lot closer than before," I smiled, sipping cold water.

He nodded, smiling to himself, brushing his finger on his glass of water. I had told him to order wine or champagne, but he didn't want to because I would drink water or soda.

Today seemed like a great day so far. We showered together, had lunch together in my office, then I waited for him at the bleachers like old times. We even dressed together for the date, eyeing each other the whole time with a heated promise of the passionate night between our unsaid words.

I eyed the navy-blue suit, his white shirt, and the golden skin appearing between the unbuttoned top two buttons. I crossed my legs, my satin beige dress tightening around me. Ethan's eyes trailed down to my chest when the bodice of my dress tightened, showing off my cleavage. I blushed, looking away.

"Do you want to have dessert?" He asked, his fingers entwining mine and squeezing my hand.

Dessert? Sure, I want you.

Clearing my throat, I smiled at him. "We can have ice cream on our way back home?"

"Sounds perfect."

We walked together after sharing two ice creams. His arm was wrapped around my waist, my nose pressed against his shirt as I breathed in his musky scent.

"I love how you smell," I commented, the light cool breeze brushing over us.

He gave me an amused look and lightly tugged at the strand of my hair. "Good to know. I love how you always smell like coconut and something . . ." I held my breath when he leaned down to kiss my neck and took a deep breath. "Something *exotic*."

The hot whisper of his breath tugged at my belly. Ethan didn't even need to do anything to turn me on. It wasn't fair.

"Come on, I want to show you something," he held my hand and dragged me to a closed shop.

I studied the closed doors and watched Ethan pull out a key from his pocket to open the locked doors. *Is he the owner of a shop?*

I followed him inside and blinked when he turned on the warm lights, closing the door behind me. The vast space was empty, without any furnishing or carpet. Except for one thing. The walls were framed with paintings.

Tears welled in my eyes, and my heart shuddered loudly as I noticed each painting framed under beautiful light, contrasting each stroke and a swirl of the colors, blending perfectly. My mother, Damini, had painted them.

I found Ethan watching me with a small smile, "They're all yours if you want them."

I bit my lip from sobbing as I walked to each of the paintings, smiling and remembering my mother in her art studio. The scent of linseed oil and oil paint wafted in my nose as the memory of my mother became stark and she was all I could think about. Her calloused fingers from holding a paintbrush for almost half a day, every year. Her long hair, darker than mine, coiled in a bun or braid so they wouldn't bother her while she painted. Her paint-stained face and hands. Her warm smile and kind eyes.

Pausing at one painting she had done before she married my father, I saw my reflection in the frame. I looked just like her, with sharp features and sad eyes with a tear-stained face. Wiping my tears, I forced myself to calm down.

"How did you find these paintings?" I asked. "They were sold or kept in her studio."

Ethan stood beside me, his hand holding mine, lacing our fingers together. I noticed how perfectly our hands fit each other. He pressed a kiss on my knuckles, his lips cold.

"I bought them from your father and found the sellers when I knew I could afford them."

I breathed out, "Why?"

He looked between my eyes and cupped my face, wiping away tears with his thumb. "Because I know how special they are to you."

They were. I remembered every story behind them because whenever I wasn't writing or running around as a child, I was with my mom in her art studio, watching her paint and listening to her stories.

Ethan had done this for me.

Love is never complicated, it's easy and simple. You love him? Yes, Mom. *Then tell him.*

I held his hands, which cupped my face. I whispered, "Thank you, Ethan."

There were a million things my mind was opposing, but my heart knew that I wanted him. It was too late. I was falling for him.

Ethan smiled, the corners of his eyes crinkling as his blue-green eyes gazed at me with adoration. "Anything for you, Bella."

19. I LIKE YOU

ETHAN

Seeing Kiara's gorgeous face crumble at the sight of her mother's painting stung my heart, but it soothed on its own when I noticed that her tears were happy tears. I rubbed her back when she gazed at the last painting, her amber eyes taking in each stroke and swirl of the paint.

I was captivated by her.

Kiara.

My Kiara.

Fuck, how badly I wanted her to be mine.

I clenched my jaw and tried to control the urge of spilling out how much I wanted her. Not just regarding her body, although I was very much in love with her shape. I wanted her the way I have always wanted her since I watched her apply cherry Chapstick on her first date with that asshole Paul who broke her heart when she was thirteen. I had hated the way she had dressed up for him and wanted to take her for an ice cream date with me instead.

But I knew I couldn't have her. So, I would rather cherish these brief moments with her and do anything to see that beautiful smile on her lips with a dimple. I would capture these moments in my heart and my mind until the sun turns to dust.

"Ethan." I looked down at her, her golden-brown eyes glowing. "Thank you."

I squeezed her waist. "You don't have to thank me, Bella. It's getting cold in here." I turned to see if anyone had installed a heater in here. As the pieces were framed two days ago, there was no decoration or any necessities placed in this small art gallery.

"Are you cold?" I asked and removed my suit coat to drape over her bare arms.

"Not at all," Kiara said, her tongue wetting her pillowy lips. Her hands tightened on the front of my shirt, "I feel very warm right now."

"Warm, *hmm?*" I teased, pulling her closer, my hand sliding down to cup her perfect round ass. Her breasts pressed against my shirt when she arched up to me, her arms winding around my neck.

"Yes," she breathed, "Can I kiss you?"

I smiled, "Kiss me, Bella."

Her palms cupped my face. I closed my eyes when her lips pressed against mine. I savored her mouth, her soft fingers brushing tenderly against my cheek. I let a soft growl slip when she captured my bottom lip between her teeth in a slight tease.

I couldn't help myself when her lips and tongue tasted of chocolate. Her exotic black vanilla and coconut scent intoxicated me. I needed to have her.

Pushing her against the wall, I slammed my lips against hers, devouring her gasp when she wrapped her legs around me. Her heels dug into my lower back.

"*Ethan.*"

Kiara whimpered softly, her sweet moan urging me to make her moan again and again. My lips traveled to her ear, licking and biting the soft earlobe before pressing a soft kiss on the crook of her neck. Her hands feathered my hair while my hands tugged the hem of her dress to her waist. I pressed my fingers on the wet spot of her thong.

"So fucking wet for me, Kiara," I groaned, her hips arching for my touch as I rubbed her through the lace.

"*Need you*," she panted, her fingers working on the zipper of my pants and stroking my hardened length.

I leaned back to stare at her hazy eyes, her flushed face and rosy lips, "Are you sure?"

Kiara pulled me out, my jaw clenching at the lack of control. "*Please*," she whispered, her sultry voice urging me to press her against the wall.

I had said that I would do anything for her, and I had meant it.

Our carnal groans echoed in the art gallery as I took her against the wall before splaying her down on the floor. On my suit. Her legs trembled against my waist, her fingers sinking into my back when I moved as we both tethered off the orgasmic edge.

We both moaned each other's names when we climaxed together. I stayed buried inside her and lifted my forehead from her chest to have my eyeful of her beautiful post-coital face. Her chocolaty eyes glistened with tears. I wiped them away and hugged her to my chest.

Kiara didn't move an inch, instead watched me with her bleary eyes, a small smile playing on her lips. The lips I had kissed moments ago. I leaned down and kissed her again.

We ended up sleeping in each other's arms on the floor of the empty art gallery surrounded by her mother's paintings.

THE NEXT DAY, I woke up to sunlight streaming over our bodies, the musky scent of our arousal in the air. I ran my hand through her hair as she tried to hide her face on my chest and sleep some more. But it was six in the morning and we both had work to do.

I took sleepy Kiara back to our home and made her shower while I forced myself to get ready without thinking too much about last night. I wanted her more now than ever.

I liked her. I liked my best friend.

Who wanted me to get her pregnant.

"Ethan!" Kiara knocked on the bathroom door, "Open up, I want to talk."

Shaking my head, I wrapped a towel around my waist and stepped out of the bathroom. I licked my lips at the sight of Miss Kiara, the teacher. *Fuck me.* Her shirt was tight, and I wanted to know what kind of lingerie she was wearing. Especially underneath her tight trousers.

"Am I getting punished, Miss Kiara?" I asked playfully, walking to my wardrobe. When I removed my towel and wore boxers, I heard her take a sharp breath. Looking over my shoulder, I found her cheeks and neck blooming with a pink hue as she looked away, her bottom lip between her lips.

"I, *uh*, wanted to talk about last night."

"What about it?" I asked nonchalantly, focusing on zipping up my pants and buttoning my shirt.

"Can we focus on having sex?"

I gave her a deadpanned look. "Then what were we doing last night at the art gallery, Kiara?"

She sighed and crossed her arms, "I like you, Ethan, and I don't want to complicate things between us."

She liked me.

Fuck yes!

Clearing my throat, I started knotting a tie and muttered, "As if a baby won't complicate things between us."

"It won't."

I clenched my jaw, my gaze hard. "Really? Then what will your baby call me? *Uncle?* Is that how you will introduce me to our child? 'Meet Uncle Ethan, we had sex to have you.'" I huffed and turned to the mirror, fixing my collar and straightening my tie.

Her hands wrapped around my torso, "Please don't say that, E. I just need some more time." She made me look at her, her palm softening a crease of the shirt on my shoulders. "You are more important to me, Ethan."

"More than making you pregnant?"

"Yes, I care more about you more than having a baby with you," she smiled up at me, her eyes swirling with emotions. "Where are you going? You never wear a tie."

"I have a meeting with my sponsors to talk about my endorsement deal. They know I saved Emma so they are letting me off the hook," I replied and wondered if she realized what she had just said.

A baby with me.

"That's great news, Ethan!" She grinned, "I hope the meeting goes well." Her cell phone rang from her room, and she kissed my cheek, wishing me good luck before she left to pick it up.

I chuckled to myself and touched my cheek where her lips had been a moment ago. She said she wanted to have a baby with me. *Together.*

I might become a dad.

Fuck.

"I think I like her," I said with a shy smile and twirled the pasta on my plate.

My mothers shared a knowing smile, sitting across from me in the restaurant while Eveline shook her head at me. After the morning meeting, which had gone great, I had a small chat with my agent, Elliot, before I met my family with Liam to have lunch at an Italian restaurant. I had asked him to join me, but he had a date with his wife, and he didn't want to miss it.

"You have liked her since you were a child, Ethan," Liam said, "Big deal."

I kicked his leg under the table.

My mothers agreed with him, taking his side.

"What? Don't glare at me like that. You were whipped since the day the little Indian princess moved to the apartment next door," he grinned at me, his grey eyes playful.

"How would you know?" I muttered and looked at my plate when my cheeks heated.

"We told him, of course," my mom, Lilly, said, "You never once showed any interest in anyone else but her. So, it isn't a surprise that you like her, Son."

I dropped the fork. "But I am not sure if it will work out between us."

My ma raised her eyebrow at me. "Are you not sure or are you scared?"

Even my little sister backed her up, "Please marry Kiara, Ethan. She is like an Indian princess and I adore her! You can be her Prince Charming."

Liam grinned at her and gave her a high five while my mothers grinned at them. I raked a hand through my hair and wondered how on Earth Kiara wooed my family. My ma was right. I feared losing her, but I was not sure if our relationship would ever work out. We were trying to conceive before ever going on a date or even getting married.

Marriage? Yeah, right.

I sighed and looked at my family, smiling and chattering with Liam.

I was way over my head.

20. SHE LOVES HIM

KIARA

I bit my bottom lip, my fingers clutching my handbag tightly. I told the taxi driver the directions to Ethan's home. I had been waiting for Ethan to pick me up when Liam had called me. I was not expecting to hear that Ethan had injured himself. He didn't give me many details, just that he was alright, and the personal doctor was treating him at his home.

Tipping the driver, I rushed out of the taxi and entered the house. My heartbeat was pounding when I saw Liam and another man in a suit with a stethoscope around his neck sitting on the couch.

"Where's Ethan?" I breathed, "Is he okay?"

Liam gave me a small smile as the doctor explained that he got a rotator cuff injury which was a common injury in swimmers. He would have inflammation in his injured shoulder for a few days and wouldn't be able to swim for a couple of weeks. I thanked him when he took his leave after prescribing a painkiller and asked to ice his shoulder twice a day and call him if the pain worsened.

"Thank you for calling me," I said to Liam, his grey eyes

looking anywhere but at me. He nodded, sliding his hands in his pockets when he stood up. "You can stay for dinner," I offered.

Liam's eyes pierced mine, raking over my face. He looked the same as he had before, but his jaw and cheekbones looked sharper, his grey eyes darker. "I don't want to disturb you guys," he said. "And as much as I would love to stay and see you scold him, I have to take my leave."

After locking the front door, I went to Ethan's room, knocking before I entered. I let out a sigh when I found him sleeping soundly on the bed, stacks of pillows under his right bandaged shoulder. Sitting beside him, I brushed his hair back and caressed his cheek with my thumb. His eyes stirred, and I took my hand away when he woke up, his half-lidded eyes landing on me.

"I am sorry I woke you up."

He smiled at me and took my hand in his, his fingers enveloping mine. "You didn't. Did you eat? I was going to buy you that kimchi you love, but I couldn't."

I poked his healthy side, frowning at him, "Why on earth would you over-train yourself like that, Ethan? The doctor told me this happened because you trained yourself to the point that your muscle tore itself."

Ethan leaned up, sitting on the bed with the support of pillows despite my concern. He hushed me by placing his finger on my lips. "I needed to swim, Bella. This isn't the first time I have hurt myself during training."

My eyes went wide and before I could ask him, he continued, "You don't need to worry, okay? It will heal in a week. But look at the bright side."

I furrowed my brows when he grinned mischievously. "What bright side?"

Leaning close, his warm breath tickled my ear as he whispered, "You can role-play as my nurse."

With my cheeks flaming red, I smacked him, "Is sex all you ever think about?"

He chuckled when I stood up from the bed. "Every time you are close to me, *yes*, sweetheart."

"You are insatiable," I muttered when I left his room with a small smile playing on my lips.

"*KIARA*," Ethan moaned again while I focused on typing up the last paragraph of the chapter I was working on.

"Hmm?"

"Let's fuck, I am bored."

"Okay, you go ahead," I answered aimlessly and pushed my glasses up the bridge of my nose. My fingers returned to tapping on my laptop keyboard.

"You didn't hear what I just said, did you?"

"No, I will eat later."

As I finished writing the last sentence, I felt his warm body heat radiating on my back. I smiled when he turned my chair around.

"Are you finished?" he asked, nodding at my laptop.

I murmured a small yes and wrapped my hands around his neck when he removed my glasses to press a soft kiss on my lips. I opened up to him, our tongues meeting in a soft caress. Aching desire clenched in my lower belly. I leaned back, his warm breath fanning on my cheek as his stubble grazed my palm.

"You know we will not have sex, Ethan," I tried to say that with a stern voice. But with him in front of me, looking delicious with his tousled hair and hazy blue-green eyes, my voice wavered.

His hands trailed on my waist. "Fine, let's make a baby together."

My thighs clenched, and blood rushed to my face. He was truly insatiable.

I stood up from the chair, maintaining the distance between us so he couldn't seduce me. "Your shoulder is—"

"*Healed.* You talked with the doctor, and he said that I can even start training." He gave me a mischievous smile, "*Cardio* to be precise."

I sighed and pulled my hair free from the bun. "That doesn't mean you are healthy enough to have sex—*ah!*"

I should have known better not to say that out loud. My back landed on the soft sheets and Ethan hovered above me. A soft moan poured out of my lips when he settled between my thighs, his hips pressing against mine. I felt the hard heat of his erection press into me.

Knowing he had to support himself on his hands, which might strain his muscles. I rolled us over, his eyes trailing down my top to the pebbled peaks of my nipples. Holding his jaw, I said, "We are not having sex . . . or making babies tonight. I don't want you to hurt yourself, Ethan."

He let out a defeated sigh, his warm hands stroking my thighs, "Okay, Bella. I will let you go. But only for tonight."

I smiled at him and was about to leave his lap when he pulled me back. "I need to ask you about something," he said, his thumb rubbing the pulse on my wrist.

"Remember your mother's paintings? I wanted to ask if you would like to set up an auction for them. It could be for children with cancer, like the gala we attended, or any other charity you want to support," he finished with a small smile.

I let his words soak in for a moment. A grin covered my lips, and I hugged him. "That's a brilliant idea, Ethan! I think she would want this too." I claimed his lips for a sweet moment. "But I would need to talk to my brother and father before we go further."

"Of course, Bella. I know Mr. Stone and a friend of mine, Khalid, would love to help us."

"*What?*" My breath hitched in my throat, "You know Khalid Al-Latif? *The* Khalid Al-Latif? *The* brother of the Sultan of Azmia? The artist who painted *Limerence?*"

Ethan narrowed his eyes at me. "Yes, I do. Don't be so surprised. He was my and Rio's roommate for a year. We shared an apartment when he was in New York."

"I think I might faint."

He rolled his eyes and pinched my ass, making me grin. "Talk to your family, and if they agree, we can plan the charity together if you want."

"They will," I kissed his cheek. "Thank you for being so thoughtful, Ethan. I would love to plan this with you."

The shy smile I received in return was one of the sweetest ones I have ever received, and I would cherish it in my heart. I went to my room and video called my brother and father. I told them about Ethan's idea, and as I had suspected, they willingly agreed to it.

"So, you are living with Ethan?" my brother asked, crossing his arms.

"How are things with him?" Dad asked. Folding the newspaper he was reading, he removed his glasses to look at me.

I forced my cheeks not to flush and replied, "Things are great, Dad. You know how he is."

They both nodded, narrowing their eyes at me. Karan asked, "Do you like him?"

"Of course, I like him."

"Love him?"

Yes.

I cleared my throat, "I am not sure about my feelings at the moment, Karan."

Dad pressed on, "If you could marry him, have kids with him, would you?"

You have no idea, Dad.

"Dad! You both need to stop whatever you are doing. I like him, maybe more than that, but—"

"She loves him," Karan said to Dad.

My father agreed with a small smile, *"She does."*

"When do you think they will get married?" Karan asked.

"By next year, I suppose."

With my cheeks flaming red, I shook my head at them. "You both are unbelievable. I am going. Goodnight and take care of yourself."

I ended the call and sighed, laying down on the bed. A small smile played on my lips and butterflies flapped in my stomach at the weird feeling in my heart. I giggled and hid my face with my hands.

I was so whipped it was embarrassing.

21. TWO HOURS OF PLEASURE

ETHAN

"So are you guys dating?"

My hand squeezed Kiara's underneath the table when Jake looked between us, my jaw clenching. When Kiara received a call from him yesterday, she decided that it would be a good idea to talk it out with him. Kiara wanted me beside her and I couldn't refuse.

"Why would it matter to you?" I said, my voice cold and clipped.

His blue eyes softened. "You're right, it shouldn't. I . . . I wanted to apologize for acting like a jerk that day, Kiara. For not telling you about Ben or Stacy."

The waiter interrupted us yet again for the umpteenth time asking if we needed any more water or wine. I should've known meeting him at a restaurant for lunch was a bad idea. I was sure the waiter wanted nothing more but the latest gossip. *Looks like all three of us are going to be in tomorrow's celebrity headlines.*

When the waiter left, Kiara replied, "I wish you had told me earlier. But it doesn't matter now. I hope you are mending things with her and especially Ben. He thinks of you as a superhero."

Jake looked away when I noted a hint of sadness and hurt flashing in his eyes. He must be overcome with guilt for not knowing about his son until it was too late. I wondered how it would have been for me and Kiara if she had the baby and told me about it after a year. I would be mad for missing out on helping her during her pregnancy, miss the labor, miss the first time he or she spoke or walked.

"Jake," Kiara whispered, "Take care of your family, okay? You, as well."

He smiled at her, "I will, Kiara. How have you been?"

Her golden flecked brown eyes glanced at me, a warm smile tugging at her lips. "I am happy."

Her reply made me smile and after our lunch and making small talk, we finally said our goodbyes. Jake patted my shoulder and said, "Take care of her. She really likes you."

I SIGHED, running a hand through my hair, "Yes, Mom! I am not twelve. Yes, I am fine."

Kiara snickered, dimples poking her cheeks as she raised her eyebrows and came toward me. My eyes followed the soft curves of her lithe body. Her messy long hair, her nipples poking against my t-shirt she was wearing and her long, tanned legs. I was hard just looking at her. Especially when she held my arm and sat on my lap, her hand massaging my shoulders. I bit my lip from sighing and tensing when she leaned down, kissing the base of my throat.

"You don't talk to your mother like that, Son."

I closed my eyes, my hand tightening around Kiara's round ass, stopping her from grinding on my hard-on while I was talking to my mother. I narrowed my eyes at her as her brown eyes were sparkling with mischief. She unbuttoned my shirt, her hands splaying over my chest. She kissed me, making all the dirty sounds from her mouth. I felt like the luckiest man on this planet.

Ignoring the tension building in my abdomen, I replied, "I am sorry, Ma, I am a bit busy and Kiara is—" I stared at her hair, she was trailing her kisses down my body, removing the belt. "She is eating food. I mean, cleaning the dishes of the food we ate. *Yes, mmhmm.*"

I was confused, angry, and aroused.

I heard my mom mutter something to her wife and said, "Don't forget to arrive early, Ethan. Eveline misses you, and she will be surprised because we told her you have work to do."

Kiara stopped, leaned over me and stroked my hardened length through my pants. I almost choked, my eyes going wide. Holding her wrist, I stopped her. I ignored her pout and replied, "I won't forget, Mother. *Ahh*, look, I have to go. The faucet is leaking."

"I didn't hear it breaking—"

"*Ma*. How about I call you later? It is flooding the kitchen and Kiara is freaking out."

She was laughing, hiding her face in my neck while her hair tickled my skin.

"Don't forget to bring your girlfriend when you come here, or you won't get to eat the cake." She hung up the phone, and I put it on the coffee table, rolling Kiara underneath me on the couch.

"You think this is funny?" I pinned her hands above her head when she kept laughing. Her eyes were closed, and soft bubbly laughter poured from her throat. I loved hearing that sound.

Kiara said, in between her chuckles, "Your faucet . . . leaking. *Ah*—Ethan!"

I tickled her, her infectious laughter echoing in the room. As I stared down at her petite frame thrashing in my arms, a light flared in her brown eyes. I felt content. I wanted nothing else but that.

Kiara laughing in my arms. Every day and night for the rest of my life.

Stopping, I spread her legs to wedge myself between them. Her breathing grew erratic. I loved how responsive she was to my touch. She stared up at me as if she felt the same way.

My blood pounded in my ear when she cupped my cheek lovingly and whispered, "Come here."

Smiling, I leaned down, capturing her lips in a soft caress while her body arched against me, wanting me to press against her. I gave what she wanted. Her soft sighs against my cheek and neck made me grind against her, eliciting a soft moan. One thing I learned from living with Kiara was that she has a very high sex drive. She was almost insatiable until she begged me to fuck her.

I pulled away first, her eyes wide and cheeks flushed. She frowned. I looked down. Her t-shirt was lifted, her thong on the side. I had done that, but no idea when. When we kissed, every inch of her being possessed me. Shaking my head, I pecked her lips and straightened her clothes.

"What happened?" she asked, leaning on her elbows, and it took all the self-control in me not to unzip myself and slide inside her.

Swallowing the lump in my throat, I straightened my shirt, buttoning it. She had sneakily unbuttoned it. "Not now, Bella. I have to be at the studio in half an hour and talk with Elliot."

It had been weeks since my injury, and I was in much better shape. I had told her about the new sponsors who were impressed with my volunteer work. They were a new athletic wear brand but had blown up in a year because of their organic, comfortable clothing. They wanted to partner up with me and possibly have my photo on the front cover of a magazine. She was so happy that we made love on the couch. She had ridden me from heaven to hell until I took the lead.

Kiara didn't seem pleased. "But you have half an hour."

A chuckle escaped my throat as I helped her up. "Not right now, Kiara. I can't be late for this shoot."

A twinkle formed in her eyes and I knew I shouldn't have said that when her hand wrapped around my crotch, throbbing with need when she stroked me. The saucy vixen licked her lips and whispered, "You won't be late if we—"

I shook my head, clearing the daze from my head, "I meant when I said no, sweetheart." I gave her a pointed look, and she politely took away her hand and stepped back, still pouting.

"Okay, I apologize. I have to get ready for my appointment." She walked back to the room, removing the t-shirt, and I groaned looking at her perfect ass, the slight red hue of pelts from the day before.

This woman will be the end of me.

Like a wounded puppy, I followed her. "What appointment?" I asked and wondered if she was . . .

I watched her get dressed when she replied teasingly, "My dick appointment, of course."

Raising my eyebrows at her, I slowly walked toward her and pushed her against the dresser, her ass pressing against my hips. I asked, "Does he know what turns you on? That making you laugh while being deep inside you makes you cum?" I ground out, a moan slipping past her lips. "Or that you love being spanked like the bad girl you are, *hmm?*"

It took a little time for her to answer when she shakily replied, "N-No."

I pressed my body against her, my hand fondling her breast as I kissed her neck and purposely left a hickey while she melted in my arms, my fingers pinching the hard nipples. "Then I suppose you should cancel that dick appointment and wait for me when I come back."

"*Ethan!*" she shrieked when I smacked her ass and squeezed her butt. Kiara turned around, her brown eyes already turning dizzy as she licked her lips. "When will you be back?"

I grinned, loving how easily she got sexually frustrated. "Getting eager, are we?"

She glared at me and, looking away, and started braiding her hair. I kissed her cheek. "I will be back after dinner, so don't wait for me." I knew she would want to cuddle, talk, or have sex so I added, "I will bring something for you."

Her eyes lit up looking at my reflection in the mirror. "Alright, Ethan. Now, go before I pounce on you and tie you to the bed." She turned, winking at me, and smacked my ass when she left the room.

I chuckled, rubbing the stinging area, and took my car keys. "God, I love it when you talk dirty to me. Come on, I will drop you off."

I knew she was going for her therapy session. She told me it helped her before, but now it was monthly visits, because she wasn't having any anxiety attacks and didn't have to dose up on sleeping pills to get a few hours of sleep. I smirked at her, knowing well why she got a good night's sleep. Kiara blushed and looked away, still holding my hand, which was over her thigh, and squeezed it.

THE MEETING and photoshoot went perfectly well. When my agent, Elliot, asked me if I was dating a teacher and the bestselling author, Kiara Sharma, I ignored him. When he asked me if I could update my Instagram and post a picture with Kiara for publicity, I glared at him and left.

I would not pull a stunt like that just to get publicity and have my name in the headlines.

Still, I couldn't help myself and checked my camera roll to see hundreds of our pictures together. Cuddling, kissing, her laughing, or when she was writing. I shook my head when I found a picture of me sleeping on her lap, my mouth agape, and another similar one but with her lips pressed against my cheek.

With flushed cheeks, I texted Kiara, asking if she was home or if I could pick her up. I started my car and checked her reply, saying that she was waiting for me. I smiled, going to the nearest bakery and buying a chocolate cake for her.

Parking my car in the garage, I wondered what we would do today. I checked her period cycle on my app. It showed her fertile window for the next ten days, and she was in her ovulation period for today and tomorrow.

This is it. I will get her pregnant.

Thoughts of how I would tie her up and make her come on my mouth, hands, and dick ran in my head. Licking my lips, I opened the door and frowned when I saw no lights in the living room. Closing the door behind me, I found Kiara in the kitchen. My eyes widened when I saw she was wearing black sheer stockings and my t-shirt covering her body, the hem brushing her thighs.

I sneaked in behind her and whispered, "Hey, Kiara."

She screamed, turning around and swatting my chest. I cackled with laughter as she saw me and took a deep breath, her hand over her chest. She closed her eyes and leaned back on the counter.

"*Hai Bhagwan.* You scared the shit out of me, E."

"Didn't you hear me open the door? Walk in?"

Kiara pursed her lips and shook her head, blush blooming on her cheeks. "No, I didn't," she mumbled. "How was the shoot? Did you make anyone pee their pants today?"

"Not really. Why are you so jumpy?" I asked. "How was the appointment?"

Gulping nervously, she looked away and walked past me, so much so that she even ignored the bakery bag. *Okay, something is wrong.* I followed her after keeping the cake in the fridge and asked, "What happened, Kiara?"

Ignoring me, she opened the door to my room. (Technically, it was ours as she slept with me.) I blindly followed her, holding her wrist in my grip. I whirled her around.

"*What.* Happened?"

This time she had enough sense to look at my face and bit her bottom lip. "Promise you won't be mad at me?" She looked guilty and her expression was wounded. I was taken aback. *Did something happen during her therapy?*

Furrowing my eyebrows, I rubbed my thumb over the pulse of her wrist, her heartbeat increasing. I asked her worriedly, "Tell me what happened, Bella."

She looked down and mumbled something incoherent.

"I can't hear you, Kia."

Kiara looked up from beneath her lashes. "I may or may not have touched myself."

My hand froze, and I let go of her hand. She stilled, noticing the change in my gaze and looked down, her shoulders slumping.

That was one thing I did not like.

"What did you do?" I asked, my voice stern as I walked around her, putting down my phone and keys. I wanted to reward her today and probably watch a movie while eating the chocolate cake, but it looked like I had to change my plans.

When she didn't reply, I turned around and saw her

linger on the doorframe. I pursed my lips. "Remove that t-shirt and get on the bed, Kiara," I said firmly, crossing my arms.

Her legs moved, her shaking hands removing the t-shirt, allowing me to gaze at her petite body in black lace lingerie and garter belts. *Fuck.* I clenched my jaw and kept it in my pants.

This was not for my pleasure.

I stepped toward the bed and she didn't meet my eyes, her eyes facing down. I made her look at me, holding her jaw in a light grip. "Tell me exactly what you did, Kiara, and I may consider punishing you less," I said, leaning down and unclasping the hooks of her bra and removing it.

"I . . . *uh*, I used my fingers." Her cheeks flushed red, her blush creeping from her neck. "I touched myself, imagining you telling me what to do and I—"

I laid her back on the bed. Kiara cried out when I smacked her pussy through the lace and growled, "What did you imagine? I asked you to tell me everything, Kiara."

Kiara took a sharp breath, her eyes flaming with lust. "I thought of you having me in every position, making me beg and edging me to orgasm."

I raised my eyebrow, my eyes twinkling with desire as I licked my lips and leaned down. My hand wrapped around her throat, a breathy gasp escaping her lips when mine brushed her ear. "I would have done exactly that and more, but unfortunately someone broke one rule." I pulled away, watching her bite her bottom lip and continued, "You could have called me, and I would have made you come, but you didn't. I even bought a chocolate cake for you, Kiara."

Her eyes widened, and a small pout covered her lips. "Can't we do this after eating the cake? *Please?*"

I chuckled, shaking my head, "Not before I punish my bad girl."

Trailing my hand down, I found her lacy thong soaking in her juices. My fingers massaged her sex, soft hums escaping her lips. The scent of her feminine arousal was in the air, musky and tangy as Kiara licked her lips, spreading her legs wider.

I glared at her, clenching my jaw, and turned her around, smacking her ass before I took her wrists in my hand. "Don't try to seduce me, Bella. You are not getting out of this without getting punished," I chided and took the small nylon rope which was thick and sturdy but felt comfortable on her skin without bruising her. "Keep your hands over your back."

I knew exactly what to do with my naughty vixen.

Taking the rope, I tied it around her wrists and made sure that it wasn't too tight or too loose. I asked her after each loop of the rope if she was alright, because she had her therapy session today and I didn't want to do anything too drastic and hurt her emotionally.

My eyes averted to the thong which was snugly placed between her ass and the garter belts, which were fastened over the thin garment. Hooking my finger on the belt, I purred, "Did you do this for me, Bella?"

She nodded, looking over her shoulder, her eyes hazy. "Yes, Ethan."

I noticed she was already going down into her subspace as she sighed softly when I snapped the garter on her ass. After retrieving the toys from the chest, I walked back to the bed and put them beside her legs.

Kiara moaned instantly when I moved the thong away and slipped a finger inside her. Her velvety walls clenched my finger helplessly when I slowly moved it in and out, her legs squirming as a wet gush of liquid coated it. Removing my finger, I inserted a remote-control vibrator inside her with a tapered curve end which settled on her clitoris making her groan. It would pleasure both her sensitive spot and pleasure nub at the same time as I made sure it was secure. She let out a breathy gasp, jutting out her hips at me.

Taking another coil of the rope, I tied her ankles together, looping it perfectly around her taut skin and tying a knot before moving onto her thighs. I was proud of my work when her thighs and ankles were bound together. I knew she wouldn't get out of them, but I made it comfortable enough for her.

"How are you feeling, Bella?" I asked, turning a notch on the vibrator snug inside her.

I held her face and passed two loops around her neck, a long moan slipping past her lips. "Like I-I have been tied up."

I smiled at her and kissed her cheek before tying the knot behind her neck and attached the bit of rope over her tied hands, asking her if it was too tight or not and if she was comfortable.

When she nodded, I opened her palm and placed a black cloth on her fist and said, "Drop this cloth when you want to say black, alright?" I asked and made sure she was clenching it in her hands.

She nodded obediently. "But why the cloth?"

"Because it's a safe gesture. You won't be able to use your voice because I am using a gag." I said, and a gasp left her lips, her body trembling with need. Seeing her read her erotic stories, I figured out there was much she wanted to try but didn't have guts to say it to my face. I was here to oblige and make her fantasies come true.

I placed a red ball gag over her mouth and wrapped it over her hair when she bit into it. I placed her body on the edge of the bed in such a way that her legs were facing the headboard. Holding another bit of rope in my hand, I twisted it in half and looped it over her tied arms and ankles. A muffled hum released from her throat, her body writhing when I tied her in a hogtie position, effectively binding her arms and ankles together. I checked again to make sure she was comfortable and put a pillow underneath her breasts.

"I know you couldn't wait for me to touch yourself and relieve yourself of an orgasm. But as I am such a nice boyfriend at the moment, I decided to let you orgasm for however long you want," I said and stood up, walking to the edge of the bed. Her eyes were wild with lust when I leaned down and kissed her forehead. "This is your punishment. I am not going to stop the vibrator until you learn your lesson."

Standing tall, I checked my watch and cocked my head to the side, "I think two hours would suffice, right?"

She tried to snap back, her eyes wide, but her voice was muffled due to the gag. Placing the blindfold over her eyes, I turned off the lights of the room, a small smile on my lips.

22. YOU LOOK LIKE HEAVEN

KIARA

I didn't know how long it had been since Ethan left me like that, but it felt like it had been hours. He had turned on the vibrator which was pressed tightly against my throbbing clitoris and the worst part was that I couldn't orgasm. I knew I was soaking wet, but he had made sure I was on the edge the whole time. I tried to move my hips or rub my legs for some friction so I could come and end this torture, but I couldn't. I clenched the cloth in my hand.

Is he going to make me suffer like this and keep me on edge for two hours?

My muffled moans of frustration echoed in the room, my hands of no use. I bit down the rubber ball in my mouth and tried to hear anything other than the cruel vibrations swirling inside and over my most intimate part. *Nothing.* Sometimes I would feel the vibration of the vibrator inside me increase and I would buck for an orgasm, but it would die down as fast as it had started.

I was sexually pissed off at Ethan, but then again, I couldn't blame him. I did fuck myself with my fingers and came when all he had wanted from me was to orgasm after his permission. He didn't have any strict rules of what to wear or not, like some dominants I had read about in books and blogs. Ethan wasn't harsh or cruel with his sadistic methods and I knew that because I had felt it. He had explained to me that what he liked was light bondage, nothing extreme like I was reading.

I wanted to push his buttons and see what would happen, but I did not expect him to tie me up and edge me to orgasm for hours. The rope around my body was digging softly into my skin but not hurting me. It was a soft pressure, and I relished it, clenching the cloth in my fist, my hums surrounding me.

I wondered if he was in the room, sitting on a chair and silently watching me as I squirmed helplessly to relieve the burn in my nether region. I wanted to know how I looked in front of him.

Did the ropes around my bound body excite him? Was he hard? Could he sense my feminine musky scent in the room?

I shivered.

"*Mmhmm!*" I groaned when the buzzing inside my pussy increased a notch and my body froze, ready for the orgasm that was building inside me since he had tied my hands. With a soft buzz, they both slowed down to level one, making me sob through the gag. I tried twisting my hands to get rid of the knot and rub myself, but, of course, I couldn't do that. The ropes were too tight and if I lowered my hands down, my neck would come up because of the collared rope around it.

I jerked when I felt warm fingers trailing over my calves, my skin tightening. I helplessly told Ethan to let me out of the misery even if I hadn't dropped the cloth. Somehow, I knew this was not my limit. I was just sexually frustrated. *Badly.*

"Tsk, tsk, tsk, Kiara. You look like you're about to cry." I heard him mock me and felt his dominating presence near me as he leaned down and removed the blindfold.

My eyes blinked at the sudden light as I glared at him through my glassy eyes. I stilled when he moved a dial on the remote, my brows furrowing to let me come this time. Ethan moved the strands which were falling in my face, his index finger trailing over my cheeks. I suppressed a shudder. It was a wonder how much he aroused me by just touching me.

He stood up, and I saw how hard he was. His stiffened shaft pressing against the confines of his pants. Ethan removed his shirt while I watched, my eyes taking in his marvelous muscles. I hummed in appreciation when his fingers unzipped his pants. My mouth watered at the sight of his veiny dick, already leaking with a bead of pre-cum.

I sighed when he removed the gag and looked at me before pushing himself inside my mouth. I moaned when his exotic male scent exploded in my mouth. The girth of his length was bigger than the ball gag as I hollowed my cheeks to fit him in. I swirled my tongue around the bulbous head and flicked his underside, just how he liked as he let out a breathy moan.

My body shivered with pleasure when he increased the dial of the vibrator and I started sucking him off, relaxing my throat and taking him deeper. Ethan's groans of pleasure encouraged me and turned me on all the same when he wrapped his hand around my hair, fucking my mouth slow and deep.

I was at the brink of orgasm when I deep-throated him. Ethan forced me to take all of him when he swelled and jerked inside me with a long groan of my name. There was nothing like hearing a grown man moan your name when he came. A second later, a warm spurt of his seed made its way down my throat, making me greedily swallow. Some of it slid down my neck when he pulled away and I licked my lips, staring up at him through my lashes.

Sighing, he bent down and rubbed his thumb over my lips, my eyes meeting his piercing blue and green. "Did you learn from your punishment?" he asked, his voice soft but firm.

Gulping nervously, I nodded, "Yes, I did."

Now, please fuck me to oblivion and back.

Ethan kissed my lips, his large hands cupping my face. He tucked my hair behind my ears, his eyes widening when he pulled away. "*Kiara* . . . why are you so hot?"

"*Uh* . . . I ask that to mirror every day." I resisted a smirk, but now that he mentioned, I was shivering.

His eyes flashed, and he quickly stood up, untying the ropes from my ankles and hands. Ethan gently laid me down on the soft sheets. "What happened?" I asked, frowning when he removed the ropes from my thighs, along with the vibrator.

I closed my eyes when Ethan leaned over me and checked my forehead. "Are you feeling feverish? You're shivering, Kia, and you didn't tell me you were sick!" he exclaimed, his forehead creasing.

I was feeling so loopy that I grinned and lazily poked his nose. "If you remember correctly, you had gagged my mouth and your cock inside me a moment later. How would I have possibly said that?" I asked innocently, pouting at him.

Holding my head down, he checked my pulse as if I was dying, but I giggled, feeling his warm touch on my neck. *God, why did his touch affect me so much?* He was my personal heater. *Very* useful during the winter.

"*Ethan*, no!" I whined when he tried to tuck me into bed, asking me if I wanted to change into something comfortable. I held the belt loops of his pants and forced him down on me.

I whispered, staring into his blue-green eyes, "Please fuck me."

Ethan gave my body a once over and I spread my legs a bit more, biting my bottom lip when he met my eyes.

He swallowed a lump in his throat. "You need to rest right now."

"I am as healthy as a horse."

I sneezed.

"*Right* . . ." he drawled and stood up, "Stay here. I will check if I have any cold medicine." He walked out of the door before I could stop him.

I checked my forehead and even though my skin was warm, I didn't feel feverish. It was just one sneeze, and he was being too overprotective. I wanted him to stay here and have sex with me until I passed out, not look for cold medicine.

I stood up and before I could walk in the kitchen, Ethan glared at me, walking in the room with a tablet and a glass of water. "Why the fuck are you standing? You are ill right now, and I don't want you to feel—"

Chuckling, I took the tablet and glass from him, putting it on the nightstand and promising him I would take it if I sneezed again.

I held his hand and dragged him to the bed, making him sit down on the edge. I kneeled in front of him and removed his pants, "Now, *fuck me.*"

His eyes clouded as he lifted me on his lap, his hands holding my waist making me suppress a shiver. "As much as I would love to fuck you to sleep, I can't do that because you are not in good—"

Cupping his face, I slammed my lips on his, kissing him and rubbing myself on him like the sex-starved woman I was. Gasping, I pulled away and asked, "Do you want to do this or not? I am not sick, E. That was just one sneeze."

Ethan was horny, judging by the erection that was poking on my inner thigh, but I didn't want to force myself on him. If he said no, I would go to the washroom, take a shower and go to sleep cuddling him. If he said yes . . . *well.*

He tucked my hair away and tightened his hand on my waist, "Are you sure? You are not feeling sick?"

I ground on him, holding his shoulders. He let out a guttural growl that had me feeling wild. The sound of him receiving pleasure was one of the most erotic sounds ever. I could come listening to him.

"Does this feel sick to you?" I asked, biting my lip.

Ethan's eyes flared with lust. The blue was like a storming sea and the green was of the dark forest as his pupils dilated. A small yelp escaped my lips when he turned me around, holding my throat and my waist.

He growled, his warm breath on my ear, "Look in the mirror."

I did and bit my cheek when I saw our reflection. My legs were splayed over his as he spread them wider, his hand lingering on my inner thigh, so close to my wet cavern as I moaned, gripping his muscular thighs.

"Look how wet you are," I gasped when he grabbed my hair and made me look. "I am going to fuck you exactly like *this*," he whispered, and my pussy clenched at his words.

Feeling him shift underneath me made me tense as his hand on my throat loosened. His thumb gently circled over my skin and made me quiver with want. When I looked at him in the mirror, I bit my lip at his glazed expression of desire, passion, and intensity as if he couldn't get enough of me.

"Feel how hard you make me, Kiara," he muttered, licking my neck. I sighed, our musky scent hovering in the air. His voice dropped to a smoky whisper, making my toes curl when he added, "You make me so hard it hurts, Bella. I can't even think straight when it comes to you."

"*Please*," my voice a small whimper as I saw in my reflection how dizzy I was with lust, my face flushed. "Ethan, I need you right now."

Ethan raised his head and held my waist, lifting me and lowering me on him. "Watch me take you, Bella. Look in the mirror and see how beautiful we look together . . . *as one*."

As I saw myself enveloping him in one slow thrust, my walls aching and pulsing at his girth, I lost all the control I had. We both groaned at the feeling and the sight. It was beautiful and erotic. Especially Ethan. He was naked and holding me, a small scrunch in his dark eyebrows and a slight blush on his cheeks when he was inside me. His pupils dilated as he watched us. His clenched jaw made him look much sharper when he licked his full lips.

My God. He is art.

"Wait," I breathed out before he could raise me and thrust inside me. "Let me have a look."

"Look?"

"I want to remember this so I can paint us."

He chuckled, and a small rumble of vibration rolled down my spine to my core. I clenched him, biting my lip. As much as I liked how joined we were, my main focus was Ethan and how he looked in that moment. I wanted to run my hand through his dark locks and draw them. His eyes were two diamonds of galaxies that I could never forget and never wished to. They were different, unique, and made my heart and pussy pulse faster. Especially when he looked at me like that. As if I was worth looking at. As if I was everything he had wished for.

It made me cry, and I blinked when my eyes became blurry. Ethan noticed the tear and wiped it, making me look at him. His lips were soft when they brushed against mine.

He kissed me, his tongue licking my bottom lip, and I opened up for him, moving back and forth. His growl was the fuel to my lust as I pulled away only to move up and sink on him.

"*Oh, fuck*," Ethan groaned, my eyes on his face when I rode him. "You look like heaven, Bella."

His words and his intense gaze did nothing but turn me on. Our groans echoed in the room, the scent of our arousal and sex hovering over us in a heavy blanket. Ethan's hands were on my breasts, rolling my nipples and flicking the clitoris as I rode myself on him. He took the lead when my head fell back on his shoulder, my eyes closing and my mouth panting and heaving with breathy moans each time he slammed inside me from behind.

His hold tightened on my waist when our breathing increased. I was about to say something to him when I felt an itch on my nose and I sneezed.

Loudly.

We both paused for completely different reasons. My eyes widened with embarrassment, but then I felt the warm sensation under me, and I looked in the mirror. Ethan's face was clenched and surprised as he came, holding me close.

"Did you . . . did you just orgasm?"

His face reddened. "Sorry, your sneeze took me off guard . . ." Ethan lowered his hand on my clit, and I jumped when I felt my abdomen clenching. "You clenched me too hard when you sneezed."

I raised my eyebrows at him when he lazily rubbed me. "I didn't know that. How about now?" I fake coughed, and he froze, groaning when I stopped and he glared at me.

"Don't do that, Bella," his eyes lowered to my pussy, rubbing the swollen nub faster. I came when white-fiery lust burned in my lids, moaning his name and trembling in his arms.

When I tried to avert my eyes from the mirror, he made

me look at the mirror as he held my hair and whispered, "No, watch yourself cum, Kiara. See how fucking beautiful you look right now."

My hands tightened on his hands and I was so in a haze that I didn't realize I was scratching my nails on his fore-arms. Gulping some air, I looked down on his arms and noticed the redness of what my nails had done against his tan skin and whispered, "I am sorry. I didn't mean to."

That looked like it hurt.

Ethan kissed my neck and rubbed my stomach and breasts in a way that I was ready for round two. "Don't be. I will wear your marks proudly," he smirked and licked the hickey on my neck.

I blushed and hugged him, turning around when he pulled himself out of me. "Thank you," I whispered in the crook of his neck and relished in his scent, woodsy and spicy.

He rubbed my back and kissed my hair, pulling me closer, "Why are you thanking me, Bella?"

I grinned. "For taking care of me when I am sick."

His eyes sparkled, and he looked fucking beautiful in post-coital bliss as he lowered me down on the bed, snuggling beside me. "Of course, I would, Kiara. I am your personal doctor bitch."

A snort escaped my lips as I chuckled, hiding my face in his chest, and trailed my hand over his abs. "Yes, you are my personal bitch."

Ethan grinned, kissing me on the lips. "Now, as your personal doctor bitch, I would recommend you go to sleep. Right now. You need to rest."

I smiled, kissing him right above his heart. "Okay, mother hen."

ETHAN HAD to wake me up early as he had a match along with Liam. I had asked to go with him and he had agreed, warning me that there would be reporters and paparazzi outside the main pool. Nonetheless, I was there to cheer him on when he won the breaststroke match against his opponents, scoring first. He had improved since the school days. There were a lot of fans wanting to take a picture with him when he changed into a black shirt and pants, his hair damp from the shower.

"Do you like kimchi?" He asked, serving me some more with his chopsticks.

I nodded, flashing him a small smile.

We were at one of his favorite restaurants, sitting on the upper level for lunch with his teammates and their girlfriends or wives. One of them was already pregnant and Ethan had squeezed my hand while introducing me to her. I ate my food, watching how happy all of them were, joking and drinking saké. Soda for me.

"Ethan, is that you?"

I peered up to see a stunning dark-skinned woman, her curvaceous body wrapped in a silky blue dress that hugged her wide hips, ending on her knees. I swallowed the lump in my throat when she smiled at him, her skin glowing, her sharp features contrasting against her warm smile. She was gorgeous.

Ethan stood up, his chair creaking. "Aretta, it's been a while," he said with a small smile and to my surprise embraced her in a hug.

I looked away, sipping some water, knowing that my appetite had vanished. I clenched my hands in a fist on my lap, not liking this feeling of being jealous of someone. He just hugged her. Of course, it didn't mean anything. It wasn't like I had the right to be jealous, anyway.

"How have you been?" Liam asked cheerfully.

Oh great. Even he knew her.

"This is Kiara, my girlfriend," Ethan introduced me to her, his hand squeezing my shoulder as warm flutters ignited in my belly.

We had decided that it was better to let our friends and family know that we are boyfriend and girlfriend rather than drop the bomb that I was pregnant. So, I was used to it by now, but he had never said it out loud, so it felt new to me. Me, Kiara Sharma, *the* girlfriend of Ethan Kane.

"Hello," I greeted her with a smile, unsure how to react as I had never been this jealous of someone.

Aretta was looking at Ethan, a small frown etched between her brows, while Ethan gazed down at me with a warm smile.

"Girlfriend?" she asked in disbelief, her date checking the time on his watch, his hand planted firmly on her hip, trying to intimidate Ethan who had an inch over him.

Ethan gave her a look that made her eyes avert to me. *"Yes.* Kiara has been my best friend ever since I remember. We are dating," he said with a firm voice.

I held his hand on my shoulder when she raked her dark brown eyes over me, clearly judging me. I was wearing high-waisted jeans and a white flimsy blouse with a sweetheart neckline and lace details, but she made me look like I was no way equal to the man standing beside me.

"It's nice meeting you, Aretta," I said sincerely, wanting to know her better if she was his friend.

She looked at our hands and smiled at me. "You too, Kiara." Turning to Ethan, she said, "It was nice seeing you here, Ethan. And Liam. I will be leaving. Take care of yourself."

Aretta left, holding her clutch tightly. Ethan sat beside me, and the conversations started as before with little tension hovering between me and Ethan. I tried to pretend that seeing Aretta didn't affect me, but Ethan knew it had. He kept our talk to minimal until we were alone in his car as he drove.

"You can ask me about her, Kiara," he said when the silence between us grew.

Pursing my lips, I turned to him, watching the night lights dance across his handsome face. "I don't know what to ask. Is she your ex-girlfriend? She looked torn when you mentioned I am your girlfriend."

His knuckles turned white when his grip on the wheel tightened. "No, not my ex-girlfriend. I used to sleep with her."

"*Oh.*"

Warmth surged in my body when Ethan entwined our hands on my lap. "I ended it before the gala because she had feelings for me. I couldn't give her what she wanted."

"But she's beautiful."

He smiled, "She is, but not more than you."

Heat flooded my cheeks, making me look away from his different colored eyes.

"Aretta enjoyed being controlled in the bed and as you already know my kinks, we both agreed to sleep with each other. But it was a mutual decision when we ended things, because she knew she would get hurt if she kept wanting more from me."

Ethan explained, his thumb making patterns on my knuckles. I lifted our adjoined hands and pressed a soft kiss on his knuckles. "You didn't have to tell me anything, E, I trust you."

"I know, but if you are going to have my baby, I wanted to make sure nothing makes you doubt me regarding my past."

"I don't doubt you, Ethan." I cleared my throat and said, "But can I ask you a question?"

"Of course, Bella."

"The things you did . . . I mean, with Aretta were the same—"

"No. I know what you're trying to ask, but no, Kiara." He squeezed my hand, "She liked more pain while I liked to delve in light bondage and BDSM. I find myself suited well with your needs and limits than I have ever been with anyone else. Can I ask why did you ask me that question?"

"I wanted to know if I was enough to please you."

The car came to a screeching halt, and my breath hitched in my throat.

Ethan's hands held my face, his piercing eyes pinned on me. "You are more than enough, Bella. I am very lucky to have you and I wish I could show you just how much in the backseat, but we will have to wait till we get back home."

My eyes widened when he planted a firm kiss on my lips before leaning back and starting the car, driving us back home. His words echoed in my mind, my heart beating faster.

More than enough, Bella. Very lucky to have you.

I wished I had enough courage to confess the same, but decided I would rather show it through my body.

23. HOW'S THE VIEW?

ETHAN

It was, dare I say, funny to watch Kiara squirm the entire ride to my mothers' house. She kept wriggling in the seat, biting her lips, sighing and clutching my hand. I had to bite my lip from chuckling when she glared at me, gripping my hand.

I was sure that she wanted to bite my head off.

I had woken her up with my tongue lapping over her wet cavern, groaning at her delicious feminine taste. But I wanted to tease her to the edge, so when she cried out that she would do anything to make her come, my mind went to the gutter. Today was Eveline's birthday, and we were driving to my moms' house. I had wrapped Kiara as my own personal gift.

After showering, I had taken care of patting her body dry with a towel and applied lotion all over her body without making any sex jokes or innuendos. It was a turn on for both of us to let me touch her in such an intimate way. It also meant that she had gone halfway into her subspace, and it made my ego boost that her body and mind reacted in such a way just by my mere touch and how much she trusted me.

I let her stand in front of the mirror, the same one we had sex in front of, and started wrapping a black-colored nylon rope around her petite body. With her arms raised and eyes closed, I had passed the rope under her aching breasts, making sure it was tight enough to make her aware of the rope on her skin and comfortable enough that she could move around easily.

Kiara had squirmed when I twined the rope over her hips, thighs, and the sides of her slick folds, but she let me without using any safe words. It was a *Hishi Karada* rope dress, and she looked stunning in it. She had complained that it was too much for her and she would curse me in front of my mothers if I teased her too much.

I had simply grinned at her and told her to ditch the bra. She wore a velvet wrap dress that hid the minor bumps and coils of the rope underneath. Every step she took made the rope tighten around her and I relished in the small sighs she made.

My mothers were excited to see us when they opened the door, hugging and kissing us on the cheeks. Everything was decorated in baby pink, blue, green, and yellow. Keeping the gifts, I walked upstairs to find my little bean who was supposed to be combing her hair all by herself.

"Hey, Evey," I grinned, looking in the mirror and crouched down beside her.

She hugged me, burying her face in my neck as I lifted her and rubbed her back. We talked for a while, sitting down on her twin-size bed. She was getting taller and reached my hips while her blonde hair was getting straighter and brushing her shoulders. Eveline asked me to braid her hair when Kiara knocked on the door and asked if she could join us.

"I brought some cupcakes for the birthday girl," she said excitedly and watched Eveline blush, her bubbly cheeks getting red when she saw Kiara grinning at her.

I leaned back on my hands and watched my little sister talk with my girlfriend. They talked about hair, nails, and dresses. I loved how comfortable they both were around each other, and I almost didn't hate the part when Eveline talked about her boy crush. *Almost.*

"Did you just say *boy?*" I asked, straightening up. They both turned toward me and Kiara gave me a let-her-be-it's-her-birthday look.

But I ignored that look and being a good brother, I asked her who was her crush.

"His name is Mark, and he shares his lunch with me," she chirped and held my face in her small hands, "He even has blue eyes like you, Ethan!"

"If he reminds you of me, then he should be considered your brother, sweetheart," I explained, but Kiara took her away from me, spoiling my sister with cupcakes and talking about boys.

Man, she grew up too fast.

WE HAD lunch with Eveline's friends, including Mark, who I couldn't stop glaring at until Kia pinched my butt. The cake was of Thor, her favorite superhero, and it was a fun time hanging out with kids except for the amount of noise and screaming or the flirtatious smiles of cougars.

The lunch went much better as I kept teasing Kiara when she served slices of pizzas to kids. She gave me the stinkiest glare she could muster and told me to piss off and help while I tried keeping my hands to myself. She looked hot when she was angry.

It was dinnertime and Eveline's nanny, Carol, had arrived with her twin daughters much to my dismay. Her daughters were seniors in college who sometimes babysat Eveline if both my moms had the same shift and I had to work. It was good because she was a great nanny and loved taking care of Eveline.

The bad part was that I had slept with her in my second year of college when we both were home. I was so not proud of myself at that moment.

"Why does Eve's nanny and her daughters keep glaring at me?" Kiara asked, taking out the plates and turning to me. "Do I have something on my face?"

Like a charmer, I pecked her cheek. "Why, *yes*, of course. It's called being beautiful, Bella." I leaned in to kiss her, but she stopped me, her brows furrowing.

"What's wrong?" she asked, crossing her arms.

Uh oh.

I sighed, running a hand over my face, "I may or may not have slept with her."

"*What?*"

"And the twins," I mumbled.

Kiara didn't say anything, so when I looked at her, she seemed speechless. Her eyes were wide with disbelief. "Together?"

"What?" I exclaimed, "Of course, not!" I remembered something, "Well, maybe one time with the twins, but . . . *no*, not really."

"*Hai Bhagwan,*" she said something in Gujarati and I only caught something like 'my God.'

I held her arm and raised her chin to make her look at me. "Does it matter that I have slept with so many women?"

Kiara shook her head, "Of course not, E. That was your past and it was your choice. I don't care if you wanted to wait until marriage or take part in orgies. You are an adult and you made choices that helped you cope."

She tipped on her toes and gave me a brief kiss on my lips. A wild and sexy look clouded her brown eyes as she whispered, "Because at the end of the night you are warming my bed and body."

My eyes widened when she squeezed my butt before letting go. Winking at me, she left the kitchen and took the plates with her to the dining room. I looked down and realized I was getting turned on by Kiara's words as I readjusted myself.

Holy shit, that was hot.

There were eight chairs placed around the dining table, three on either side and two at the center. My mothers sat across each other while Carol and her daughters sat across from me. Kiara was on my left and Eveline was on my right. The sexual tension around the table was increasing tremendously until my mom started talking about me and Kiara.

Eveline asked small questions about us throughout the meal, wondering how gorgeous our babies would look together. I had to pat Kiara's shoulder when she coughed on water, her face red while I tried to concentrate on the piece of broccoli. But now I was wondering about it too.

Would they have my different colored eyes or chocolaty brown like Kiara's? Would they have dimples? Would they have dark onyx hair like mine or wavy brown like Kia's?

I was chewing my food when I felt something weird on my ankles. Swallowing the food content, I realized it was Carol giving me a flirtatious smile and trailing her toe over my leg. A second later, Kiara's hand landed on my thigh, laughing about the time when I went to India with her together and giving a stink eye to Carol in a flicker of a moment.

Biting off my smirk, I ate my food, watching my woman take the lead as she teased me, massaging my thigh and trailing her hand up. I held my breath when she wrapped her hand around my crotch, giving me a slow squeeze. I twitched underneath the ministrations of her palm.

I grinned at what my mother said and leaned over to whisper in Kiara's ear, "I am going to spank your ass red when we get alone, Bella. Unless you stop teasing me this instant."

Her eyes twinkled when she gave me a hard squeeze underneath the table and replied, "Make me, Ethan."

Holding her hand, which was stroking me, I squeezed it and could not wait to get her alone after dinner. She was asking for it, and her wish was my command.

They further talked about Kiara's book, and my mothers were surprised when they received a signed hardcover from her. Not to mention, she had brought more books for each of them and children's books for Evey.

Smiling at my parents, I finished my dinner, helping them put the dishes in the dishwasher. I let them chat with Carol and the daughters while I held Kiara's arm and took her upstairs to Evey's room as mine was filled with birthday presents and decorations.

"Not your sister's room, Ethan," she whispered when I locked the door behind me, her eyes widening.

I gave it a thought. "We won't fit in a bathroom and it will be too risky."

I nodded toward the bed, removing my belt and unzipping my pants, "Face down, ass up."

"Say please."

I stared at her, raising my brow.

She sighed. "I was joking, E."

Kiara propped herself on her elbows on the small bed and bent down. "How's the view?"

"Fucking marvelous," I whispered, standing behind her. I admired her submission and how much she trusted me to take care of her.

I untied the dress and raised it to her back so I could gaze at her perfect round ass pushing toward me. When I touched her lower back, her hips moved involuntarily asking for more. I found the remote of the small television and turned it on because I didn't want my parents or sister to hear us going at it. Increasing the volume, I stepped back a little and held her hair.

"Are you ready?" I asked, tugging them back, her back arching deliciously.

She gasped, "*Please*, Ethan."

My hand stung as it came down on her ass, her entire body moving with a jerk, but I held her, striking her in alternate smacks, giving her little time to breathe. Her soft cries and the sound of my hand striking against her ass surrounded us. Each time my hand retreated, she pushed her hips back asking for more.

Letting go of her hair, I squeezed and massaged her red burning skin with my palm. I leaned down and kissed her soft, sore skin, eliciting a moan from her.

"*Ethan!*" she cried out, looking over her shoulder. "You did not just bite my ass."

I smirked and stood up to my full height, "Sure did, Bella."

Her tongue seeped out, wetting her pink lips when I pulled myself out of the confines of my pants, positioning myself over her heated core. My eyes flickered to her and waited for her permission. She looked down, pushing herself back slowly, taking the red bulbous head inside her as we both groaned in unison.

Holding her waist, I sunk myself inside her in one slow thrust, clenching my jaw. Her walls clamped around me in such a way I thought I would come inside her without even trying. Taking a deep breath, I reared back and slammed inside her.

"Oh, *shit*." Kiara gasped, "Harder, Ethan."

My eyes flared with lust, and I gave her what she craved. Driving myself in and out of her, each time bumping against the rough scrap of her g-spot as her hips moved back toward me. I leaned over her, holding the ropes and knots of the *Hishi Karada* dress. I fondled her breasts when my hips rolled and thrust inside her, eliciting foreign carnal sounds.

My hand trailed down to roll her clitoris as she came, groaning my name and wringing the sheets in her fists. Pulling back, I increased my pace, elongating her orgasm, and spanking her ass as her cries of pleasure grew louder.

"Come for me, Kiara," I growled, our skin slapping against each other and her walls clenching me each time the smack reverberated through her skin to core.

Kiara whimpered, "I-I can't. I am too sensitive." But her hips moved back each time I reared back.

Squeezing her ass, I muttered, "Come on, Bella. Give me one more orgasm."

I moved slowly because I did not want to orgasm until she came. As my thrusts got deeper and slower, rocking her body against me, her moans increased. Even the small bed thumped against the wall with each thrust.

"Ethan."

I swelled inside her and gave a small jerk to her body as she clenched me, her walls convulsing when she orgasmed. Coming inside her, I grunted and gave a few sloppy thrusts and held her waist when her legs trembled from the aftershocks.

Licking my lips, I smacked her butt, sinking on my knees and laving my tongue over her soaked pussy. "Oh, fuck, fuck, fuck!" she grumbled when I squeezed her ass and ate her out, driving another orgasm from her. Her scent intoxicated me when she came again, crying out my name and begging me to stop.

Finally, accomplished with her dizzy about-to-pass-out state, I licked her dry and stood up. Gently holding her in my arms, I laid her down on the bed and tucked the strands away from her face as she gazed at me from her half-lidded eyes.

"You look so fucking beautiful in post-coital bliss," I murmured, pecking her lips, and squeezed her hand. "Makes me hard just looking at you."

Kiara chuckled, her voice husky. "You and your stamina. Do you ever stop talking dirty, Ethan?"

My eyes roved over her half-covered body. I shook my head, "Not when it comes to you." I noticed the small shivering in her body and asked if she wanted me to remove the *Karada* rope dress.

"As much as I like it . . . not right now, I feel like I am going to faint," she murmured and for a second, I got worried, so I removed it from her body. Where the rope was tight and looped in knots, her skin had small prints, and I felt bad that I couldn't shower her and tuck her in. But Kiara stood up after a while telling me she was fine, orgasming three times in ten minutes had made her dizzy.

I fixed the bed, knowing I had to put the sheets in the washing machine. She went to the washroom to clean herself up. I had messed up her hair, dress, and a bit of makeup. I couldn't help but smirk proudly.

PART FOUR

"I want a soccer team."

24. A SURPRISE

KIARA

I was feeling nauseated for about a week, and Ethan was convinced that I had eaten too much cake at his sister's birthday. But you don't puke, have migraines and tender breasts if it's food poisoning. *Yes, maybe it is food poisoning.* I was throwing up as soon as I woke up and didn't let Ethan massage my aching breasts with coconut oil which was saying a lot.

But, deep down, I *knew* it was something else.

"Do you want me to drop you off?"

I snapped back to reality when I heard Ethan's deep voice when he entered the kitchen. He was wearing a soaking grey t-shirt and sweatpants, a towel around his neck.

I ate my cereal and shook my head. "It's fine. I need to contact the editor and see that apartment I was talking about." A few days ago, a landlord contacted me asking me about the apartment I had seen after the breakup with Jake. Ethan would come with me if I wanted, but he was going to talk with his agent and Mr. Stone.

So, the reason for my sickness could be stress-related because of my second book and the auction.

Licking my lips, I watched his muscles bulge and clench when he gulped water from the water bottle and my pussy twitched for some attention. *Not now*. I scolded my inner hoe, shamelessly staring at him like I always did when he came back from the gym. Something about getting dirty with him as soon as he came back from working out and lifting weights turned me on.

"Done eye-pussying me, Bella?" Ethan asked, his voice low and smoky as he sat across from me.

I rolled my eyes. "Will you ever stop saying that word? And to answer your question, no, never." I stood up from the stool and pecked his lips, keeping the bowl in the sink.

"Then why don't you move to my room? I have a bigger bed." Ethan said, grabbing my hand and pulling me between his legs.

"You will distract me from my work."

He raised an eyebrow, "Me? Distracting? Have you seen yourself?" His eyes averted to the thin tank top I slept in last night. A soft moan slipped past my lips when his hands cupped my breasts, tweaking the pebbled nipples. "It's hard for me to walk around you without *bending* you over the nearest surface and drive myself inside you whenever I lay my eyes on you."

My fingers threaded through his hair when he looked at me with pure hunger in his eyes, his hand trailing over my throat, making me gasp when he whispered, "You are that fucking distracting, Bella." His hard-on poked over my thigh when he used his knee to spread my legs, pushing me into the island and grinding himself on my core.

My back arched and tightening my fingers over the back of his neck, I pulled him down on top of me and kissed him. I wrapped my legs around his torso, removing his t-shirt and kissing him on the crook of his neck, his stubble scratching against my skin, turning me on. His musky woodsy scent intoxicated me when my nails raked across his back. I licked the hickey I had made on his neck, my lips trailing down. Lower.

"*Kiara*," Ethan groaned, yanking my hair back to stop me and devour me with his hungry mouth. He swallowed my moans when he ground against my heated sex, my panties dampening at the heat of his muscular body pressing against me.

We both pulled away when the ringtone of my phone blared in the kitchen.

"Sorry, I have to take that." I pulled down my tank top and tugged my cat pajamas to my waist which Ethan had successfully lowered to my knees.

I swear this man has sex magic when he is horny and wants clothes to disappear.

After the call with my agent, I told Ethan about the change in my plans and ignored his frown when he pulled himself away, "Not even a quickie?"

I gave him a look. "Ethan, we don't have 'quickies'. We have scenes which end up with me being sleepy or straight up blacking out." He scowled, crossing his arms as if it was his fault, which it was. "I meant that in a good way . . . or that sounded much better in my head."

Tipping on my toes, I pecked his lips, "We need to talk tonight."

He followed me to the room. "About what?"

I stuttered. "I-it's a surprise."

He narrowed his eyes at me, stripping out of his clothes. "Fine, I will bring a small surprise for you too. But don't eat cake for dinner like last night. Wait up for me or no more cakes for you."

I would have laughed at a grown naked man telling me all that while we were showering together, but I grinned at him. "You are such a dad."

THE APARTMENT WAS WAY TOO small for me, so I thanked the sweet old landlord before going to the nearest drugstore and buying three pregnancy tests. I wanted to be sure before I could let Ethan know.

Back at home, I was pacing in my room and wondering if I should wait for him or do it before and then surprise him. *Fuck it.* As I closed the bathroom door behind me, I heard Ethan enter.

Oh, great.

Without waiting, I followed the instructions on each pregnancy test and kept them on the sink after washing my hands.

"Kiara, I know you're in there. Come out, I have a surprise for you!"

Swallowing the lump in my throat, I stepped out.

"Why are you looking so pale? Are you alright?" Ethan asked, his hand checking my forehead, which made me grin.

"It's nothing, what's the surprise?"

"Khalid and I talked to Mr. Stone, and he agreed to the auction as soon as I told him about you and that you are Damini Sharma's daughter." He grinned as he explained that Mr. Stone would help set up the auction and Khalid would help with the media and security. While we had to bring her paintings. All the money raised in the auction would go to different children charities all over the world.

"I am so proud of you!" I grinned and hugged him, his soft laugh filling my ears when he hugged me tightly.

The beep went off in the bathroom. My eyes widened when Ethan frowned, "What was that?"

I couldn't wait. "I took three pregnancy tests, Ethan."

He raised his eyebrows, "No way, I bought one for you. *Look.*" He showed me the test, and I asked him why he bought met one. He smiled sheepishly, "Because I thought you might be pregnant with all the puking. Not to mention, your breasts have gotten bigger."

"*Really?*" I asked, looking down at them. "Are you sure?"

"I might need to feel them just to be sure—" he grinned when he saw my face. "Sorry. Now check the test. I am impatient."

I clutched his hand, "Come with me."

He squeezed my palm, his eyes softening, "Of course, Bella."

Taking a deep breath, I opened the door and bit my bottom lip to keep it from trembling when we both saw the results. A sharp exhale left my lips as I checked all three of them, tears welling in my eyes. I turned to see Ethan, his hand squeezing mine tightly.

"*Kiara,*" he whispered, blinking at the tests. I let out a nervous chuckle when he picked one up and saw the plus sign, a huge grin covering his lips. "I can't believe it. Come here."

I let out a soft laugh when he hugged me, pressing me to his chest as happy tears streamed down my face. Ethan pulled away only to keep his hand on my stomach. "You're pregnant," he said, kissing my temple.

"I am pregnant," I said, my voice sounding different to my ears. "Thank you, Ethan."

He had a dreamy look on his face, his eyes crinkling when he smiled at me. "Don't thank me, Bella, we both made this baby."

Keeping the positive tests on the sink, I tipped on my toes and kissed him. Our lips met in a slow languid kiss, our tongues dancing together with soft touches, tasting each other. His arms tightened around my waist, pulling me closer as his tongue swept over my bottom lip.

"Can I make love to you?" he murmured between our kisses and joked, "Make another baby, perhaps?"

Gazing at his handsome face, I said, "In that case, I want a soccer team. Bunch of little Ethan and Kiaras running around."

I chuckled when he scooped me in his arms and laid me down on the bed to make love to me.

IT HAD BEEN a week since I realized I was pregnant. We had gone to the doctor and Ethan was with me the whole time when she did my check-up and told a sour-faced Ethan to get out. If I wasn't on the bed, I would've laughed at him.

I was six weeks in, and my breasts were getting bigger. Never thought I would like them big, but they hurt at night. Ethan promised to massage them whenever I wanted him to, but I knew he just wanted to grope my breasts. *Perv.*

"Not this one either," Ethan frowned at the crib which I had found the cutest. He held it and gave it a little shake, "It's not sturdy enough."

I sighed, "Babe, we are having a human baby. It is sturdy."

"We will look for another one. Come on, I saw one at that side." He held my hand and dragged me to another aisle of baby cribs. I awed and cooed at all the cute, tiny stuff while he made sure the crib we were going to buy would last along with the baby car seat.

I had told him to wait until my first trimester passes before we buy anything. He gave me a stern look and said that we were reserving things for the future and the store would deliver it to us once we were ready.

When he talked to another scared employee, asking for a sturdier crib, I smiled up at him. The employee scurried away to find the crib he asked for, leaving us alone. "You'd make *the* best baby daddy ever," I whispered in his ear.

He smiled down at me, his eyes taking in my small bump through the dress. "You bet I would. He or she is going to deserve the best we have to offer," he said, caressing my stomach.

"I have you, so I am not worried."

He kissed the top of my hair as we looked through different pregnancy pillows. "When should we tell our parents? Liam already knows I am hiding something because I try to be with you as much as possible."

"Anya and Katherine are the same. They know I am hiding something. We can tell our parents in a few days?"

"Sure, Bella."

25. INSATIABLE

ETHAN

"*F*uck," Kiara moaned, bracing her hands on her desk when I thrust into her from behind. Her legs trembled, and the desk bumped into the wall attached to her classroom.

My hands smoothed down to her thighs, squeezing the soft skin when I reared back and rammed inside her. "Oh, God. Ethan!"

I groaned, and she whimpered, my length caressing her velvety tight walls. The warm pressure of her weeping pussy was enough to drive me to the edge as I throbbed achingly inside her.

"Come on, Kiara!" I growled, lightly smacking her ass and yanking her hair. I gradually increased my thrusts, her breathy moans echoing in her office, her blouse ruffled, and pressed her breasts down on the cold wooden surface.

"Please, Ethan. *Oh, fuck*," she let out a sweet whimper, my thrusts aiming at her sensitive spot when her body started trembling, her orgasm teetering on the edge.

"I am right there with you, Bella," I panted, releasing her hair and holding her hips with both of my hands. Her delicious walls clenching me when she started spasming and came with a groan. I pushed deeper, grunting softly, and released my load inside her wet cavern, her body convulsing and withering when I caressed her back.

I pressed a kiss to her neck, my hand caressing the taut belly bump. "Are you okay?" I asked, pulling out of her. I took a handful of tissues from the box on her desk to clean her up, then dropped them in the dustbin.

She sighed, giving me a small hum, not opening her eyes. With a small smile, I turned her around and smoothed my hands down her waist. I kissed her neck, giving soft kisses to her pert nipples, her breasts bigger and more tender than before as I kneaded them and covered them with the cups of her bra, fixing her blouse.

"I *really* love your cock, Ethan," Kiara whispered, her amber eyes hooded.

"I am glad you love me for my cock, Bella," I teased, straightening her underwear and pulling her trousers over her legs. I buttoned them, making sure they weren't too tight for her bump. I pressed a kiss to her growing stomach and stood up to my full height.

She cupped my face, her thumb stroking my cheek lovingly. "I could easily fall in love with you, Ethan."

I smiled at her. "I already have, Kiara."

She froze, knowing my confession was out of the blue. I squeezed her waist, "*Shh*, stop thinking. Take your time, you don't have to answer right away."

Kiara relaxed, her warm eyes glinting with golden flecks. "I am halfway there, E. I took the biggest fart on the heart for you," she grinned, pressing a close-mouthed kiss on my lips.

"So did I, sweetheart. Now finish your lunch before you need to get to your class."

Her eyes dropped to my pants. She licked her lips and batted her lashes at me, "Will I get the dessert?"

A chuckle poured out of me as I pulled out a chair for her, "You are insatiable."

She truly was. She was eight weeks pregnant and ever since we found out about it, we had been having sex like wild animals and our libido had increased ten folds. We had planned for a small lunch date in her office during the lunch hours, but as soon as I opened the door to her office to greet her, she had pounced on me, begging me to fuck her like a wanton woman.

I hadn't complained one bit, wanting to satisfy all her needs.

I loved and cherished her, what was there to complain about?

"ARE you sure you can finish all that?" I asked, watching her eat chicken like a starved woman.

"Babe, I am growing a child inside me. Do you think that's easy?" she licked her lips, eyeing my plate, "Are you sure you will finish it?"

Shaking my head, I pushed my plate toward her and took a sip of my beer, changing the channel on the television. We had taken a warm shower together, making her come three times in a row after she sucked me off. We ordered some fried chicken and cuddled on the couch.

I caressed her stomach, already excited to talk to the tiny human being growing inside her and read them stories. We didn't have the time to tell our parents, as we were both busy with our work and preparing for the auction, which was happening in a couple of weeks. So, we decided to break the good news to our friends and family together at dinner that day. If all went well, Karan wouldn't try to punch me for getting his little sister pregnant.

There was a very intense look in her eyes when she sipped on her glass of water, her appetite full.

"What are you thinking, Bella?" I whispered.

She blinked her eyes at me, a small smile curving on her lips before she shook her head. "I need to go pee," she groaned, frustration ringing in her voice as I watched her amble to the washroom. She hated living in the washroom for half of her day.

As we cuddled on the bed later that night, my hand caressing her bump, we both talked about the baby names, wondering if it would be a girl or a boy. I told her it would be a little princess, but she frowned at me and said she wanted a son like me, which made me blush.

We couldn't be happier.

But late in the night, when it was cloudy and dark, I woke up when Kiara shuffled in her sleep. That was normal, but what wasn't normal was the blood on the sheets. Her face was scrunched in pain. I gently woke her up.

"*Bella*," I said, her eyes opening up to me. "You are bleeding."

26. LET ME SEE YOU

KIARA

I sat up on the bed, my lower belly aching with unbearable cramps. Tears welled in my eyes when I saw the mattress and my sweatpants were covered in my blood. Ethan was kneeling beside me on the edge of the bed trying to say that little bleeding was normal. But I knew it was not normal.

Something was wrong.

"It's alright, sweetheart. *Shh*, don't cry, I will talk to the doctor."

He wiped the silent tears from my face and helped me stand up. He gave me some space in the washroom while he changed the sheets and asked me to call for him if it hurt too much.

We were silent on our drive to the hospital. I was clutching his hand tightly with both hands while he silently drove the car. We both didn't know what to say, especially after we had just decided on names.

It's my fault.

No, no, no, don't think like that, Kiara. The baby is fine.

I can't lose another child.

"It will be alright, Bella," Ethan whispered, squeezing my hand while I sat patiently on the bed. The nurse and doctor had checked up on me and we were waiting for the doctor.

I nodded and tried to smile at him, but I couldn't smile. I straightened up when the doctor came in, and looking at her face, I knew what she was going to say. My heart broke into tiny pieces. My throat ached and a soundless sob escaped my mouth. I shook my head, not wanting to hear what she was going to say. Wanting to deny the truth. Tears blurred my eyes and pooled down my face.

"We are sorry for your loss," she said, trying to be polite as she held my shoulder. Ethan squeezed my hand. He looked like he was about to cry when he scooted to the bed and hugged me to his chest.

My sobs pierced through the room, and the doctor left us alone, closing the door behind her. It was hard listening to myself cry while I felt the hospital gown getting wet over my shoulder. Ethan was crying too, but didn't want to make a sound.

I kept muttering, 'I am sorry' through the heaving sobs as I clutched my stomach and squeezed my eyes shut, wanting to stop the pain.

IT HAD BEEN a week since the death of my second unborn child and it was taking a toll on me. I tried to be the best teacher I could, focusing on my job even though it made me cry every time I was alone. Ethan had tried asking me to go to therapy, but I didn't dare to speak up about it. I kept the façade up that I was alright. That I was fine. But both Ethan and I knew I wasn't.

"Morning, Bella," I heard Ethan's hoarse voice and tensed

up. I served the eggs on a plate for him, keeping it on the island.

"Morning," I mumbled and moved my head, closing my eyes when he pecked my cheek.

I heard him sigh, and my hands balled in fists when he sat down on the stool, his unmatched eyes searching for mine.

"Where's your breakfast, Kiara? Come on, we can share," he nodded at the stool next to his.

I shook my head as I removed the apron, "I already had breakfast." I said. I had a glass of protein shake.

"You're lying," he glared at me, pain flashing in his eyes. "Please come and sit beside me. Let's talk."

I ignored him, my feet taking me to my bedroom, ready to hide. He followed me.

"Look at me, Bella."

I did and noticed the bags underneath his eyes, remnants of pain behind those diamond eyes. I remembered the tears leaking from them after hearing the news.

I swallowed the lump in my throat and shook my head. "I am going to take a shower."

"Do you want me to—"

"No, Ethan."

I didn't let him reply as I rushed to the washroom and turned on the shower, throwing up in the toilet. *There goes my breakfast.* I wiped the tears and flushed the toilet as I finally looked at myself in the mirror, hating what stared back at me. Sullen, gleamy eyes, pale face, and my cheekbones and jaw looked sharper than ever. Hollow. I stripped out of my clothes and whimpered, cupping my mouth when I saw my pale skin. Tears brimmed my eyes when I saw how thin my body looked.

This is what I did to myself.

Still silently crying, I turned on the warm water to

shower, swallowing the sobs and whimpers that threatened to escape.

"Kiara? Can I please come in?" I heard Ethan's voice, laced with worry.

Of course, he would be worried, Kiara. What did you think? You haven't allowed him to touch you or even hold you whenever you were together, ignoring his kisses and sleeping in separate beds at night.

"No," I said firmly, but my voice was weak. Just like my body, which can't bear any child.

He sounded angry. "Yes, I am coming in."

I turned off the shower and wrapped the towel around me even though I knew he was watching me.

"*Kiara*," he said, his voice strained. He stood in front of the door when I tried to get out. "Talk to me, Bella. We haven't talked about the miscarriage—"

I glared at him. "I don't want to talk about it."

"But it happened, Kiara. You can't ignore it and it's hurting you. *Please* talk to me. Or anyone."

"I don't want to, Ethan. Please move."

"Let me see you."

He was begging.

I looked away and shook my head.

He stepped closer, "Why not?"

My fists tightened over the towel as I didn't reply. I stilled when his warm hand landed on top of mine, "Please? I won't . . . I won't touch you, Bella, if that's what you want, but please let me see you."

I didn't reply and squeezed my eyes shut when he gently pried the towel away from me. I turned around, hiding my face with my wet hair. I shrugged away from his hand when he tried to touch me, a tear escaping my eyes.

"I don't want you to see me, Ethan. Or touch me, because I am ugly." My voice broke when I said that. "I can't even take care of my body or my . . . *our* children, Ethan. I can't even look at myself as a woman—"

"*Stop*," he hissed. He turned me around and grabbed my face. "Stop saying that. You are beautiful to me and you are my woman. I don't want to hear you say that." His thumbs wiped the tears as his eyes trailed down my body, still fueled with lust and adoration as if I had something worth looking at.

"Please stop looking at me, Ethan."

"No, I want to show you how beautiful you are."

He gently pressed his lips to mine, his large hands caressing my body sweetly. We kissed. He took me to bed, whispering sweet nothings in my ear. Kissing my body, worshiping it with his hands and mouth. But I was too shaken up, and I cried and pushed him away. If I couldn't love myself, then how could I ask him for it?

"Let me touch you, Bella. We won't have sex." He gently pried away my hands, his body covering mine, and pulled me to him. He kissed my hair and covered us both with blankets. I relaxed under his warm hold, my mind running through all the times we had spent together.

I slept in his arms when he whispered sweet things to me, promising me it would be alright and that we can try again. I didn't reply.

When I woke up after a few hours, it was well past noon and Ethan was nowhere in sight. He had left me a note saying that he would be back before dinner and I should have the spaghetti he had made for me. My stomach growled at me as I changed into my sweatpants, and his t-shirt while I made my way into the kitchen.

After devouring my lunch, I asked Dr. Sabrina if she would have a session with me right now. I needed to talk to someone before Ethan came back. Anya and Katherine were busy with their work, and I felt that I would need to tell them personally.

"KIARA?"

"I'm in here!" I said from the guest room where I had been sleeping for the last week. It seemed cold and barren without Ethan's musky cologne, like in his room.

He appeared in the doorway, smiling at me. "Hey."

I managed a small smile, happy to see him. I patted beside me, wanting him to sit with me on the bed. "Can we talk?" I asked, my heart pounding in my ears.

Doctor Sabrina's words rang in my mind, if you are interpreting and have negative thoughts, ask the person for the facts.

Ask him, Kiara.

Ethan nodded, settling beside me, his sandalwood scent wafting in my nose making me scrunch the sheets. "What did you want to talk about, Bella?"

I swallowed the lump in my throat, forcing myself to be stronger for us. For him. And for me.

"I wanted to talk about the miscarriage."

27. MORAL SUPPORT

ETHAN

I watched Kiara struggle to be open with me, but I was proud of her for asking me to listen to her. Her hands clenched the sheets of the bed she had been sleeping on for the past week until this morning. I was relieved to know that she hadn't harmed herself even though she had lost some weight. I knew whatever happened when I was gone had brought some kind of acceptance from her.

"Did you have a session while I was gone?" I asked, wanting to know if she had talked to someone about what had happened.

"I talked with my therapist," Kiara nodded. "I wanted to ask you something, Ethan."

When I waited for her question, I noticed how she fiddled with her hands, taking time to form the question. After taking a deep breath, she asked, "W-will you, I don't know, um, leave me?"

Knowing how important this was to her, I bit back my question. "Never, sweetheart. I wouldn't leave you. Can I ask why you asked that?"

Kiara sighed as if my answer relieved her. She met my

eyes for a brief second before looking down on her lap. "I was worried that you would leave after . . . after I couldn't keep the baby. I know it sounds stupid, but I am trying not to overthink or interpret those thoughts. Dr. Sabrina wanted me to clear those doubts by talking to you, so that is why I asked."

I took her hand in mine, squeezing her palm. "Bella, I won't leave you like that. Ever. I am glad you are talking to me." I brushed my lips on her knuckles.

"Aren't you offended? That I am asking you about all of this?"

"Not at all, sweetheart. I told you to talk to me whenever you are in doubt. I care about you more than having or not having a baby with you."

A small chuckle left my lips when Kiara hugged me, her arms wrapping around my torso as I pulled her closer, breathing in her black vanilla and coconut scent. I sighed and ran my hand through her hair. Even though I knew she was having a hard time for the past week, I was relieved that she talked to me.

"Ethan," she pulled away, her hands tightening over my t-shirt. "Thank you. For being here with me."

My eyes softened at the raw emotions glinting in her warm chocolate eyes. I kissed the corner of her lips and said, "There isn't anywhere else I would rather be."

FOR THE NEXT FEW DAYS, the tension between the two of us increased despite living under the same roof. Yes, we had talked about the miscarriage and we're slowly growing together in our relationship, but we were also making sure that we were taking it slow this time. There were kisses, but either of us stopped before it escalated to stripping each other out of our clothes. We slept on the same bed with clothes on and woke up cuddling but we didn't get intimate with each other. I wanted her to feel comfortable enough to initiate it, even though it meant cold showers every morning.

The auction for her mother's paintings was a week away, and I had to be in New York for a weekend for the shoot of an athletic brand. We both had worked on it together in the evenings as she had school in the morning. Even though I was not a volunteering coach in the school anymore, I still went to drop and pick her up. Sometimes surprising her with lunch and eating at her office table, enjoying myself when she ate with a flushed face remembering how we had tainted the desk.

"So what's he like in real life?" Kiara asked, her curious eyes wide, "Is he rude and cold?"

"Khalid is . . . well, *Khalid*. Why are you so interested in him?" I narrowed my eyes at her.

"Can you blame me? He is a prince. Brother of the sultan. His paintings are worth over a billion dollars, yet he is going to visit the auction. Why?"

I sighed, running a hand through my hair. "Because he is kind, Kiara. Even though we lived in the same apartment for a year, I know little about him. He is a private person."

She hummed. "I would be private too if I was as famous as he is."

Before I could argue with her, someone rang the doorbell to the house, and I wasn't surprised when Liam opened the front door, peeking in. Kiara waved at him as he sheepishly hid the key to my house and entered the living room. But I was surprised when Anya followed him with Katherine waddling toward her friend, her one hand on her baby bump.

"What are you guys doing here?" I asked when they made themselves at home. Anya was even putting takeout boxes of delicious sushi rolls on the kitchen island while Liam started pouring saké in shot glasses with a soda bottle for Katherine.

"We are here to have a tea party as the ladies put it," Liam replied. I shook my head at them and helped bring everything to the living room as all of us sat down on the floor around the coffee table with Katherine on the couch.

Anya broke the silence. "Kiara and Ethan, we all know you have been hiding something from us so I would advise you both to spill it."

Katherine nodded while Liam drank his saké. "I am here for moral support," he looked at the sushi and added, "And sushi."

I squeezed Kiara's hand and let her tell them what had happened. I held onto her hand when she told them about the miscarriage with tears in her eyes and how it almost shattered both of us. She even confessed how she was afraid how I wouldn't want her if she couldn't bear any children. I kissed her temple, proud of her for being brave enough to talk to her friends about it.

"Aw, Kia," Anya patted her hair when she cried on her shoulder, Katherine sniffling into a tissue. "You could have told us earlier."

Liam patted my shoulders even though he wished I had told him about it. I was glad for all their support as we talked about it and ate. Kiara was smiling and laughing with our friends after lunch. They helped us with the auction, giving us their honest opinions as we made minor changes.

When they left with a threat to call them when we needed them, Kiara smiled up at me.

My cheeks burned with heat at her warm gaze. "What are you staring at, Kiara?"

"I am staring at you," she said. "I am sorry, Ethan."

I frowned, "What are you apologizing for?"

She stepped closer to me, her brown eyes gazing up at

me. "I was so selfish in my guilt that I never stopped to think it was your child too. I am sorry for not thinking about you. Before you say something else, I want to confess."

I raised my eyebrows, waiting for her to continue. She licked her lips, "I love you, Ethan. I have been in love with you for so long and I never once forgot about the way you make me feel when we are together or alone. I want to spend the rest of my life with you, even if it is filled with lots of difficulties."

My heartbeat thundered in my chest when she cupped my jaw. "I am made for your love, Ethan Kane."

I kissed her. Her lips melted against mine when I caressed them. My arms tightening around her, holding her close when she feathered my hair, pulling me close. My breathing wavered, and I felt lightheaded.

This is real.

I pulled away, my voice husky and breathy, "I have been dying to hear that, Bella. I love you so fucking much it hurts. Every night after telling stories to the baby, I said it to you when you were asleep, but now hearing you say it to me." I shook my head. "I am crazy for you and I don't want anyone else but you. God, I love you so much."

We were grinning as we kissed again, falling on the couch when I made her say it again and again until it was a mantra between us. She moaned those words against my lips when I asked her to, thrusting inside her in a slow, loving caress. Our bodies pressing against each other, too afraid to let go as we kept whispering the words of love until we were satisfied.

I pulled her sleepy body closer to me, snuggling her to my warm chest. Smiling down at her gorgeous face, I kissed her forehead and whispered, "I am made for your love too, Kiara Sharma."

28. TOOK A FART ON THE HEART

ETHAN

I fixed my tie for the umpteenth time, my eyes wavering over the people in flashy, luxurious clothes, finding one woman for whom my heart still beat wildly. Where did she go? My eyes searched for her in the crowd. The hall was covered in velvet and satin drapes, giving it a rich feeling, which blended perfectly with the golden lights and the paintings. Kiara was responsible for the display of paintings and their introduction while I worked with the lighting and decoration coordinator. Mr. Stone handed me a flute of champagne, his eyes approving of the suit I was wearing. It was, of course, in black.

"Looking for Ms. Sharma?"

Heat creeped up my cheeks as I scratched my neck, "Is it that obvious?"

Mr. Stone chuckled at me, patting my shoulder. "Take care of her. I am sure Mrs. Damini would be proud of her daughter's choice."

I smiled at him when he left to talk with the other guest and looked for my girlfriend. When I found her laughing with Anya and Andrew, my heartbeat came to a halt. She looked stunning in a red *saree*. The black blouse hugged her curves while the folds of silk fell over her petite frame, golden *jhumkhas* donning her ears. Kiara looked more beautiful than I have ever seen her donned in a *saree*.

I knew I would have a hard time keeping my hands off of her tonight. I made my way toward her, greeting Anya and her son but I didn't miss the way my Bella gazed at me from beneath her lashes.

I couldn't wait to get her alone tonight.

The auction went well, with billions of dollars going to a children's charity. Mr. Stone was more than happy with the outcome, congratulating us. I couldn't keep my hands from her waist when everyone couldn't stop gawking at her. She was the only one who was wearing a *saree* and resembled her mother. Her father and brother were proud of the entire event. Even my mothers seemed happy.

"She is truly beautiful. I could see why you love her," a deep voice said over my shoulder from where I was watching Kiara meet and talk with the people who had placed a bid for the paintings.

I turned with a smile, his sharp face melting into a teasing grin as we hugged. "Nice to see you too, *Prince* Khalid," I said. "Stop staring at her, she is taken."

He smiled down at me, his six-foot-five tall figure looming over me. "Not staring, Ethan, appreciating the efforts of the daughter of Mrs. Damini. She must be proud of her."

"Yes, she would be," I whispered, loving the small dimple poking her cheek when her brother and father embraced her in a warm hug.

Sliding my hands in my pockets, I turned to him knowing well enough that people, mostly women of all ages, were eyeing him. "What about you? Dating anyone?" I asked, curious if anyone had captured his heart of steel.

He let out a hearty, deep laugh. "Not at all. You think my rebellious sister will let me relax and have the time to date anyone?"

His voice was deep yet firm when he spoke in English and it made him sound British as he was born and raised in Azmia. His brother was the Sultan of Azmia, and his little sister was a rebel, running away from their country and making him worry. If he loved anything more than his country and the art of painting, it would be his sister.

"I thought you found her in New Zealand last time?"

Khalid Al-Latif shook his head, a small smile curling over his face. His bronze skin glowing. "We did, but she wanted to travel to Australia and then Sri Lanka. She is a wild spirit. I worry about her sometimes."

"Which brother doesn't worry about his sister? Let her see the world. She will come back on her own."

Kiara walked up to me, her eyes wide and mouth agape when she saw who was standing beside me. I frowned at her when she stuttered greeting him, her hand digging in my arm when Khalid congratulated her by kissing her knuckles. I glared at him. He winked at me before he walked away when Mr. Stone called him over to meet other people. He would have joined us for dinner, but he had to leave for San Francisco tonight.

"You never told me how hot he is in person," Kiara said as soon as he was out of our earshot.

"I will pretend I did not just hear that."

She grinned up at me, her golden-brown eyes sparkling, "Oh, come on, you know I was just appreciating his beauty. I took a fart on the heart *for you*, Ethan."

I smiled, looking down at the woman I loved dearly, "So did I, Bella."

AFTER THE AUCTION and the dinner with our friends and family, we were driving back home. I squeezed her thigh, smiling at her as I recalled my conversation with her father and brother. They had given me their blessings when I had asked them for something, even though Karan, her brother, didn't fully trust me to keep his sister happy. I could understand his feelings as I have a little sister of my own.

But I loved her and her father could see that, so he had approved of me.

Not Dharmesh from Delhi, ha!

Before I could whisk her away to our bedroom and strip her out of her *saree*, Kiara led me to the guest room wanting to show something to me. I followed her into the room as she moved to the covered frame and removed the white cloth to reveal the painting. From the start, I knew she did it. She painted us. Together. United. *As one.* I swallowed the lump in my throat, clearing the memories from that night.

"Why did you paint that?"

"I told you I wanted to paint *us*. Together."

I fucking loved it. So much so, I didn't want anyone else to look at it. It showed us how intimate and vulnerable we both were together. Each stroke of the brush was precise, our skin glinting with a small glow. She sat on my lap, my arm covering her breasts and holding her throat while the other held her hip. I was embracing her from behind, her tumbling waves brushing our naked skin with the rumpled bed sheets in the background. The most detailed part was our faces. I was looking at her, my face tilted and blue-green eyes gleaming with adoration, watching her when she took all of me, our faces showing the throes of our passion.

I met her amber eyes. "It's fucking beautiful, Kiara. I love it," I whispered as I awed at the painting once again.

"Really?"

"Let me show you how much I love it."

Closing the distance between us, I pressed my lips against hers. She sighed in relief, melting in my arms when I pulled her closer, my hands digging in the bare skin of her waist. Our lips met in a heated kiss. Neither of us complained when we fell on the soft rug, which had dried paint streaks all over it. We both said the words of love again and again. Kiara moaned those sweet words against my lips when I asked her to, thrusting inside her in a slow caress and making love with our painting staring back at us.

29. BEFORE I CHANGE MY MIND

ETHAN

It had been a month since the auction. We were living together, in the same room and sleeping in the same bed. We had talked to each other about conceiving and decided that both of us wanted to wait till marriage to have a baby. Her ob-gyn was positive that we both could have children again if we wanted. We were using protection and talked to each other after each intimate moment.

We were closer than ever. It seemed like our relationship was finally on the right path and we were growing together.

I called Rio. "Please tell me everything is ready. I can't mess this up."

He chuckled, and I heard Liam and Volt yelling in the background with a loud crash.

I sighed when he replied, "Haha . . . *ha*, funny, Ethan. Everything is going as planned, don't worry. Katherine, Anya, and even Becky will be there in an hour. Oh and have some yogurt if you can or else Kat will start crying. I swear, man, pregnancy changes a woman."

I remembered Katherine was nine months in and her due date was in a week. I checked the fridge, "Yeah, we have yogurt, but please take care of Liam and Volt. I will be there as soon as I can."

"Where?"

I almost jumped out of my skin when I turned and saw Kiara. She was leaning on the island, her arms crossed. I stuttered, "I . . . *uh*, I. To the restaurant, Bella. Remember, we are having dinner tonight?"

She frowned. "Yes, I remember. Katherine said she will be here to get me ready, why?"

"How would I know? Maybe she wants to talk to you or something." I checked the time and stepping closer, I pecked her lips. "Listen, I have to leave right now. I am taking the clothes with me so I will change there. Anya will come here and pick you, Becky, and Katherine, alright?"

When she nodded, I smiled and kissed her once again. Squeezing her ass, I leaned down and whispered in her ear, "Don't wear underwear."

Her soft gasp made my dick twitch with excitement. Her eyes widened with mischief when I pulled away, "And what if I wear it?"

"Then I have to punish my bad girl."

Kia chuckled and tipped on her toes, kissing me. "I love you."

Like every time, my heart melted hearing those words. "Love you more, Bella. See you soon."

My plan was ruined.

Volt and Liam started fighting with each other as soon as they got there, crashing the decorations around the room I had booked for the surprise. Rio had tried to stop them, but he tripped on a wire, wrecking the music system.

"Well, no one is dead," Liam grinned, wiping blood from his split lip. "*Yet.*"

Rio glared at him and mimicked him in a small voice, rolling his eyes at the man in a grey suit who stood beside me. We were all wearing suits today, but even though we looked grown-up, two of us were still acting like children, bickering.

I closed my eyes and shook my head. "You guys had one fucking job, and you ruined it!"

"We are sorry, Ethan." They all mumbled in unison.

"Damn right you are!" I exclaimed, running a hand through my hair.

"Whose kid is this?" Liam asked, raising Volt's three-year-old son, who was chewing a plant.

Volt did a double-take, "Does he have an 'I am Ken and Touka's son'?"

"Yes, he does. And just so you know, this is not how parenting works. But you do you, man." He handed the crying Joshua to his dad, who promised to give him chocolate if he stopped crying.

I shook my head and asked the restaurant employees to clean up the mess my immature friends had made and gave them a hefty tip for helping me out. I could feel the tie tightening around my neck and removed it, unbuttoning the top two buttons. Walking out of the sliding doors, I stood on the roof's balcony, watching the sunset as I leaned against the railing.

"You know, she would have never liked it anyway," I heard Liam say as he stepped beside me, handing me a glass of whiskey.

I gladly took it, clinking it with his glass, and took a huge gulp. The warm clench of the liquid made me relax as I asked, "What do you mean?"

"Kiara is a complex person, but she always loves

simplicity when it comes to everything. She would love it if you proposed to her in there with her friends, but it would make it special if you two were alone so she could be more herself."

I was dumbfounded. I didn't know if she wanted to marry me after what had happened a month ago or wanted to wait. But knowing our past together, a little part of me hoped she would say yes. Her family had agreed and given me permission. Even my mothers had given me blessings, but Kiara would be the one to accept or reject me.

"Thank you for the advice, man. I will ask her here."

KIARA LOOKED stunning in the dark maroon dress and not just because it hugged her body in all the right places, accentuating her curves. It was the way she grinned and laughed with everyone, playing with Joshua and his baby brother.

Man, I was whipped.

"Stop eye-pussying her." My head snapped at Ryan, who was sipping his wine. "It's uncomfortable."

I frowned, "Don't tell me Katherine tells you everything they both talk about."

He shrugged, his green eyes averting to his pregnant wife who was chatting with Kiara, Anya, and Becky. "Not everything, but enough to learn the weird vocabulary they use." He looked back at me and said. "Take her out on the roof and ask it. If you keep thinking about it, you will never propose. Heck, I *almost* bailed on the marriage, yet here I am."

"You did?"

His cheeks reddened, "Don't tell her that, but I had my doubts that I would let her down and I was not good enough for her. But it doesn't matter anymore. She has stayed with me for more years than I can count. I still can't believe I am going to have a family with that woman."

I nodded, gazing at Kiara because that was exactly how I felt with Kiara and more. We have been together since we were born, sharing our cribs and colors. Even now, she wore my clothes, shared my bed and our home. I knew I wanted to marry her and I would ask her with a proper ring this time.

Buttoning the suit, I walked toward the women as they laughed at something they were whispering about when I squeezed Kiara's shoulder. "Excuse me, ladies, do you mind if I take my girlfriend away for a while?"

Kiara frowned, but Katherine looked so excited that she nodded hurriedly, "Sure, sure, go ahead. *Take her away!*"

I gave her a look, and she zipped her lips shut when Kiara raised an eyebrow. Anya smiled at me and raised her wine-glass at me.

Becky smirked, wiping the drool from her newborn son's lips as she said, "Don't take too much time, desserts are on the way."

"I won't," I promised.

Holding Kiara's hand, I walked out of the sliding doors into the cold air of the night. Her fingers tightened on my hand as I pulled her against me. She chuckled, her hand holding the lapels of my suit when I nuzzled my face in the crook of her exposed neck.

"You smell so fucking good, Bella," I said, my voice lowering an octave as I kissed her neck. Her coconut and black vanilla scent surrounded me, and I felt dizzy, wanting to push her against a wall and claim her like a wild animal.

I almost did that.

"Ethan! What are you doing?" Kiara shrieked when I trapped her petite body against a wall. I pressed myself against her and sank to my knees, her eyes widening.

Bunching the hem of her dress over her legs, I pushed it

past her navel, exposing her in the cold air. The music of the restaurant muffled in our ears. I growled at the scent of her feminine arousal numbing my senses when I saw how wet she was.

"No underwear, *hmm?* God, look how wet and ready you are," I teased, her hands tightening around the dress she was clutching when I parted her thighs.

"You asked me not to wear it, and I didn't want to disappoint you," Kiara said, her brown eyes wild and sexy with lust as she gazed down at me, her voice sultry.

My hands trailed over her bare legs. "You can never disappoint me, Bella." My eyes zeroed in on her dripping pussy as I pulled her against my mouth, holding her ass and whispered, "I would like to have my dessert."

Kiara licked her lips and pushed her hips forward, her back arching. *"Dig in."*

Smirking, I kissed her nether lips, and she tried to not make any sounds but failed miserably as small whimpers and mewls escaped her red lips. I swirled my tongue around her slick lips before pushing in and tasting her sweet nectar on my tongue.

I pulled away only to look up at her and asked, "Will you marry me, Kiara?"

She gasped, her eyes widening. *"What?"*

I squeezed her ass. "You know, marriage? Two people saying vows and promising to stay with each other forever until they die or . . . get divorced." I shook my head at her confused expression, "Not the point. You want a soccer team, and according to my statistics, I am the perfect man who should marry you and fulfill your wish. *All* your wishes."

"You can't just ask me like that, Ethan."

"But I did," I leaned down and flicked her swollen clitoris with my tongue, her back arching as she moaned deeply.

"What's your answer, Bella? Because I can do this all night." I smirked when she glared at me through her lust-filled eyes.

"It's a yes. I will marry you, Ethan!" she grinned, arching her hips toward me. "Now, make me come before I change my mind."

I grinned and before she could say anything, I ate her out, holding her dripping pussy over my mouth. My lips, teeth, and tongue nibbled over her soaking cavern and she came, groaning my name and bucking her hips over my tongue.

Licking her clean, I straightened her dress and bent down on one knee, pulling out the ring from my suit when her eyes widened. Kissing her knuckles, I whispered, "I took a fart on the heart since we kissed, Kiara." She chuckled, her eyes glistening with tears when I squeezed her hand. "I am made for your love, Bella. You will make such a beautiful bride, and I can't wait to marry you." I slid the diamond ring on her finger, her hand shaking when I kissed it.

"Come here." Her voice cracked as she pulled me up. I chuckled and kissed her softly, her fingers threading through my hair.

Kiara pulled away first, and I wiped the tears from her face, her eyes glittering under the moonlight as she whispered, "I can't believe this. This feels so unreal."

"I know a couple of things to make you believe that this is true. I have lost you once, and I am not making the same mistake twice."

She giggled, hugging me as I kissed her hair. I was about to say something when she pulled away. "Oh, I almost forgot."

My eyes widened when I saw that her dress had pockets. My jaw went slack when she pulled out a plain platinum band from her dress and bent down on her knee.

"What the fuck, Kiara?"

Kia grinned, holding my left hand, "It seems like you are

not the only one full of surprises." She looked down at my hand and I felt my heartbeat race when she said, "I mean, I would love to give you a blowjob and ask you to marry me, but you beat me to it. So, Ethan Kane, my boyfriend, my lover, my best friend, will you marry me and honor me to be your wife so we can make our soccer team?"

I couldn't help but grin. "Of course, Bella. Now, hurry with the ring, I want to let everyone know that you are mine and I am yours."

Grinning, she slid the ring over my left finger, and surprisingly it fit. She was about to stand up when someone slid the door open.

Katherine saw us, her green eyes widening, "Are you guys . . . *what the—?*"

I looked down and realized we were in such a position that to others it might seem like Kiara was blowing me off. I shook my head at Katherine and helped Kiara stand up. Before I could stop her, she rushed to her best friend and hugged her.

"We are engaged!"

"I am so happy—*oh*."

All three of us gasped when the water splashed on the floor, Katherine's face turning into a wide grin. Ryan rushed out and saw that his wife's water had broken. We all congratulated them when Katherine asked to have dessert before going to the hospital.

WE WERE BACK HOME after making sure Katherine and Ryan were in the hospital. They had asked all of us to leave and said they would call us if we were needed, so we complied. I was removing my suit when Kiara walked in, completely naked, her dress pooling around her ankles as she stepped toward me. My eyes widened looking at her beautiful body, her face when she kneeled across from me.

Looking at me, Kiara whispered, "I want you, Ethan."

My cock pressed against the confines of my pants when I heard the pleading in her sultry voice as she gazed up at me, her eyes half-lidded and wild with passion. My eyes roved over her naked form. She wasn't completely naked. She was wearing a diamond ring.

Leaning down, I tilted her chin, "Are you sure?"

She nodded, "Yes, Ethan."

I smirked, "Then who am I to deny the pleasure of my fiancée."

THE END

Click HERE to read the Extended Epilogue or type this in your browser: https://mailchi.mp/6faf86177ce9/epilogue

Thank you so much for reading Don't Date Your Ex Best Friend! If you enjoyed reading this book, I would be grateful if you could leave a review on the platform(s) of your choice.

Reviews help other readers like you find this book and are hugely appreciated by authors!

Love always,

Mahi

EPILOGUE

"Daddy!"

"Hmm."

"Daddddddddddddyyyy, wake up."

I shook my head and grumbled, "I don't want to, Bella."

"No. Bad Daddy!"

A small smile tugged my lips hearing the scream of my little demon. She learned that from her gorgeous mama. I opened my eyes and saw one of the most beautiful grins even if it was missing one front tooth.

"Morning, Daddy!" She jumped on my chest, her small arms wrapping around my neck.

I sat up and cradled her small body to my chest, her pink pajamas smelling like coconut and candies. "Good morning, cupcake," I mumbled when she kissed my cheek.

Her wild brown hair was in a mess. Her mother or I was going to have a field day with it. Whoever caught her first.

"Do you know what day it is, Daddy?" she asked cheekily, a small dimple poking her left cheek and her beautiful mismatched eyes blinking up at me.

I gathered her small body in my arms and stood up. Her

small giggles melted my heart when I rubbed my face in her tummy, my hair tickling her face.

"Daddy, stop, you are being silly." She grabbed my hair in her small palms, effectively stopping me.

I walked into the bathroom and kept her down on the counter, applying toothpaste on her pink toothbrush. After wetting it with the water, I handed her the small toothbrush. "Come on, you need to brush your teeth."

She grumbled, "I don't want to. My mouth freezes when I drink water, Daddy."

I grinned at her excuse. "Your mother will have our bums if you don't brush your teeth this instant."

"What does that mean?"

"Start brushing, Aethra," I said in a warning voice. She pouted but started cleaning her teeth.

After brushing our teeth, we both walked downstairs. I smiled leaning on the door, watching my gorgeous wife make the batter of cake. Her curvy, lithe body swayed in the peach slip dress she was wearing. My other head twitched in my sweatpants when I saw the thin fabric shaping against her ass, stomach, and accentuating the hips I loved so dearly. I held back my groan when I noticed she wasn't wearing a bra, and all I wanted to do was remove that dress and slide myself home, sucking on those beautiful tits.

The squeal of Aethra brought me back to reality when she launched herself on her mother's legs but tripped on the rug.

"Aethra! How many times have I told you not to run? You will hurt yourself, sweetheart," Kiara helped her up and checked if she bruised her knee. She ignored her mother's concern and climbed on a chair at the island.

I took my wife in my arms and kissed her on the lips. Her round stomach made a gap between us. I felt the small kick of our child on my abs and we chuckled, kissing clumsily. My hands trailed down her waist to her stomach. I forced myself not to squeeze her ass in front of our children and ignored the fake gagging over my shoulder.

I pulled away, pecking her once more, and licked her lips which tasted of strawberries, "Good morning, Bella."

Her brown eyes twinkled and averted down my neck, successfully undressing me in her mind. "Good morning, Ethan."

"Gross, Dad. Your kids are watching."

Kiara chuckled, looking over my shoulder and patted my chest. I missed the warmth of her body pressing against me when she winked and got back to making the cake for the kids.

I ruffled our son's hair, sitting down beside him at the island. "Elijah, you won't say that when you have a girl-friend." I thought for a moment and added, "Or a boyfriend for that matter."

He scowled, hiding his flushed face in the sketchbook, "Dad, I am six and too young to talk about this with you."

"Daddy, can I have a boyfriend?" Aethra asked, eating the frosting sneakily and pouting when Kiara gave her a stern look.

Even Elijah narrowed his mismatched eyes at her and we both said in unison, "*No*, you can't."

I added, "You know you can't date boys until you are thirty. You promised Daddy, princess."

She grumbled something about not waiting to get to thirty and rambled to her mother about how I was being unfair. I couldn't care less if she liked it or not, I had made her promise me that as soon as she learned to speak 'yes'. I was not letting some immature boy hurt my little angel's heart.

I looked down at what my son was sketching. "What is it?" I asked, "May I see it?"

Biting his bottom lip, he slid his sketchbook toward me,

his mismatched eyes flickering between my face and his drawing.

They both had heterochromia in opposite eyes. One brown and the other green and blue. I remembered we both had cried tears of happiness seeing their eyes for the first time. It was a long day with twenty-seven hours of labor, but it was all worth it when we held the crying twins in our arms for the first time.

"Mom was telling me a story about a boy who saved a girl from drowning. How is it?"

I smiled looking at the mini drawing of a big stick figure helping a tiny stick figure from drowning in water full of goldfish with sharp teeth. "It is creative, Elijah, but I am sure goldfishes don't have sharp teeth," I pointed out, giving it back to him.

His cheeks turned red, and he continued coloring the sky a dark grey color. "In my head they do."

"Why are you embarrassing my son on his birthday?"

I turned around, guilty as charged, a grin splitting my face. Her hair was in a braid, a few wisps of them framing her face when she narrowed her light brown eyes at me. Standing up, I walked toward her, easily towering over her and held her hand, admiring the ring on her finger. I kissed her cheek and admired the body which was growing another human inside her.

"Come on. Dad and Mom are doing the gross stuff. *Again.*" Elijah pulled down Aethra from the counter who was busy eating the batter of the cake, remnants of it caking her small face. "I will show you new flowers in the backyard."

"I heard that!" I said as they held their hands, rushing outside and giggling.

"Don't go on the road and keep the door open!" Kiara shouted worriedly, looking over her shoulder.

I frowned, "Let them close it. They are six years old now, Kiara. Elijah takes care of her better than us."

"Yes, I know, E, but he has been acting weird ever since he came in our room to sleep with us—"

"When I was inside you?"

I remembered that night vividly. All we wanted was a quickie, so we had cared little about removing our night-time clothes. When I was about to pull out after a mind-blowing orgasm, Elijah had walked inside the room, complaining about the volume of our TV, which was playing Tom and Jerry. With a much awkward position, I had quickly pulled out when Kiara distracted Elijah with the cartoon.

"Yes, Ethan. I think he is too mature for his age."

I smirked, trailing my hands down her soft arms, "Remind you of anyone?"

She chuckled, threading her fingers in my hair, and I almost purred. "Yes, babe, I remember. Everyone keeps pointing out that Elijah is following in your footsteps while—"

"Aethra is stubborn like you."

"I am *not* stubborn."

"Yes, you are."

"*No*, I am not!"

I raised my eyebrow and hid my smile when she scoffed, "Whatever. You are distracting me, I have so much to do." *Uh oh, there she goes*. She turned into full-on mama mode and walked out of my arms, "I have to bake the cake, the frosting, snacks for children, ohmygod."

I laughed and wrapped my arms around her stomach. "*Shhh*," I whispered in her ear, kissing her neck, "My mothers, Anya, Katherine, and everyone are on their way and they will be more than happy to help you. Don't stress yourself too much right now."

I stroked my hand on her stomach as our child kicked

and we both grinned, feeling it. She hugged me, "I am sorry, Ethan. It's just that it's their sixth birthday and I want it to be perfect."

I held her jaw and tipped her face toward me, crashing my lips over hers and kissed her soundly. She moaned when I gently kept her on the island, my hand sliding over her bare legs until they reached between her thighs. Her eyes widened and grabbed my shoulders when my fingers rubbed against her underwear. I let out a small groan when I felt her wetness.

"Don't apologize, Bella, I can punish you later for this," I whispered, teasing her entrance with the fabric. When her rounded belly pressed against mine, the baby kicked his or her leg and I chuckled, looking down between us, "*See?* The baby loves that idea."

Kiara gazed up at me, her chocolate brown eyes twinkling with mischief and lust, "So does her mama." She pulled me close, swiftly removing my t-shirt, "*Please*, Ethan. I need your cock inside me right now."

Hearing those sultry soft words from my wife and mother of our two children (third on the way) I wanted to be on my knees and worship every inch of her strong body. But I controlled myself.

"Greedy, are we?" I teased playfully, tugging the hem of her dress upwards and moving the underwear to the side to watch my fingers rub against her slick lips, eliciting a soft moan from her.

This was one of the best things I loved about pregnant Kiara. She would jump me or want me during any time of the day. Even though I had fucked her until she was exhausted, I would rub her back, and a minute later, she would beg me to fuck her on her knees.

Kiara purred, bucking her hips, "Yes, Ethan. Please, I need you."

I groaned, "We can't have sex when our kids are awake."

Her face fell, and missing the dimple on her cheek, I leaned closer and kissed her cheek, jaw, and neck. I licked the flush creeping up her neck. Her exotic scent of coconut and black vanilla wafted up my nose, making me sigh at the thought of not being one with her. Controlling my desire, I fixed her underwear and lightly kissed her stomach, covering her body with the dress.

"Don't worry, Bella. We will have this entire house to ourselves tonight. And I want to take my time worshiping my wife's body."

She hummed, "Okay, Ethan. I will wait for you tonight."

"You better."

"I love you."

Nuzzling my face in her neck, I kissed her soft skin, "I love you more, my sweet Bella."

Click HERE to read the Extended Epilogue or type this in your browser: https://mailchi.mp/6faf86177ce9/epilogue

THE UNFOLDING DUET

PREVIEW - KIARA

I laughed more. Chortles and snorts escaping my mouth while his icy blue and green eyes kept glaring at me. That was too funny. I realized I was laughing too much when he clamped his hand around my wrist and dragged me away from any peering eyes.

"Ethan!" I squeaked and giggled when he pressed me against the wall, his muscled body pressing against me, trapping me from running away. "What are you doing?"

"So, now you decide to sober up from all that laughter?"

I looked around and saw that he had taken me on the hidden stairway to the roof where no one would find us until they looked for us or went to the terrace.

My eyes widened when he whirled me around, raising my hips so that I had to support myself with my palms on the wall. I let out a gasp when I felt his hardened length through my *sari*, his hands roaming over my bare waist.

I shivered.

He couldn't possibly be thinking...

"Ethan, stop," I moaned when he yanked my hair back, his

lips landing on my neck, his fingers undoing my blouse. I didn't want him to stop. "S-someone might catch us."

"Let them," he growled, grinding himself on me. "Let your family realize how naughty their sweet daughter is." I couldn't help my gasp when his warm hand wrapped around my breast, tweaking the nipple roughly, punishing me. "Getting fucked against a wall by her soon-to-be husband under their roof."

I whimpered, clenching my legs.

Ethan's dirty talk humiliated me, embarrassed me, and aroused me. I wanted that. I wanted to be fucked against a wall by him in my parents' home. I didn't care if anyone found us when Ethan was deep inside me, my blouse tangled over my waist, my *sari* hanging up in the loose swirl.

"Oh, please, Ethan," I groaned out when his warm hand cupped me through my soaking underwear, his fingers rubbing my slick lips through the lace while I tried to grind myself on his hand.

Ethan chuckled, his voice raw and deep sending shivers down my spine when he yanked my hair to stay upright and not move. "Look at you, Kiara. You are soaking and begging me to take you here. Do you want that? Do you want me to fuck you here, like this, hm?"

I was nodding, moving my hips back and forth, making small sighs when he rewarded me by slowly rubbing my clitoris. His warm breath fanned my neck. He kissed my jaw before letting go of my breast and removing his hand from my *sari*.

EXCLUSIVE CONTENT

Want more exclusive content? You can sign up for Mahi's Patreon to read steamy one shots every Saturday!

As a supporter, you get access to early drafts, exclusive VIP content, deleted scenes, deleted chapters, cat pictures and YOUR NAME in the Acknowledgements of my books.

www.patreon.com/mahimistry

DIRTY WILD SULTAN PREVIEW

NASRIN

Zain chuckled, his laugh devoid of any humor making me shudder. He leaned closer and my eyes widened when his lips went past mine to press against my ear as he whispered, "I don't want to know why you think so lowly of me but I assure you, future *wife*..." A slither of pleasure rolled over my spine hearing his rumbling velvety voice, his lips brushing over the shell of my ear, "That you would be the one begging me to touch you."

He was so right, he had no idea.

I would beg. For him. *Only* him.

My eyes were glazed when they roved over his powerful, lean body, the muscles on his biceps moving when he leaned back on the stool. I pressed my teeth on my bottom lip, the air around us thickening with the steam, exotic oil, his musky cologne.

I met his eyes. "Then I beg you to touch me, Zain." I swallowed the lump in my throat and added in a soft whisper, "Please."

His eyes widened a little with shock, and something darker coursed through them. My heart thudded loudly when I realised what it was. Pure lust. Desire. If I could move back in the bath, I would, because his gaze turned predatory, and I felt like his prey. Naked in the bath, while he was covered in clothes.

I watched when he unbuttoned the top two buttons of his dark shirt, revealing the tan skin underneath. My tongue seeped out to wet my lips. A hint of a smirk grazed his lush lips when he said,

"Spread your legs and show me your cunt, Princess."

PREVIEW OF TWISTED THERAPIST

IVY KNIGHT

"I am so sorry, Aiden, the traffic was so bad," I heaved, taking support of my knees to control my breathing. So much for dressing up in cute dress, applying light makeup and curling my hair in waves just for the session. I wiped down the sweat from forehead and straightened up, daring to peek at him.

Aiden looked like he always did. His face stern and no emotions showing on his face. His eyes travelled down my body and I held in my shiver when they raked over my bare legs.

He made a dramatic point of checking his wristwatch that cost more than the car that I drove and hummed. "We will talk about your tardiness after the session. *Sit.*"

I quickly sat down and drank some water, the breeze of the air conditioner cooling my skin. The session started, and we made usual talk about my day, what happened that week or if anything exciting happened that I wanted to share with him.

"How did your journaling go?"

We talked more about the days where I would write two-three pages a day or days when I could barely write a paragraph. He listened to me and asked questions when I would stop talking, urging me to drink water and keep going.

"Do you mind if I see what you've written?" He asked, his dark eyes soft.

My muscles tensed as I met his obsidian eyes. They ran over my body and noticed how stiff I had become. My eyes lingered on his crisp white shirt, stretching over his shoulders, the sleeves rolled up to his elbows with a dark-coloured tie. Maybe it was my imagination when I thought his eyes had stayed far too long on my chest and my legs. I shuffled in my seat and tucked the strand of my hair behind my ear.

Aiden's eyes flickered to my face, and he closed them for a moment, as if he was taking his time. He finally said, "You don't have to if you don't want me to read. I will understand and respect your privacy."

I licked my lips, trusting my instinct. "I-it's okay, I don't mind. You can read it."

I handed him the diary, frowning at the ruffled separate pages that I had shoved between them. He silently read the entry of my first day while I squirmed in my seat. I may or may not have drunk too much water, so I excused myself to the washroom.

When I came back, I could feel the change in the air. Aiden was sitting on the couch, but his posture was stiff. He barely addressed my presence when I sat down in my seat. I saw the diary was placed beside him and his jaw was clenched.

"Is everything okay?" I asked, my voice small.

He finally looked at me and the corner of his lips twitch. Leaning back on the couch, he said, "Yes, I suppose you could say that. I want to ask you something, Petal, and I want you to be honest about it."

Frowning, I nodded.

His eyes darkened, and he said in a stern voice, "Use your

mouth."

"I—*um*, yes, Dr. Aiden."

I didn't know why I *felt* the need to address him seriously.

"What were you doing this morning?"

My eyes widened, my heart pounding in my ears. I glanced at the diary and it struck me. Those ruffled pages. *Shit, shit, shit.* After journaling every day for a week, I wrote my fantasies regarding Aiden, my brother's best friend, on different torn pages. I always tucked them back in the diary, reminding myself to pull them out before I brought it to the session. But I was in such a hurry that I had completely forgotten about them.

Did he read it? I hope he didn't. I would rather eat raw broccoli than have him read all those pages.

Looking away from him, I lied and carelessly shrugged my shoulder, "I was meditating."

I mentally winced at my lie. He had tried coaching me to meditate, but I could never do it.

He is right. I am a terrible liar.

Aiden raised his eyebrows. "Is that so?"

I didn't like the tone of his voice. He seemed serious, and I prayed that the ground would swallow me up. He waited for my answer, crossing his arms over his chest. I got distracted by the way his biceps bulged, the veins on his forearms getting prominent.

He noticed me staring. I glanced down at my lap, twiddling my thumbs. "Y-yes, Dr Aiden, I was meditating and I-I focused on my breath like you taught me—"

"Why are you lying to me, Ivy?"

My head snapped at him. I shook my head, "I-I am not lying."

Aiden tilted his head and my throat went dry when he said, "Then why did I hear your voice moaning my name when you orgasmed with your fingers inside your pussy?"

ALSO BY MAHI MISTRY

Have you read them all?

Alluring Rulers of Azmia Series

Dirty Wild Sultan

Filthy Hot Prince

Tempting Rebel Princess

Charming Handsome Sheikh

Alluring Rulers of Azmia Complete Series Books 1-4

The Unfolding Duet

Don't Date Your Best Friend: Best Friends to Lovers

Don't Date Your Ex Best Friend: Second Chance Best Friends to Lovers

The Unfolding Duet Books 1-2

Dominating Desires Series

Twisted Therapist: Brother's Best Friend Age Gap Romance

Tempting Teacher: Student Teacher/Dad's Best Friend Age Gap Romance

Scan to easily access all of my books:

ACKNOWLEDGMENTS

I wish I could give *gulab jamuns* to each and every reader who supported an indie author like me and gave a chance to Ethan and Kiara's story. It means the world to me you spent a day or two reading this book.

To my family, thank you for believing in me and telling strangers to buy my book.

To my cats, thank you for teaching me patience and cuddling in my lap at three in the morning while I wrote this duet.

To my editor, Jeanie, thank you for your constructive feedback and being one of the best editors any author can ask for.

To all my wonderful friends, beta readers, proofreaders, bloggers and book lovers who helped me perfect this series with your love and support. I couldn't have done this without you.

To all the wonderful Patreons who constantly support me with your sweet messages and uplifting comments: Skylar M., Tisha L., Madi L., Tracey B., Tina W., Sara L., Celia M., Natashia M., Katie M., Andrea A., Wendy C., Anita A., Kim L., Erin R., Christine N., Grace, Katie U., Jessica C., Leslie D., Hope M., Michelle M., Priscilla S., Jenny T., Mariah B., Alicia D., Nabihah A., Anna, Mya C., Lana K., Angela E., and Amanda V.

Thank you to everyone who accepted the ARC edition of this book and helped me share this book baby to the world.

If you enjoyed reading this book, please don't forget to leave a review. I would really appreciate it.

ABOUT THE AUTHOR

Mahi Mistry has been writing since she was in middle school. Soon, she fell in love with writing passionate, steamy romances. Her stories have elements of humor, suspense and character development. Mahi's main purpose in her life is to make one person happy every day, even if that is a stranger reading her book and rooting for the main couple or her cats by giving them extra treats.

She enjoys simple things in life, like spending time with her family and friends, cuddling with her cats, reading and writing drool-worthy characters while sipping on hot chocolate from the wineglass to validate herself that she is actually an adult. She is an avid reader of fantasy, romance and thriller books and thinks writing about yourself in third person is atrocious. She firmly believes that cats rule the world.

www.mahimistry.com